GRAVEYARD RULES

Gary Cook

POCKET BOOKS

New York   London   Toronto   Sydney   Tokyo

Another *Original* publication of POCKET BOOKS

POCKET BOOKS, a division of Simon & Schuster Inc.
1230 Avenue of the Americas, New York, N.Y. 10020

ISBN: 0-671-65234-6

First Pocket Books printing October 1988

10 9 8 7 6 5 4 3 2 1

POCKET and colophon are trademarks of
Simon & Schuster Inc.

Printed in the U.S.A.

Praise for
Gary Cook and
Graveyard Rules . . .

"*GRAVEYARD RULES* is the story of two undercover cops who cannot or will not escape what they become in Vietnam, and who bring the killing home to the mountains and back roads and honky-tonks of Montana. Make no mistake, this is the real stuff. These guys are *out* there, and Gary Cook knows them well. A haunting and important book, brutal and absolutely authentic. You'll know that as soon as you start reading."

—Kent Anderson, author of *Sympathy for the Devil*

"Two Vietnam vets working undercover as narcs discover that the drug war isn't all that different from the one in Southeast Asia and that enforcing the law doesn't always mean obeying it. . . . *GRAVEYARD RULES* is cover-to-cover excitement."

—James Crumley, author of *The Last Good Kiss*

"Gary Cook has skillfully blended scenes of the protagonists' Vietnam experiences into the story, horrible and compelling scenes, that make their particularly brutal crime-fighting methods understandable. *GRAVEYARD RULES* is an exciting, enlightening and unforgettable book."

—Robert Mason, author of *Chickenhawk*

To Terry Lambert
Thanks Barney.

GRAVEYARD RULES

> Sometimes you eat the bear;
> Sometimes the bear eats you.
>
> —The Bear

CHAPTER 1

Graveyard Rules

Three in the morning and Barney's dented and rusting 1966 cream-colored Chevy Nova rumbled through the long, curving sweep of the Interstate into Hellgate Canyon. Barney reached down and pulled the tab off the Olympia gripped between his legs; beer smell filled the interior of the Chevy.

Cookie Monster yawned and hauled himself upright. Beyond the glare of the headlights, one wall of the canyon loomed massive and black, a faint tinge of indigo delineating the ridgeline against the lighter black of the sky. He wrinkled his nose at the beer smell and rolled the window down. The night smelled of pine and fresh mown hay, and of the river that coursed hidden off to their right in the murk of the canyon wall. He thrust his head out the window, eyes closed, feeling the wind press his straggly beard flat against his face, ponytail laid out behind him.

"Kiss my ass, world!" he yelled into the wind.

Barney smiled and drank his beer, keeping one eye on the highway over the tilted beer can. Up ahead, between the Interstate and the river, the blurred outlines of a new condominium complex shone gray and white, like some huge cluster of mushrooms.

"Kiss my ass, condominiums," Cookie Monster shouted as they passed them and came out of the curve and out of the

1

canyon, headed for the Blackfoot. He sat back in the tattered seat, yawned again, stretched, and pulled the fourteen-shot Browning automatic from the shoulder holster concealed beneath his frayed and ripped Levi's jacket. Nonchalantly, as they approached a lighted exit sign, he aimed the pistol, arm fully extended out the window. "Bam-bam . . . bam."

"Quit fucking around," Barney said.

Cookie Monster looked over at Barney. He replaced the automatic in its holster. "Quit fucking around. Quit fucking around," he mimicked.

Barney took another drink of beer. "Quit horsing around."

Cookie Monster looked over at Barney for a moment, at Barney dressed in a leather vest, Grateful Dead T-shirt, jeans, and an old camouflage bush hat. "You even look like a narc," he said, and sat up, dragging his boots off the dash, "like one used to look anyway," and crushing his empty beer can, tossed it into the back seat where it rattled and tinked for a moment among all the other empty beer cans. "Sorry fuckers."

Two beers later, Barney pulled the Chevy off the highway onto an old road overgrown with weeds and grass and a few tiny fir trees, and they bumped and clattered—"Hey, where you goin'? I'm spilling beer all over the fucking place"—across a meadow and up onto a little bluff that overlooked the Blackfoot River.

Barney killed the lights and engine. "We're early. Relax," he said, as they coasted to a stop. He opened his door and they could hear rapids, the slap of water against rocks invisible in the hard, moving blackness of the river.

"When I worked uniform patrol—graveyard shift—and things were slow, I'd come out here and sit and listen to that river."

Underneath the sounds of the rapids they could hear water against the riverbank, could feel the steep mountains of shale pressing in against each other, leaving little room for anything but the water and highway and an occasional hay field or meadow at a bend in the river. "Dark," Cookie Monster murmured, looking up at the dense mass of the mountains. "Really dark in here." A breeze, inexplicably warm and moist against their skin, rippled up the canyon; the pines at the edge of the meadow shifted, creaking and groaning in the darkness.

Barney picked up a small rock and threw it far out into the river. They waited, but the sound of its splash was lost in the rapids.

"First place I ever went fishing was up here somewhere," Cookie Monster said. "My uncle took me. All I remember is hooking a fish and falling off a rock into a pool of that green, slimy algae and pollen stuff."

Barney laughed. "I'd like to pollinate some of the stuff you been falling into lately."

"Oh, no, you wouldn't."

"Oh."

"Yeah." He picked up a rock and threw it out into the river.

"Well, shit," Barney said. "Better go. Got to get the sheriff reelected."

"Graveyard," Cookie Monster said as they pulled slowly back out onto the deserted highway. "I used to like graveyards, too. Only you and the assholes out and about late at night, early in the morning. Whole different world when the citizens aren't around to watch. Make up your own rules."

"Graveyard rules," Barney said.

The Chevy puttered around a sharp curve. Bright specks of emerald gleamed out of the darkness at the edge of the light from the headlights. Barney flicked on the brights and three deer stood trapped in the gravel and on the pavement at the edge of the road. He slowed the car and swerved out into the middle of the highway, missing the blinded and paralyzed deer by only a few feet.

"You're under arrest," Cookie Monster shouted out the window. "Lurking with intent to commit mopery.

"Crazy deer," he muttered. "Never around during hunting season, but the rest of the year they're everyfucking-where, standing in the middle of the road at all hours of the day or night—"

"Might as well have one of those beers," Barney said.

Cookie Monster popped one open and handed it across. "I got to take a whiz pretty soon," he said.

"We're almost there." Barney took a long drink of beer, letting the Chevy wander across the center line.

Cookie Monster pulled the 9mm Browning from the shoulder holster. He pointed it up out the window and, reaching across with his left hand, in one quick movement pulled the slide back and released it, jacking a round into the chamber. With left thumb and forefinger holding the hammer, he pulled the trigger and eased the hammer down. He thumbed the hammer back to half-cock and reinserted the weapon into the holster.

He glanced over at Barney. "Habit. Just habit."

The Chevy grumbled down a long, straight stretch, tall pines and firs crowding out the shadows on both sides of the blacktop, making it seem as though they were driving through an alley in the forest. A metal guardrail unraveled out of the darkness and into the beam of the headlights; squat wooden posts flicked by like railroad ties seen in the shadow of a moving train.

"This part of the Blackfoot just don't feel right," Cookie Monster said. "Even the Indians didn't hang around in here long. And nowadays it seems like every little gulch and canyon is full of Okkies—little kids running around with big bellies, bare feet, raggedy clothes. Reminds me of some of those villes—"

"We're here," Barney said, and pulled the Chevy off onto the dirt road of a small rest area. He stopped the car about midpoint between where the road left the highway and where it reentered. Just ahead and to their right was a large memorial made of river rock and concrete that looked like a giant grave marker. Directly opposite Barney's window was a lone pine tree; a few yards ahead of that, a rock twice the size of the Chevy. Barney shut the engine off.

The exhaust pipe ticked and popped.

They could hear the river on the other side of the highway, the wind in the trees.

" 'LaFray Creek Rest Area,' " Cookie Monster read. " 'Blackfoot Garden Club, Hellgate Lions Club, 1969.' " He laughed, a short sarcastic bark of sound. "One year after Tet, muh-man—1969. We was still in the 'Nam while people back here were building fucking gravestones made out of river rock."

Barney took a drink of beer. "You extended in Vietnam."

" 'Nonpotable water. Unsafe for drinking,' " Cookie Monster continued reading from a small white metal sign attached to a chain-link fence that stretched from the rock memorial to a U.S. Forest Service–green wooden outhouse about thirty yards away. "Kiss my ass," he said. "Something did die here in 1969—the water."

"I'll drink to that," Barney said, and drained his beer.

Cookie Monster opened the door and stepped out. He walked a few steps away from the Chevy, unzipped his fly, and began urinating onto the dirt road. "Pisses me off, anyway," he said, and snickered.

Barney got out of the car and took a step toward the pine tree. "I hope they don't bring that silly cunt with them," he said, relieving himself onto the pine tree. "What an idiot."

"L. L. Bean hiking boots—but the best-looking ass I've seen in a looong time."

Barney snorted. "She might look good, but I'll bet she's . . ." His voice trailed off as they heard the sound of a vehicle approaching, still about a mile away.

Cookie Monster zipped up his trousers. "How do you want to work this?"

"Oh, play it by ear. These are a bunch of fun hogs, not those Okkies you were talking about." He paused. "I'll leave the lights on. You stand behind the rear fender, and I'll stand behind this here door."

They could hear the vehicle getting closer. A powerful engine. A truck with a modified exhaust system. They could see lights hitting in and out of trees across the river as the vehicle negotiated curves farther down the highway. Light appeared on the telephone lines across the road, and a pickup—yellow fog lights under the front bumper, headlights on bright, a row of little orange lights on top of the cab— blasted around the corner.

"All right!" Cookie Monster said. "Get on it!"

The truck downshifted and roared into the other end of the dirt turnoff, brakes locked up, gravel and dirt, dust and twigs and rocks billowing from the fat off-road tires sliding from side to side and finally stopping thirty yards in front of the Chevy, engine burbling like an inboard motor.

Dust washed over them, the yellow fog lamps baleful through tendrils of dirt.

A man tall and big, as tall as Cookie Monster and at least twenty-five pounds heavier, climbed out of the passenger side and walked up even with the front bumper. "That you, Barney?" he asked. "Monster?"

"It's us," Barney answered, voice calm and easy.

Southern syrup, Cookie Monster thought.

"You bring the money?"

"You think we're out here at this time of the morning to go fishing?"

The big man laughed and went back to the cab. A moment later, he walked out in front of the right fog lamp, a small briefcase in one hand. "Well, c'mon over here, then, and see what you caught so bright and early."

Barney walked out between the two vehicles and up to the big man. Cookie Monster moved up even with the Chevy's door, thumbs hooked over his belt buckle. Barney was at least a head shorter than the other man. Puny in comparison.

The man opened the briefcase toward Barney, so that Cookie Monster, squinting against the glare of lights, could not see what was in it. The big man reached in and said something to Barney, and Barney's back went rigid, his arms perfectly still at his sides, and Cookie Monster reached for the 9mm, his stomach suddenly hollow, as two aircraft running lights, mounted high on the pickup's roll bar, exploded on, blinding him.

"Freeze, Monster!" a female voice, high and shrill, shouted from his right, and a short, incredibly loud burst of automatic-weapon fire—an M-16, he immediately knew—cracked and snapped over his head, the explosions echoing across the river and against the mountains. He looked down at the ground, the beer in his stomach sour. The dirt and gravel were sterile-white in the intense light. His eyes blinked rapidly.

"Put your hands on top of your head!"

The smell of cordite hung in the air.

He put his hands on his head and heard the driver get out of the pickup and walk toward him, gravel crunching under heavy boots. Two nearly new hiking boots halted in the dirt in front of him, the driver's body momentarily blocking the light. The 9mm was jerked out of the shoulder holster; one solid clank as it landed among the beer cans in the back seat of the Chevy. "Up against the car," a nervous voice said. "You know how to do it."

"You rippin' us off?" Barney asked, his voice outraged. Cookie Monster could hear the bluff in it.

"Shut up, narc," the female voice said, and screamed, *"You slime!"*

"Left hand. Give me your left hand," the man said to Cookie Monster, and Cookie Monster felt the hard thin edge of a handcuff encircle his left wrist, heard the ratchet sound as it tightened, "Now the other one."

All the pickup lights except the fog lamps went off. Cookie Monster blinked, looking down at the Chevy's rooftop. White and red spots pulsed in front of his eyes.

"Turn around," the nervous voice said.

Cookie Monster turned around and leaned back against the car. "Hello, Harold." Harold was short and muscular, long dark hair and full beard, plaid shirt and baseball cap. Cookie Monster knew the patch on the cap read John Deere in big green letters with a little green deer underneath the letters. "How you doin', Harold?"

Harold giggled.

"They never knew I was there!" the female voice said. "They got out and took a pee and never knew I was here!" A figure wearing a jumpsuit mottled with the brown patterns of desert camouflage walked toward them from beside the rock memorial, her long dark brown hair gleaming in the Chevy's lights. Cookie Monster could see the barrel tremble; her eyes were wide with excitement. The black ugly barrel pointed at his stomach.

"Desert camouflage," Barney said.

"Debbie." Cookie Monster grinned. "Don't you look swell—"

"Shut up! Just shut the fuck up!" The barrel of the M-16 jerked from Cookie Monster to Barney, handcuffed in front of the truck. "I heard you talking about me! Chauvinist fuckers."

Barney laughed, slumping against the bumper of the pickup, arms behind his back.

"Turn the Chevy's lights off, Harold," the big man said.

The Chevy's lights clicked off, leaving only the deep yellow of the fog lamps to see by.

She walked over to Barney. "I'd like to blow your guts all over the road." Her voice stilled Barney's laughter. "Blow your gut—"

"Cool it," the big man said from the shadows next to the truck's bumper. "Bring him over here, Harold." He stepped up next to Barney and shoved him out into the space between the two vehicles. Barney took two faltering steps forward, hands cuffed behind his back, but unable to keep up with the force of the shove, he fell, chin and chest skidding in the dirt and rocks. Dust from the force of his fall swirled in the yellow light.

He rolled onto one shoulder, arms behind his back, knees pulling up to his chest. He pushed off with his shoulder and rose to his knees.

"Laugh now, motherfucker!" Debbie said, and kicked him in the small of the back, slamming him chest down into the dirt again.

The big man walked over and grasped him by the chain that held the two handcuffs together and effortlessly picked him up. Cookie Monster could see the pain ripple across Barney's face as Barney's arms were pulled straight back, his shoulderblades nearly touching. He staggered upright, pants and shirt and lower face dark with dirt.

Harold shoved Cookie Monster up next to him.

"You drank beer with us; you ate with us," the big man intoned. Freckles on his balding head and round face made his skin appear blotched, unhealthy in the yellow light. "You smoked dope with us." He stroked his walrus mustache, one side and then the other, studying the two men. "Can you believe that? You even smoked dope with us."

Barney and Cookie Monster watched him.

"A warning," he said. "Keep working narcs and you'll be dead."

Cookie Monster's eyes narrowed.

"Tonight it's your word against ours," the big man continued. "And you know who our lawyer is." He paused, matching Cookie Monster's stare, and grabbed a handful of beard on the right side of Cookie Monster's face. "You asshole." He laughed, shaking Cookie Monster's face. "You still think

8

this is the rinky-dink seventies, don't you? And his other hand came up and, twice in rapid succession, smashed into Cookie Monster's mouth. "You got that, smart mouth?" He released the beard.

"Oh, yeah," Debbie breathed.

Harold giggled.

Cookie Monster was silent, eyes never leaving the face of the big man.

Debbie reached forward with the barrel of the M-16 and lightly rapped Cookie Monster's crotch with the flash suppressor. "You better answer the man."

Cookie Monster's head slowly swiveled to look at the M-16.

"We heard you," Barney said.

"Move back," the big man said to the woman, and grasped Barney and Cookie Monster by the shoulder. He pivoted them back to back. "Sit," he commanded, and pushed down, making them sit on the ground, their legs sprawled out in front, sideways to the vehicles.

Harold removed Barney's hat.

The big man took the M-16 from the woman. He pressed the flash suppressor against Barney's temple.

Barney jerked his head away.

The big man laughed and moved the flash suppressor in front of Barney's face, barrel pointed toward the trees, and fired a burst, the muzzle blast and flash blinding Barney, numbing his ears, causing his head to reflexively snap back, the back of his head colliding sharply with the back of Cookie Monster's head.

The woman and Harold laughed.

The big man pressed the flash suppressor against Cookie Monster's head, pushing harder as Cookie Monster sat unmoving.

"Next time," the big man said, jabbing the flash suppressor against Cookie Monster's temple.

Cookie Monster's neck muscles tightened, holding his head rigid.

"Next time." He jabbed again. "Shit! I ought to fucking do you right now." And his hand tightened around the M-16's pistol grip, the large muscles of his forearm in sharp relief as his finger pressed against the trigger. He moved the flash suppressor fractionally above Cookie Monster's head and fired the remainder of the magazine, the barrel climbing as the rounds cracked into the darkness of the hillside.

For a moment he glared at Barney and Cookie Monster, cordite eddying in the yellow light.

Barney and Cookie Monster sat rigid, staring straight ahead.

The big man abruptly wheeled, tossed the M-16 to Harold. "What the fuck you looking at?" he snarled at Debbie. "Let's get out of here." And they walked to the truck, big man to the driver's side, Debbie and Harold to the passenger's side.

The engine rumbled into life. Headlights and landing lights exploded into white incandescence.

And the truck backed up, bellowing, all four tires churning and digging, throwing rocks and pine needles, branches and dust, over the two figures sitting in the middle of the LaFray Creek Rest Area. Rubber squealed and the light wavered and shifted as the truck reached pavement, faded into darkness again as they heard the truck howl around the corner and up the highway.

For several minutes neither man moved or said anything. In the east, the direction the truck had gone, the star-filled sky was turning deep violet above the black mountains. Their ears were still numb and buzzing, but they could hear the river and the pines again, smell the water and forest, the dust and cordite. And their sweat: that sour sweat.

"I don't suppose you've got a handcuff key?"

Cookie Monster sighed. "In my coat pocket."

CHAPTER 2

Hair Monsters

The sky had lightened considerably, the trees and buildings of the city becoming distinct and gray. Cookie Monster sat leaning against the car door, staring blankly out the window, watching vacant city streets slide past, his eyes automatically checking dark alleys.

Going to be one of those summer days, Barney thought. Hot, dry, only a few clouds in the sky. One of those days for fishing and drinking beer; one of those days that made it hard to remember February and March, and easy to remember why he'd traded Virginia for Montana.

"Let's just go kill them," Cookie Monster said. "Right now. Just turn around and go waste them right fucking now."

Barney turned the Chevy into the shadows of the parking lot behind the courthouse. On the other side of the lot, floodlights still shone bright and sterile down onto three strands of barbed wire strung above a metal fence and gate.

Cookie Monster turned toward Barney. "I said—"

"Later," Barney said, looking at the gate and the lights. "Maybe later."

The gate and fence closed off a cul-de-sac about seven yards wide and fifteen deep, a small indentation that separated the old courthouse from the four-story addition that housed the county bureaucracy, and led to the rear entrance to the sheriff's department.

Barney shut the engine off and they sat looking at the building. The old courthouse was made of marble and granite and had a massive bell tower with a huge lighted clock. Radios in the unused squad cars crackled with squelch breaks and mumbled with not quite intelligible radio traffic.

Cookie Monster slouched back down in the seat. He rolled the window down. The early morning breeze felt cool and soft on his face. It always, even now, made him remember listening to the city band perform on pleasant summer nights—martial music, sometimes, that years later as a marine, in spit-shined shoes and dress blues, he'd marched to. A covered stone bandstand had been located in one corner of what to a young boy had seemed a huge expanse of green lawn. He'd liked to run along the cement wall that surrounded the lawn—the wall, big and fat and solid then, but now barely up to his shins and crumbling in places—run along the wall to the corner and look up at the statue of a World War I doughboy attacking, rifle in one hand, and near the doughboy an old cannon and an unbelievably tall and white flagpole, the American flag stirring lazily in the breeze while John Philip Sousa or Beethoven urged the doughboy on. Now the fine, thick lawn was sparse and scarred in places where mock graves had recently been dug by nuclear war protesters. The new addition, a glass and cement box, had replaced the stone bandstand and much of the lawn.

The corners and crevices of the cul-de-sac were filled with little piles of dirt and grit and small bits of paper that had been blown across the parking lot and trapped between the two buildings. An aluminum canoe with a jagged hole in the stern, several bicycles missing tires and chains and with bent handlebars and frames cluttered the cul-de-sac. From three positions, remote control television cameras stared down onto the lighted area.

"What the hell are we doing *here?*"

"Might as well get the report over with," Barney said, rubbing stubble on the side of his face. He gingerly touched his chin. "The lieutenant knows we were supposed to make a buy." He opened the door. "And besides, we've got to turn the buy money back in."

"I wonder why they didn't take the buy money?"

Barney shrugged. "Who knows? Probably figured it was marked or recorded. Like he said, this way it's their word against ours."

"What're you going to say in the report?"

"We'll say they didn't show. As far as anybody else is concerned, they didn't even show up. We drank some beer—too much beer—got pissed at each other, and wrestled in the dirt . . . typical drug team."

"Why say anything?"

"We won't, unless somebody asks. Shouldn't be anyone around this time of the morning, anyway."

They climbed out of the car and threaded their way between patrol cars to the gate. Cookie Monster pressed the button on a black box, small black speaker on top, set against the wall just inside the gate.

"Who's there?" a metallic voice coyly asked.

"Open the gate," Barney said.

"Why, I declare," the metallic voice replied, "It must be Smartsky and Hunch. For a minute there, we thought you were a couple of *transients* looking for a free meal and bed."

They both looked up at the television camera mounted above and to the left of the gate. "Open the fucking gate," Cookie Monster said.

"Hey, Barney," another voice yelled through the speaker, "what happened to your chin? She close her legs too hard or something?" They could hear loud laughter in the background.

The gate buzzed and Barney pushed it open. Self-conscious under the scrutiny of the cameras, they walked to the end of the cul-de-sac, to a metal door set into the side of the building. Cookie Monster grabbed hold of the doorknob and waited for the door to buzz.

Nothing happened.

He sighed and reached into his pocket.

"Assholes," he muttered, and pulled out his key ring. The door buzzed just as he inserted the key into the lock; Cookie Monster quickly pulled it open.

"Smart asses," Cookie Monster said, as they stepped into the elevator. He pressed the fourth-floor button.

They were both silent, impassively watching the closed elevator doors.

The doors opened, revealing the blank institutional-beige wall of a narrow hallway. Laughter and conversation echoed from the left. "Sounds like the whole graveyard shift," Cookie Monster said, following Barney out of the elevator. "Wouldn't you know it."

The hallway ended at the door to the combination radio and jailer's room. Another doorway opened immediately to the left. Two uniformed deputies stood just inside the door to the radio room, both young and overweight, bellies beginning to push over the top of wide, polished gun belts. The gun belts were festooned with black leather mace holders, handcuff cases, ammo carriers, and holstered four-inch Smith and Wessons. Both deputies were grinning. "Man, if I saw that in my house, I'd call for help," one of them said with a laugh. "Monster, he's so ugly, it boggles the mind."

"You're supposed to lock your pistols in one of the gun lockers when you're in there," Barney said.

Conversation died inside the room.

"We were just leaving," the deputy said, but Barney had already turned and walked through the other doorway, Cookie Monster behind him. Through a large and extremely thick window they could see the radio and television and teletype consoles, and a civilian jailer seated in a padded gray swivel chair, staring at them. Several more deputies stood on the other side of the radio console; one of them, sergeant stripes on his shoulder, held up his hand, two fingers extended in the peace sign.

"Can you believe that bunch is all that stands between the fine citizens of this country and chaos?" Cookie Monster said, following Barney around several more corners toward the narc room. "Imagine if they got in any real shit."

"Yeah. Like us."

The narc room door was open, fluorescent lights turned on, illuminating the clutter of too many metal desks, filing cabinets, typewriters. Portable radios, walkie-talkies, bongs and water pipes, and all manner and shape and color of other drug paraphernalia littered the windowsills and tops of the radiators and file cabinets. A bearded man, hair to his shoulders, plaid shirt and jeans, sat on top one of the desks in the corner, logging boots dangling toward the tile floor. Next to the desk he was sitting on was a large, very healthy marijuana plant growing in a grotesquely patterned yellow and orange clay pot, "Mascot" printed in large white sloppy letters on the pot.

"What are you doing here?" Barney said.

"Desk called. Said you two got in some kind of trouble. Some girl called and said someone beat the bejesus out of the both of you." He looked at Barney's chin and Cookie Monster's mouth, their dirty clothes.

Barney shook his head. "Leave it to the desk. Asshole here"—he nodded toward Cookie Monster—"made me drink too many beers while we were waiting to make a buy, and then tried to show me some weird Oriental wrestling hold and threw me on my chin." He walked over to a desk, pulled the chair out, and sat down, one leg on top of the desk. He smiled. "Had to smack him in the mouth—just to let him know who's boss."

Cookie Monster smiled.

"That right?" the man said, and stood and walked over to the window. He picked up a two-foot-high red plastic bong. "I suppose the dopers didn't show, either?"

Cookie Monster watched him play with the bong.

"Win some, lose some." Barney shrugged.

Bruce actually looks like a logger, Cookie Monster thought. A little over six feet, well-muscled back and shoulders and arms, but almost no chest. Thick wrists and callused hands. No way he looks like a narc, but his busts aren't very good, or often—small quantities of grass and speed. Well, he'd never worked with Bruce, and neither had Barney, so maybe it was just bad luck and poor training.

"I'm going to the head," he said. There was just no telling who'd make a good narc, he thought. Barney looked like a cop trying to look the way a doper was supposed to look, but since he did, and because of the southern accent he exaggerated when he was around dopers, people fell all over themselves trying to sell him dope.

In the men's room Cookie Monster looked at his face in the mirror: hair pulled severely back from a receding hairline and tied into a pony tail with a piece of old leather shoelace, scraggly beard and huge, sloppy mustache, crooked teeth behind the split and swollen lips, blue eyes. Christ, he looked like an aging hippie. Too mean and ugly and fucked-up looking to be a cop, let alone the way narcs were supposed to look today. Just another hair monster—a spaced-out child of the sixties and seventies become cynical and mercenary.

He ran water into the sink. Splashed some on his face and beard, but it only made him feel grubbier. He hadn't felt like this since Vietnam. Once, in 'Nam, they'd gone for nearly a month without a shower. Flying every day. Landing and taking off in the red dust. Patched and worn and shot-up helicopters. Oil and grease and hydraulic fluid. Everywhere flies buzzing from sawed-off fifty-five-gallon barrels underneath the shitters to the mess tent to the helicopters to the cans of C rations he'd eat because there were so many flies in the mess tent the food always seemed to be full of raisins. Everybody had the shits. The pilots and crew chiefs and gunners would crap in their pants and fly all day like that, changing clothes when they could, sick with fever and dysentery and who knew what else. No showers until the Seabees put in some chemical showers. Little metal spigots that dribbled tepid, foul wetness that was equal parts rice-paddy water and chemicals. No flies in the shower tent, though. Just mosquitoes.

Cookie Monster splashed more water on his face, then dried it with paper towels from the dispenser. His eyes were red and puffy—from the dust generated by that fucking truck. *Don't think about it.* He wet a crumpled paper towel with cold water and held it to his lips. *Think about Vietnam: keep things in perspective.*

He threw the wet paper towel into the wastepaper basket in disgust. Perspective: he'd had to shoot an entire squad of South Vietnamese soldiers, once. Massacre the poor fuckers.

"If any of them turn around when they get out of the helicopter, shoot them," an officer had told them at briefing. "We've been having trouble with ARVN troops getting out of the plane and turning around and shooting it up, or throwing a few grenades back inside. And check the radio compartment. They've been leaving grenades in the tail section, the pins pulled and a single rubber band holding the spoon on."

And sure enough, they'd flown in a squad of Vietnamese,

little brown-skinned men, frail and childlike in their steel helmets, flak vests, and American uniforms, rifles seeming too massive and unwieldly for them, and the last man out had turned around and he'd wasted him, and then the next man had turned around, and then the next and the next and the next until he'd wasted all of them.

They'd probably just wondered what all the shooting was about.

Cookie Monster shivered, staring with bloodshot eyes into the mirror. He could still see and feel the elephant grass rippling away from the helicopter in silver and green concentric waves. The helicopter bellowing and thrashing, radio traffic crackling and popping in his flight helmet. The fatigues pressed tight against the thin bodies of the Vietnamese as they turned around one by one. The M-60 machine gun vibrating in his hands, tracers disappearing into the waving grass, and into the bodies snatched backwards and down into the grass, rifles, helmets, and other bits of gear thrown like chaff into the wind. The helicopter rose, and the figures on the ground didn't move at all. Target practice.

Cookie Monster smashed at the swinging metal door to the john, hitting it twice before it rebounded against the cement wall, his fists leaving dents in the metal. *Why couldn't it have been those fucking dopers, all the fucking dopers and hair monsters, child molesters, murderers, rapists, all the people who deserved it?* He took a deep breath. *Don't think about it. Not now.* He caught his reflection in the mirror. God, he looked awful.

Barney was typing and Bruce was still sitting on the desk, playing with the bong while he gazed moodily out the window, when Cookie Monster walked back into the narc room. "Who called the desk tonight?" he asked, looking over Barney's shoulder at the report.

"Some chick named Debbie."

The report was nothing more than a note to the lieutenant: Officers Monster and Barney drove to the LaFray Creek Rest Area at 3:00 A.M. in the morning to meet suspect dopers and make a buy of dangerous drugs (see report #4719, 21 June). Dopers did not show up. Officers returned to station house. Officers returned $3,000.00 of buy money to narc safe. Officers went home.

" 'In the morning' is redundant.''

Barney laughed. "The lieutenant is redundant."

"Report number forty-seven nineteen? I don't remember writing anything about these guys, except in the log to account for mileage and time spent."

"I just threw that in to make this read a little more professional . . . fuck with the lieutenant's mind.'' Barney yanked the report sheet out of the typewriter. "Here. Sign it."

"You write reports like old people fuck," Cookie Monster mumbled, and signed the report: C. Monster, senior deputy.

"Say what?"

"You don't."

"Sign your real name, asshole. You want to upset the lieutenant?"

"That's the realest name I got at the moment."

Barney signed the report with a huge illegible scrawl. He took a stamp pad from the desk drawer, opened the pad, and rolled his right thumb across it. He pressed his thumb down onto the report next to his scrawled signature. The print was clear and neat.

"Not bad, Barn. Don't upset the lieutenant."

"The desk called the lieutenant, too," Bruce said. "He's on his way in."

"How long ago was that?" Barney asked.

"Ten or fifteen minutes before you guys got here."

"That means he won't be here for another fifteen minutes," Barney said. "I'll just go to the can, and then we can get out of here," he said back over his shoulder to Cookie Monster.

Cookie Monster sat down in Barney's chair and put his feet on top of the desk, the heel of one battered cowboy boot lying on the signed report.

"What really happened, Monster?" Bruce asked, his deep voice inviting confidence.

Cookie Monster laced his hands behind his head and leaned back in the chair, looking up at the off-white acoustic tiles. He detested that tone of voice: man-to-man, get-it-off-your-chest. "How long you been a narc now?" Cookie Monster said.

"Six months or so."

"Hmmm."

"What's that mean: Hmmm?"

Cookie Monster dropped his feet to the floor and swiveled his chair to look over at Bruce. Bruce's neck was flushed, the heavy muscles of his shoulders looked tight.

Cookie Monster stared at him. "Somebody told me you been to Vietnam?"

Bruce frowned. "Yeah. Yeah, I been." His eyes narrowed. "Why?"

"See any action?"

His eyes narrowed even further. "I was in the artillery—army artillery."

Cookie Monster was silent for a moment. "You ever think much about it anymore? Dream about it?"

"Sometimes. Not often." He shrugged. "It was a long time ago."

Cookie Monster nodded.

"Why do you ask?"

"You ever kill anybody? See anybody get killed?"

Bruce smiled and walked to the window, looked down at the street below. He turned back toward Cookie Monster. "Well, not exactly." He grinned, his teeth big and square, and yellow from chew. "But we fired plenty of artillery rounds—105, 155, 175. Some of them killed people." He paused. "I reckon killing people with an artillery round or with your bare hands, it's all the same thing." His gaze slipped past Cookie Monster and he reached into his back pocket and pulled out a red and black can of Copenhagen.

He removed the tin lid and took a pinch of dark brown tobacco and inserted it between his lower gum and lip. He smiled and put the can in his shirt pocket. "So how's Gerri?" he asked, and grinned again. "Man could settle down with a woman like that."

"Are you serious?"

"Of course. She's a special lady."

"I mean about killing people."

"Well, sure," Bruce said, his eyes smiling like a salesman's on the road.

Cookie Monster stood and stretched. "She's all right. Still doesn't know I'm a cop, though."

Bruce smiled.

Cookie Monster kneaded the back of his neck. "Hey, Bar-

19

ney," he yelled. "Let's go. You-know-who is going to be here any minute."

Barney come out of the john.

"Later," Cookie Monster said to Bruce. "Be sure to give the lieutenant our report."

"Let's take the main elevator," Barney said.

Back in the Chevy, they both opened a beer. The sun was just coming up, rays of heavy golden light filtering down the street on one side of the parking lot, through the maple trees on the other side. The wet grass and bushes next to the old courthouse sparkled. The sky was clear and blue.

Barney took a drink of warm Olympia. "Bruce know anything?"

"He knows that killing someone with an artillery shell is just like killing someone any other way."

Barney looked at Cookie Monster.

"I'm not joking; that's what he really said."

Barney frowned. "Well, what about what happened last night? He know anything about that?"

"No. Nothing." Cookie Monster looked across the courthouse lawn, across the far street where he could see the marine recruiter's office, a poster in the window: The Marines Are Looking for a Few Good Men. "I'm sure he doesn't know anything about that bunch we been working on . . . unless the lieutenant told him."

"The lieutenant," Barney said. He started the car.

"What are we going to do now?"

Barney backed the car out of the lot and into the sunshine. "Right now we're going to go out to your place and do a little fishing in that trout pond of yours that is full of big, fat trout, all of them too well fed and lazy to be caught because you insist on feeding them too much, and get drunk and crazy so we won't do anything we'll regret later. How's that sound?"

"Reasonable."

Barney gunned the Chevy around the corner and ran a red light—amber until they hit the intersection. A green sheriff's cruiser was stopped at the light, headed straight toward them. Barney honked the horn and waved; Cookie Monster held up the middle finger of his right hand. "Oh. We is going to hear about that, too," he said.

Barney smiled and turned the Chevy onto the Interstate on-ramp, headed for Nine Mile and Cookie Monster's place.

"What the hell's wrong with us lately?" Cookie Monster said.

Barney threw his empty beer can in the back. "Don't think about it," he said.

Cookie Monster's face darkened. "Don't think about it," he repeated.

"How you fixed for beer? Think on that."

"Better stop and get some."

They were silent, both of them watching the Interstate wind toward Frenchtown and beyond Frenchtown to Superior and Spokane and finally to Seattle. Go west, young man, Barney thought.

"It'll drive you crazy," he said.

CHAPTER **3**

Win Some, Lose Some

W hat happened to your mouth?'' she asked, and Ben opened his eyes. Dust motes floated in yellow-white beams of sunlight streaming through three large windows only a few feet from the mattress he lay upon. Fu Manchu, black except for white paws and a white marking that resembled a drooping Chinese mustache, sat sharing the dusty center windowsill with four or five desiccated flies.

"Kiss my ass, Fu," he mumbled automatically.

Fu Manchu yawned, exposing his teeth and throat, and stretched, careful not to place his paws on any of the dead flies.

"What are you doing here?"

"The door was open." She was behind him, fooling around with something in the dresser. "And that's not all that's open. There're empty beer cans everywhere. In the yard. The bathroom. The kitchen. The backyard."

"Barney was here yesterday."

"Is that why you haven't called or come over?"

Fu jumped from the windowsill and sauntered across the hardwood floor to the edge of the mattress.

"Go away. Don't even think about it."

She stopped digging in the dresser. "I beg your pardon."

"Fu," he said, still lying on his side facing away from her, the blanket pulled up under his beard. "I'm talking to the cat." Fu was black and sleek in the sunlight, his eyes arrogant and yellow. He reached out a paw and gently tapped Ben on the cheek. "I'm up, dammit. Can't you see I'm practically already up?" The paw paused and then tapped him again, more insistently this time. "Go play in the traffic or something."

"Somebody named Debbie called me at the hospital this morning."

Ben groaned. An image of Debbie dressed in camouflage jumpsuit, black, ugly barrel of an M-16 pointed at his guts, flashed through his mind. He rolled over onto his back and sat up, blanket falling to his waist. "Oh?" He held his head in his hands, elbows on bent knees. His mouth tasted of stale beer and coconut macaroons and vomit. His lips felt thick and swollen, and his head hurt. He hadn't taken a shower for two days. Should have taken one when they got back from the Blackfoot, but they'd started drinking and . . . "What time is it?" he asked.

"Eleven. What happened to your mouth?"

"I hurt it fishing yesterday." Fu crawled under the blanket and lay down next to his thigh. He started kneading Ben's skin with his claws. "Ouch. Dammit, Fu."

"It looks as if you were fishing for beer cans and catching them with your mouth."

Cookie Monster reached under the covers, grabbed Fu's front paws with one hand and pulled him out. He scratched the cat's belly and then swung him off the bed and toward the doorway. Fu landed lightly, stretched, and sauntered toward the doorway. Ben looked up.

She was still wearing her nurse's uniform, shoulder-length blond hair curled and soft looking. Her blue eyes watched him intently, a tiny furrow across her forehead. She nervously brushed unruly hair away from her forehead.

"Somebody named Debbie?" he said.

She held up what looked like a black wallet. His sheriff's badge, set into thick leather, glinted next to the laminated I.D. card.

He wouldn't meet her eyes; just stared at the gold badge as if he'd never seen it before. His stomach felt enormously hollow: a feeling that melded perfectly with the sour taste in his mouth. The same feeling he'd had when that M-16 went off.

"I was—" he started to say.

But she turned back to the dresser drawer, reached in, and held a tiny pair of silver wings up over her shoulder. His AirCrew wings. He'd forgotten he even had that stuff.

She held up a medal. "Purple Heart?"

He nodded.

"Why couldn't you have been straight with me?" she said. " 'Let's go slumming tonight, check out all the dives,' " she mimicked. "Don't you know me better than that? Obviously not."

"I couldn't . . ." he started to say, but realized how silly that would sound. "You can't under—"

"Oh, go take a shower. You stink." Her eyes filled with tears, and she quickly walked out of the room.

". . . stand," he said to the empty doorway. He grabbed a towel off the floor next to the bed and stood up, forgetting for the moment how hung over he was.

"Shit," he muttered and hurried to the door. "Shit. Shit. Shit." He wrapped the towel around his waist and ran into the living room and then onto the porch of the old farmhouse. Her orange VW was just pulling out of the yard, thumping across the metal cattle guard.

"Hey!" he shouted, running down the steps, one hand holding the towel up. "Hey, wait a minute," and caught a glimpse of her blond hair as the car turned out onto the county road and built up speed. She shifted gears, and the tiny orange car began to disappear behind a cloud of dust, a sandy fog that hovered over the pasture and trees long after he could no longer hear her car.

Fu purred and rubbed against his leg.

He picked the cat up and gently scratched its neck and chin, and looked for a moment across the fields in the direction she had gone. "Well, win some, lose some," Ben said, and put the cat back down. "C'mon, turkey."

Dopers, Barney thought, as he sat in an aluminum lawn chair, the orange and white plastic webbing new and clean and garish against the green of the front lawn and the wet, shining leaves of the maple tree that dripped water onto his bare chest and feet. *Dopers seen too much TV, read too many books.* In the distance, thunder rolled like volleys of artillery fire; lightning cracked nearby, sounding like the vicious slap of a 106 recoilless rifle. Raindrops splatted against his chest and stomach and face. *Dopers don't know it but movie time is about over.* The air under the tree was humid. Beer cans, crushed and bent, littered the grass around the lawn chair. *I wonder what the ex-old lady is doing.* Without warning, the rain abruptly became gray sheets of water that hissed and bounced against the pavement. *Monsoon,* he thought, reaching under the lawn chair for the last beer. The rain soaked and darkened the old faded cutoff camouflage fatigue pants he was wearing. "Rainy season," he muttered. "That's what it is." Water dripped from his chin and nose and fingers, and from the bill of his baseball cap. "What it is," he murmured again, one arm hanging limply over the arm of the lawn chair, hand curled around the can of beer, as he stared blankly into the rain and the water that made the street look like a canal full of silver water. Or a flooded rice paddy. He remembered another rainy season when he'd been out in the bush, in the shit, for five days, and fuck *that,* he didn't want to think about it: Lang Vei. Better to remember something like the time he was enjoying a can of Pabst Blue Ribbon beer that wasn't even rusty, lying in another Japanese-made-bought-in-America lawn chair atop an ancient concrete bunker constructed by the French and later owned by the Special Forces of the Army of the United States. Of which he'd been a first lieutenant and therefore, even though only twenty years old, entitled to sit on top of the bunker and watch the Artillery of the Army of North Vietnam rocket the shit out of the docks.

Rockets had screamed out the dull gray sky, wailing through the steady rain, plowing into the docks and ships and into the fat, swollen, ugly brown river. The explosions were wonderful. Pieces of crates and ships and maybe even people flying into the air. Once in a while one of the ships—navy landing craft, most of them—would be hit and the sound would be different: a heavy metallic blang, and gray and silver pieces of ship would arc into the air and splash into the river. The river was disgusting, so muddy and brown and fat it looked as if you could cut pieces out of it.

"Hey, you better get down from there. You want to get hit

or something?'' a corporal, flak vest, helmet, and camouflage fatigues, had shouted at him. "What the fuck you doin' up there, anyway?''

More rockets screamed and whistled overhead through the rain. *Wham! Wham!* The corporal flinched. *Blaang! Wham! Wham! Wham!*

"I'm working on my tan. What the fuck do you think I'm doing?'' And he grinned and raised his beer at the corporal. But inside he felt sick and hurt. Like a piece of that river was inside his guts.

The rain was already letting up. Several cars splashed past in the street, pale ovals in the wet and steamy windows—the drivers looking at him lying in the lawn chair. Barney sighed and sank back into the chair, with one hand wiping the rain off his face. He popped open the last Oly and took a drink. It tasted sour.

The rain stopped completely, and for a moment there were no cars and it was quiet.

He could hear drops of water falling from the maple tree onto the lawn and the chair and him.

The bushes and grass and maple trees began to glow obscenely green and tropical in the intense light filtering through the thin, leaden clouds. Shreds of slate-gray clouds hung at the base of the mountains across the valley.

Barney took another drink of beer. The sawmill across the river screeched and groaned.

At first they hadn't realized it was tanks. They'd thought it was one of the generators acting up, growling and roaring in the wet night over the sound of the battle.

"What the hell's that noise?'' he'd radioed the colonel.

"One of the generators, we think.''

"Well, I don't know. Sounds like it's coming from out front, somewhere down by the river.''

It sounded like a tank, but the Vietnamese had never used tanks before. And they were blowing their bugles, screaming, shouting, preparing to attack. Bangalore torpedoes were going off in the wire. Mortars and B-40 rockets and artillery incoming and outgoing. Flares and illumination rounds, machine gun and automatic rifle fire. Tracer rounds arcing out into the dark mass of jungle and bamboo; the river turgid and fast, orange in the glare and flicker of the illumination rounds.

Napalm. Jesus Christ, napalm bombs were going off in the wire, in the first line of bunkers and machine gun pits. A wave of men clad in black ran toward the wire, absorbing an amazing number of tracers and the bright flash and crump of mortar rounds. Shadows flickered everywhere in the orange light. Things were burning, the napalm and fresh illumination rounds. Another wave, uniforms this time, screaming, bugles blowing, pith helmets, Chinese steel hats, here and there branches and leaves attached. Incoming artillery stopped. Rounds snapped and cracked everywhere. Men shouting and screaming. Explosions. And that sound.

Under the orange light, three stubby black hulks roared and gnashed, screeching as they hit the first wire. One of them, its short, thin barrel tracking malignantly toward a machine gun firing an unbroken stream of red tracers, spurted a long finger of orange flame, and *crak-whuk,* the two sounds almost one, the machine gun post was gone, just gone, as the black hulks rolled across the wire. Four rows of wire. Concertina and razor wire and metal X's strung with wire, claymores and fixed charges, and the tanks just ignored it all and kept coming, growling and clanking, stopping momentarily to spit orange flame, their rounds firing and hitting with a sound like breaking a board with a rubber mallet.

The radio operator disappeared in one unbelievable smash of light and sound. Only twenty-five Americans—two Special Forces A Teams and one spook. And four hundred Vietnamese Ranger and Civilian Irregular Defense Group, and two other Americans already dead that he knew of, one shot through the neck, the other half his head blown away.

"Get as many LAWS as you can carry," he'd shouted at Cheney, and the two of them had run down into a lower bunker with about sixteen Light Anti-tank Weapons Systems. The tanks were through the wire. Orange. Everything shadows and shades of orange, flashing, streaking, burning, exploding. The fucking LAWS wouldn't work. Sixteen, and only three went off, one of them hitting a tank and exploding and burning against the metal, but the charge too old or wet or something to penetrate. The tank kept firing, and hitting things with that terrible sound.

The Vietnamese mortar team behind him had the mortars cranked all the way up and were using minimum charges,

27

shooting the rounds almost straight up into the air and down into the mass of charcoal-gray figures following the tanks through the wire. The mortar rounds had so little charge that they seemed to flutter toward the ground. A light wind blew some of them back into their own positions. The mortar crew's powder pit, behind and just above him, started burning.

Five divisions of the North Vietnamese Army out there, fifty thousand or so men, and it seemed as if all of them were coming through the wire.

"Two grenades each," he said to Cheney and the other sergeant on his left. "You two throw to the sides and I'll throw mine to the front. And then we'll get the fuck out of here," and as he threw, saw out the corner of his eye Cheney rise and throw a grenade and a round catch him in the side through the flak jacket and spin him around, and Cheney start to get up and throw the other grenade and two or three rounds thuk into his chest and stomach between the unzipped flaps of the flak jacket, and Cheney fall backward real quick like someone had a rope tied around his chest and had jerked hard on it. They carried him up to the concrete bunker and on the way the other sergeant took a round in the hip. Cheney was dead, of course, but you know . . .

He could still smell the sweat and blood and cordite and burning things against the organic, wet smell of Lang Vei during the rainy season.

"Was he a friend?" Cookie Monster had asked. Shit. They were all friends, and later the fucking colonel, in country only a few days, had charged a tank with grenades and been cut down, and Barney had gone out and pulled the stupid son of a bitch back, and some war correspondent had written a book and mentioned Lang Vei and the colonel and the tanks and the napalm, but he hadn't said anything about Cheney's chest and stomach and guts glistening on the cement floor in the flickering orange light, or Smitty's neck, or Amondsen's brains all over the wet dirt, or Powell who wasn't even hardly pieces anymore.

Barney took a long, hard drink of his beer and looked down at the scars on his knee.

Well, somehow they'd broken out, some of them, and walked and fought their way through the night and the jungle, the bush wet and dank and no fucking movie then, to Khe

Sahn only five klicks away. Only he and four other Americans and about twenty-five Vietnamese had made it to Khe Sahn that night. In the morning they'd gone back out to look for survivors. All told, ten Americans, including the spook, had made it out, and about fifty Vietnamese. Barney had taken mortar shrapnel in the knee, but nothing serious.

When they tried to get back to Khe Sahn again, they couldn't. Too much shit. So they walked to Dong Ha. Five days in the bush—rain and bugs and snakes and crotch sores and blisters and fighting all the time. But it didn't matter, none of it. He'd welcomed it. By then, he'd just wanted to kill people. When they reached Dong Ha, there was just him and two other Americans and about eight Vietnamese, and maybe ten clips of ammunition left among them. They'd killed people, all right.

Barney drained the beer, drinking thirstily, as if it were his first in a long time. He'd become so used to the sound of the sawmill that he hadn't noticed it for weeks.

An approaching pickup, obviously with a defective exhaust, blotted out the noise of the sawmill. He could see the truck down the street, high and thin and solid looking. Roaring and splashing past, a 1957 dark green International four-wheel-drive pickup, log rack on the back, large, faded Olympia sticker on the door, and Cookie Monster, his upper body out the driver's window, waving with both hands.

". . . beer!" he heard Cookie Monster shout over the noise of the truck, and the truck continued down the street. It sounded like a tank, he thought, even looked like one. Squat. Ugly. Tuned to the grind and screech of the sawmill. The truck turned around down the block and came back, stopping in front of his yard.

Cookie Monster climbed out of the truck.

"Incoming!" Barney shouted, and sat forward in the lawn chair and threw the empty can at the pickup.

Cookie Monster crouched theatrically, spun, and ran behind the truck. Barney saw his head peek above the truck bed. Cookie Monster vaulted into the bed and stood crouched, looking fierce, arms spread like a wrestler. "Gooks," he shouted. "Surrounded by slope motherfuckers," and dropped to his knees, tearing frantically at something, throwing yellow-orange and white bits of cardboard into the air. "Hippies, slant-eyes, hair monsters . . . You'll never get me!'' and began lobbing full cans of Olympia at Barney. ''Fire in the hole.''

Barney blinked as the first can arced through the air and smacked the aluminum support next to his elbow. Three or four more were already high in the air, arcing down toward the maple tree and him. ''Hey,'' he blurted and tried to catch the cans, but Cookie Monster kept lobbing them faster and faster. They were falling out of the maple tree, slicing through the leaves, thudding into the ground around him, hitting the chair. ''Ouch, goddammit . . .''

''Mortars!'' Cookie Monster shouted, and Barney fell sideways out of the lawn chair and scuttled on all fours behind the trunk of the maple tree. ''Nuke the whales!'' Cans thunked off the other side of the tree, one of them popping open, hissing and spurting foam into the yard.

Cookie Monster jumped out of the truck and ran zigzag across the lawn and picked up the beer can. He pulled the tab all the way off and took a healthy drink.

''Boy, you sure looked silly out here on that lawn chair in the rain,'' he said, leaning against the tree and looking at Barney, wet and bedraggled, grass stain on one shoulder, crouched behind the tree. ''Lucky I came by.''

Barney stood up. He rubbed the top of his thigh where it had been hit by a beer can.

''Have a beer,'' Cookie Monster said.

Cookie Monster squinted toward the sunset. They were still out in the yard, Cookie Monster sitting propped up against the maple tree, Barney lying in the lawn chair, the dark lenses of his aviator sunglasses refracting the bright reds and yellows of the setting sun. The sky had cleared completely; overheard it was a deep azure blue. Only the tip of the sun still showed above the mountains.

''I need another beer,'' Barney said. Beer cans were still scattered under the maple tree like so many metallic apples.

''I shot a woman once. I ever tell you that?'' Cookie Monster said. ''Shot her right through the head.''

''Hand me a beer, will you?''

''I never knew it was a woman, though. I mean, we were taking rounds. You know, those big blue-green tracers they had. Big fucking blue baseballs that seemed to float toward the helicopter. I just pointed at where they were coming from and fired—''

"A beer. Give me a beer, will you?"

"—like pointing a hose. Sometimes I could hardly hear the M-sixty over the helicopter and radio noise. Couldn't hardly feel it sometimes—just a dull sort of vibration, that old *machine* gun pivoting easy, like an oar in an oarlock. Brass flying everywhere."

"If you're going to get poetic about it, hand me a beer."

Cookie Monster took a drink of his beer. "Down on the ground, the grunts dug this gook body out of the plane. Her head was a real mess, eyes, nose, forehead gone. Slimy shit in her hair. She was the machine gunner, they told me. They thought it was great. . . . Wanted to see what my reaction would be, I suppose."

Barney groaned and got up off the lawn chair. He walked toward a beer can tilted into the grass. "Looks like a fucking Easter egg hunt," he said. "What will the neighbors think?" He shook the beer several times and walked over to Cookie Monster sprawled under the tree, and popped the can open, spraying Cookie Monster with beer. "Gives you bad dreams, does it?"

"Nope. None that I know of." A couple of fat little clouds, lit yellow and gold on the bottom, were caught in the middle of the sunset.

Barney laughed and walked back to the lawn chair. "Well, why should it? It was you or her."

They were silent, watching the horizon turn blood red, the little clouds becoming dark clots above black mountains.

Down the block someone started a lawn mower.

"How do you suppose they found out we are narcs?" Barney finally asked.

"Somebody told them, I suppose."

They were silent again, watching the sunset as it began to die.

"Movies," Barney said. "I read this book by a war correspondent, not a bad book, really, but he says we were just acting out a movie, or some such shit. And maybe we were at first. Sometimes. But I never seen a movie about the shits and jungle sores. Or about Mr. Charles blowing the shit out of everything and everybody. Brains and blood—really fucked up corpses. What it sounds like to hear a bullet hit someone you know.''

"What's that got to do—"

"But I sure have seen a lot of movies. Western movies. War movies. Man! Remember? It was supposed to be *fun*. Danger and adrenaline, wasting slant-eyes and fucking Suzie Wong. Coming home a hero. You know: finally getting to fuck the high school cheerleader, or some such shit.'' Barney stood and started pacing in front of Cookie Monster, gesturing with his beer. ''But the high school cheerleader was a doped-up, burned-out hippie chick. And we were baby killers, committers of atrocities.'' He threw his half-full can of beer at the dark hulk that was Cookie Monster's truck, but missed, the can hitting and sliding out into the street, beer spewing after it, hissing like a smoke grenade. ''So why the fuck not be a narc? Danger. Intrigue. A little fear, a little adrenaline. Let you know you're alive. About fucking time!'' He picked up another beer from the lawn and popped it open. ''But now. Now those ex-fucking hippies have screwed *everything* up.''

"Hey . . . jack down. Relax. Drink your beer.''

Barney stared down at Cookie Monster. He walked over and sat on the lawn chair again. ''Ahh, shit,'' he said. ''It's not just that. There's a lot of good people out there, too. People who don't never need to know what it is.''

"They called Gerri at the hospital. Told her all about me.''

Barney was silent.

"Well, anyway,'' Cookie Monster said. ''I guess you know we can't touch them with the law—they've got too much money, too much lawyer.''

"I know,'' Barney said. ''I know.''

"It's not just the dope—I don't care abut that—it's what they did and said to us. I won't be able to handle that if I don't do something about it. Especially since I believe them.''

"Yeah. But I care about the dope, too.''

"Well, whatever . . . that M-sixteen certainly had real bullets in it . . . for a while there . . .''

Barney grunted.

"On the other hand, we were real sloppy and don't have much excuse for letting ourselves get in such a predicament.''

"That's for sure."

"It all sort of boils down to just us and them, doesn't it?"

"And whoever told them we were narcs," Barney said. "Don't forget about that; that's the most important part."

Cookie Monster smiled at the darkness. "Why don't you finish your beer?" he said. "And put some clothes on, and we'll go get something to eat and talk about it."

CHAPTER 4

Ants in the Flowers

Cookie Monster turned the engine off and let the truck coast the last half-block. It was late and he didn't want her to know he was coming. The heavy mud and snow tires rumbled against the pavement. Gravel crunched next to the curb as the truck slowly came to a stop. He and Barney had talked for a long time, eating steak and eggs and drinking coffee, but nothing had been resolved. No real plan of action, except to head up toward Kalispell, to the bar where they'd first met the three dopers, and trace their steps back, see if they couldn't figure out who'd burned them, and why, before they did anything to the dopers. Play it by ear, Barney had said, one way or another they'd find out.

He smiled to himself, feeling the adrenaline just thinking about it. He had a feeling—that old feeling. . . .

There was a light on in her bedroom; all the other windows of the two-story four-plex were dark.

The night was clear and crisp, smelling of mowed lawns and irrigated gardens, already a hint of dew in the air.

He paused at the steps and looked up at the sky, remembering summer nights when he was a boy, sleeping out in the backyard and staring for hours up at the bottomless star-filled sky. Sometimes other kids would sleep over, and they'd talk about people from other planets and, looking up at the stars, try to solve the riddle of how the first, the very first, anything came to be. Then they'd go raid gardens, creeping bent over and on hands and knees through rows of corn and strawberries and beans, smearing dirt on their faces and pretending to be commandos stealing from the enemy.

At the top of the steps, he looked out over the wrought-iron railing at the houses and lights covering the hillsides surrounding the city. When he was a boy, none of those lights, except the ones in a few farmhouses, had been there. Just fields and gullies and forests filled with squirrels, chipmunks, birds—hawks and owls and even a few eagles—deer, porcupine, and once in a while a bear. Just him and his dog. Hours of exploring, of being alone, enjoying the solitude. But now it was low-income housing on one hillside, the rich and ostentatious on the other hillsides. Paved streets, kids, cars, noise. The wild animals gone. The valley nearly always full of air pollution. No solitude in those hills anymore. But that was okay. Being alone was no longer enjoyable: his mind seemed as clogged and polluted as the valley.

He raised the brass knocker and sharply rapped it several times against the wood door. He pictured her reading in bed, wearing one of the ridiculously large T-shirts that she liked to sleep in. Her blue eyes—flecked with gold and with a double row of eyelashes—startled, but probably already guessing who it was. Throwing on her old white terry-cloth bathrobe. Walking to the door.

"Who's there?" her muffled voice asked.

"Me. It's me," he said, surprised that his throat and mouth were so dry. The first "me" was almost a croak.

The chain rattled and the porch light went on. The door opened.

She was sleepy-eyed, dressed in the old bathrobe. "Come in." She turned and walked toward the kitchen, paused momentarily next to the couch, and switched on a table lamp. "Want a beer?"

"No, thanks," he said, and sat down on the couch.

She opened the refrigerator. White light flooded around her, and he could see how fine and silky and thick her hair was. She closed the refrigerator door and walked out of the darkened kitchen toward him, handed him a can of Olympia.

He automatically popped open the beer and took a drink.

He really didn't want it; still too full of coffee and toast, steak and eggs.

"Look," he said, leaning forward, elbows on knees, forcing himself to look up at her. "It was for your own good I didn't tell you I was a cop." She was wearing his favorite perfume. "We might have had a fight or something, and in a moment of anger you might have told someone who I was and . . ." His voice trailed off as he watched her walk across the thick carpet to the bedroom door and reach in and switch off the bedroom light. She walked back across the carpet and seated herself cross-legged on the floor on the other side of the glass-covered coffee table and looked at him.

He frowned. He needed a Rolaids or something. He looked around the room. The colors were warm. Heavy oak furniture, chairs, end tables, couch. Clusters of pictures, of all different sizes, with wood frames. One wall almost entirely covered by shelves full of books. He stifled a belch and moved the can of beer from side to side on the coffee table, watching the thin trail of water as the can slid across the glass surface. He rubbed his beard, looked around the room again. Flowers and plants. Ferns. Bamboo. Jade plants. Comfortable.

Usually. Her eyes glittered. He took a long, hard drink of beer, watching her to one side of the uptilted can. Full of pity, her eyes were. Wet. Abruptly, for an instant, he wanted to leap up and smash his fist into her face. He carefully set the can down on the glass tabletop.

"Maybe it's for the best," he said nastily.

She picked at the carpet. "Maybe."

"Someone has to do it," he said. "It's not all peace and love and 'hey, man have a toke.' . . . There are some nasty people out there, lady. Blow-you-fucking-*away* people. People who love to hurt or kill and just happen to be selling dope, too." He could hear his voice getting out of control.

"Is that why you do it, Ben?" she asked quietly, looking down at the carpet. "Is that really why you do it?"

"Someone has to. At least I understand that kind of person."

"Ben . . . I've seen too many like you." She looked up at him.

"Just like me, huh?" He despised the pity and knowledge in her eyes. He laughed, and reached behind his head and flapped his ponytail up and down. "You don't even know what I look like without a beard and long hair."

She stood up and glared down at him. "How *could* I know you?" She pointed a finger at his head. "*You* don't even know you." She walked over to the bookshelves.

"I hate you," she said. He could see the tears. "All of you. I hate all of you who like to fight and con and play with guns." She walked to one of the chairs and sat down, feet braced, hands firmly gripping the chair arms—as if she were in a plane about to crash, he thought—and stared directly at him, tears running down her cheeks.

"No, that's not true, I don't hate you. You just like what you do."

Cookie Monster leaned back in the couch. "Terrific. I'm not supposed to like it every time we stop a murderer or rapist or help an accident victim."

"Oh, I know more about it than you think I do. Your . . . your generation of veterans was uniquely prepared for combat—"

"What the hell are you talking about now?"

"It's no secret. I learned about it in psychology class. You were taught to want to fight. To like it. You were made into a kind of addict—addicted to . . . to a special excitement."

"Yeah, that's right. All of us. Especially all the guys in the psycho wards."

"No. Not all of you—and don't use that tone of voice with me; you can get out right now. Most of you who experienced combat . . . there's really not that many of you, I know that."

"Well, you sure seem to know it all." No tears—or pity—in her eyes now.

"It made you emotional cripples. You don't want to, or just plain can't, understand normal feelings, normal desires—stable job, house, wife, kids—"

Cookie Monster jumped to his feet. "What!" he shouted. "What the fuck do you know about it?" He crouched, arms held away from his body, trembling. "I don't give a fuck what your psychology professor said. What the fuck do you know about how I felt? Feel. Friends dead. Fucked-up bodies. Dead, lady. D-e-a-d, dead. Guys I went to boot camp with, vibrating like Jell-O on the floor of my helicopter.

37

Missing legs, arms, heads. Holes in chests, stomachs. Burned. Rotten. Full of maggots . . .

"What the fuck does your psych professor know about maggots?" he shouted and moved around the table toward her, right hand balling into a fist. "Tell me that, you know so fucking much!"

She pressed back into the chair. "Ben . . . don't—"

"Don't," he screamed down at her, spittle hitting her face. "Fuck 'don't,' " and took quick steps toward the bookshelves and smashed his right arm into a row of paperbacks, a forearm smash that sent books and shelf cascading onto the floor. "Shit," he yelled and kicked at the fallen books. "Shit. Shit. Shit."

He stopped and stood staring blankly at the mess, his chest heaving.

He took a deep breath.

"Oh, man," he said. "I've never done anything like that before."

He looked over at her, still pressed into the chair. Another fucking deer, he thought. Too stupid to get out of the way of the headlights.

"I'm sorry," he said.

He picked up the fallen shelf and set it back on the metal brackets and began picking up books and placing them on the shelf. His hands trembled, his legs felt weak, and he didn't know if it was because of what she'd said or the way he had reacted to it.

He knew he should say something like "I'm not really that way anymore; you're plenty of excitement for me, I love you," but instead, mostly just for something to say, he said, "Not everyone is like me and Barney. A high school buddy of mine went to Vietnam and came back after only a few months because he was the sole surviving son. Mentally he was a wreck, even after such a short tour. Afraid of everything. He got married. Got a solid job. Now it's all he can do to cope with that."

"You know what I'm talking about," she said.

"Another high school friend came back and got heavy into drugs—LSD, heroin, speed, anything he could get his hands on. From what I've heard, he's practically a basket case now."

"You know," she said again.

And of course he did, even if she didn't. His father and uncles had been marines. He had expected to fight in a war when he grew up. He'd never even really thought about it, just assumed it. When Drill Instructor Lopez walked into the Quonset hut and told half a platoon of shaven-headed marine recruits sitting on the cement floor that he just couldn't wait to get to Vietnam and kill gooks, Cookie Monster had found that attitude completely natural. A given.

"Those dopers—the ones who called you—really did a number on us," he said. "A real number." He put the last of the books on the shelf and turned to face her, hands in his pockets.

Her lips were soft and full, and he could see the swell of her breasts under the bathrobe. He wanted to just hold her, but knew he was feeling the chemistry only because it was going to be good-bye. Another movie, he supposed: what could be, if only all the other wouldn't intrude.

"You'd better go," she said.

At the door, he grinned uncontrollably. "I'll see you," he said.

"Don't do anything stupid," she said, staring up at him. "Please don't do anything you'll regret."

All the way to the pickup, he could feel her eyes on him—blue eyes with gold flecks. He opened the door and climbed in, feeling as if he was going to choke.

The truck rumbled to life and he drove slowly down the street. He waved his left arm out the window, afraid to turn around and look. Afraid if he saw her still framed in the light coming out the doorway, he would turn around and go back.

"Kiss my ass, world," he muttered, and turned the headlights on. He shifted into third and headed for home.

Unaccountably, he felt better.

"Coffee ought to be done," Barney said, leading the way toward the kitchen. The house was an old wooden, made-before-the-Second-World-War house that Barney had remodeled himself: bookcases made out of old barn wood, new tile and cabinets and appliances in the kitchen, new paint, and a carefully tended yard. He loved flowers. Every year his mother sent him hundreds of dollars' worth of flower bulbs from Virginia. "How'd it go last night?" he asked, pouring coffee for himself and Cookie Monster.

Cookie Monster shrugged. "Lot more fish in the sea," he said, accepting a mug.

"Better sit in the living room," Barney said. "The ex-old lady came by the other day and took the kitchen table and chair."

"Got any doughnuts or anything?" Cookie Monster opened the refrigerator and bent forward to peer inside. "Bacon. Eggs. Beer . . ." He carefully held the coffee mug away from the interior. "Wilted lettuce, wilted carrot . . . Something breeding in here, Barn. Something green and white and terrible . . . No cookies, even."

Midmorning sunlight filtered through the maple trees and through the picture window, blotches of sunlight and shadow like camouflage on the furniture and walls and bookcase, and on Barney, making it difficult to see him sitting in a large upholstered chair.

Cookie Monster leaned against the bookcase. "What happened to all the ferns? And that plant used to be in front of the window?"

"Ex-old lady took them, too." Barney drank from his mug. "Looks like she's going to get the house—everything except my personal possessions." He glanced up at Cookie Monster. "Depressed you, did it?"

"Nah." Cookie Monster shifted his feet, looking down at the carpet. "I dunno. Maybe."

Barney sipped at his coffee.

"Your house, too," Cookie Monster said. "That's a real screw."

Patterns of light bobbed and weaved as a light breeze moved the leaves of the maple tree.

"Felt like a piece of whale shit when I woke up this morning," Cookie Monster said.

"Nothing lower than whale shit." Barney took another sip of coffee.

"She really is special," Cookie Monster said. "I might ought to be in love with her, even." He laughed nervously.

Barney rolled his eyes and looked out the window. "Every time you knock off a piece of ass, you fall in love."

Cookie Monster stared into the mug.

40

"And now you feel guilty."

Cookie Monster sighed. "Well, didn't you—" he began, but the phone, on the floor next to Barney's chair, rang.

"Guess who," Barney said.

"Probably."

Barney picked up the receiver and leaned back in the chair. "Huroh," he said. "Honorable Barney not home. Can take message?"

"Oh, good morning, Lieutenant, sir, what a sur—" He paused, listening. "I did write a report; we have been around." He paused again. "Out at Monster's. Here. Around, just around. Shit. What are you—our baby-sitter?" He squinted in the direction of Cookie Monster, his knuckles tightening on the receiver. "Get our asses down there? What are you talking about? We're supposed to be under cover."

Cookie Monster placed his coffee mug on one of the shelves.

"Nothing happened. No one showed up. It's all in the report." Barney sat up in the chair. "I don't know who it was. Some crazy broad . . ." He stopped and looked over at Cookie Monster. "Oh . . . she said that, huh? Met us up at Kalispell . . ."

Cookie Monster cleared his throat and walked to the door. He stood inside the screen door, gazing innocently out at the front yard and porch, rocking back and forth on his heels, hands clasped behind his back.

"Well, that's probably why she called, then: just trying to get Monster in trouble."

Cookie Monster began to whistle tunelessly.

"We didn't need any backup. Like I said in the report, they didn't show. . . ."

Barney listened intently.

"Let me explain—" Barney began. Cookie Monster could hear the southern accent beginning to creep into his voice. "Lieutenant, this phone line is recorded all the time. It might not be wise to—"

Cookie Monster smiled and turned back toward Barney.

"Well, yes, sir, Lieutenant, sir, I certainly realize that is an order—" Barney stood up and mouthed "fuck you" at the mouthpiece, his face flushed and angry. "Yes," he said. "But—" He held the phone away from his face. Cookie Monster could hear the dial tone. Barney slammed the handset down.

"I've had about all I can take from that asshole," he said.

"That makes two of us."

Barney leaned back in the chair, his eyes narrowing as he looked up at Cookie Monster.

"Sure are a lot of beer cans out on your lawn, Barn," Cookie Monster said hurriedly, his eyes not meeting Barney's.

"Monster. Monster, is there something you neglected to tell me about Debbie? You know: Debbie. The sexy little number who fired about half a clip of two-twenty-three right over your head."

"Ah, well . . . actually." Cookie Monster grinned. "I meant to tell you . . ." He shrugged, arms out from his sides, palms up. "But . . ."

"You screwed her, didn't you?" Barney jumped up and walked toward Cookie Monster. "You crazy son of a bitch; the lieutenant was right. You screwed her."

Cookie Monster cleared his throat. "Actually . . ."

"You did it that first night we met them up at that bar outside Kalispell," Barney said. "When you went outside with her . . . 'to talk about a buy,' " he mimicked.

"Well . . ."

Barney grabbed handfuls of Cookie Monster's faded orange tank top, EP water-ski logo on the chest. "What am I going to do with you?" he said in his southern voice, the same voice he loved to use making a bust: "Ah'm sorry to ruin y'all's evening, but . . . but y'all are under arrest," and he'd flash the gold sheriff's badge, laughing at the stunned, mouth-gone-slack, watery-eyed looks. He gently shook Cookie Monster. "What am I going to do with you, Monster?" He shook harder, and the shirt ripped along the neckline.

Cookie Monster grinned down at him. "So solly," he said. "Won't hoppen again."

Barney shook him again; the shirt ripped a little more. Cookie Monster continued to grin, his eyes wide and blue and guileless, like those of a puppy that doesn't know why it's being beaten. Barney let go and turned away. "The lieutenant wants to see us in *exactly* one hour."

"You're just jealous."

"Jealous!" Barney shouted and spun around. "Not jealous, you fucking idiot. But I might have been seriously in fear if I'd known you'd porked her."

"A woman scorned . . ."

Barney looked at him.

"Uh . . . Well, why's the lieutenant in such an uproar?"

"He says someone—one of the sheriff's old cronies—heard the shots—don't change the subject, asshole—and saw the car and us. Called the old man, personally."

Cookie Monster smiled. "And the sheriff wanted an explanation from the lieutenant. And the lieutenant only had that report to show him. What's wrong with that?"

Barney retrieved the coffee mugs and walked back toward the kitchen. "The lieutenant is going to use this as an excuse to give us our monthly ass chewing. That's what's wrong with that."

"You mean the too many expenses, too much drinking, too much unaccounted time, poor police procedure lecture?"

"That's the one."

Barney walked out of the kitchen, two beers grasped in each hand. "Here," he said. "Let's go out on the porch." He held the screen door open. "I can't believe you really porked her."

"Heat of the moment, I guess."

Barney shook his head. "Oh, you're something, you are."

"You're one to talk."

Barney sat down on the steps, counting the empty beer cans spread around the yard. He stopped counting and sat for a moment thinking about it. "I suppose so," he said. Right after he'd gotten out of the Special Forces, he'd gone in on a bar with two other guys. But all the people—his family, friends, customers—and the drinking and carousing every night had gotten to him, and he'd sold his share in the bar and come out to Montana to get away from it all. Hunt. Fish. Hike. Camp. He'd always wanted to see Montana, ever since he was a kid hunting deer in the family's fruit orchards.

But Montana had been too much too soon. He'd moved to Hamilton, where there were almost no women his age—they all moved or married as soon as they got out of high school—and with no women around, he'd decided it was time to get married. He called up a girl he used to date—they'd always

43

had a good time together—flew back to Virginia, married her, and drove back out to Montana.

Barney leaned back on his elbows, feeling the morning sun on his face. He closed his eyes.

"Middle-class America just kind of crept up on me," he said. "I felt suffocated. Like I was being eaten by some insidious disease or something."

"Insidious disease. Is that sort of like the clap?"

"Sort of." His wife had hated Montana. Wanted to go back to Virginia. No way he'd go back. No way. So, instead, she got religion, and pottery, and auctions, and concerts at the university. And they bought more things and never had any money. Doctor and dentist bills. Things. "Like jungle rot," he said. And guilt, he thought, ministers and marriage counselors, and it was always *all* his fault, they said.

And they were probably right.

He stood and walked over to a gigantic chrysanthemum bush covered with white flowers growing next to the house—the ex's pride and joy. "Ants on these flowers," he said.

He poured beer over the flowers.

"VC ants," he said, watching the ants suddenly appear out of the center of the blossoms and rush around, up and down the stems and leaves, running over one another. "The more you wash off, the more there are."

"They'll like that beer," Cookie Monster said. "Go right to their heads."

"What d'you suppose they think about us?" Barney said. "Crazy fucking people messing up their world."

Cookie Monster peered at the ants on the flowers. "I think they probably wish we'd leave them alone and go see the lieutenant."

CHAPTER 5

Dead to Rights

Hi, Brenda," Cookie Monster said to the narc secretary. She was standing next to the desk he and Barney had used the night before last. Five feet five, short curly hair, wearing a tight knit top and tight black slacks. "You're sure looking good today."

"Ben." She smiled. "And Barney. What are you two doing here?"

"Our lord and master beckons," Barney said.

Bruce was seated at a desk in the corner, a manila folder open on the desk in front of him. He held up a hand in greeting.

"I don't remember asking you to come in," Brenda said, seating herself behind the desk.

Barney laughed. "I meant our *official* lord and master."

"That top is indecent." Cookie Monster leered.

"He's in talking to the sheriff." She smiled at Cookie Monster. "You're supposed to wait for him in the conference room."

"C'mon in and wait with us."

She laughed, a throaty, good-natured sound. "You know the rules. No fraternizing among employees."

"What are you guys doing here?" Bruce asked, watching Brenda and Cookie Monster.

"What are *you* doing here?" Barney asked. "Aren't you supposed to be working undercover, too?"

Bruce grinned his big yellow grin.

"The lieutenant's idea," the secretary said.

Cookie Monster leaned toward Barney, cupped his hands around his mouth, and loudly and theatrically whispered: "He's got a thing for Brenda, Barn. Wants to fondle her body."

Brenda laughed, and Bruce blushed, his neck and cheeks on either side of his beard turning red.

Cookie Monster waggled his fingers at Bruce and followed Barney into the other room.

The room served as both conference room and interrogation room, and occasionally as a classroom used by patrol commanders. The carpet was military green; the walls off-white; the table long and dark brown, chips and scratches at the edges, seven or eight steel chairs with gray padded backs and seats scattered around it. In one corner of the room a pile of books and tapes and a color television set and a videotape system were heaped on top of a long green wooden box. There were no windows. Barney walked around the table and sat down facing the doorway. A small green blackboard hung from the wall facing him, diagrams of possible robbery situations chalked in yellow on it. Cookie Monster began drawing something next to the diagrams.

"What's that supposed to be? Chinese?"

"Yup."

"What's it say? Fuck you?"

"Yup." Cookie Monster put the chalk down and took a chair across from Barney.

"Are they here yet?" a loud they-better-be-here voice asked.

"Yes, sir," the secretary replied, her voice tinged with respect. "The officers are in the conference room, as you requested."

Cookie Monster looked at Barney.

"I'm expecting a call from Seattle," the voice said. "Let me know if it comes in."

"Yes, sir."

"Yes, sir!" Cookie Monster said, a stricken look on his face. "Oh, no. Tell me it's not true."

Barney nodded. "About a month now."

Cookie Monster let his head fall forward onto the table, arms splayed to the sides. "Arhh," he said, his voice muffled against the tabletop. He lightly banged his head up and down, ponytail bouncing as his forehead struck the wooden surface. "Arhh. Arhh. Arhh. He's got kids and a wife and everything . . ."

Barney smiled sourly. "So's she. Except she's got no husband—no man."

"Her and about half the women in this city," Cookie Monster said. "Too bad. The prick."

The lieutenant walked into the room. "What was that, *Officer?*" His tone reminded Cookie Monster of the first time Lopez had called him "recruit." A dirty word. The lieutenant closed the door and took the chair at the head of the table.

"Nothing, Lieutenant, sir, I was just remarking to *Officer* Barney here that there sure are a lot of divorced women in this here city. Heck, sir, you can't hardly walk into a bar anymore without being besieged by sex-starved divorcées. 'Course, being a married man and all, you probably don't know about that."

The lieutenant looked stonily from Cookie Monster to Barney. Six feet, medium build, tan cotton sport coat cut too big and padded at the shoulders, crew-neck cotton shirt—turquoise to emphasize his green eyes—baggy cotton pants that matched the coat. Blond hair, mustache. Sunglasses hanging from the coat pocket.

" 'Besieged,' " Barney said. "What kind of a word is that?"

"Same kind as 'insidious.' "

"Do you two have to dress like that, when you report in here? You don't have to come to the station dressed like that."

"When we report in here?" Barney flared. "We shouldn't even be here—"

"What's wrong with these clothes?" Cookie Monster interrupted, catching Barney's eye. "In case you forgot, Lieutenant, sir, we're supposed to be *under cover. Deep* under cover." He put one rubber sandal–clad foot up on the table. "And Ho Chi Minh sandals and cutoffs are uniform of the day for any undercover person worth his salt." He folded his arms across his chest. "These clothes are a *disguise*, Lieutenant."

"That's right, Lieutenant," Barney said, watching the lieutenant. "We wouldn't want anyone finding out we are narcs, or anything like that, would we?"

"But don't worry," Cookie Monster said. "We're not like this in real life."

Barney put his feet up on the table, not taking his eyes off the lieutenant. Barney was wearing dirty gold-colored low-cut Converse basketball shoes without socks. His T-shirt had a design on the front that from a distance looked like the Olympia beer trademark—horseshoe surrounding an old brewery with a water wheel—but instead of "Olympia," it said "Opium" across the top, written in the same calligraphy as the usual "Olympia," and across the bottom instead of "It's the Water," the shirt read "It's the Poppies."

"Ain't nobody ever realized we were narcs until after we busted them," Barney said. "And sometimes they won't even believe it then."

"In real life, we're a lot worse," Cookie Monster said.

"Are you two done?" The lieutenant looked from one to the other.

"Never been burned," Cookie Monster said.

"Please don't look at us like that, Lieutenant," Barney said. "You'll frighten us."

The lieutenant leaned forward, looking intently from one man to the other. "You two are in serious shit," he said. "This time the sheriff is really pissed off." His smile was like that of a banker repossessing a new car. "I just talked to him."

"I just talked to the secretary," Cookie Monster said. "How're the wife and kids, Lieutenant?"

The lieutenant jumped to his feet, metal chair banging into the wall behind him. "Goddammit, I've had enough bullshit from you two. I'm fed up with your smart-ass remarks!" He pointed at Cookie Monster. "I am sick of your attitude." He pointed at Barney. "And I'm sick of your impertinence and insubordination."

He ran a hand through his hair. "You're supposed to be a sergeant," he said to Barney. He gestured toward Cookie Monster. "Providing an example for this idiot. Officer Anderson says you ran a red light right in front of him and then gave him the finger in front of civilian witnesses. Is that right?''

Barney nodded.

"Anderson can kiss my—" Cookie Monster said, but was silenced by a look from Barney.

"Why didn't you have a backup? You know the procedure."

"We didn't need it."

The lieutenant raised his eyebrows and looked meaningfully at Barney's chin and Cookie Monster's mouth. "Don't bullshit me. I listened to the tape of that woman's call. You fucked up." He smiled, exposing his perfect teeth. "You guys went up the Blackfoot to make a buy, and you fucked up."

Barney and Cookie Monster were silent.

The lieutenant coldly looked from one man to the other. "That got your attention, didn't it? Nobody puts a hurt on you two. Not unless they have you dead to rights. Not two trained killers like you."

Barney and Cookie Monster looked at each other.

"You see the top the secretary is wearing?" Barney asked Cookie Monster.

"Ohhh," Cookie Monster rolled his eyes upward. "Did I see that top?"

Barney held both hands up, palms outward, one on either side of his face, closed his eyes, and shook his face from side to side. "Bwwwww . . ." He opened his eyes and looked at the lieutenant. "Just get in there between those things." He closed his eyes, shaking his face again. "Bwwwwww . . ."

"Okay, that's it." The lieutenant leaned forward, fists on the tabletop. "I've had it with you two." They could see a customized .45 automatic in a brown Bianchi shoulder rig concealed beneath his sport coat. "You're through. You're back on patrol tomorrow."

Barney sighed and pushed his chair back. He slowly stood.

The lieutenant straightened, watching him.

Cookie Monster stood also.

"Look," Barney said, his voice even and reasonable. "You're right. We fucked up." He stepped toward the lieutenant. "We fucked up because someone *burned us!*"

Cookie Monster gently tugged on the lieutenant's coat sleeve. "Pay attention, sir."

The lieutenant jerked his arm away from Cookie Monster. "Sit dow—"

"Not many people knew we were even working on these dopers," Barney said. "Just me and Monster, you, the sheriff, and anyone else you or the sheriff might have told. Asshole that the sheriff might be, I can't believe he'd do anything like that, can you?"

"He likes us," Cookie Monster said. "Our busts get him reelected."

Barney smiled. "You see our problem, don't you, Lieutenant?"

"Now, look—"

"No, *you* look," Barney said, allowing a little of the anger to leak out. "This is no big-city police department. Lieutenant doesn't mean anything here, except how far you got your nose up the sheriff's behind. *We* do the work. *You* hang around the office, take the credit, cheat on your mileage and expenses—"

"Wouldn't some of the commissioners love to find out about that," Cookie Monster said.

"—and fuck the secretary. The rest is all bullshit stories about you in Miami."

"We met a cop from Florida last fall," Cookie Monster said. "Took him hunting."

"He checked up on you for us," Barney said.

"Got him a real nice five-point elk," Cookie Monster said.

The lieutenant swallowed, his Adam's apple moving above the turquoise shirt. "That's bull—"

"It's not bullshit," Barney said. "You know it; we know it. So don't tell us we're through. We don't care what lies you told the sheriff; this place needs someone like you. All we care about are those dopers and who burned us. Especially who burned us."

"Pretty expensive threads, Lieutenant," Cookie Monster said. "Always wondered how you managed to buy land, build a house, and support a wife and kids and horses and all the toys you have."

"I don't have to take this."

Cookie Monster's hand shot out, and the lieutenant flinched.

Cookie Monster picked an imaginary piece of lint from the lieutenant's shoulder. "Let's not start any cowboy shit. What do you say?"

"We don't think it was you," Barney said. "You're not *that* dumb. And anyway, if you had, we'd be hearing about it from our snitches."

"Those hippies threatened to kill us," Cookie Monster said. "And they were serious."

The lieutenant's eyes narrowed. "So arrest them."

Cookie Monster smiled at Barney. "Now, why didn't we think of that?"

"This is between us and them," Barney said. "Our report stands: nothing happened. Monster and I drank too much waiting for the dopers and got in a fight. That's all."

"You'd better—"

"You say word fucking one to anyone . . ." Barney smiled. "Well, you know us well enough by now.

"Tell the sheriff you chewed our ass good. And we are sufficiently chastised and promise not to do anything like it in the future. Tell him you sent us on another out-of-town trip—to Kalispell; that's close to where everything seems to have started—to work off some of our excess energy." He paused, considering. "We'll be gone anywhere from a couple of days to a week or so. We'll take Monster's truck."

Cookie Monster opened the door.

"After you," Barney said.

The lieutenant cleared his throat. He glanced from Cookie Monster to Barney. "If anything goes wrong, it's going to be your asses, not mine."

"We go, you go."

The lieutenant looked hard at Cookie Monster, and turned and walked through the door.

Barney watched him retreat into the narc room. "Don't underestimate him. He might be small-time, but he's mean and smart like a—"

"Like a snake," Cookie Monster said.

When they walked out of the conference room, the secretary was alone, typing at another desk, gazing blankly toward

51

them, thin gray earphones in her ears, a wire connecting the earphones to a tape recorder.

"Bye, Brenda," Barney said, and waved as he walked out of the narc room.

"Bye," Brenda called after him, and took the earphones out of her ears. She smiled at Cookie Monster.

"Brenda," he said, "I *am* surprised."

Her eyes darkened. For the first time he noticed the lines at the corners of her eyes and around her mouth.

"Fuck you," she said. "What do you know about it?"

"You asked for it," Barney said as they walked down the steps inside the rotunda of the old courthouse, past the faded and cracking Paxon murals of Lewis and Clark's West, and out through the glass and aluminum doors.

"I guess so," Cookie Monster replied, squinting in the bright, hot sunlight. The conference room always made him feel dirty. Ugly. It felt good to be outside in the heat and noise and pollution. "Why'd you say we were taking my truck?"

Barney stopped and turned toward him. "Because we're not." Behind Barney, off in the corner of the courthouse lawn, Cookie Monster could see the statue of the World War I soldier, white birdshit on his darkened helmet, looking as if he was running away from them, headed across the intersection, through the traffic, and into the bar full of Indians and rundown cowboys and ranchers already drunk at noon. They wouldn't even notice.

"Say what?" he said.

"It's time we cleaned up our act," Barney repeated. "A change of appearance won't hurt." He looked Cookie Monster up and down. "Besides, I'm sick of looking at your dirty, grubby, hippie face. Go get a haircut, shave off your beard—it looks like hell, anyway—and get some other clothes. Try to look like a normal person . . . if it's possible."

"Now?"

"I'll meet you back at my place. Put your truck in the garage and lock the garage doors." He turned and began to walk away.

"You think the lieutenant burned us?" Cookie Monster said.

Barney turned back toward him. "Maybe. I don't know. I don't think so. But from now on we're not taking any unnecessary chances."

He turned and walked toward the street.

"Hey, Barn . . ."

"Later," Barney said without turning around.

". . . you sure are getting fat."

CHAPTER 6

Running in Circles

CHAPTER 6

Running in Circles

Oh, man," Cookie Monster said. "I can't ride in *that!*"

"AM-FM, cassette deck, power everything. Real leather bucket seats that swivel." Barney patted the front fender of the jet-black Ford four-wheel drive short-bed pickup. "Roll bar." He kicked the front tire. "Look at these babies. Go anywhere."

"This is the most useless excuse for a truck I ever seen. Jesus Christ, Barney. What if someone sees me riding in this . . . this cowboy pimpmobile! Look at this thing: you can't even haul hay in it."

"You drive." Barney walked around the front of the truck, admiring his image in the mirrorlike finish. "Look-ing *good,*" he said, and climbed into the red leather interior.

"Yeah. You go real fine with this piece of junk." Barney was clean-shaven, styled hair cut above the ears. He was wearing cowboy boots, clean, slightly faded jeans, a blue cowboy shirt with mother-of-pearl snaps, and a new straw cowboy hat folded and creased in the style of a salty bull-rider. "But you must've missed a turn. It's about a thousand miles that away." Cookie Monster flung his arm loosely toward the western horizon. "You can't miss it. It's called Hol-ly-wood."

Barney swiveled the bucket seat toward Cookie Monster.

"Quit crying and throw your stuff in the back and let's get going."

Cookie Monster shook his head. "Oh, man," he muttered, and threw a new white canvas bag marked Nike into the bed of the truck. Barney's old green duffel bag and some camping equipment—down sleeping bags, tent, Styrofoam cooler—and a large padlocked wooden box were stacked neatly behind the cab, taking up almost half the space offered by the short bed. "Can't believe you're doing this to me . . ." He climbed into the cab.

"Just take your time. Get used to all these modern conveniences." Barney punched the radio on, and Waylon Jennings boomed out of six speakers.

Cookie Monster jumped. "Holy shit!"

Barney turned the radio off. "Try the engine. It's even better."

"I don't know if I can drive in these shoes." Cookie Monster looked through the steering wheel at his gray and black nylon running shoes, inch-thick rectangular rubber protrusions covering the soles.

Barney pulled his straw hat almost over his eyes. He tilted his head back and looked down his nose at Cookie Monster, who was wearing gray gym shorts and sky-blue tank top, Adidas emblazoned in large white letters across the chest. "How'd you get such a tan, anyway?"

"How'd you get the money to buy all your cowboy duds?"

"Where'd you get the money to buy yours?"

"I charged it to my uniform allowance."

"So'd I." Barney smiled. "You're not so fucking clever."

"What you going to do if you have to go back on patrol someday?"

"What *you* going to do?"

"I'm not."

"Well, how about that? Me neither. At least not in this fucking department, I'm not."

"So where'd you get this truck? From Fred the Car Salesman, alias Fred the Part-Time Dope Dealer and Full-Time Snitch, I'll bet."

"You betcha."

"Poor son of a bitch. What if we wreck it?"

Barney took off his straw hat and placed it over the left

55

side of his chest. "Sometimes you eat the bear," he said piously. "Sometimes the bear eats you."

"Yeah. I can hear the concern in your voice. Where's the damn key?"

Barney put his hat back on and pointed at the key. "You sure look funny with just that little-bitty mustache and that short hair," he said. "Joe Jock. I forgot you had a chin."

The engine rumbled to life, the truck vibrating slightly. Cookie Monster goosed the throttle, and the truck broke into a deep-throated roar. "Ah, so," he said, turning with wide eyes toward Barney. "Ah fucking so." He stepped on the throttle again and jammed the gearshift into drive. The truck roared and inched forward, dirt and gravel from the alley showering Barney's garage door and roof. Cookie Monster let up slightly on the gas pedal, and the truck gathered speed, howling as the tires dug trenches into the dirt alley. The truck began to drift sideways, fishtailing, Cookie Monster frantically spinning the steering wheel. "Power steering," he shouted, and the truck straightened and rocketed out of the alley and onto the pavement, across the pavement and into the alley of the next block.

"Missed the turn," Barney said.

"Yahoo!" Cookie Monster yelled. "Get back in the wagon, woman!" He took his foot off the gas and pulled the gearshift into low. The engine shrieked, and Barney braced both hands against the dash, fighting the deceleration. Cookie Monster touched the power brakes, stomped on the gas as he cranked the steering wheel to the right, and the truck drifted slightly sideways out of the alley, engine roaring, dust billowing off the spinning rear tires and the skidding front tires.

"Crazy fucker," Barney yelled as the truck lurched onto the pavement, tires screaming, dust cloud changing to blue smoke, and slid completely sideways, gliding across the pavement, engine bellowing, rear tires completely obscured by smoke, and then shot forward, the smoke around the rear wheels disappearing as the truck gained speed.

Cookie Monster took his foot off the gas. The truck whined and popped down to twenty-five miles per hour. He shifted into drive, and the whine became an effortless burble as they motored sedately down the street.

"You can sit back now," he said, turning on the radio.

Barney pushed himself back from the dash. "Not any of that boogie-woogie shit."

"Kiss my ass if I'll listen to country and western all the way to the lake." Rock music reverberated through the cab. "Only people really like country and western are tourists and foreigners."

Barney switched the radio off. "We'll flip."

"Shit. We always do this."

"We'll buy some tapes. Take turns playing tapes." Barney swiveled toward him. "How's that? We never had a vehicle with a tape deck before."

"That's for sure." Cookie Monster turned the truck onto the Interstate on-ramp and stepped on the gas, the truck effortlessly gaining speed. Coming up onto the Interstate, they could see the city spread out below them: maple trees, pine trees, fir trees, church steeples, house roofs, the larger buildings of the downtown area. And in the background Lolo Peak, 9,096 feet, big and massive and solid blue to the treeline, white innocent-looking thunderheads massing around the gray peak.

"Shotguns are behind the seat," Barney said.

Twelve miles later, the jet-black truck eased off the Interstate and up the exit lane onto Highway 93.

"I drive Highway Ninety-three, pray for me," Cookie Monster said. To the left, they could see a range of mountains stretching west toward Idaho, the largest nearly as tall as Lolo Peak, but with a sharp conical peak bare of trees or snow.

"Maybe we ought to forget this and go climb old Squaw's Tit over there," Cookie Monster said.

"Stop at the truck stop. We need gas and tapes."

"Look for elk. Go fishing. Get away from people for a while." He turned the pickup into the truck stop. "Get our heads straight." Semis were scattered and lined up around the restaurant and gas station. A gold and brown van—Washington plates, custom wheels and paint, blackened windows—was parked at the gas pumps.

"Get our heads straight," Barney said. "That's a laugh."

"What's this thing take?"

"Regular. Pull in next to that van over there and I'll fill her up while you go see if they've got any tapes."

Cookie Monster guided the truck up next to the gold and brown van and shut the engine off. Two men stood at the rear of the van, one of them filling the tank, one hand on the gas nozzle, the other hand in his pocket. "Tourists," Cookie Monster grunted, and opened the door. "Just like you." He climbed down out of the cab and headed for the convenience store.

Barney opened his door and stepped down onto the cement island. Both men looked at him. Both wore aviator sunglasses with silver lenses that made it impossible to see their eyes. He pulled the gas nozzle out of the pump and pushed the start bar upward. The pump whirred and the numerals behind the plastic face clicked to zero. Both were about five eleven, blue jeans and hiking boots. The one pumping gas had on a faded green fatigue shirt, USMC stenciled above the right breast pocket, a rectangular patch, darker green than the rest of the shirt, above the left pocket. "How you doin'?" Barney said. The other man was wearing a green and yellow plaid short-sleeve shirt. Neither had his shirt tucked into his pants. Both had short hair, brown and blow-dried. Barney turned back to the pickup, looking for the gas cap. It was on the other side.

"It's on the other side, cowboy." Both men laughed.

Barney turned back toward them and grinned. "New truck," he said. The mountains and Squaw Peak were distorted and bent in Green Shirt's glasses; the pickup and pumps and himself in the glasses of the other man.

Neither man answered, their mouths humorless beneath the glasses.

Barney climbed up on the running board and into the bed of the pickup, stretching the hose and nozzle across the equipment in the back. He sat on the edge of the truck bed and undid the gas cap, inserted the nozzle and began pumping gas into the tank. With his free hand, he pushed the straw cowboy hat back on his head.

One of the two men said something Barney couldn't quite hear, and they both laughed again. Green Shirt pulled the nozzle out of the van's tank and, as the other man put the cap back on, replaced the nozzle in the pump.

"Nice van," Barney said. "You guys are from Washington, huh?"

Plaid Shirt stepped up onto the cement island, between the

two pumps. "Uh-huh," he said, looking into the bed of the pickup. He leaned forward against the truck, the top of the bed hitting him in the chest just below his armpits.

"Whereabouts?"

"Seattle." Plaid Shirt reached in and opened the lid of the Styrofoam cooler.

"Have one," Barney said. "You, too," he added as Green Shirt came up next to Plaid Shirt. Both pairs of sunglasses looked at him, Squaw Peak clear and sharp-pointed in the center of all four lenses.

"Don't mind if I do," Green Shirt said, and reached in past Plaid Shirt and pulled out two cans of Olympia, bits of ice caught in the pull tabs and the indentations of the tops.

Gasoline overflowed, gushing for a second out of the pickup's gas tank before Barney could release the trigger on the nozzle. He jerked the nozzle out. Both pull tabs popped open. "Damn," he said, replacing the gas cap. He handed the nozzle across to Green Shirt. "Put that back on the pump, will you?" He smiled.

Green Shirt's sunglasses stared at the nozzle, then at him, and then back at the nozzle. "Well, sure, cowboy," he said. "I reckon a cold beer's worth that."

Plaid Shirt removed his glasses, holding them in his left hand, the Olympia in the other. He smiled as if he felt obliged to lessen the impact of his pale blue eyes. "Where you from, cowboy? You from around here?"

"My partner is. Ah'm from Virginia. Just out for the summer." He hadn't seen many eyes like that, not since Vietnam, anyway. "Where you all headed?"

Plaid Shirt shrugged. "Kalispell. Glacier Park. Wherever we feel like." He tipped his beer up, his eyes watching Barney over the bottom of the can.

Green Shirt turned and stepped off the island, up to the back of the van, and banged a fist on the doors. "Wake up, asshole," he yelled. "I need money for the gas." He opened the rear door and leaned inside, a bulge beneath his shirt just above the belt at the small of his back.

"Must be nice." Barney grinned. "You all know people in this part of the state, have a place to stay?" Green Shirt straightened up, the shirt covering the bulge again. He closed the door, pushed a wad of money down into his pocket, and turned and walked toward the station.

Plaid Shirt drained his beer. The muscles on his forearm flexed as he crumpled the can with one hand. He put the sunglasses back on. "A few," he said. The sunglasses stared steadily at Barney.

"Might just as well have another beer," Barney said. "My partner drinks most of my share anyway."

"No, thanks." The glasses continued to stare at him.

"Your friend must've been in the marines, huh?"

"Yeah." The sunglasses turned away from him. "Both of us."

"Went to Vietnam, huh?"

The glasses turned back toward him. "Uh-huh."

"They wouldn't take me." Barney looked sheepishly down at the truck bed. "Bad back." He brightened. "But my partner was in the marines. A gunner or crew chief or something." He smiled apologetically. "Always felt like I should've gone, anyway."

"Shit," Plaid Shirt snorted.

Barney cleared his throat. He shuffled his feet on the metal flooring. "Say," he began. He removed his straw hat, held it between his knees, and rotated it nervously in his hands. "You guys wouldn't happen to have any good smokin' stuff . . . being from the Coast and all."

The glasses stared, silver and unblinking. "What are you talking about?"

"You know . . . grass, hash. Smokin' stuff." He smiled. "Nevah mind. You don't know us." He frowned. "I just thought since you and my partner were ex-marines and all . . ."

The sunglasses stared steadily at him.

Barney put his hat back on. "I'm sick of drinkin' beer and listening to my partner's country and western music."

Plaid Shirt turned and walked around the far side of the van. Barney heard the front passenger-side door slide open, and a moment later Plaid Shirt walked back around the van carrying a brown paper sack folded into a small package about eight inches long and two or three inches thick. He offered it to Barney. "Seventy-five bucks," he said. "California home-grown."

"Hey, wow . . ." Barney unwrapped the sack and pulled out a plastic Baggie filled with marijuana. He opened the Baggie and sniffed. "Smells good. *Real* good." He smiled at his reflection in the sunglasses.

Plaid Shirt smiled back.

"Sure appreciate it," Barney said.

"Man, you see that dude back there in the marine fatigue shirt?" Cookie Monster said, as he pulled the pickup back out onto Highway 93. "Baaad-looking dude."

"He was in that brown and gold van parked across the island from us," Barney said. He rolled his window down. "Whew!" he said. "Smell that." Behind and to their left the silvered stacks and metal buildings of a pulp mill belched white steam and smoke, the steam and smoke rising and billowing, spreading down the valley, back toward the city.

The stacks and buildings disappeared as the truck crested a small hill and started down the other side, but he could still see the smoke and steam silhouetted against the blue mountains across the valley. It reminded him of an air strike. Napalm or white phosphorus.

"How could anyone put something like that in the middle of a valley like this?"

"That, my man, is a question that will truly make you crazy. Here. Check out the tapes."

Barney opened the sack and peered inside. "You must be feeling rich or something." He pulled out a pair of sunglasses, red and yellow frame around silver one-way lenses. "What the fuck are these?"

"That dude looked so bad in his, I just had to have a pair. . . . Make me feel like a *real* narc. You know: lurking in dark alleys, offering candy to little girls, ruining people's lives. Real sinister shit." He reached over and took the sunglasses from Barney and, steering for a moment with his knees, put them on. "Hee. Hee. Hee," he cackled. "Narc. Narc."

Barney looked into the sack. "Nigger music," he said. "A package of chocolate chip cookies." He put the sack on the floor and pushed a cassette into the radio.

The deep, heavy drums and strident guitar of Jimi Hendrix

filled the cab. "Hey. Hey," Cookie Monster said. "I can't believe *you* are playing *that!*"

Barney slouched in the seat, polished cowboy boots up on the dash, one arm and elbow out the window, hand beating on the outside of the door to the music. "Purple haze up in my brain," Hendrix sang, and Cookie Monster turned up the volume, shouting the next line of the song: " 'Lately things don't seem the same.' Hee-yah!" he shouted and floored the pickup. "S'cuse me while you kiss my ass, world!" he yelled out the window. He let his foot off the gas pedal and grinned fiercely at Barney. "Man, I haven't listened to this for *years.* "

Barney smiled.

"Memories," Cookie Monster said. "Memories: all we need is some dyno-mite dope and some willing women."

Barney pulled himself upright and reached underneath the seat. "Almost forgot," he said, and unwrapped the paper sack and pulled out the plastic bag of grass. "Gave those guys back at the truck stop a couple of beers, and one of them sold me this 'California home-grown' for a mere seventy-five dollars." He offered the Baggie to Cookie Monster.

"Seventy-five dollars!" Steering with his knees, Cookie Monster opened the bag and sniffed. "You got ripped off." He looked slyly at Barney. "Where'd you get the bread?"

Barney shrugged. "I took five hundred dollars of buy money out for expenses."

"Well, what're you buying dope for? We're not interested in making any cases."

"Because they were assholes."

Cookie Monster laughed and turned the volume up until he could feel the heavy bass vibrations like adrenaline in his thighs and buttocks and in his hands on the steering wheel. He turned toward Barney. "Hey, Barn, you better run," he sang.

Barney turned the volume down. "What do you think we really ought to do?"

"When in trouble or in doubt, run in circles, scream and shout."

"Those guys I got the dope from are from Seattle."

"So what? Turn the music up."

"One of them was packing."

Cookie Monster took off the sunglasses and put them on

the dash. "This is the Wild West. You ought to know that by now."

"Didn't we hear the lieutenant say he was expecting a call from Seattle?"

Cookie Monster laughed. "Barn, muh-man, that is some *real* paranoia, if I ever heard any."

Barney shrugged. "Well, not too many people'd recognize us now, that's for sure. And the lieutenant knows we're not going to back off."

Cookie Monster looked incredulously at Barney. "What are you saying?"

Barney shook his head. "Just being weird," he said, and turned up the volume again as the black and gleaming pickup motored past the sign that said Flathead Indian Reservation, headed toward the silent crags of the Mission Mountains. "Just being weird."

CHAPTER 7

The Pass

$\mathbf{N}$ever seen a sunset like this," Barney said forty-five minutes later. He was sitting on the open tailgate, legs dangling toward the ground, a beer loosely held in his hands between his legs. Red light surrounded the truck parked on a gravel turnoff at the top of the hill. The red light made it appear as if the truck had been dipped in a dark viscous fluid. That special color, he thought. Goose bumps ran up his arms. He took a drink of beer.

Orange and red beams of light shot across the ridgeline behind them, disappearing into the blood-red sky.

"Well, there's something to be said for pollution and forest fires," Cookie Monster said. He was lying spread-legged in the bed of the pickup, his head and shoulders propped up against the rolled-up canvas tent, like Barney, a can of beer held in his hands.

Across the valley, cliffs and peaks rising almost perpendicular from the floor of the valley glowed an intense gold, as if Cookie Monster and Barney were looking at them through the lenses of shooting glasses.

Cookie Monster tilted his head back and drank. A thin trickle of beer, glistening red in the light, dribbled out of the corner of his mouth, across his cheek.

They could smell asphalt, still hot from the day's sun, and

under the smell of hot asphalt, the scent of fresh-cut hay. A semi groaned over the hill and trundled down toward the valley, dark, sooty smoke blossoming from its exhaust stacks as it shifted gears, gaining speed.

"Lawyers are fucked. Juries are fucked. The laws are fucked. . . ." Cookie Monster took another drink. "We be busting people for hundred-lots of speed or acid, or for a few lines of coke, and what happens? The courts dump on them. But bust somebody for boo-coo dope and he's got *money*—just like those bastards up the Blackfoot—and the courts don't do anything. . . ."

Barney squinted down the fence line. Barbed wire sparked and glinted red in the rays of the sunset. Who gives a shit? he thought. Two hundred yards down the fence line, just inside the game preserve, two bucks, their antlers thick and soft with velvet, lay side by side, watching the two men.

"It's all a bunch of shit," Cookie Monster said. "All a fucking game. Vietnam or here; it don't matter. We're still doing some politicians' shit work."

The deer hadn't moved. Barney jumped off the tailgate and walked twenty yards through the knee-high grass toward them. They still didn't move.

Cookie Monster looked toward the mountains, his eyes following the jumbled line of their march toward Flathead Lake and beyond, to Glacier Park and Canada. "But what the hell?" he said. "I figure the community is doing us a favor."

"What are you mumbling about?"

"It's all a big game. Cops and robbers. Judges and juries. But at least it provides some excitement now and—"

"Was a game," Barney said. *"Was* a game."

"But what's the game: a home run is catching an armed robber coming out of Seven-Eleven with a gun pointed at you and his finger on the trigger. Fat chance he has. Blow his shit away." He stood up and stretched. "It's legal, though."

He vaulted over the side of the truck bed and walked through the grass toward Barney. "Let's see how close we can get to those two deer."

"They'll run soon as we start for them. I didn't think I'd get this close."

"Want to bet?"

"Fifty dollars."

Cookie Monster smiled and went back to the truck and rummaged around in the back and pulled out the Browning 9mm in the leather shoulder holster. "Okay," he said. "It's a bet."

"What are you going to do, shoot them to keep them there?"

"I want to see if the sights are still on after that asshole threw it into the back seat of the Chevy."

They walked down the hill toward the two deer. The side of the hill was in shadow, but even the shadow seemed permeated by the red light, the air oppressive, filled with something undefined that made the hairs on the backs of their necks tingle, like walking down a jungle trail knowing, just knowing, there'd be an ambush up ahead, but going ahead anyway. The deer lay unmoving, their ears twitching and rotating like tiny radar dishes. A fragile breeze began to move down the hill, stirring the knee-high grass.

Barney picked up a rock.

"That's cheating."

Barney dropped the rock. Both deer had large racks—four or five points, at least.

They continued walking. The blood-red sky was fading toward orange and pink.

Abruptly, the deer stood and backed a few feet farther up the hill, away from the fence.

Cookie Monster cleared his throat.

"Damn," Barney said.

Cookie Monster jumped up and down, flapping his arms and the straps of the holster. "Booga-booga," he yelled. "Booga-booga."

The deer stared, their ears flicking back and forth. One turned its back toward the two men and ambled a few feet up the hill and began grazing.

"They know where they're at," Cookie Monster said. "They know one step on the other side of that fence and they're safe. Just like old Victor Charlie. Even the Indians won't shoot at them in there." He pulled the Browning from the holster, dropped the holster to the ground, and assumed a shooter's stance, feet parallel and slightly more than shoulder width apart, arms extended, pistol gripped with both hands. He cocked the hammer back with his right thumb. "Watch this."

Barney put his fingers in his ears. "People can see us from the highway."

Cookie Monster took a slightly deeper breath, exhaled halfway, then held his breath, both eyes open. He fired twice, the sound of the shots almost one single *crack*. Five yards downhill from the deer and twenty yards in front of the two men, splinters flew from a fence post. The two deer froze for a moment and then, white tails up, bounced erratically up the hill, stiff-legged, necks rigid, and racks thrown back, splitting away from each other as they ran. Cookie Monster fired four more rounds, the shots stuttering like a short burst of automatic weapons fire, firing one after another the instant the barrel dropped back to the horizontal, spent brass ejecting, flipping through the air in front of Barney. Splinters flew. The top strand of barbed wire parted and twanged away from the post.

"Oops," Cookie Monster said. He let the smoking pistol drop loosely to his side, slide locked all the way back, short, ugly barrel exposed.

"What the hell did you have to do that for? We'll have half the reservation down our necks."

Cookie Monster released the slide lock; the slide clunked forward around the barrel, and he replaced the automatic in the shoulder holster.

"Fucking cowboy. Lot of good your target practice did us when it counted."

Cookie Monster turned toward Barney. "Yeah . . ."

"Yeah," Barney said, the skin at his cheekbones stretched tight. "Cowboys and Indians bullshit. Head the deer off at the pass."

"Hey, you got something to say, say it. But you better—"

"Better what! Better fucking what!"

"Better—" Cookie Monster abruptly stopped and stared at Barney—at Barney dressed in cowboy clothes, at Barney angry and frustrated and out of shape. "Better we don't get to acting like this."

Barney glared at him.

Cookie Monster spread his arms, palms up. "Go ahead, if it'll make you feel better."

"Ahh . . ." Barney turned and started up the hill toward the truck. "Cowboys . . ."

"Actually—" Cookie Monster laughed, following behind him. "Actually, I'd take a shotgun full of double-ought and slugs any day. Blow that fence post right in two. No self-respecting cowboy'd do something like that."

"Probably too much listening to the Sons of the Pioneers on my way to school," Cookie Monster said. " 'Ghost Riders in the Sky' every morning five days a week."

They were sitting on the front fenders, listening to Willie Nelson and watching the headlights of the traffic struggle up the hill.

"Want to field-test that dope you paid such an outrageous price for?"

Barney swiveled on the polished fender.

Cookie Monster jumped down. "I'll bet there're papers in the glove box."

"Nah. I always get a headache from it."

"And it just puts you right to sleep, too, I'll bet."

"As a matter of fact . . ."

Cookie Monster rummaged around in the cab, singing along with Willie.

"You're ruining a good song," Barney said.

He heard the clatter of the tape being ejected and, "Hey!" he said, smelling the sweet, pungent odor of marijuana. "You idiot. What are you doing?"

Cookie Monster, squinting against the smoke, was sitting behind the steering wheel, puffing on a fat and crudely rolled joint. He waggled his eyebrows, eyes big and wide, as he held the smoke in. He exhaled, a long slow exhalation, the smoke sifting and curling around his head. He climbed out of the cab and offered the joint to Barney. " 'Ere," he said.

"What are you doing? We can't do this . . ."

Cookie Monster blew smoke in Barney's face.

Barney coughed. "You—"

"Whoa. Halt. Desist."

"Put that thing out."

"Whoa. I say, whoa." Cookie Monster held the joint out over the hood, out of Barney's reach. "Goddammit. Quit fucking around. This is it. We're finished. You know it; I know it.'' Smoke from the joint coiled upward. ''So cease this Mom-and-apple-pie shit. We haven't been saving the world by putting dopers in jail any more than we were saving the world by shooting gooks. All we want to do is get even and split.''

He offered the joint to Barney. ''Anyway, it ain't the dope; it's the people who sell it.''

Barney waved it away.

Cookie Monster's eyes glittered. ''Look, my man, we don't owe a fucking thing to anybody but ourselves. We paid our dues—more than once. So fuck it.'' He paused. ''If you don't want to smoke this, that's fine with me. But let's keep the proper perspective, okay?'' He again offered the joint to Barney.

Barney stared at it for a moment and then gingerly accepted it. He took a long, easy pull, gazing up at the ridgeline as he held the smoke in. Stars were beginning to show, but just above the ridgeline the sky was a deep and ugly purple. Off to the left, one of the deer was silhouetted, slowly picking its way down the ridgeline. He exhaled.

''Really does put me to sleep,'' he said.

CHAPTER 8

Bones

Barney lay on top of the two unrolled sleeping bags, feeling nylon soft and fluffy against his skin. Warm wind snapped and eddied around his head, ruffled his hair, slid across his face, plucked at the nylon. He smiled, stoned to the max, looking up at the huge star-filled sky, tuned to the mechanical exertions of the truck vibrating beneath him.

A tinge of pink still colored the western sky.

It's out there, he thought, and silently cackled up at the sky, "It's everywhere, it's everywhere."

He giggled. "And it's not Chicken Man."

He'd never seen it, but it was out there, all right, kind of like those dragons the Chinese are always talking about—never see it, but sure can feel it when it's there.

He raised his arms straight up, hands above his face, wiggling his fingers toward the stars and dark. He squirmed a little against the nylon sleeping bag.

It felt so soft.

He moved his fingers: pale white worms wiggling in the stars.

He giggled.

First met it when my father died. Eleven years old and I didn't understand.

He dropped his hands back into the soft, soft nylon. The warm wind felt wonderful.

But in Vietnam it was around all the time. Hovering like a Huey gunship.

Everywhere! Everywhere!

Always there. Warm and soft like the wind and the sleeping bag. Hard and bright as the stars. But mostly pink like the horizon . . . and red and orange like Lang Vei . . . rushing straight at you. . . .

His hands tightened, grasping handfuls of nylon sleeping bag.

You shot and stabbed and choked, surrounded by blood and stench and liquid rubbery things. And all of a sudden you were alive and everything else was dead.

But it was still there.

Still there in the blood covering your body.

In the corpses.

In the wounded.

A thrill that felt sick, like hitting his elbow on a sharp edge, coursed through his body.

Their death is my death.

He looked at the pink horizon and forced his face and hands to relax.

Sometimes. Sometimes I still feel like when I was eleven years old.

I still don't understand.

And he fell asleep as the truck vibrated through the warm night.

And the pink on the horizon faded to gray.

CHAPTER 9

A Nice Place

Friday night traffic—ranch kids in beat-up pickups, spitting Copenhagen in between sips of beer, yahooing and shouting at the girls; middle-aged cowboys and ranchers in new, shiny four-wheel-drives, their wives or girlfriends sitting close against them; summer people from the lake, driving Fiats and Camaros and Daddy's Thunderbird, suntanned girls and boys, open-shirted necklace-clad lawyers and doctors and accountants in Z cars; Indians packed into ten-year-old Fords and Chevys, and new evil-looking Trans Ams—cruised the main street, yelling, screaming, shouting insults, racing engines, or saying nothing at all, just staring with quiet faces at suntanned bodies and bleached hair and new cars. Clumps of tousle-haired men and women, wearing expensive but fashionably sloppy and ragged hiking shorts, day packs, T-shirts, and hiking boots, stood on the sidewalks talking politics and sociology and saying things like "Righteous" and "You should've seen this place before it got commercial" and "Me? I'm from Connecticut, man, doin' some rock climbing backpacking mountain biking water-skiin' fishin'." And a female voice: "I need a Heineken." And another: "There's a ten-K and a full marathon next week." And: "Oh, yeah. Yeahhh. Do a line of this." Drunken Indians, ancient and weathered, wearing Stetsons and cowboy shirts and boots, wandered from bar to bar. "Hey, I like White Eyes, White Eyes is okay, got a dollar for a true American Native?"

"Hey, Barn!" Cookie Monster shouted. He was standing beside the pickup, parked diagonally at the curb, looking into the bed at Barney. "Wake up. Look at all the cowboys and Indians and fun hogs."

Barney lay flat on his back, arms spread away from his sides, palms up, legs straight out, heels on the metal flooring. His toes pointed inward, meeting in an inverted V. His head was bent back over the rolled-up tent, his mouth open; he was snoring softly.

A dark blue Trans Am blasted by, chasing a trio of cowboy-hatted high school boys in a well-used pickup, straw broom sticking straight up behind the cab.

"Incoming!" Cookie Monster yelled, and slapped the side of the pickup with the flat of his hand. *"Incoming!"*

Barney's head slowly tilted forward and one eye and then the other opened. "Whazzat?" he croaked. "Wherethefuck-arewe?"

"Port Polson, muh-man. Montana's answer to Tahoe. C'mon. Let's get a beer." He grinned down at Barney. "I know a place."

Barney's head tilted toward him. "A place," he said thickly and suspiciously. "The last *place* you knew was up at Kali-spell." One eye closed again. He cleared his throat. "And look what happened because of that."

Monster opened his gym bag and took out a pair of off-white canvas trousers and a light blue nylon jacket with a terry-cloth collar. "This is a genuine Montana bar," he said. "Cowboys, Indians, hippies, ranchers, dopes, bikers . . ." With one hand, he pulled his gym trunks off. He threw the trunks into the gym bag and pulled his pants on. "Shit, I forgot a belt."

Barney sat up, his body like a puppet with the strings re-laxed. "I think I got stoned," he said matter-of-factly.

Monster pulled on the jacket. "Hi, girls," he yelled as a carload of girls with bleached hair and suntans slowly mo-tored by. "Must be the duds," he said to Barney.

"It's not your looks, that's for sure."

"Shee-it. If I was an orange, I'd be stamped Sunkist."

Barney giggled. "Sunkist. Sun kissed." He struggled upright and gingerly vaulted over the tailgate. "You been out in the sun too long, all right."

"Grab that stuff in the back and throw it in the cab," Cookie Monster said, putting his derringer in the side pocket of the jacket. "We don't want to get it stolen. Not no self-respectin' cops like us." He paused and looked at Barney—at Barney's shirttail hanging out, his tousled hair, the unbuttoned pearl snaps on one shirt cuff.

"You'll fit right in," he said.

"Tuck in your shirt," Monster said, as they stopped outside the door of the bar. "This is a nice place."

"I'll bet."

"Where's your hat?"

"Dunno." Barney struggled with his shirt. "Must've blown out the back of the truck."

An overweight middle-aged lady came out of the door. A rush of voice and smoke and rock-and-roll music sifted out around her. Caucasian, Barney thought, and giggled to himself: five feet eight, green and white and black plaid cotton shirt, pink and black and white bell-bottom pants—too short—and penny loafers without socks. She bumped into him.

"S'cuse me, sonny," she said, bleary voiced. "But get the fuck out of my way." She pushed past him to the curb and stood, hand on hip, surveying the traffic. She pushed lank brown hair away from her eyes.

"A real Montana bar," Barney said. "I can hardly wait."

"You seen my old man?" the lady asked him, as if Barney had hidden him somewhere.

"He went into that bar across the street," Monster said, and pointed toward a bar on the other side of the street.

"Oh, yeah?" She wandered out into the street. "That old fart—"

Barney closed his eyes as a Z car screeched to a stop inches from her ample hip.

"You fucking tourist," she yelled. "Go back where you came from." She started toward the driver's door.

"C'mon," Monster said, and grabbed Barney's arm and pulled him through the door.

Smoke and music and voice assaulted them as they stepped inside. The room was rectangular with a high ceiling. Old-fashioned light fixtures dangled from the ceiling, the light faded and weak like the light inside an old train station. Tanned and weatherbeaten ranchers and ranch hands, wearing jeans and cords, rolled-up shirtsleeves, and baseball caps that said John Deere and Caterpillar and Ceretana Feeds, stood elbow to elbow at a magnificent hardwood bar with cowboys wearing fancy western shirts, Stetsons pushed to the back of their heads; Indians with long hair, short hair, in jeans and dark tank tops; bikers in soiled denim jackets, leather vests, black T-shirts, with folding buck knives in black leather cases; fun hogs with their hiking shorts and boots and tousled hair; and women—old, young, fat, slim, and everything in between—wearing pants and jeans and shorts and halter tops, polyester pullovers, cat-eye glasses, rings, necklaces.

A crowd stood watching the play on two pool tables in the center of the room. Dark wood paneling covered the lower portion of the walls, pink paint the upper. Pinball machines rattled and clanged. People shouted, laughed, screeched, roared, squealed. Barney giggled. Elk and deer and moose heads and antlers lined the pink wall; a giant Rainer beer opener hung from the antlers of a bemused-looking whitetail deer.

"Holy shit!" Barney yelled.

Cookie Monster shouldered his way through the smoke and people toward the magnificent and ancient hardwood bar. Music blared out of the jukebox, but it was impossible to tell if it was rock and roll or country and western.

Barney squeezed in beside Cookie Monster. "S'cuse me," he said to a very large and stocky Indian wearing bib overalls, white T-shirt, and blue stocking hat.

The Indian stared down at Barney for a moment, his eyes black and shiny. About as full of life as one of the deer heads mounted on the wall, Barney thought. The Indian seemed to be staring at his stomach.

I've got to lose a little weight, that's for sure.

The Indian grinned, exposing a massive row of perfect, brilliant white teeth.

Better to eat you with, Barney thought. "This is a great bar, isn't it?" he said, running his hands over the scarred and pitted wood surface. He leaned back, holding on to the edge of the bar with both hands. " 'Jim T. plus Deb M,' " he read.

The Indian kept grinning at him.

Polly want a cigar, Barney thought.

Cookie Monster leaned across the bar toward the bartender. "Two Coors." Behind the bartender the usual array of bottles and glasses stood in front of a huge mirror flanked by polished hardwood pillars.

"Really old bar," Barney said to the Indian.

"Couple of shots of bar whiskey," Monster said.

The Indian had a large tattoo of a bull sitting on its ass, leering and smoking a joint. The tattoo was on a large and obviously well-exercised bicep. The bull stared directly at Barney. It tilted sideways, stretching all out of proportion, as the Indian took a drink of beer.

Barney giggled.

"Want a beer?" Monster shouted at the Indian. "Hey, Chief, you want a beer?"

The Indian grinned and nodded.

Barney's giggle turned into a laugh, which he tried to stifle by looking at the floor. The floor was dirty black and burgundy squares of tile. He started laughing uncontrollably, leaning his elbows on the bar, alternately looking down at the floor and up at the Indian. Tears formed in the corners of his eyes.

"Don't mind him," Monster said over Barney's bowed head and quivering shoulders. "He's just a little stoned is all."

Barney tilted his head up toward Cookie Monster and laughed even harder, pounding one fist on the bar.

The Indian started laughing, too. Slowly at first and then harder, his chest and shoulders shaking.

Barney looked up, laughing. The bartender was young and overweight and white, with a Prince Valiant haircut, his plaid cotton shirt unbuttoned to expose a faded black T-shirt.

"Another beer over there," Cookie Monster said, gesturing toward the Indian.

Barney stopped laughing. He pointed at the bartender. *"That man killed Chicken Little,"* he shouted.

Conversation near them ceased as cowboy hats, baseball caps, necklaces and earrings, and a beehive wig turned to see where Barney was pointing.

The bartender rolled his eyes and turned to get the other beer.

Conversation resumed, a few people casting wary glances toward Barney.

"You're okay," the Indian said, grinning his terrible grin again. "Hit us again," he said, as the bartender placed a beer in front of him. "Probably crazy, but so's everybody else in here."

"Oh, not just in here," Barney replied soberly. "Outside, too."

Several beers and shots of whiskey—"I can't believe you're drinking that rotgut"—later, the three of them stood clustered at the bar, telling North Dakota jokes.

The big Indian's name was David; he was a logger who owned a small fleet of trucks. "Why'd the North Dakotans put Astroturf on their football field?" he asked Barney.

Barney laughed.

The big Indian looked at Cookie Monster.

Monster shrugged.

"So they could keep the cheerleaders from grazing at half-time." He grinned his huge white-toothed grin.

Barney and Cookie Monster laughed. "That's pretty good," Barney said. "Why'd the—"

"I think it's terrible!" a female voice said, and a thin white arm and fist flashed out from behind Cookie Monster and smacked into the side of the big Indian's bib overalls.

The Indian grunted from the impact. "Aw, shit, Marianne . . ."

Cookie Monster moved to one side. Marianne was about five feet eight, thin and blond. Nice firm breasts. Short, curly hair. Gold earrings, blue jeans, cowboy boots.

"You big, ugly 'skin, you still think women are just a bunch of squaws."

"Aw . . ."

Barney's mouth dropped open. "I hate housework," was emblazoned across the front of her T-shirt.

"Get me a beer, will you?" she demanded.

"Marianne," the big Indian said, "why are you so pissed?"

"Those assholes." She nodded toward the pool tables. "That redheaded son of a bitch." She grabbed the beer out of his hand and took a drink.

Barney and Cookie Monster and the Indian looked toward the pool table. Through the smoke haze, beyond the moving crush of people, they could see Green Shirt bent forward over the far pool table into a circle of white light from a low-hung, red and green plastic Schlitz shade. Plaid Shirt stood on the other side of the table, chalking a cue. Another man, short and stocky and red-haired, leaned one hip against the table, hands around the end of a pool cue planted against the floor, his lips curled into a sneer.

"What about them?" the Indian said. "You been beat before."

Monster looked at Barney. "Is that who I think it is?"

Barney nodded. "Yup."

"Not by someone like that. He kept talking to me when it was my turn to shoot. Asking me if I'd like to fuck a *real* man."

"Well, can't blame him for that," the big Indian said, but he looked once more toward the pool table, his eyes flat and dark and glistening like the eyes in the mounted elk head above the pool table.

"Are those three guys together?" Monster asked.

Her blue eyes looked him up and down, taking in his clothes, as if to say, What's it to you, Jack?

"These here're my friends," the Indian said. "Ben and Barney. This here's Marianne," he added.

"Pleased to meet you, ma'am," Barney said in his best southern drawl.

Her blue eyes widened. "Oh, wow," she said, her voice abruptly girlish and amazed. "Say that again."

"Pleased to meet y'all, ma'am."

"Ohhh. You hear that voice, Dave? Wow." She looked up at the Indian and frowned. "Why'n't you learn to talk like that?"

The three men laughed. "Look what I have to put up with," the big Indian said and pulled her toward him, his arm around her shoulders, forearm as big around as her neck.

She slipped her thin white arms around his waist and hugged him.

"I'm hungry," she said, gazing softly up at him. "Let's go get a burger."

"I just ordered you a beer."

"Aw, Dave. I'm hungry." She freed her arms from around his waist and stood back away from him. "Besides," she said, her blue eyes flashing darkly. "I don't want to be around when something bad happens to that redheaded shit."

The big Indian grunted and looked helplessly from Barney to Monster. "Wait'll we're married," he said. "I'll never have any peace then." He glanced toward the pool table and sighed. "Got to watch the women around here. . . ."

He shook his head. "A friend of mine was in here drinkin' one night, and his girl called, wanted him to come and see her, do something together or something. He said no and hung up. Stayed in the bar drinkin' and talkin' and playin' pool—"

"Sounds like a Willie Nelson song," Barney said.

"Yeah, something like that. He walked outside a while later, and his girl blew him away with some little no-account pistol."

"Tough ladies around here," Marianne said. "You better watch out." She put her arm protectively around the big Indian's waist.

"You don't have to tell us," Barney said.

"Well, I guess we're going to go eat," the Indian said. "Want to come?"

"Think we'll pass," Monster said, glancing toward the pool table. "Thanks, anyway."

"You know those guys?"

"Barney met them today." Monster smiled at the Indian. "Bought some dope from them."

The Indian nodded. "We ain't got to worry about them, then," he said. "Not between you two and the fact that the people around that table sure aren't taking a shine to them."

"Nice to meet y'all," Barney said, as they turned to go.

"Oh," the big Indian said to Barney, "I forgot to tell you." He grinned his grin. "I knew you was a cop as soon as you walked in." He nodded to Monster and turned and shouldered his way into the crowd, pulling Marianne by the hand behind him.

Barney's mouth dropped open. "How'd he know?" he said. "How'd he know? Did you say something?"

"Well, ah think . . . Ah think, it has something to do with that cute li'l PPK in your pants pocket. Ah guess he could see the outline clear as anything, y'all."

CHAPTER 10

Nothing Ever Changes

Barney stared at his reflection in the bar mirror. Behind him, the noise and smoke and jostling continued unabated. Had increased, if anything, he thought. Cookie Monster stood next to him, his back to the mirror, watching the dopers play pool. Son of a bitch, how could he have walked into this place forgetting he had a pistol in his pocket? Stoned, that's why. All these ranchers and Indians and cowboys would never miss a detail like that—his pistol practically hanging out. Fucking Monster. Just like him not to say anything.

"Thanks for telling me, asshole."

"I did tell you," Monster replied, not turning around. "I could've waited until tomorrow, you know."

"You knew it the whole time."

"I forgot until the Indian reminded me."

Barney stared at his beer can. "I'll bet the rednecks around here don't appreciate that big buck sporting around a blonde."

"Like you say, he's a big buck."

Barney grunted.

The fat Indian lady next to him said, "It's not that I got anything against people with long hair. Everybody's got a right to do what they want, don't they?" Her glasses were huge and thick and round. Like an owl, Barney thought.

"Whatever's right," he said.

Her eyes, lost in pools of magnification, blinked at him. "It's like my old man and me," she said. "I got a right to split if I want to, don't I?"

Oh, no, he thought.

"He don't own me, you know." She leaned forward on one elbow so that he'd have to look at and listen to her. "I mean, shit. Who'd ever want to be a hippie? All they do is eat vegetables."

"Your old man's a hippie?'

"No, but you can't live on just vegetables, can you?" Her eyes, little brown almonds caught in a plastic whirlpool, peered unblinking at him. "Just like me and my old man, if you know what I mean."

"You from around here?" Barney asked.

"My old man is."

"And you?"

"I'm from Maine."

Barney laughed. So much for local color, he thought. A real live Montana squaw from Maine. Help.

"Those are some nasty dudes over there," Cookie Monster said. "Especially that redhead. Going to be a fight for sure, the way he's strutting around like he's king rooster or something."

Barney looked over Monster's shoulder. "We could always go bust them."

"Who you goin' to bust?" the woman said. "I'd like to bust that redhead myself."

"C'mon," Monster said to Barney. "Let's go sit in one of those booths across the room."

"Right in the mouth," she called after them.

"What a zoo," Barney said as he slid into the low horseshoe-shaped padded booth. The view of the pool table was unobstructed; most of the crowd was on the bar side of the pool tables.

"Yeah. I told you we'd fit right in."

"Where'd you put the rest of the dope?"

"Left it for the deer."

Barney raised his beer bottle in greeting to Green Shirt, who was leaning against the wall about fifteen feet away, watching the game between Plaid Shirt and the redheaded man. "I haven't ever been to Vietnam—or even in the service," he warned Monster.

Green Shirt pushed off from the wall and walked over. "Well, if it ain't the cowboy from Virginia," he said. "How you doin'?"

"Set down and rest your feet," Barney offered. "We doin' fine . . . jes' fine. Thanks to your partner over there."

Green Shirt sat down across from Cookie Monster, his back to the pool tables. The red-haired man had just beaten Plaid Shirt, and a young-looking ranch hand had the challenge. The ranch hand had his worn straw cowboy hat pushed back on his head; his forehead was a lighter shade of brown.

"This is my partner, Ben." Barney laughed nervously. "My name's Barney; guess we never got around to introducing ourselves back at the truck stop."

Green Shirt nodded to Cookie Monster. "Howdy." Even in the dim light, Monster could see a web of fine white scars radiating from just above the right eyelid, across his temple, and into the hair above his ear.

"Howdy," Monster replied.

"Call me Lucky," Green Shirt said.

Monster raised his eyebrows. "As in love?"

Lucky smiled. "As in Vietnam." He touched his right eye and temple. "Took a piece of my skull, but never hurt my eye or my hearing." He looked at Barney. "So how was it?"

Barney rolled his eyes upward. "Oh, wow—"

"A rip-off," Monster said.

Lucky's eyes snapped back to Monster and stared at him. His eyes reminded Monster of the deep pools of water along the Blackfoot.

"Your little friend here says you were in the Crotch."

"That's right."

"Helicopters, huh?"

"Uh-huh." Even in the dim, smoky bar, Monster could see his eyes darken perceptibly, the pupils widening just as Fu Manchu's did when he was angry or getting ready to kill something. "A real rip-off," he said again.

"My partner and I . . ." Lucky nodded backwards. "Ears is his name—for all the ears he used to collect. We were in Recon."

"I carried a lot of you in my helicopter." Monster smiled.

83

"KIA. WIA." He paused. "So tell someone who gives a shit."

Lucky laughed. "Once a marine always a marine," he said.

He reached into his shirt pocket and pulled out a wad of bills and peeled off twenty-five dollars and threw it onto the tabletop. "No hard feelings," he said, extending his hand toward Monster.

They shook hands, smoothly changing from handclasp to thumb and palm grip to finger clasp. "Why'n't you get Ears over here?" Monster said. "And I'll buy us all some beers with Barney's money."

"Did you know the ceiling's really painted white?" Barney said. "That's old nicotine and tar up there."

The other three men glanced up at the ceiling. "How d'you know that?" Ears asked.

"Bartender told me."

"Shee-it," Ears said. "Bartenders."

"You must be from around here," Lucky said to Monster. "What do you do for a living, anyway?"

"Oh, I rustle a little cattle," Monster said, and they laughed. "As opposed to a big cattle."

"What do you guys do?" Barney asked.

"We sell dope," Lucky said.

"How much dope?"

Both men looked at him and then back to Monster, as if to say, How do you put up with this chump?

"Lots," Ears said. "More dope than *you* ever seen."

"That's all you do?" Monster asked.

Ears smiled. "Oh, you know . . ." He waggled his right hand over the table. "This and that."

"Saw some graffiti in the can," Lucky said. "It said, 'If you think we had fun playing Cowboys and Indians, wait'll we start playing Cowboys and Niggers.' "

"I saw that." Monster laughed. "But you probably already know who'd win. And it sure wouldn't be the cowboys."

"That's no shit." Lucky glanced over his shoulder. "But don't say anything like that to Nasty over there. He hates niggers."

Ears snorted. "Niggers! Man, he hates everyone, regardless of race, religion, or political affliction."

"Nasty?"

"That redhead playing pool," Ears said, swiveling to look in the direction of the pool table. "At least I think he's playing pool. Got to watch him all the time."

"Nasty ain't the half of it," Lucky said.

The ranch hand had already lost, and a monstrously fat woman had the challenge. She was wearing new-looking blue jeans, a belt with a huge silver buckle, and a thin black top with short sleeves. Her breasts were massive. About thirty, Monster estimated, hard eyes and mouth. And a good pool player; she'd just put three straight balls in.

"Some guys, they learned to like to kill in Vietnam," Lucky said. "You know. But that dude, he never been to 'Nam. He was just born liking to hurt things—people, animals, bugs, never mind, if it's alive."

"So what're you guys doing with him?"

The fat woman was running the table. She walked from one side of the table to the other, sizing up her next shot, her immense thighs jiggling even in the tight jeans.

The red-haired man leaned back against the wall, one foot up on the wood paneling, knee bent toward the table. Five feet eight, stocky—maybe 180 to 190—but only a slight paunch. Heavy forearms, reddish hair catching the bright light from the table lamp, skin pale and freckled.

"We had to take him along," Lucky said.

"Oh?"

The fat woman bent over to take her shot, huge breasts almost falling out of the black top, spread soft and obscene across the green felt.

The redhead reached out with his pool cue, slowly inching it toward the fat woman, the muscles in his forearm flexed with the strain of holding the cue steady. The woman drew her cue back and forth several times and shifted her feet and monstrous buttocks, making sure of the shot. The pool cue inched toward the side of her left breast, its hardwood surface shiny as it inched into the bright light over the table.

"Oh, shit," Ears said.

The fat woman drew back her cue one final time, and just as it started forward, the redhead's cue jabbed hard and deep into her breast, popping it out of the black top, the breast flopping like some beached sea animal onto the green felt.

85

"Arrrrh!" she screamed and her cue bit into the felt, ripping through it, the cue ball bouncing off the table. She dropped her cue and straightened, grabbing her breast with both hands. The red-haired man kept his arm extended, the pool cue held still in the circle of bright light. Like a snake poised over a trail, Barney thought. It flicked forward again, jabbed between her fingers, into the breast, the blue felt tip of the cue striking her nipple dead center.

"You cocksucker!" she screeched.

The bar was abruptly quiet, people pausing in mid-conversation or mid-drink, hats and caps and hairdos turning toward the action. Elvin Bishop on the juke box; a low mutter from the people nearest the pool table. "Get that redheaded prick, Kathy," a female voice shouted. Elvin Bishop and his band worked out on the jukebox, jivin' and happy. "Welll, the joint is jumpin'."

Two-fifty. Maybe three hundred, Cookie Monster thought, as she crouched like some huge, slow-witted sumo wrestler, her massive breast hanging out of the black top. They could see the red welt on the side of her breast, the blue chalk on her nipple. Her arms slowly extended away from her sides, the breast bouncing like white Jell-O.

The red-haired man leaned, relaxed and grinning, against his cue, planted on the floor, his foot still against the paneling.

"Go get him!" Ears said, and pushed Lucky out of the booth. He scooted after him.

"Kill him, Kathy!"

Kathy reached over to the nearest table and grasped the neck of a tall beer bottle. With a surprisingly quick motion, she broke the bottom of it against the pool table, beer and brown shards splatting out onto the green felt. Not much fat on that arm, Barney thought.

The redheaded man dropped his other foot to the floor. He grasped the pool cue with both hands, holding it across his body.

"Don't!" Lucky yelled.

"Get back," the fat lady warned, the jagged edges of the bottle extended toward them, stopping them in midstep, and the red-haired man, stepping right foot forward, throwing his right arm and shoulder into it, hit her square in the mouth with the butt end of the pool cue, a dull chunking sound that snapped her head back as if someone had tied a rope to it and connected the other end to one of the cars in the street outside. Monster and Barney and Lucky and Ears all thought of bayonet practice in boot camp. Parry. Thrust. And chunk: a mouth that already hurt to look at. Her body didn't even move, just jiggled a little.

"Son of a bitch," someone said.

"Jump. Jump," Bishop sang. "Jump . . ."

Her mouth drooled blood and saliva and teeth. She edged forward, the broken bottle still tightly clasped in her hand. She moaned, a deep mewing sound that made Monster think of a cow elk that Barney had gut-shot, the elk moving a step forward and stopping, trembling with the pain and sickness of the 30.06 slug that had smacked into her at 2,900 feet per second. The woman's head shook a little from side to side and she shuffled forward, moaning and drooling. Her breast looked slack and gray.

"Holy shit!" Monster said, and both he and Barney climbed up onto the back of the booth, standing on the foot-wide ledge of upholstery to get a better look. "Jump. Jump. Jump . . ." The crowd edged forward, forming a semicircle around the shuffling woman and the pool table and the red-haired man. They could see bikers and cowboys, ranchers and Indians. Women as well as men.

"Jump. Jump. Jump . . ."

The red-haired man stepped forward again and this time speared the butt end of the pool cue into her midsection, grunting with the effort. The cue disappeared almost to his leading hand. In almost the same movement, he jerked it out and, raising the butt end high in the air, brought it down sharply against her wrist. There was a loud snap, like the snap of a rubber band against a wooden tabletop, and the rest of the beer bottle shattered against the linoleum floor.

Elvin Bishop and the jukebox were silent.

Her arms dropped to her sides, and fighting to get air, she began wheezing and then coughing as she swallowed blood, ignoring, probably not even feeling, her wrist. Her eyes crossed and rolled up into the back of her head and she slowly collapsed to the floor, sinking into a huge ball of fat and blue jeans, sucking in great loud *huh's* of sound for breath.

Lucky and Ears rushed forward and grabbed the redhead, one on each arm, just as he was lifting the pool cue over his head like a baseball bat, preparing to hit her again as she gently settled sideways into a table and chairs, knocking them over. They had him halfway through the crowd before anyone really realized what had happened. The redhead fought, twisting, turning, kicking. *"You cunt fuck animal,"* he screamed. Ears stepped back a full step and, not letting go of his arm, kneed him between the legs. "Fucking—ahh . . .'' The redheaded gagged, and they propelled him through the door, lifting him as his knees bent toward his chest.

People shouted and screamed and crowded around the woman.

"Well," Cookie Monster said. "On that note, I suppose it's time we left, too.''

"I know you're going to laugh," Cookie Monster said ten minutes later as they drove across the bridge at the edge of town, headed for Kalispell. "But in the old days those old bars were more like a community center than anything else.''

Barney snorted and looked across the bridge railing at the lake stretching like a black mirror toward the dark mountains, the black mirror shot with long slivers of white and orange and red from lights and campfires across the bay.

"Loggers used to float huge caravans of logs to a sawmill at this end of the lake, and bars were where people gathered in the evenings and slow times of the year." A ski boat slashed out from beneath the bridge and headed directly across the bay, its wake a white phosphorescence, ghostly against the black, shiny surface. "Not many women then, though.''

"Alcoholics," Barney said. "Criminals. Low-lifes.'' He watched the boat move across the water against the lights on the other side.

"Well, I just mean to say, things haven't changed much— at least around here, they haven't.''

Barney laughed, a short, sarcastic bark. "Change? Nothing changes. Nothing *ever* changes! Not here, not anywhere. People just been beating and killing and generally fucking over each other since time one. Why do we even bother to pretend we're different?''

"You're sure in a pissy mood all of a sudden."

"All of a sudden!" He looked over at Cookie Monster. "All of a sudden! God damn! We've been beat on, and we don't know how or why or because of who. I just got divorced; you just lost your girl. We're nearly forty now, and we still can't do anything but hurt or catch or shoot people." He banged his fist on the padded dash. "And I'm fucking sick of it," he said. "We never do anything positive."

"Well, I don't know about that, but I'm *positively* amazed at your attitude.'

Barney sat back in the seat and looked out the window, silent for almost a minute. He rested his head on the cool glass. "It seems like since 'Nam nothing really happened," he muttered. "Bits and pieces."

"You're still stoned."

Barney raised his head. "We've been leaking time or something."

"Really stoned."

"Fuck you. Look out there." He nodded at the lights across the lake, at all the people in their summer homes, sitting around campfires, drinking beer and vodka collinses and telling their kids to go to bed, it's past, way past your bedtime.

"Ahh, shit," he said. "I can't fucking talk to you."

Cookie Monster pulled the truck off onto the shoulder. He eased the gearshift forward into park and turned toward Barney. "Look, Barney, muh-man—"

"Don't call me your man; I'm not your fucking man."

"—I hear what you're saying. It gets to me sometimes." He looked ahead into the darkness beyond the headlights. "Maybe I don't say it the way you do, but . . . you ain't so unique, muh-man, you ain't so unique at all."

"Yeah?"

"Yeah. So let's not be feelin' sorry for ourselves, stoned or not, just because we been beat on a little and just because we watched some absolute asshole trash a fat lady." He put the truck in gear and eased back out onto the highway.

He stepped on the gas and the truck surged forward. "It's like I was talking to a chick a few weeks ago—a chick I haven't seen since high school. 'You went to Vietnam right after high school, didn't you?' she asked. 'Uh-huh.' 'Well, I always wondered what happened to you,' she said. And she didn't mean just me personally. She meant all of us who went to Vietnam and found out what it is. All of us who dropped out, faded out, weirded out, or just died." He brought his fist down twice on the horn button, honk, honk, and turned toward Barney. "Well, here we are, Barney, muh-man. And if we ain't here, we're somewhere else where we don't have to be like all those people out there sitting around those lights."

"Sometimes those lights—"

"Yeah. Sometimes. But only sometimes. Because it's always the same. When you're in the shit, you're sayin' to yourself: 'Self, what am I doing here? I *hate* this.' And you're ready to piss your pants. Your stomach feels like that red-headed fucker just put his cue into it. And you're startin' to think about prayin' . . ."

Barney smiled.

". . . But two days later you're craving it again, lookin' for ways." Cookie Monster abruptly swerved the truck from shoulder to shoulder, the big tires squealing in protest. "Like that," he said. "Only it's never enough. There's never an end to it. You want more and more of it. More and more intense. And someday you know—and *you,* Barney, you really know— you're going to get it all. A hunk of meat, just like all the others."

"Thanks for cheering me up."

"Hell, we be just like some slope motherfucker caught in the wire and not able to get free, just waiting for a flare or daylight or our own panic to let some other Barney or some other Monster know we're there. And then, *zzot,* just like a fly—only with gunfire, if we're lucky."

"Let's hear it for gunfire."

"And maybe we don't like ourselves sometimes, but the fact of it is we didn't have much to do with it." He looked across at Barney. "We got potty-trained too well, that's all."

"Potty-trained!"

"But even if we'd've had something to do with it, we'd've still gone ahead and done about the same thing anyway . . . because what it is, is we're just human beings. Things really haven't changed, just like you say. So if we don't like ourselves sometimes, it's because there ain't much difference between the best of us and that redhead."

"I don't know about *that*."

"Yeah, you do. That's why you like animals and flowers better than you like people. Hell, I'm the same way . . . only, I don't like flowers that well; flowers are for faggots."

Barney laughed and rolled his window down, letting in the damp, humid smell of the lake and the sweet smell of fresh-mown hay. "You sure have a line of bullshit," he said, and slouched in the seat, head against the headrest. He closed his eyes and concentrated on the lake smells.

"Might not be the time to having a midlife crisis," Monster said. "Mental menopause, as it were."

Barney cracked one eye open. Cookie Monster, a frown creasing his forehead, was intently watching the road as he drove.

"Speak for yourself," Barney said.

"Uh-oh," Monster grunted a few minutes later, flicking the headlights on bright. He took his foot off the gas, and the pickup decelerated.

"What?" Barney said, sitting upright. Ahead, caught in the headlights, the brown and gold custom van was pulled off onto a gravel turnoff, parked at an angle facing the highway.

Monster dimmed the lights and pulled the pickup off the highway, making a shallow turn to bring it up parallel with the van. As the pickup swung toward the van they could see Lucky and Ears caught in the headlights. The redhead was standing on the far side of the van, peeing onto the gravel. A small white cat darted out of the weeds and thistles at the edge of the gravel and ran between the men and pickup to underneath the van.

Monster turned the lights off and shoved the gear shift into park.

"Kitty, kitty," Barney called, peering out the window. "Hey, what's happening?" he asked, as a dark, shadowy figure walked up between the van and the truck.

"Oh, it's you," Lucky said, and Barney and Monster could see him fumble with the back of his shirt.

"Was that a *gun*?" Barney said. "Holy shit, what've you got a gun for?"

Cookie Monster slowly reached for the 9mm in the shoulder holster wedged between the console and his seat. He clicked the hammer back.

"I thought it might be someone who followed us from that bar," Lucky said. "Don't think we were too popular."

"Man, you guys better stay out of town for a while," Barney said. "Especially your friend there. I think the cops are looking for him."

"Noooo shit, cowboy," the redhead said. "No fucking shit."

Monster sighed. "Enough is enough," he muttered, and climbed out of the pickup and walked around the front. He leaned against the fender. "You're lucky you had that pool cue," he said.

"Shit." The redhead spit into the gravel between himself and Cookie Monster.

"Where you guys headed?" Lucky asked.

"She would've pinned your balls to the wall with that beer bottle," Monster said.

"Shit." This time the spit landed a foot closer to Monster. The cat mewed, a thin, pleading sound.

"We thought we'd camp out somewhere next to the lake," Barney said. "What about you?"

"And then handed them to you for breakfast," Monster said.

"Shit!"

Monster straightened away from the fender.

"We got to make it up to Kalispell tonight," Lucky said, watching Cookie Monster. "Got to meet somebody up there."

"Then they would have stuffed you and put you on the wall right next to that sheep head," Monster said.

"Shit!" He drew his head back to spit again.

"I sure hope that doesn't land on my shoe," Monster said.

"Knock it off," Lucky said to the redhead. "Or Ears and I are going to kick the shit out of you right here and now. I'm sick of your act, anyway."

"Just climb in there and sit nice and quiet behind the steering wheel," Ears said.

The redhead looked from Monster to Lucky to Ears. His body tensed.

I don't believe it, Barney thought. The asshole is really thinking about it.

"Do it!" Ears said. "The man is going to be pissed, as it is."

The redhead climbed into the van and slammed the door, sullenly staring straight ahead.

Barney saw the white kitten scramble up onto the front tire.

"The man?" Monster asked. "The cops?" He laughed. "Traffic tickets, spitting in public—"

"Fuck you!" the redhead said out the open window. "Cops don't fuck with me." He spit out the window. "I blow away cops."

"No. Someone else," Lucky said wearily. "Our boss . . . unfortunately."

"Oh," Monster said. "I thought you were in business for yourselves."

"Not exactly," Ears said.

"How much stuff you got with you now?" Monster asked. "That you got to pack guns around."

"Not much," Lucky said.

Ears stepped out from behind Lucky. "Why do you ask?"

"Well, I might be interested—if the price is right."

Lucky and Ears were silent, studying him in the dark.

"Besides rustling cattle, you never did tell us what you do for a living," Lucky said.

"Oh, this and that." Monster waggled his hand. He laughed. "I own a little ranch up Nine Mile, just west of where you turned off the Interstate. At the base of that mountain that looks like a big tit."

Barney stifled a laugh. Cookie Monster's ranch consisted of twenty acres of pastureland gone to weeds and bushes and thistles, and another twenty of steep mountainside covered with pine and spruce and larch, blowdown, and thick stands of lodgepole. His livestock consisted of Fu Manchu the cat, a pond filled with big fat trout he fed instead of caught, and deer and elk, which he refused to shoot if they were on his land. And a weathered house at least eighty years old with wood shingles. Some ranch.

"No shit?" Ears said. "How'd you manage that?"

"I inherited it."

"Must be nice."

Monster shrugged.

Barney watched the cat climb slowly backward down the tire tread. It crouched behind the tire, looking up at him.

"Well," Lucky said, "we can't sell you any more of this; it's not ours. But if we was to get some more, how much would you be interested in?"

"Oh, a couple of kilos," Monster said. "Probably all the Thai-stick you can get—if it's real Thai-stick. But I'm most interested in coke."

"We can get a lot," Ears said.

Monster shrugged. "Well, then . . ."

"We might be in Kalispell tomorrow night," Lucky said. "If you're headed that way, maybe we can work something out."

"Yeah," the redhead said. "That'd be nice."

"Shut up," Ears said.

"Where at?"

"Name it," Lucky said.

"How about Moose's? If you're not there by closing time, we'll know you aren't going to make it. You know where it's at?"

"We'll find it."

"Okay," Monster said, "tomorrow night, then." He walked around the pickup and climbed into the driver's seat.

"Later," Barney called, as the two men opened the back door and climbed into the van.

Monster started the pickup; the redhead started the van.

The cat, Barney thought. He looked under the van. It was climbing back up the tire, clinging spreadeagled to the tread. "Hey!" he yelled.

The redhead looked over at him.

"Hold it. There's a cat on your tire."

"A what?"

"A cat on your front tire," Barney opened the door and started to climb out.

The redhead leaned out the window to see the cat. He gunned the van forward. The brake lights flared red.

Muffled shouts came from the back of the van.

"Where's it now?" the redhead asked.

Barney stood with one hand on the open door. The cat was a shapeless white lump flattened into the gravel between the front and rear tires of the van. He looked up.

"Tiger Paws," the redhead called back to him. "Better gription," and he gunned the van again, rocks and gravel and cat squirting away from the rear tires, striking Barney and the open door. The van hit the pavement, tires squeaking, swaying from side to side.

Barney watched it recede down the highway, until the crest of a hill blotted out its taillights, and then it was silent except for the muted idle of the pickup, the faint ticking of the tappets. The air was cool and fresh, smelling of lake and hay, and he couldn't even see any of the cat.

He silently climbed back into the pickup.

Cookie Monster put the truck into gear, and they motored smoothly and effortlessly out onto the pavement and down the highway in the same direction as the van.

CHAPTER 11

Clowning Around

Barney opened his eyes. The inside of his mouth tasted rancid, like buttermilk left too long in the refrigerator. Less than an arm's reach away a chipmunk sat on its haunches eating a grape nearly a third the size of its head, rotating the purple fruit with tiny front paws, stripping the skin away with its sharp teeth.

Chip and Dale, Barney thought.

The purple skin disappeared as if the grape were on a lathe, the chipmunk's dark, glittering eyes watching him.

Barney swallowed, ran his tongue over dried and cracked lips. Morning sun slanted over the jagged mountaintops across the lake, beat against the side of his face and the down sleeping bag. He felt suffocated. Hot and clammy, sweaty and dry all at the same time.

The chipmunk popped the entire grape into the side of its mouth and sat considering Barney.

The grape popped out into its paws again.

Too much to drink last night, Barney thought. He and Monster at the edge of the lake, drinking beer for an hour or so before they unrolled the bags and went to sleep. Sitting, not saying much. Watching the lights wink out one by one across the black still water until the bulk of the mountains seemed to lean forward, shrinking the lake, and the sky became more stars than dark.

Barney threw the unzipped sleeping bag off his bare chest and legs.

The chipmunk squeaked and darted to the side. It ran in a tight, erratic little circle, tail raised, and then stopped and chattered at Barney.

Barney groaned and sat up, feeling the morning breeze against his legs and arms and chest, but instead of cooling, the breeze only dried his body sweat and oils, making him feel as if he were encapsulated inside a layer of plastic wrap.

He ran a hand across the stubble on his face, and lay back down. The sun throbbed against him.

Drinking too much lately, he thought. Not this much since Vietnam. Always got drunk after an operation, waking up in a steaming tent, or in a hot room over a Da Nang bar, or just lying in some sandy, suffocating bunker smelling of piss and vomit and sweat. It helped then. Helped to be drunk. You didn't feel so alone. You weren't ashamed to talk about death and fear and all the things that were too hopeless to talk about when you were sober.

Never did any good, of course. Never answered anything. Because even back then you knew you'd just have to learn to live with it. With yourself. But at least talking about it made it retreat back into its own little corner—a small dark thing you never notice. Well, what was he thinking about all this for?

He sat upright. His mouth tasted awful. His head hurt. His bowels felt loose. He was unbearably hot. And there was fucking Cookie Monster standing waist deep out in the lake, head a white mass of soapsuds, face covered with white lather, carefully scraping lather off the side of his face and rinsing the shaver in the lake. Small blobs of lather bobbed around him.

"You're polluting the lake," Barney croaked. "You fucking hypocrite."

Monster threw the shaver up onto the shore and disappeared into the water; a mound of white suds rocked gently where he'd been standing. Ten yards further out, he abruptly reappeared, snorting and shaking his head. He squirted a stream of water out his mouth toward Barney. "It's biode-gradable."

Barney shuffled over to the Styrofoam cooler sitting on the open tailgate. Cans of beer floated in tepid water.

He fished one out and popped the top; warm beer foamed out and over his hand. He swilled some of the sour liquid around in his mouth. Threw his head back and gargled for a few seconds. Spit it out onto the grass and pine needles.

Fuck me, he thought, my fucking existence has become nothing but a never-ending stream of Oly cans. "Feels great," Monster yelled, treading water. "C'mon in." Barney tilted the can up, feeling the warm beer and carbonation working like Drano down his clogged throat and into his stomach. He belched and threw the empty into the bed of the pickup.

Monster began swimming with powerful strokes, slow and easy.

"Disgusting," Barney muttered. He looked around.

In the dark, he hadn't been able to see what the place really looked like. Tall ponderosa pines right up to the pebbled shore. Soft layer of pine needles and grass underneath the trees. Low bushes and stands of quaking aspens.

It was so perfect, and he was so hung over and curdled, it made him almost yearn to see something like a rusted car body along the lakeshore. Something besides the small, dark dot that was Monster's head disappearing around a point where tiny waves lapped at gnarled and bleached tree roots.

Barney walked toward the shore, flinched and almost fell as he stepped on a pinecone. Water blue and clear. Clean enough to drink right out of the lake, Monster had said, ninety-eight percent pure. But who could believe that idiot? What about the other two percent? Lake huge and deep. And even though the Special Forces had taught him to swim, he shivered: somewhere, way down, hard, cold currents.

He gingerly waded out into the lake, trying to ignore the cold, and dived in.

Underwater it was cold and green and mottled with sunlight. He felt his hand touch a slick greenish-yellow rock. His hand recoiled from the slimy surface, and he fought to get his feet underneath him. He flailed about, the resistance of the water making him swim in slow motion, and kicked for the surface. He broke the surface, sucking in great mouthfuls of air, feeling his heart hammer against his ribs. Even this close to shore, the lake was way over his head: the currents were cold and would take you away forever.

He turned and kicked toward shore, swimming until his knee hit a rock. He thrust his feet downward and bruised his toes on the rocks. Knee deep in the water, panting, he held himself up off the bottom with his fists, arms extended as if he were doing pushups in the water.

Fucking water, he thought. Clean and clear and cold, and it scared him more than that thick brown shit in Vietnam ever had.

Something strong locked around his ankles, jerking him back out.

"Huht!" he grunted, hands scrabbling at the rocks, fingernails scraping, and he swallowed water, was underwater, green and eerie, cold on his face and shoulders. He couldn't breathe, wanted to cough, Monster's voice a muted rumble above him. He twisted and the pressure on his ankles was gone, but his feet wouldn't touch bottom.

He clawed and splashed to the surface, fought his way toward shallow water; water cascaded around him, stinging his face.

He struggled into waist-deep water. "You motherfucker," he said. "You shitass son of a bitch bastard—"

"A drowned rat," Monster said, and backstroked easily out into the lake. "A chubby little drowned rat."

Barney waded toward shore. Without turning around, he raised his hand, middle finger extended upward.

"Ah, so," Monster called, treading water. "Numbah one chubby rittle drowned rat." He laughed, rolled over, and swam away.

A few minutes later, Barney lay on the hood of the pickup, on a worn but clean wool blanket, USMC in large letters along one edge. He was wearing a pair of Monster's gym shorts—way too big—and Monster's Ho Chi Minh sandals—also way too big—just lying there, feeling the sun and breeze against his bare chest, looking at the blue lake and green tree-covered mountains, smelling the water and pines, a hint of sage.

Monster was still wallowing around about three hundred

yards down the shore, swimming on his back, arms rising and falling in slow, languid strokes.

Barney smiled. Clowning around was just Monster's way of relieving pressure.

"We ought to run a check on those guys," he'd said to Monster.

"What for?" Monster had replied. "Nothing the computer is going to tell us we don't already know about them. What we ought to worry about is how we're going to find out who burned us, and then we ought to worry about what we're going to do after we find out."

Monster was right, but the only solution they'd been able to come up with was "Play it by ear. These things usually have a way of working themselves out."

Well, why not? When had things ever been in control? Even predictable? All they'd ever had was themselves and others like them. At times like this, all you could go on was experience and intuition. Luck and reflexes.

Monster understood that. Maybe sometimes he clowned around too much, but at least he understood that.

Barney leaned back against the hot window of the pickup. Monster slowly worked his way past him. To his left a canoe with two people in it came around the point.

Barney tilted his face up toward the sun and closed his eyes. A red-orange haze blotted out the lake and people. Voices wafted across the water, carried by the hot breeze. The heat and red-orange haze inexplicably triggered a memory: the bullet that hit the forward observer passed just under his steel helmet, grazing the camouflage cover. Quarter of an inch higher, it would have struck the steel, probably knocking the helmet off, but leaving the redhead unhurt, his brains still in his head instead of mixed with the paddy muck.

Now, why that, of all the things he had to think about? Probably because of the other redhead they might see again tonight. Too bad it wasn't his brains all over the paddy.

Leaning forward, he opened his eyes. The canoe was only about sixty yards from Monster who, swimming on his back again, still hadn't seen it.

The women looked interesting, the one in the stern tall and dark-haired and wearing what looked like a blue one-piece swimming suit or Danskin top, the one in front wearing a fluorescent yellow bikini, long blond hair and dark tan.

He jumped down off the hood and ran to the back of the truck, fished around in the clutter of gear and beer cans, and ran back to the front of the pickup, a pair of field-green U.S. Army–issue binoculars clutched in his hand.

He scrambled back up onto the hood and raised the binoculars. The blond was— Jesus, look at that, he thought. A slight frown furrowed her forehead as she paddled toward Cookie Monster, her breasts— "Oh, oh, oh," he muttered. Her stomach flexed as she dug the paddle into the water.

Keeping the binoculars to his eyes, he waved one arm in the air. "Hi, there," he yelled. "Sombitch," he said. "Sombitch."

The dark-haired one looked at him and waved, a flash of white teeth as she smiled. Slim with shoulder-length black hair glistening in the sunlight, but older, her face showing the beginnings of creases and wrinkles that people who spend a lot of time outdoors get, skin lighter at forehead and above mid-bicep, but still olive. A little Indian there, maybe. Not as good-looking as the blonde. He rotated back to the blonde, intersected her left breast with the meter grids in the left lens, the vertical and horizontal lines meeting precisely on her nipple. She laughed, pointing at him. They stopped paddling and watched him. The canoe drifted forward.

"Hi, there," he yelled again, and almost lost his balance on the bumper.

"Take a picture, why don't you?" the blonde shouted.

"I would if I could."

Monster was treading water about thirty yards from the bow of the canoe. He slid under the water.

Barney put the binoculars down on the USMC blanket and jumped off the bumper. He walked to the water's edge, Monster's Ho Chi Minhs slapping against his heels. "Where y'all going?"

"Down the shore," the dark-haired one said.

"Looks like hard work," he said. "C'mon in and have a beer."

"Too early for a beer," the blonde replied.

"Well, y'all better c'mon in, anyway. There's a Monster out there."

They both laughed.

And Cookie Monster shot above the surface, rising out of the water, roaring and slapping the water with his arms, splashing water into the canoe behind the dark-haired woman.

The two women screamed, nearly upsetting the canoe. They clutched wildly at the sides, their paddles clattering.

Monster disappeared beneath the surface of the water.

"I told you," Barney shouted, laughing.

The dark-haired woman picked up her paddle and held it like a baseball bat. She peered over the side of the canoe.

The canoe rocked, an unseen force pushing up and from side to side just in front of where the blonde sat. The blonde screamed and clutched at the metal sides; the dark-haired one beat at the water with the paddle.

"Better get in here," Barney yelled.

The canoe settled back into the water, and a few seconds later Monster surfaced ten yards from the canoe. "Hee, hee, hee," he said, and disappeared again.

The two women grabbed their paddles and quickly turned the canoe toward shore.

Monster surfaced a yard behind them, flailing the water with his arms.

The dark-haired one glanced behind. "Faster," she said, and the canoe pulled easily away, toward the shore. The two women shipped their paddles and the aluminum canoe rattled up onto the pebble beach.

"Hi, there." Barney grinned as they stepped ashore.

"There's a monster out there, all right," the blonde said, slightly out of breath. She looked Barney up and down.

Barney blushed, aware suddenly of how he must look: gray gym trunks big enough to be Bermuda shorts, black rubber sandals at least two sizes too big. Ten pounds of lard around his waist. He bowed slightly at the waist. "At your service, ma'am," he said. "The clothes belong to that creature out there."

Monster, waist deep in the water, smiled and held up his right hand, fingers in a V. "Huroh. Didn't mean to scare you like that."

"Oh, of course not," the black-haired one said. "You're lucky I didn't bean you with my paddle."

"You asked us if we wanted a beer," the blonde said to

Barney. "And I thought we were going to get the whole lake."

"Ninety-eight percent pure," Barney said, and turned and walked to the pickup. "But part of the other two percent is standing out there, so I wouldn't drink any of it if I were you." He opened the Styrofoam cooler.

"I guess I could use a beer after all," the black-haired one said.

"Don't worry. He won't come out; he doesn't have any trunks on. I'm wearing them."

The two women looked at Monster.

"Is that right?" the blonde said.

"Is that right," the black-haired one repeated. She smiled at Cookie Monster. "Let's just sit here and drink beer and watch him shiver."

"Barney," Cookie Monster said, "throw me my shorts, will you?"

Barney carried a six-pack to the shore. "Monster?"

"Barney."

"Was my scope broke or not?"

"Oh, man . . . not now."

Barney smiled. "You want some pants . . ."

Monster retreated a few feet out into the lake. "Scope. *Scope.* You're such a lousy shot, you need *laser* sights."

"Okay." Barney shrugged and walked back to the two women. "Here you go, ladies." He tore two cans out of their loops and popped the tabs. The cans hissed and puffed little white tongues of beer foam. "One for you. And one for you."

"A real gentleman." The blonde smiled.

Barney smiled back. "Barney," he said, and offered his hand to her, thinking it was always good to break the touch barrier immediately.

Her hand was warm and soft, her grip firm. "Sarah," she said. "And this is Evy."

Evy grasped Barney's hand. "Howdy, y'all," she said, mimicking his accent, and grinned, tiny, fine wrinkles appearing at the corners of her eyes. Part Indian for sure, he decided. Her eyes were big and soft and brown, but not defenseless, and for some reason he wondered if she had children.

"Hey," Monster shouted. "Throw me some pants."

"Come and get them," Evy said.

"I can't."

"Oh? Modesty got the best of you?"

"No, it's not that. It's this wound I got in the war. . . ."

"I see."

"I hope not."

Evy laughed, a throaty sound. "What're you called? Besides the Monster of the Lake."

"Monster."

She looked at Barney.

"Ben. But everyone calls him Cookie Monster, or just plain Monster. Monster fits."

Monster put his mouth half in the water and blew hard, making a loud whistling and bubbling noise. "The Monster is getting cold."

The three of them sat down at the edge of the pebble beach.

"C'mon, you guys."

"Such modesty," Evy said.

"C'mon, Barn. I'm freezing. I could die of hypothermia or something."

"Not to worry, Monster, *my man*. It will without a doubt be the 'or something.' " Barney winked at the women. "Monster, I'll tell you what: you say, 'Barn, I knew your scope was broke all along, and I apologize, you're a better shot than I am,' and I'll throw you your pants."

"Oh, man . . ."

"What are you talking about?" Sarah asked.

"The scope on my rifle was broke, and I accidentally shot an elk in the wrong place. Isn't that right, Monster?"

Sarah grinned. "That sounds horrible—to even shoot an animal, I mean."

"You eat beef, don't you?"

"Yes, but—"

"Well, you ought to see how they kill beef. They—"

"Shoot them in the head with a twenty-two, which only stuns them," Evy said. "And then they slit their throats. That way the heart is still pumping and there's not so much blood in the meat when the animal finally dies."

Barney looked at her in surprise.

"Oh, that's *terrible!*" Sarah said.

"Elk and deer are a lot better for you," Barney said. He patted his stomach. "Less fat in the meat."

Evy smiled. "Is that why you go hunting?"

Barney looked at her.

"I like to hunt, too," she said.

"I'm going to catch pneumonia. Dammit. C'mon." Monster held his hands up out of the water. "I'm going to look like a prune if I stay in here much longer."

"This beer sure hits the spot," Evy called to Monster.

"I think most people just rationalize it," Sarah said to Barney, the same little frown of concentration on her face that he'd seen through the binoculars.

I'll bet she has that same look on her face when she's fucking, he thought. "Pardon me?"

"I think the reasons for hunting are just excuses; people just like to shoot things."

"Okay," Monster said. "Okay. Your scope was broken. You can get these ladies to sign a statement that I admitted it."

Barney stood and walked to the water's edge. He cupped one hand to his ear and leaned toward Monster. "What was that? I'm not sure I heard that."

"Your scope was broken."

"What?"

"Your scope was broken! Throw me my pants!"

The two women laughed.

"I didn't hear an apology." Barney smiled at Sarah. "Did you hear an apology?"

"I'm sorry all to hell," Monster said, his teeth beginning to chatter slightly. His lips were turning purple.

Barney shook his head. "Not good enough, Monster. You're not being sincere." He walked back to the two women, trying not to be obvious as he looked at Sarah, again conscious of how ridiculous he must look in Monster's shorts and sandals.

"What happened to your knee?" Sarah asked.

He self-consciously rubbed the shrapnel scars. "Just a skiing accident."

"Well," Evy said. She stood up, tugged on the edge of her swimming suit. "We'd better go. We're already late, Sarah."

"Oh, that's right." Sarah jumped to her feet. "We said we'd be right back." She smiled down at Barney.

"Well, hey. Don't rush off," he said, struggling to his feet. "Maybe we can get together, go swimming or dancing or . . . something," he finished lamely.

He blushed, and the two women laughed.

"Maybe tonight," he said. "We have to go into Kalispell, tonight."

"Well . . ." Sarah looked at Evy. "We were planning on going into town tonight."

"We have to meet some people at Moose's," Barney said. "But it'll just take a few minutes. . . ."

"Maybe we'll see you there, then," Evy said, helping Sarah push the canoe into the water.

"Here. Let me help you," Barney said as they climbed in, both of them managing to look graceful, the canoe barely rocking.

He pushed the canoe out away from the shore.

"No fair peeking, ladies," Monster said.

"I don't see anything," Evy said. "A lot of little minnows swimming around, that's all. You see anything, Sarah?"

"Nope, nothing at all. No big trout, that's for sure."

Monster laughed.

Both paddles bit into the water, and the canoe pivoted smoothly, and pulled away, headed back around the point.

"Tonight," Barney called, and Sarah waved.

"Hot damn," he said to himself. "Can you be—" he started to say to Monster, and stopped in disbelief.

Monster was walking out of the lake, water streaming from his new tan all-purpose swimming trunks.

"Fooled you, huh?"

CHAPTER 12

Something in the Air

Sunset in Kalispell: warm and dry, the light bouncing yellow, like polarized light seen through shooter's glasses, off the sides of old brick buildings, energy snapping between relaxed cars and people cruising up and down, around, tuning up. The smell of fresh-mowed lawns.

"Not bad feed," Monster said, elbow out the window, two fingers limply controlling the steering wheel as the black pickup motored quietly down Main Street. "I love seafood—especially when the sheriff's office pays for it." Despite the people and cars, the light and the dry warmth made him feel as if the city were deserted, as if the pickup and they were the only things alive, full of parts, blood and oil and water, not just images.

"Not bad," Barney agreed. "What's this tape? I'd better play some music, get me in the mood for that sweet young thing."

Monster smiled, a frayed toothpick clenched between his teeth. He rolled it to the corner of his mouth. "Try it," he said. "It grows on you." He laughed.

Barney frowned. "I don't like that laugh," he said. "Don't be fucking with me again."

"Try it."

GRAVEYARD RULES

Barney pushed the tape in, turned the volume up, and music—electronic as the yellow light, damp with energy, and melding perfectly with the warm evening—boomed out of the speakers: Alan Parsons singing about something wrong in this house. Violins and drums. Bass, huge and sinister.

"Where'd you get this?" Barney asked, raising his voice over the music.

Monster looked at Barney, Monster's eyes flat and blue and glistening, the sunset making a light golden halo in his hair.

Barney felt the skin tighten and prickle at the back of his neck.

Monster grinned, and yellow light sparked off his teeth, sparked off the chrome inside the cab.

"Jesus," Barney said, and turned the volume down and ejected the tape. "I thought you liked that funky sixties and seventies rock-and-roll shit?"

"They didn't have this then."

"This is evil."

"Well, they've always had that."

Barney rubbed the side of his face and sat back, blinking at the light refracting off the buildings. "Weird music."

"Weird world," Monster said, and turned the black truck into the parking lot behind Moose's. The lot was already full, trucks and sport cars, mostly.

He shut the engine off, and they got out and walked around the rear of the truck, meeting at the tailgate.

"Hey, hey, hey," Barney said heartily. "Got some ladies coming . . . drink a little beer, have a good time. What d'you say?"

"I say," Monster replied, mimicking the music. "I say something's wrong." He smiled without humor. "Something's been going on." He pointed a finger at Barney. "And there's going to be a price to pay."

Barney stared at Monster. "Noooo shit," he finally said, and with both hands shoved Monster in the chest, propelling him backwards in the direction of the door.

Monster stumbled and caught himself. Laughing, he turned and walked to the door.

"You asshole," Barney said. "I never know when you're serious."

With a flourish, Monster opened the door. "Welcome to the Magical Mystery Tour, sir," he said, and bowed and gestured Barney ahead of him.

Barney shook his head.

And they went inside.

CHAPTER 13

A War Story

The barmaid, a harried-looking woman of twenty-five or so—no doubt a single parent, Monster thought—dressed in jeans, hiking boots, and flannel shirt, sleeves rolled up above her elbows, took their order—beer—and delivered it, pushing damp hair away from her eyes. Barney smiled and y'all'd her, but it didn't do any good.

The bar was finished in barn wood, sawdust on the floor, booths built like stubby cattle chutes along the far wall, a fireplace ringed by wooden benches. An oval bar took up nearly a third of the room. People sitting around the fireplace were eating pizza.

"This is nuts," Monster said.

Most of the men wore hats—straw cowboy hats creased salty-dog don't fuck-wit-me style, leather cowboy hats, felt cowboy hats, baseball hats, "Case" lettered on one. Clean hats. Clean people. Rolled-up sleeves, tank tops, clean and smooth and tan skin everywhere.

Girls in nylon running shorts. Red shorts, green shorts, blue shorts, fluorescent and shimmering. Curled hair and Nike-Adidas-Brooks running shoes. Tight T-shirts. Girls in western shirts, tight jeans, boots, curled hair.

"Look at those red shorts," Barney said. "Mmm-mmm."

"Remember the last time we were in here?" Monster said.

"That guy that was bartending: big, fat, crazy bartender."
He nodded toward the bar. "Now they've got a fucking basketball player for a bartender." He raised his mug of beer
and took a drink, looking at Barney over the rim. He put
the mug down. "Remember? The place was full of at least
halfway real cowboys and thousands, it seemed like, of long-
haired, burned-out doper sons of bitches. And we was freak-
ier than anyone." He smiled. "But the bartender knew who
we were, and the silly shit kept giving us free beer and peanuts, and naturally everyone noticed, and we couldn't buy
Hershey bars, let alone dope."

He laughed, eyes glinting, as he looked around. "I'll bet
we could stack these idiots outside like cordwood."

Barney took a drink of beer.

"In fact . . ." Monster said. His hands trembled slightly.

"Don't start fucking around, now."

Monster looked across at Barney: Barney about sixty
pounds lighter, chubby and out of shape.

"I mean it," Barney said.

Monster's eyes narrowed. "You little shit."

Barney waited.

"Well, then . . ." Monster said, and Barney tensed.

Monster raised his beer. "To long legs and firm tits."

Barney smiled. "I'll drink to that."

Monster drained his mug. "Ah," he said. "I—" He stared
toward the doorway. "Oh, no."

"What?" Barney turned quickly in his chair.

"Look what just came in."

Bruce stood just inside the doorway, looking from side to
side, quartering the bar with his eyes. In the dim, smoke-
filled light, his T-shirt was the same black as his beard and
hair.

"He's looking for us," Barney said.

"Sure is." Monster slouched back in his chair. "But I
don't think he's ever seen us without beards and long hair."

"The secretary has a bunch of before and after pictures of
the drug team."

"Let's see."

Bruce walked along the bar, back rigid, arms tensed and
held out from his sides. The woman in red shorts threw her

head back and laughed, blond curls bouncing, and stepped back and bumped into Bruce.

"Oh," her mouth said, and smiled, "I'm sorry," but Bruce just stared at her, his face expressionless. Her smiled faded, and she turned back to the two men she'd been laughing with, glancing at Bruce out of the corner of her eye.

"What a jerk," Monster said.

"The Incredible Hulk in Dodge City," Barney said.

Bruce resumed walking along the bar, not bothering to thread his way between knots of people; instead, he simply walked up to a person, and stood staring until that person moved.

"I'll bet he's wonderful in uniform," Monster said.

"Don't look him in the eye." Barney looked down at his beer. "He'll recognize you."

Monster stared at Bruce.

Bruce's eyes swept the room, checking people around the open fireplace, the booths, the tables, finally locking on Monster. His eyes were hooded, reptilian in the orange light from the fireplace.

Monster smiled sardonically and silently mouthed "fuck you," and even in the poor light he saw Bruce flush, his neck swell.

"What're you doing?" Barney said. "Those women might be here any minute."

Bruce walked over to their table. "You got a problem?" he said to Monster.

"A problem?" Monster asked in mock surprise. "You stupid fucker. Sit down before I give you a real problem."

Bruce frowned.

"Sit down." Barney sighed. "You're making a spectacle of yourself."

"Jesus. I didn't recognize . . ." He pulled out a chair and sat down. "What happened to your hair, your beards . . . ?"

"What're you doing here?" Barney asked.

Bruce looked from Barney to Monster. "Man, you sure don't look like cops anymore—like narcs, I mean."

Monster leaned forward. "You want to go outside with me, Bruce? You feel big and bad enough? Or is it just that badge in your pocket?"

Bruce flushed, his eyes looking everywhere but at Monster.

"Shit, Monster. I didn't recognize you. I thought you were some jock with a hard-on for loggers or something."

"Don't make a damn." Monster leaned farther forward, forearms on the table. "What do you say? Just me and you."

Bruce looked sullenly down at the table.

"Maybe you were going to pull your gun on me?"

The muscles in Bruce's biceps twitched under the tight T-shirt. He slowly looked up into Monster's eyes. "Some-day . . ."

Monster grinned, and Barney thought, This ought to be interesting. Monster's bigger, but Bruce has that look—feral eyes more cunning than intelligent, a pit bull you'd have to kill to free the jaws. But it'd be Monster, for sure, because Monster was fast and when he did it, it was never halfway, and because Monster's eyes were cold and blue and too fucking smart sometimes.

Bruce looked away, his eyes gone watery. "What's with him?" he said to Barney. "The lieutenant sent me up to check on you, back you up if you need it, and"—he glanced at Monster—"you're treating me like I was a fucking hair monster or something."

Monster leaned back in his chair. He looked around: people laughing, talking, eating, drinking, sawdust on the floor, pert little asses in running shorts and tight designer jeans, cowboy hats, fake fire in the fireplace, Bruce. He pushed himself to his feet, his chair scraping the floor through the sawdust. "Take a whiz," he said to Barney.

Barney and Bruce watched him ease his way into the crowd at the bar. He paused to smile and say something to the blond woman in the red shorts, and she laughed and looked toward Bruce.

"He's a little uptight," Barney said, wondering what Monster had said to the blonde.

"Well, still . . . we're in this together. I mean, we're cops and veterans, and if we can't stick together, help each other . . ."

"That's right, you were in Vietnam, weren't you?"

Bruce nodded.

"Where were you at?" Monster had probably used his remark about the Incredible Hulk.

"The Delta, mostly."

"Saw a lot of action, I suppose."

"A little." Bruce shrugged. "Nothing like you."

"The first body is always the worst."

Bruce's face creased into a grin, the skin at the corners of his eyes folding into a delta of wrinkles. "Yeah," he said, and right then Barney knew Cookie Monster had been right. "That's right. Exactly."

Fuck you, Barney thought. "So the lieutenant sent you to watch over us, huh? Give us a fire base in the rear, so to speak."

Bruce nodded. "You guys are so independent, he worries a little." He smiled. "Cowboys, he calls you."

"He would. Well, stick around town if you want, do your thing, but we don't have anything going. We came up here for a little R and R, is all. In fact"—he looked toward the doorway—"we've got dates. And they should be here any minute, so . . ." He smiled. "Y'all know how it is."

"You guys really aren't working?" He frowned. "I can go back and tell him you're just taking it easy?"

"Why don't you just tell him to go fuck himself?"

Bruce laughed. "Sometime I'd like to work with you guys. You have more fun and make more busts than the rest of the team put together."

"Just seems that way."

"Yeah, well . . ." He stood. "Tell the Monster I'm sorry about pissing him off."

"Later," Barney said.

"Later," Bruce echoed, and unconsciously squared his shoulders before making his way back through the press of people, cold and hard and mean, a man's man in logging boots and jeans and T-shirt that showed off his biceps.

Barney grimaced. "Asshole," he muttered.

"Say what?" Monster asked, sitting back down. He passed a fresh mug of beer across to Barney. "A real piece of work, that man," he said. "Just naturally pisses me off."

Barney slid the mug of beer back and forth, from hand to hand, across the tabletop. He looked up at Monster. "After that little talk we had, it's hard to believe the lieutenant would send that idiot up here to keep an eye on us."

Monster shrugged. "I wouldn't put anything past the lieutenant."

Barney was silent for a moment, staring at Monster.

"Well, anyway," he said. "Bruce's never seen any action."

"That's what I told— Here comes your little blonde."

"My little . . ." Barney turned to look. Sarah and Evy were standing just inside the door. Barney waved, and Sarah waved back, and the two women made their way into the crowd. "Hel-*lo,*" he said. "Look-ing good."

Evy led the way—black hair gleaming even in the poor light—tall and graceful, jeans and boots and tailored blue western shirt, but it was Sarah who attracted attention.

She tossed her long blond hair as she edged through a group of cowboy hats, her breasts moving unfettered beneath a shimmering purple blouse.

"I can't take it," Barney said. "I can't take it." He jumped up. "Get some chairs."

"We've got chairs."

"Get some beer, then."

"Calm down," Monster said. "Jeezus."

"Hi, there!" Barney grinned at Sarah. "Glad y'all could make it."

"Have a seat," Monster said, and looked up and found himself staring straight into Evy's large and brown and slightly Oriental eyes.

"Hello, Monster," she said. "You look different without your lake."

"What do you two do, anyway?" Sarah asked a few minutes later. "You're so tense . . . in a funny sort of way."

"It's just that we're not used to such good-looking ladies," Monster said. "You make us nervous."

Evy raised her eyebrows.

Sarah giggled. "Really. What do you two do?"

Barney and Monster looked at each other. Monster shrugged.

"We're undercover cops." Barney smiled. "Narcs."

Sarah laughed. "No. Come on. What do you really do?"

Monster reached into the pocket of his windbreaker and pulled out a thin black leather case and threw it onto the tabletop.

Evy flipped it open. His gold badge, dull and heavy-looking in the dim light, stared out of black leather, I.D. behind clear plastic on the other side. *"Why couldn't you have been straight with me?"* Gerri had said.

"Oh," Sarah said. "Oh, neat." She looked at Barney. "You really are," she said. "Do you have guns on, too?"

"I knew it," Evy said.

"Knew what?" Monster asked.

Evy shook her head.

"I think it's neat," Sarah said.

Monster shrugged. "Well," he said, "if you don't like cops . . ."

Evy put her hand on his forearm. "I didn't say that."

Monster looked at her hand, fingers long and slim and warm, but nails blunt and uneven. "You didn't look too happy when you saw that badge." He could feel calluses on her palm. Gerri's hands were soft.

"I just didn't want you to turn out to be a cowboy."

"Cowboy!" Barney said. "He won't even ride a horse. Hates them."

Evy smiled and pulled her hand back from Monster's arm. "Oh, I don't mean like that," she said. "Some men, but especially cowboys—I have a brother-in-law who's one—never grow up. They just ride horses and drink and chase women, fight, get into trouble with the law. When they get older they beat on their wives and kids, do as much dope as alcohol, and get fat and old and lazy, not necessarily in that order." She looked down at the tabletop. "When they hurt someone they love, they get hard and tough, and later they cry." She paused and looked up and smiled at Monster. "My sister's thirty going on a hundred and thirty, I think."

Sarah looked sideways out of the corner of her eye at Evy.

"And you think cops are like that, too?" Monster said.

"Well . . . I don't really know any cops." She blushed. "But some of the ones I see . . ."

Monster laughed. "No. You're right," he said. "A lot of them are like your—the guy you're talking about—but without the dope or the crying. At least a lot of the ones I know are.

"But don't worry, Barney and I aren't like that." He hesitated, and smiled. "We're worse."

Everyone laughed. Evy squeezed his arm. "Can we start over?"

"We already have." Monster looked at Barney. "But first we've maybe got some business to do?"

"What do you think?" Barney said.

Monster shrugged. "We said we weren't going to make any cases."

"Well, why don't we wait for a while, anyway," Barney said. "Maybe they'll show."

"Can we stay, too?" Sarah asked, wiggling in the chair, her breasts moving beneath the silk blouse. "We won't be in the way. I promise."

"Maybe we'd better not," Evy said. "We can meet somewhere else, later."

"These are not nice people," Monster said and, as soon as he said it, knew it was exactly the wrong thing to say.

"Oh, please!" Sarah pleaded.

"Look," Barney said. "This isn't television." He frowned at Monster. "I don't think—"

"You have the cutest accent," Sarah interrupted. "Where are you from?"

Evy and Monster laughed.

"Virginia, ma'am."

"Seriously," Monster said. "You can stay if you want. But these really are not nice people. Worse than cowboys, for sure," he said to Evy. "Two are burned-out Vietnam veterans, and the other is just naturally rotten."

"Are Vietnam veterans rotten?" Evy asked.

"We're veterans," Monster said.

"I thought so."

"Of course," Monster said. "That doesn't mean anything: we could be rotten, too."

"Just like everyone else."

"Well, not exactly . . ."

"Did you go to Vietnam?" Sarah asked Barney.

"How'd we get on this subject?" Barney said. "Who is this woman, anyway?"

"He's a hero," Monster said to Sarah.

"Really?" She impulsively put her arm through Barney's, hugging his arm to her breast. "You know, for a long time nobody would talk about Vietnam. But I always wondered what it must be like.''

Ah, fuck, Monster thought. I did it now: war stories. He drained his beer, watching with expressionless eyes Evy over the rim of the glass.

Evy smiled politely.

''No war stories,'' Monster said.

''Please,'' Sarah said to Barney.

Monster leaned forward. ''No war stories, *please.*'' He leaned back and picked up his glass of beer.

The two women glanced at each other. The damp smells of beer and sawdust and cigarette smoke eddied about them, rock and roll on the jukebox, people shouting, talking, arguing.

''Excuse me,'' Monster said. ''But it's a personal thing.'' His eyes met Evy's.

She smiled, her brown eyes warm.

He hated that look. Warm for all the wrong reasons. Knowing nothing. Knowing everything. Women.

''My, my, my. Isn't this cozy?'' a male voice said from behind Monster. ''Mr. and Mrs. All-America out for an evening of beer and peanuts.''

Barney's head jerked up.

Monster stared at Evy for a moment and then pushed himself up, hands on the armrests of his chair, and turned to face the redhead and the other two men.

''Hey,'' he said. ''Pull up a couple of chairs. Barn, grab us some glasses and another pitcher of beer, will you?''

''Yeah, Barn,'' the redhead said, brushing past Monster to the other side of the table. ''Get us some beer, will you?'' He reached across to an empty table and pulled a chair over between Sarah and Evy. ''Nice,'' he said, sitting down. He looked from one woman to the other. ''Very nice.''

''Hey!'' Barney said and jumped up. ''How's it goin'? Excuse me,'' he said to Sarah. ''Three glasses, one pitcher of beer coming up,'' and headed for the bar.

Bewildered, Sarah stared after him; Evy watched Monster.

''Sit down. Sit down,'' he said to the two men, gesturing them to the table.

The two men pulled chairs into the space between Monster

and Barney and sat down. Both were dressed in gray slacks, Lucky wearing a light blue short-sleeve knit shirt, Ears a cream-colored shirt. The redhead leaned back in his chair, trying to look down Sarah's blouse. "Mmmmm." He said, leering, "No bra."

"We'd about given up on you," Monster said.

Sarah straightened in her chair, holding herself so that her blouse fell flat against her chest.

"Sarah and Evy," Cookie Monster said. "This is Lucky, and this is Ears." He gestured toward the two men.

The two men smiled thinly.

"Really snuck up on us." Monster smiled, thinking they sure had. "Didn't even see you come in." Not your run-of-the-mill dopers, he thought, and felt a thrill of adrenaline. Going to be interesting arresting these two. Worth it, maybe.

"Didn't mean to," Lucky said.

Ears smiled.

"And that creature sitting between you," Monster said, "is called Nasty—for obvious reasons."

"Don't mind him," the redhead said. "He's just jealous because I've got such a big tool."

Sarah and Evy looked at each other. Evy shrugged.

Monster laughed, thinking, They're fucking with us. "It's not the tools that make the artist," he said. "It's how you use them."

"Shit!" the redhead snorted.

"C'mon, Barn," Cookie Monster shouted at Barney, who was pushing his way through the tangle of people at the bar. "These folks be gettin' thirsty."

"Yeah, Barn," the redhead mimicked. "We be getting thirsty." He put his hand on Evy's arm. "And not just thirsty, either."

Evy jerked her arm, but the redhead held it firm against the chair arm. "Yum-yum," he said.

"Get your hand off me!" She jerked her arm again, and the redhead tightened his grip. She winced and looked wide-eyed at Monster, a woman who obviously knew some hard men but not prepared for the redhead, then up at Barney as he put the fresh pitcher on the table.

"You like it," the redhead said, his voice as intimate as a

hand between her legs. "I can tell." Evy pulled her head and shoulders back, neck stiff, as she stared at the redhead: a bad dream come to life.

"What's going on?" Barney said, forgetting to make his voice good-ol'-boy southern.

"Sit down, toad," the redhead said. "I've got a joke for the lady."

Monster looked at Lucky and Ears.

"Why do women have legs?" the redhead said, leaning forward to keep his face close to Evy's, his eyes locked on hers.

Lucky smiled, and Ears shrugged at Monster, as if to say What can we do?

"So they don't make snail tracks on the dance floor."

Evy sank the fingernails of her free hand into his wrist. "Let go of me," she said. "Let go."

"Oh, yeah!" The redhead laughed. "Pain: I love it."

Evy dug her fingernails in deeper, and Monster scraped his chair back, but as he did, Lucky and Ears also pushed their chairs back, both of them watching him carefully.

"Y'all ought to let her arm go," Barney drawled.

"Or what, Toad?" The redhead kept his eyes locked on Evy's.

Barney moved the pitcher of beer and the glasses to the far side of the table, in front of Monster. Monster relaxed back into his chair. He smiled at Ears and Lucky.

"Ben! Help me!" Evy said, looking wide-eyed and angry at him, a vein in one side of her throat prominent as she tried to squirm out of the redhead's control. The top snap of her western shirt came unsnapped, and the redhead pulled her slightly forward, causing her shirt to open, allowing him to see down inside it.

"You bastard," she said, and reached with her free hand to close her shirt, just as Barney leaned across the table, in front of Sarah, left arm and hand supporting his weight, and hit the redhead on the side of the neck below the skull and behind the ear. A short, snapping punch that popped the red-head's head to the side, stunning him, causing him to release Evy's arm.

The redhead blinked, a rage quicker than comprehension

of what had happened unfocusing his eyes. His head turned toward Barney, his mouth opening.

"Ahh—" he began, a deep, guttural scream of rage, and Barney hit him again, another snapping punch to protect his hand, fist against open mouth and lips, that split the redhead's upper lip against his teeth, blood already flowing as his head snapped back. Barney straightened and stepped back and around Sarah, and as the redhead's upper body rebounded forward, Barney dug one hand into the redhead's curly hair and pushed his face down onto the table top. With his other hand he pulled the redhead's right arm out and up behind his back, forcing his hand up between his shoulderblades. "Nuhhk," the redhead said. "Motherfuck." He tried to spit blood out of his mouth, the side of his cheek pressed into the table, eyes gone mad. He looked at Sarah.

She scrambled to her feet, backing away from the table.

Conversation had ceased in all but the far corners of the bar, people intuitively aware that the fight was not an ordinary push-and-shove, kick-and-hit-and-make-up bar fight.

"Apologize to the lady," Barney said. "Apologize or I'll break your fucking arm." He yanked up on the arm and Cookie Monster was amazed it didn't dislocate.

The redhead tried to kick Barney; his free hand searched for Barney's balls. Barney pushed, and they all saw the shoulder dislocate. Dislocate without the usual popping sound, just sort of slide out of the socket, the arm suddenly limber and unresisting in Barney's grasp.

The redhead groaned—that special groan you hear when something hurts sick to the bone.

Lucky and Ears and Monster all stood up at the same time, Monster balanced evenly on both feet, aware that at least one of them was probably carrying a gun.

Barney yanked back on the redhead's hair and half pulled, half threw him back into the chair.

The redhead squeaked, a sound part scream part groan, as he fell back against his arm and shoulder.

Barney smiled crookedly, his eyes dark and no mistaking he wanted more of it. "Well, damn," he said, watching the other two men carefully, "I don't know what got into me."

The two men looked at each other and relaxed, accepting the situation.

Barney looked down at the redhead. "Damn," he said again, false concern in his voice, "I ain't never done that before. I sure hope I didn't hurt him."

The room was silent, blurs of white faces, people edging forward to look at the groaning redhead. The bartender pushed his way toward them. Female voices, snatches of conversation, murmurs of disgust and titillation, like the crowd at an automobile accident: "Shoulder . . . did you see . . . sick . . . happened so quick . . . who are they?" and the bartender, "What happened? Outside if you want to fight," and Monster and Ears and Lucky and Barney watched one another while the redhead, white-faced and leaning forward, his arm dangling uselessly, groaned. Sarah stood back away from the table, arms crossed in front, hugging herself, eyes darting. Evy clutched her shirt and stared at Monster. A muscle jumped at her temple. The skin was stretched tight across her cheekbones.

"Just a friendly argument, sir," Barney said to the bartender. "Everything's okay now. No harm, no foul."

The bartender scowled down at Barney. "Happens again and you're out of here." He turned and pushed his way back to the bar.

"I'll kill you for this, motherfucker," the redhead whispered. "I'll fucking . . . kill you."

"Still want to talk business?" Monster said to Lucky.

"Just wanted to see what kind of people we was dealing with is all."

"Well, hey, don't get the wrong idea," Barney said. "It was just an accident. I didn't know what I was doing." He looked embarrassed toward Sarah, who was visibly trembling. "Couldn't stand him insultin' the womenfolk like that is all."

"Sure," Ears said. He glanced at Monster. "And bears don't shit in the woods, do they?"

"Maybe you should get him out of here," Monster said.

Lucky nodded. "Get up," he said to the redhead.

"My shoulder . . . fuck—"

"Just get the fuck up!" Lucky walked around the table and grabbed the redhead by his good arm, pulled him to his feet, and pushed him toward the door.

"Why don't you stay with the girls?" Monster said to Barney. "I'll be back in a minute." He placed his hand gently on Evy's shoulder. "How you doing?"

"I'm okay," she said, but her eyes were as angry as any he'd ever seen, watering a little. Her hand still clutched her shirt.

"Kill him," they heard the redhead yell. "Kill him."

Monster took his hand from Evy's shoulder and turned to Sarah. "That's why I can't handle them," he said. "They make you crazy."

Sarah frowned.

"War stories," Monster said. "War stories."

"Why don't you sort of leave him somewhere?" Monster said when they got outside. "I think Barney be for forgettin' the whole thing, otherwise."

"Won't happen again," Ears said. He and Lucky stood next to the van, which was parked in a far corner of the parking lot, streetlight above and behind them as they faced Monster, their faces and bodies shadowed and uniform. Monster knew that the opposite was true of him: the light, white and fluorescent, highlighted his features, exaggerated his expressions. Light like light from a flare.

"But it's up to you," Lucky said.

The redhead was mostly silent, shut inside the van, groaning and swearing occasionally.

"You sure you can get that much cash by tomorrow?" Ears asked.

"No problem. I can go to the bank here; it's a branch of my own."

"Well, we be for going, then."

Monster nodded, hands in the side pockets of his windbreaker, right hand gripping the derringer.

"No more games," Lucky said. "Just business." He opened the driver's door and climbed in. Ears walked around to the other side, and Monster heard the side door slide open and then slide shut, the sound reminding him of the doors they'd had on their helicopters.

Lucky started the van, nodded once at Monster, and drove the van out of the lot.

GRAVEYARD RULES

Monster stood underneath the streetlight and watched the taillights disappear around a corner. Stood there for a long moment, feeling the buzz of beer and adrenaline and, for some reason, fear.

Large moths bounced and flickered up near the white globe of light like out-of-control helicopters.

He thought of helicopters.

CHAPTER 14

The Lake

The cabin was old, made out of logs shortly after the First World War when the lake and Montana were relatively unknown and the only way in and out was by a dirt road that was little more than a path by today's standards. A fine place then, with a hand pump that brought water up from a well, even though the lake water was clean and clear. Shortly after the Second World War, during the prosperity of the 1950s, a bedroom had been added, the addition sided with cheap plywood, and the whole structure painted a uniform rust-red in an attempt to blend the plywood into the pine logs. Recently, a porch had been added, the upper half screened, the bottom half made of still unpainted rough-cut planks.

There was a double bed on the porch, an old brass bedstead with a blue down quilt on top of the mattress. Other mattresses, lawn chairs, fishing tackle, and canoe paddles were stacked neatly on the porch against the wall of the cabin, obscuring most of the cabin's one large window.

The main room was cluttered with sink and dishes, pots and pans hanging on a wall, old stuffed chairs and sofa, throw rugs haphazard on the wood floor, and a rock fireplace flanked by a stack of split wood and by fireplace tools. The thick pine mantel was crowded with framed pictures, cheap china, a coffee can full of rusted nuts and bolts and nails, bug spray, suntan lotion, and red and yellow shotgun shells. One corner of the room had been partitioned into a bathroom barely big enough for sink, toilet, and metal shower. Several suitcases, one on the floor just outside the bedroom door, one on an old wooden chair, were open, the contents mussed and pawed through.

A bare light bulb burned above the sink, the light weak, giving everything a shadowed and slightly seedy appearance.

But it was all clean and comfortable, and sitting on the couch in front of the empty fireplace with Evy, Cookie Monster had no idea what the bedroom looked like, because Barney was in there with Sarah, and they were giggling and whispering and thumping around. Just like a couple of kids, he thought.

When he'd gone back inside Moose's, Evy was in the women's room, and when she'd come back out, her eyes had been red and puffy. "It felt as if I was being raped," she'd said, but he knew her tears were because of frustration and outrage at her helplessness, and not because of fright.

They'd left Moose's and gone to the Outlaw Inn. Danced and drank, and he'd explained what was going on. Gradually, she'd loosened up and they'd had a good time, but now, even with Barney and Sarah romping around in the bedroom, she was tight again. They'd started out with some fairly heavy breathing on the couch, but somehow, he wasn't exactly sure how, they'd ended up sitting at opposite ends, facing each other, Evy with one leg underneath her, he slouched down into the corner, one leg bent at the knee, the other sprawled straight out in front of him, talking, talking about this and that, but nothing of any importance to either of them. She was divorced. It was herself, not her sister, she'd been talking about at the bar, but he'd already known that. She had a nine-year-old son. Lived near Missoula. And Cookie Monster supposed that this was merely Getting to Know Each Other. What bothered him, though, was that despite her appeal, he didn't feel that spark. And he felt that it was probably his fault.

"I think I'm afraid of you, a little bit," she said. "And I'm not sure why."

"I'm as gentle as a bear."

"That's what I mean." She laughed.

He looked down at his hands, fingers laced over his stomach. "Well, don't ever be afraid of me. I like you."

"Sure." Her voice held a hint of bitterness. "They all say that."

"After your bod, huh?"

"What else?"

"Well . . . it's a nice bod, but plenty else. You're good people. You been through some hard times. I can tell."

She smiled. "I suppose that's meant to be a compliment. But why do men always equate good with hard or tough, things like that?"

"What! You mean you don't want to be macho, too?"

She made a face.

"I guess I never thought about it," he said. "But maybe it's because men have to be sure of hard and tough . . . honorable and proud . . . all of those things, before the others can happen."

"Maybe."

He sat up and leaned forward, elbows on knees, hands clasped together. "Hell, I don't know. Or if I do, I'm not saying. Not even to myself."

"I didn't mean to offend you," she said.

He shrugged, and they were silent, he staring into the fireplace, she watching him.

In the other room, Sarah squealed and something thumped against the wall. The bed started squeaking.

He glanced toward the bedroom door. "I guess I'm not very good company tonight. Sorry."

"Oh, that's okay." She smiled. "I'm used to it."

"Used to what?"

"Men always seem to have trouble with me. It's my size or my looks, or both, I think. I intimidate men, somehow."

"You do that." He grinned, running his eyes over her.

"Oh, sure," she said, dismissing his look.

"Are you serious?"

"Of course, I'm serious," she said. "You have no idea how many men I've been with who couldn't get it up." She blushed and looked down. Her hand began picking at the sofa fabric.

"That sounds like a challenge." He smiled.

Her head jerked up, eyes flashing even in the wan light. "Thanks. I needed that."

He stood and walked to the fireplace, traced the grain in the mantel with his fingertips.

She watched him.

He turned toward her. "It's probably a tougher time for women than it is for men."

"Well . . . you don't say."

"I do say."

"Got me figured out already, huh?" She looked at him shrewdly. "Have you got a girlfriend?"

"Nope. Did have."

"Recently, I'd say."

"That's a good way to put it. Recently."

They looked at each other for a moment.

"Why do I get the idea you know what I'm going to say before I even say it?" he asked.

She smiled and shrugged, her brown eyes big and wide and guileless.

"I just hope you're not going to try to pick a fight," she said.

"Me!" he said. "Pick a fight?" He laughed.

Evy stood, her movement graceful, and walked over to him. In the other room, the bed had stopped squeaking. Her brown eyes were dark and not afraid of him at all, the pupils expanded. If he could have looked into a mirror, he'd have seen that, except for the color, his eyes looked almost exactly like hers at that moment.

"Are you finished?" she said.

"Finished?" he asked, conscious of her body heat and at the same time irritated with himself for saying things so awkwardly. He swallowed; her eyes watched him—a combination of cynicism, humor, and get-it-over-with. "I just mean it must be tough trying to become what a woman could be, without turning into a man in a woman's body." His hand went to her shoulder. "And I don't really give a damn." They were face to face, only a few inches separating their bodies.

"Umm, I know," she murmured, and moved forward and pressed her body lightly against him, hands still at her sides. "All that biology to fight." Her eyes looked sleepy, her lips slightly swollen. Putting his arms around her, he kissed her gently, experimentally, feeling the softness of her lips, smelling her skin.

"Some fighter," he said.

She put her arms lightly around his waist. "Who's fighting?" she said, and kissed his neck just above the collarbone. "Let's go to bed."

And they did, to the old brass bed on the screened porch, first shutting off the light above the sink and then groping their way out onto the porch, giggling and shivering with the night breeze blowing off the lake through the screens onto their naked bodies as they hurriedly undressed and jumped into bed, the bed groaning as their bodies came together, rubbing and squirming between sheets ice-cold, clean, and smooth. "Get me warm," she said, and he was immediately hard and ready, but he delayed, waiting for her, and as the bed warmed and it became hot beneath the covers, he inexplicably became hot also—not a normal, sweaty hot, but a dry hot, and thinking about other women and rice paddies and nothing in particular, just that dry feeling, as if his body were a husk, he lost it. Not entirely, but just enough, and no matter what she did—"What can I do?" she asked, her fears confirmed—he couldn't quite. He wanted to, was aroused mentally, he thought, but his body was dry and desiccated like rice paddies a long time ago, and wouldn't.

He swallowed hard: a wave of fear—that old fear, familiar and gray with adrenaline—smashed at him, and, her head in the hollow of his throat, she misunderstood and asked him if he was crying.

"What? No. This never happened before. I mean, I really want to, but . . ."

He lay there feeling a fool, crawly and wide awake from the adrenaline. He could smell lake and pines, hear the lapping of waves at the dock, the swish of pine needles, but all he could feel inside the dryness of his body was the adrenaline, the thump of his heart.

"This is crazy," he said. He could feel her weight against him, feel her disappointment and fatalism. "This'll sound like an excuse . . . but I feel disoriented, out of it. I used to feel in control, thought I had a handle on myself. But lately . . ." He laughed nervously. "Pretty melodramatic, huh?"

"Were you crying?" she asked again, her voice dull, her body and hands still.

"No." He turned his head away from her and then back again. "You don't understand."

"What's to understand?" she said.

"I'm afraid."

She raised herself up on one elbow and peered down at him, her face an oval darkness above him. "Afraid. Afraid of what? Of me?"

He laughed. "No. Not of you."

"Of what, then?"

He reached up and gently slid his hand along her cheek and neck, resting it on her shoulder.

She tilted her head, pressing her cheek against his hand. "Of what?"

"That's the problem," he said, withdrawing his hand. "I don't know."

She stared down at him. He could feel her eyes. And after a moment, she turned around, back and ass pressed up against him, and said, "Go to sleep. You're just being weird." She reached behind and patted the top of his thigh. "You'll feel different in the morning."

"I'm going swimming," he said.

"What?"

"I'm going swimming," he repeated. The thought of cold, dark water enveloping his body was irresistible, and throwing the covers off, he sat up, feet on the floor, not feeling the coldness. He looked through the screen down at the lake. The moon was not up, but the night was clear, and by the starlight he could see the dark mass of water through the pines in front of the cabin, sense the movement of the lake more than see or hear it.

Evy turned over underneath the covers. He felt her hand on his back, lightly rubbing. "Don't be silly," she said. "It's okay."

"It would feel good to be in the water. I'm hot."

"You *are* hot," she said, her hand held still on his back. "Is something wrong?"

He laughed, and stood and walked to the door. "I won't be long," he said, and opened the door. Walking down to the dock he noticed that his feet felt swollen and padded, hardly feeling the pine needles and rocks on the path.

The dock was old, the pilings irregular and white like driftwood, the boards smooth and soft to his feet. He walked out to the end. There were other docks and boat houses all up and down the shore, dark shapes, the same dark as the shoreline and the mass of trees and hill behind it. He could feel the mountains across the lake, barely make them out against the incredible assemblage of stars. For a moment, head tilted back, he stared up at the blackness between the stars, blackness infinite and sterile and, because of that, not as attractive to him as the blackness of the lake.

The lake was alive. Familiar. Like the mountains, a part of him. And as he dived in, he relished the shock of wet and cold already penetrating him, colder yet toward the bottom. He opened his eyes into total darkness, the deeper water and its currents only sensed. And he remembered, as he always did, water-skiing in the dark when he was a boy. Falling. Falling so fast and hard he was out of the skis before he even hit the water, his life preserver exploding apart into small squares of white foam. Underneath, turning over and over, he'd lost sense of what was up and what was down, and he'd pushed his way down, down, trying to go up, and panicked, swimming harder, down, down, into water that only got colder, sucking toward the deep, forever currents. At the last second, he'd realized his error and turned and clawed and kicked toward the surface.

It had been a lesson. Even through his panic, he'd recognized the fascination those depths offered, and now, gliding along the bottom toward deeper water, feeling the coldness penetrate his skin, tasting it, he felt that same attraction.

Smiling into the darkness, he reluctantly kicked to the surface.

On the surface, he rolled over onto his back and looked up at the sky, looked at the holes between the stars, at the stars. Slowly and effortlessly, he backstroked toward the dock.

Evy was standing on the dock, a dark form wearing running shoes and his windbreaker, a blur of towel in her arms. The nylon windbreaker reached just below her ass.

"You're crazy," she said, as he rolled over and grabbed the dock.

Monster pulled himself along the dock to shallow water, where he stood for a moment up to his waist.

"You really looked like a monster out there," she said, offering him the towel.

Monster smiled, a flash of white teeth in the dark. "Booga-booga," he said, and walked out of the water, up onto the dock. "A wet one," he said, accepting the towel. He shook his head, droplets of water spraying about him, hitting her.

She squeaked and ran awkwardly off the dock, holding the windbreaker down with both hands.

Monster carefully toweled himself off. His teeth started to chatter.

"Last one into bed has to do whatever the other one wants," he offered, and she was off, running, no longer worried about the windbreaker riding up to her waist.

Ten yards from the door, he passed her. Laughing, he snapped her on the ass with the towel as he ran past.

"Not fair," she protested as he jumped into bed.

But later he didn't ask her to do anything she wasn't already doing. And after a while, at that instant when he slid smooth and hard into her, he wondered at his feeling when he was in the water. Wondered at the attraction. So much the opposite of this, he thought, enveloped by her liquid warmth.

She groaned. "I knew you'd be like this," she said.

And he could feel her eyes.

CHAPTER 15

Attitude Adjustment

Three hours later, at that time of day when night was ending and dawn beginning, Ben sat on the grass at the edge of the pebbled beach, looking at the dark mass of mountains caught between the light gray of sky and the metallic gray of the lake, waiting for Barney.

The air was brisk, still free of frost; a sudden breeze stirred the smells of pine and lake. It was easy, sitting there, to ignore the docks and cabins and imagine the lake as French explorers had found it.

He picked up a small rock and flipped it out into the water, watching concentric circles expand from the splash and travel across the silvered surface. They hadn't gone back, most of them. The country had been too much.

He heard Barney open the screen door to the porch, the crunch-crunch of cowboy boots on pine needles.

Last night, at the Outlaw Inn, they'd explained to the two women that they wanted to get up early. Get an early start. Check the place out where they were to meet the dopers. Hole up somewhere and take a nap until the meet that night.

"What're you thinking about?" Barney sat down on the grass next to him.

"Oh, just thinking about a few good men."

Barney squinted toward him. "Sometimes I worry about you."

Ben smiled. "I was thinking about the French who first came to this place."

"The French. You just spent the night with a lady and you're thinking about the French who first came to this place?"

"I don't want to go," Ben said. "I want to stay here for a couple of days."

"Okay."

"Just go back up and go to bed."

"Sounds good."

"Get up, have breakfast. Be domestic."

"Okay."

"Fool around the lake all day. Get sunburned."

"Sounds good."

Ben flipped rocks into the lake, knowing he wasn't going to stay. Enjoying the sadness of it.

"Funny thing about Vietnam," he finally said. "It's like it was just yesterday we were there. . . ." He looked at Barney. "Like we're still partly there, or something."

Barney threw a rock into the lake, a dull plunk as it hit. "Seems like it sometimes," he said absently. He twisted around. "You asshole." With both hands, he shoved Monster over onto his side. "I just said that the other night."

Cookie Monster laughed and pushed himself back up. He threw a rock at the toe of Barney's boot. "Things have sure changed back again, though, haven't they? Moose's. Shee-it, Barn. Sarah wanted to hear a war story. She even thought the badge was 'neat.' " He shook his head. "She got a war story, all right."

"She's not so bad," Barney said.

Cookie Monster stood, brushing grass and pine needles off the back of his trousers.

"I don't want to go, either," Barney said.

Monster looked down at him, at Barney unshaven, hair mussed, shirt cuffs unbuttoned. At Barney looking more tired and burned out than he'd ever seen him. At Barney wanting something that, when he had it, he couldn't stand it, anyway.

"Why're you so afraid of the water?" he asked.

"Water?" Barney looked up at him, surprised at the question. "I'm not afraid of the water." He stood up. "I'm afraid of the fucking lake."

As the black truck crested the hill behind the cabin, turning off the rutted dirt road onto pavement, the sun broke over the top of the mountains—laser shafts of light that made the trees and bushes along the highway a lush and healthy green, the rocks and dirt of the highway cuts rich browns and tans.

The horizon appeared to stretch immense distances, the sky a huge bowl of blue. Below them, the lake sparkled and glittered, shadowed and still near the base of the mountains.

There was a bluff a few miles off to their left. The bluff was bare of trees, one side a wall of rock—a sheer drop of 400 to 500 feet. Indians used to herd buffalo off the bluff, Monster thought, the buffalo falling to their death on the rocks below. Piles of buffalo. Some of them only wounded.

"We should've been born in King Arthur's time," he said. "You know that? Then we could be like the knights were. Raping and pillaging and all that good shit. Along with being heroes."

Barney smiled. "You couldn't cut it."

"I'd love it. Sir Monster-a-lot."

"No, you wouldn't. You'd get the clap and die because penicillin hadn't been invented yet."

"Well, there's that."

They were silent again, watching the road curve and climb and dip back down, following the contour of the lake.

"What pisses me off, though," Monster said, "is that we're just sort of caught in between."

Barney sighed. "You got laid last night. It's nice out. Look at the sky. Birds are singing. Fish are jumping. Just for once relax and enjoy it, okay?"

Monster glanced at him. "Pussy-whipped," he said. "Worst case I've ever seen."

"It's not that," Barney said. "I know you, and we got enough to do today without your being depressed." He looked out the side window. "Here we go again," he muttered.

Traffic at that time of the morning was light—a few RVs, tourists getting an early start, a few salesmen in company cars that looked like FBI cars, a string of logging trucks, a cop, a highway patrolman probably coming back from a traffic investigation. Useless fuckers, Monster thought. Over-paid, overequipped, and most of them don't do shit. Only had jurisdiction on the highways. About like the Vietnamese traffic cops with their white gloves. White mice. Real nice.

He floored the pickup, the sudden acceleration snapping Barney's head against the headrest.

"What the fuck you doing now?"

Monster waved as they passed the highway patrolman, speedometer climbing past eighty.

"Oh, shit," Barney said, noticing the bubble. "You silly bastard. Don't be fucking with the Highway Patrol again. Not now."

Monster watched the rearview mirror. He let the truck decelerate. "Don't worry, he didn't even have his radar on, he's in such a hurry to get home or to have coffee with his buddies." He stared unhappily at the road, at the rearview mirror.

"All they be good for is traffic accidents." He subsided into silence, quiet for the next few miles.

"God," he blurted suddenly. "Those big brown eyes she's got."

Barney looked over at him. "Not to mention legs."

"She's got those, too. But it's her eyes." He paused. "Eyes. I don't know why, but I always notice the eyes."

"Right," Barney said. "Especially in the dark." He looked back out the window. It was going to be a hot day. Maybe a thunderstorm in the evening. "I never seen anybody fuck with himself the way you do sometimes."

"I'm serious."

"Well, I'm hungry. Aren't we about there?"

"Ten miles," Monster said moodily, and was silent again for a while, watching the road.

"Do you remember the first body you ever saw?" he asked.

"Body. *Body!* What are you talking about now? Naked body or what?"

"Dead body."

"Oh . . . shit," Barney groaned. "Dead body."

"I do," Monster said. "And it's funny: I can remember all the individual bodies if I want, but I can't remember masses of bodies." He glanced at Barney. "Know what I mean?"

Barney refused to look at him.

"Once in 'Nam I saw a pile of North Vietnamese bodies strung out in the red dust and clay. Maybe forty, but it seemed like all the bodies in the world. They didn't seem like dead people, though. Just a mass of arms and legs, heads and chests, backs and faces. Torn cloth. Flesh.

"Dead people, it seems like, come in ones and twos. More and it's just a pile of bodies." He glanced at Barney. "Do you know what I mean? Junked cars. Spare parts."

Whipping around in his seat, Barney shouted, "Stop the truck!"

The truck swerved and straightened. "Wha—"

"Stop the fucking truck!"

The truck slowed, and Monster pulled it off the side of the road. He turned toward Barney. "What?"

"Get out."

"What for? What the fuck—"

Barney shoved him, not hard, firmly. "Trust me," he said, his voice reasonable, a slight smile on his face. "Just get out for a minute, will you?"

Confused and curious, Monster got out. Barney's eyes looked funny, he thought.

Sliding across to the driver's seat, Barney pulled the door shut, slammed the locking lever down. He revved the engine and grinned at Cookie Monster.

"Hey," Monster said, reaching for the door handle. "What're you do—"

Still grinning, Barney pulled the gearshift into drive, making the rear tires spin and skid in the loose gravel at the edge of the pavement.

Monster jumped back. "Hey!" he yelled as the truck hit solid pavement. He ran for the tailgate. "Stop!"

He slowed to a trot and then stopped. "Crazy fucker," he muttered. "What's he doing now?" The truck popped and whined as it decelerated. The brake lights came on, and it stopped about fifty yards down the highway.

Barney opened the door. He stood on the edge of the doorwell, the top of the cab and the door propping him up.

"Start running, asshole," he called.

Monster started walking. "What?" he called back, cupping one hand to his ear. "I can't hear you."

"Attitude adjustment," Barney called. "Time to sweat all that bullshit out."

"What?" Monster walked a little faster. The truck was only thirty yards away. "I can't hear you. What are you doing?"

Barney grinned. "I'll tell you when to stop," he called, and eased himself back into the cab.

Monster started running, sprinting for the truck.

The driver's door slammed shut.

He sprinted harder, feeling the pavement through the running shoes, his pants pulling tight at the knee when his leg bent, windbreaker too tight at the shoulder, arms moving like pistons.

The brake lights went off, and the truck began to move smoothly away from him.

He was tightening up already, losing his smoothness, head too far back.

The truck slowed, waiting for him. He could see Barney grinning back at him in the side mirror.

A logging truck blasted by, its bed empty. Loud honk from the air horn. He was panting already. The pickup was only a few yards away, still moving. He brought his head back down, summoning up a last sprint. "Arhhh!" he grunted, and lunged for the tailgate.

His hand touched metal, and Barney gunned the truck, wrenching the tailgate out of his grasp, turning him sideways, windmilling to keep his balance. The pickup pulled thirty yards ahead and stopped when he stopped. He leaned forward, hands on knees, sweating, out of breath.

He spit at the ground and straightened, glaring at Barney again, propped between the door and roof.

"Seven miles," Barney said. "Clean your tubes."

"Fuck . . . you."

"Start running; seven miles," Barney said. "Or I'm going to drive into Kalispell and eat breakfast without you." He eased back into the cab. His face reappeared suddenly, lower down, between the door and the cab. "I'll wait for you down the road."

The door closed and the pickup gained speed and motored down the highway. Monster watched it until it rounded a bend nearly a mile away.

"Damn," he muttered, "damn," and started running, pulling the windbreaker off as he ran. "Little bastard." But before he got to the bend, he had to admit it felt good. Felt good to smell the trees and ground, even the pavement. Good to sweat. Sweat oiling his muscles, as he began to lose himself in the stretch and flex of muscle, the feel of lungs opening up, the morning sun on his back and shoulders.

He picked up the pace.

An RV, square and white, Oregon license plate, slowed as it approached him going the other way, a blur of faces behind the windshield as it drove past.

But he hardly noticed, singing as he ran: "Yo-ho-ho, you and me, sitting in the belly of a thirty-four D . . ."

And a while later, as his left foot hit the pavement: "One . . . two . . . three . . . four . . ."

And later: "I don't know, but I been told, Eskimo pussy is mighty cold."

And: "Yo-ho-ho, you and me, sitting in the belly of a thirty-four D . . . Flying all around, looking on the ground . . ." He grinned at the trees lining the highway. "Looking in the trees for the old VC."

He slowed and trotted the last fifty yards to where Barney sat on the hood of the pickup. The truck was parked in a turnout on a bluff high above the shimmering lake. He walked around the truck, hands on hips, windbreaker knotted around his waist.

"Fifty-four minutes," Barney said. "Not bad, considering that according to insurance companies you're about thirty pounds overweight."

Monster grunted and spit into the dust.

"Also not bad considering your training habits."

"I owe you one."

"Hah. You're still about fifty up." Barney hopped off the truck. "Besides, you loved it. Jump in." He opened the driver's door and climbed in. "Watching you sweat really gave me an appetite."

Cookie Monster opened the passenger door and, groaning, pulled himself up into the seat. "I couldn't eat anything now if I wanted to."

Barney started the truck. "Something happening here," he

sang. "Ain't exactly clear," his voice surprisingly good. He pulled the truck back out onto the highway and smiled over at Cookie Monster. "Didn't know I could sing, did you?"

Cookie Monster looked at him.

"Stop, children," Barney sang. "Look what's going 'round."

"You can't," Monster said.

"I'll have the Trucker's Special," he said. "Four eggs, steak, hash browns, toast—wheat bread, please—a large glass of tomato juice, and—do you serve beer?—and a beer."

"Not hungry, huh?" Barney said.

"Growing boy." Cookie Monster grinned up at the waitress. She was young and blond, and they'd already discussed her anatomy. Her name tag said Lisa. "I just ran twelve miles; that's why I'm so grody-looking."

"Twelve miles," she said. "I have trouble running—"

"Can I order," Barney interrupted, "before I lose my appetite?"

She smiled at Cookie Monster, then turned to Barney.

"I'll have the same thing."

"The same thing," she repeated. She looked at his neat clothes and combed hair. His waist.

"I'm too smart to run *twelve* miles," he said, looking pointedly at Cookie Monster.

"Don't mind him," Cookie Monster said. "He's always grouchy in the morning."

She smiled. "What kind of beer do you want?"

"I trust your judgment in these matters. Anything but Oly." She smiled.

"I suppose you have to work all day?"

Barney looked out the window. "Why me, Lord?" he muttered.

"Until four-thirty," she said.

"Oh," Cookie Monster said. "That's too bad. We're going skiing this afternoon. Soak up some sun. Drive around in the boat. Get sunburned. Drink some beer . . ."

"Oh, it sounds like fun." She moaned. "I hate working here."

"Maybe get sunburned all over."

She blushed.

"Excuse me, ma'am," Barney said. "But I'm starving to death."

"Well, you don't look like it," she said, and turned and walked toward the kitchen.

Cookie Monster laughed.

"You asshole, you have no intention of meeting her tonight," Barney said as they walked out to the pickup. "We told Sarah and Evy we'd meet them tonight, if we could."

"So what?" Monster said, putting a toothpick in his mouth and opening the passenger door. "Made her day, didn't it?"

As Barney pulled the black truck out into traffic, Cookie Monster rolled his window down. "Ah feel good," he said to no one in particular. "Kiss my ass, world."

"About time," Barney said.

Cookie Monster started chuckling.

"What you laughing about?"

In a falsetto, Cookie Monster mimicked the waitress. "You don't look like it."

"Kiss *my* ass," Barney said.

"Hey," Monster said, sitting upright, his tone abruptly serious. "I know what I wanted to tell you. I remembered it last night."

"What's that?" Barney asked sarcastically.

"Toad."

"What toad?"

"The redhead called you a toad."

"So what?"

"Cons call their guards toads; toads are cops."

CHAPTER 16

Too Many Mosquitoes

You sure you got the directions right?'' Barney asked as he turned the truck off the county-maintained gravel road onto a road that was little more than a trail, weeds and grass growing between the tire tracks. "Seems a bit extreme to come clear out here just to buy a few drugs."

"A couple ounces of eighty percent cocaine ain't anything to sneeze at," Cookie Monster said. "So to speak."

"Hmmm."

"But I have to admit this is definitely a bit extreme."

The grass and weeds turned into dirt and rocks, two ruts winding between thick ponderosa into tight stands of spruce and lodgepole and then along a creek, water flowing even though it was late summer, following the bottom of a rocky canyon no more than fifty yards wide. Talus slopes and ragged cliffs towered above them, shutting out the sunlight.

In places, the track had obviously been under water during the spring runoff, but some time after the runoff someone had taken a blade to the washed-out portions and now it was easily passable. The van wouldn't have much trouble; Barney didn't bother with the four-wheel drive.

Both men were silent, intent on the country, frowning at the shaded cliffs as the truck slowly moved farther up into the canyon.

142

The canyon widened slightly, and they broke into a tiny valley, a meadow four or five hundred yards across, a cul-de-sac bordered on the right by an almost sheer rock wall running into steep talus slope and rock outcroppings directly ahead; the left side was an uneven series of rock slides and rock outcroppings, terraces like giant steps, with clumps of pine and bushes working their way down the slope.

Barney stopped the truck just inside the meadow.

"Isn't this cozy?" Monster said.

"Couldn't guess this is back here, even as we were coming in," Barney said. "Let alone from the highway. And it's only about half a mile as the crow flies from the highway.'

The far end of the long, narrow meadow looked to be a swamp, stands of quaking aspen or birch scattered among thick bushes, tall cattails between some of the bushes, meadow grasses high and thick.

"Nothing even grazing in here," Monster said, looking closely at the ground. "No cow or horse shit. Maybe a few mule deer up on those terraces."

Barney put the truck in gear and slowly drove to the other end of the meadow, toward the swamp, stopping when the track faded into grass.

"I'm surprised so much is growing in here," he said. "Must get a lot of heat reflection off those cliffs in the late afternoon."

"Don't like this," Monster said.

"No shit."

"Maybe we ought to get Kalispell to give us some backup," Monster said, opening his door.

They walked around to the front of the pickup. Even in the bright sunlight, the meadow made them feel claustrophobic, and both of them were thinking that in the dark, when they were supposed to meet the dopers, it would seem as if they were at the bottom of a huge pit.

Monster swatted at his cheek, then scowled at a smear of blood on his palm. "Don't walk through the grass," he said. "This is mosquito city, even in the sunlight."

They could smell swamp in front of them—rotting vegetation, stagnant water.

"Fine place," Monster said sarcastically. He looked up at the terraces on the west wall. "This sucks."

"I don't want to ask Kalispell for a backup," Barney said.
"Why not?"

"I don't know. Just don't. I'd rather call it off."

"Maybe we ought to forget it, then. Because I'd sure like to know how three guys from Seattle know about this place. They didn't even know where Moose's was—unless the redhead did."

Barney looked up at the terraces.

"There's rattlesnakes sunning themselves up there on those terraces," Monster said. He smiled at Barney. "Just waiting for you to come sneaking over the top of that ridge and down close to this meadow."

Barney looked at him. "Say what you're thinking."

Monster shrugged. "I hear what you're saying. It's sort of personal between us and them—the redhead, and all." He swatted at another mosquito. "You've got one on your cheek," he said. "But at the same time, I don't think we should try to take them down in here. Too much could happen, especially with those two, and if someone got shot it would be our asses, one way or another."

Barney brushed the mosquito away. "So you think we ought to make the buy, then take them down later?"

Monster nodded.

"Only one problem with that."

"Yeah, I know. Not enough money."

They were both silent again, considering.

"Well," Barney said. "We could give them what we've got and say we didn't trust them setting up the buy in a place like this, so we've got the rest of the money stashed somewhere else."

"Sure. Then we'd have them someplace where we could probably take them down ourselves. Or at least someplace fairly public where we could explain the no-backup: we had no time, it was going down too fast, had to play it by ear, that sort of thing." Monster thought for a moment. "The parking lot of the restaurant where we had breakfast would be okay."

Barney looked up at the terraced ridge. "One of us drives in with Suzie Wong; the other comes over that ridge ahead of time and sets up."

"Sounds like a wiener."

Barney smiled. "Since you're so athletic—twelve miles before breakfast, and all . . ."

"Since you're lighter, move quieter . . ."

"We'll flip for it."

"Fuck you, flip for it! You're supposed to be the Special Forces expert on sneak-and-peek, you do it. Besides, you need the exercise."

Barney looked back up the ridge, mentally tracing a route down the staggered series of terraces. There probably would be snakes up there, he thought. Rattlers sliding out of crevices and holes so small you wouldn't think anything bigger than an angleworm could crawl out. Slipping down the rocks toward the creek and swamp, catching rodents going to and from water.

But Monster would have to drive the truck out of the narrow canyon mouth, into the open meadow. In the dark. His headlights telling the whole world exactly where he was. He'd need a backup, for sure.

"There was a road a couple miles back," Barney said. "It looked like it went up the next drainage on the other side of that ridge. We can hole up there. Take a nap. I'll start up the other side a couple of hours before dark, wait just over the ridge until dark, and then come down here. How's that sound?"

Monster frowned. "Okay, I guess."

"But what?"

"Nothing. Sounds okay." He waved his arms at the mosquitoes—silvery glints in the sunlight. "Let's go. Mosquitoes are hungry."

They were silent and tense as Barney drove the truck back down the meadow and into the dark, narrow defile.

"What?" Barney asked.

"I don't like this place," Monster said. "Funky." A branch slapped against the windshield, bending, pine needles sliding and scratching past the side window as the truck went past. "Too many mosquitoes. Not enough flies."

Barney was silent. The creek on their right splashed beneath the trees and cliffs. They knew that from up on the ridge it would sound like wind rushing through the pines.

"The light is wrong," Monster said.

CHAPTER 17

Slides

A dull rumble of thunder passed over the ridge and over their heads. Lying in the back of the pickup, they opened their eyes to a mass of gray-black streaks moving fast above pine branches. Hours before, Barney had pulled the pickup in under the pines, next to another creek that ran up the drainage next to the box canyon where they were to meet the dopers. They'd washed and shaved, neither of them saying much. Both had learned long ago that such things—life in general—are sort of like shooting at a target—the more you look at the target instead of the sights, the more you hit around it. Or sort of like looking at something in the dark—if you look directly at it, you never see it. The trick is to keep your eyes, or your mind, moving, look all around it, and whatever it is will take shape.

A raindrop hit Monster on the forehead. "Shit," he said, staring straight up at the fast-moving streaks. "It's going to rain." When they'd gone to sleep, lying on top their sleeping bags, it had been hot, the sun bright and glaring outside the shade of the pines.

Barney sat up. "That's very perceptive of you." Several drops hit his shoulders and arm.

Monster quickly slipped on his running shoes, not bothering with the laces. "Get the tarp," he said. "I'll cut some poles." He opened the wooden box lying at the head of the sleeping bags, pulled out a hatchet, leather cover on the blade, jumped out of the pickup, and headed for a stand of lodgepole.

A few minutes later, they sat once again on the sleeping bags, looking out the rear of the pickup bed. Monster had pulled on a pair of jeans; Barney was barefoot, wearing a black sweat shirt and green wool hunting trousers. A faded green canvas tarp was stretched across a long pole that lay on top of the truck, reaching from front bumper to rear end, where two shorter poles, lashed together to form a lopsided X, held the long pole up off the pickup bed. The corners of the tarp were tied to the door handles and the rear bumper.

Monster leaned forward, peering out at the gray sky. "Sure. Now it's not going to rain." Thunder rumbled in the distance.

Barney lay back, hands clasped behind his head. His eyes closed, and then slowly half-opened again. Then closed, his chest rising and falling rhythmically.

Sitting cross-legged on the foot of his sleeping bag, Monster continued looking up at the sky and the slope bare of trees, gold with tall grass. He sat that way for minutes, feeling the air turn hot and stagnant, and hearing the rain slowly begin to patter against the canvas, pattering harder and faster until, with a smash and crack of thunder and lightning that opened Barney's eyes for an instant, the wind roared down the canyon, through the pines, filling the space underneath the tarp with air, ballooning the canvas for a moment away from the truck and the poles. The wind died almost as fast as it had come, and the patter turned to drumming, the sky and the slope obscured by rain.

He watched, not thinking of anything in particular, but caught anyway, as he always was at moments like that, between the past—a childhood washed away by monsoon rains—and the present.

After a while, he lay back on the sleeping bag, pulled one side over his bare chest and arms, and fell asleep listening to the rain.

"Don't worry about all this," Monster said, motioning toward the tarp and poles and truck. "I've got plenty of time.

You'd better get going before it gets dark.'' The sky had cleared again, but water still dripped off the pines.

Barney nodded and adjusted the empty leather radio case on his belt over his left rear pocket. He wore old, battered Vibram-soled hunting boots. The wool pants were loose and baggy at the ankle—rattlesnakes would strike at whatever was closest—but because of the rain, he wasn't worried about snakes. The rocks on the other side wouldn't dry off before tomorrow; anyway, rattlers were usually shy critters. It never hurt to be prepared, though.

Monster handed him a small compact of dark brown face-paint.

Barney stepped up to the side mirror on the truck door, and began applying the paint. "I feel ridiculous. Fucking movies."

Monster laughed. "You'll be okay once you get away from the truck and start sneaking around in the woods."

"Hmmm."

From behind the driver's seat, Monster pulled out a long, slender object loosely wrapped in an old blanket. He carried it around to the back of the truck and laid it on the tailgate and unfolded the blanket. "I'll give you the Benelli," he said, lifting the shotgun off the blanket.

Barney walked back to him and handed him the compact. "Loaded?"

"Eight rounds. Slugs and double-ought. First one, when you load it, will be double-ought." He handed Barney two small, slender boxes. "Here's two more boxes of double-ought."

"We're not going to war. The white of Barney's eyes were stark in his darkened face. "Just give me one more round. If nine rounds won't do it, we best be shittin' and gittin', anyway."

Monster smiled. "Sure, and besides, it's less weight, you chubby little fucker. Here's a flashlight." He handed him a small two-cell flashlight.

Barney put it in his right rear pocket, making sure the flap was buttoned over it. "Hat."

Monster handed him an old, faded camouflage hat. "Hat," he repeated.

"Bug juice."

Monster handed him a small white plastic bottle of Cutters. "Bug juice."

"Radio."

Monster handed him a portable radio, a two-inch stub of black rubber antenna protruding from one end. "Radio. Both batteries are charged; I just checked."

Barney turned it on anyway, checking the squelch. "One, go back," he said. "Two, you're on your own."

"Roger dodger."

"UHF should have plenty of bounce in that canyon. But if for some reason you don't hear it, I'll let off four rounds."

"Farm out."

"Binoculars."

Monster unzipped a small leather case and handed Barney a pair of nine-power Nikon binoculars. "Binoculars." They fit easily into the front pocket of Barney's trousers.

"One round."

Monster silently handed him one round of double-ought, the thick blue plastic above the brass containing nine pellets, each pellet approximately the size of a .32 caliber bullet.

"Shotgun."

Monster handed him the shotgun. Black, no-scratch finish. Semibuckhorn sights. Eight rounds in the tube. Barney inserted the first round into the ejection port. Two rounds of double-ought followed by a slug followed by double-ought, and so on, nine rounds total. Ugly. Deadly, of course. The short-barreled semiautomatic shotgun was capable of firing five rounds before the first empty casing hit the ground. Five rounds of double-ought, if you wanted: forty-five pellets the size of .32 caliber bullets flying through the air before the casing hit the ground.

"I thought only the SWAT team was supposed to have these shotguns," Monster said.

"Those idiots." Barney grinned, his teeth as white as the edges of his eyes. "Later," he said, and turned and began walking toward the open slope. He hesitated and turned back toward Monster. "Watch your ass."

"Yeah," Monster said. "You, too—watch my ass, I mean."

"One long break, you get out."

"Roger dodger. Over and out."

Barney turned and walked toward the hillside, blending into the growing darkness underneath the pines at the base of the slope.

Ten meters below the top of the ridge, Barney silently edged his way into a stand of pine and spruce that stretched toward the top, careful of the mat of dry branches and pinecones beneath the trees. He sat down, sweating. The climb up the slope hadn't been that bad—his breathing was controlled—but the bulletproof vest under his sweat shirt was hot and tight against his chest and back. He was in better shape than Cookie Monster gave him credit for. He smiled at the mountain folds stretching like dark blue waves toward the last of daylight. Better shape than he'd given himself credit for.

He pulled the plastic bottle of mosquito repellent from his pocket and began liberally dabbing it on his face and hands, neck and wrists. He put the bottle back in his pocket and, careful of the shotgun barrel, stood and began easing his way toward the top, through the trees. Actually, he'd enjoyed the climb, using it to tune his senses to the forest, gradually hearing and smelling and seeing the little sounds—squirrels scratching and skittering across a fallen pine, a woodpecker tapping somewhere off to his right, breezes in the grass and bushes, the groan and sigh of trees leaning together, and about halfway up, the abrupt, shrill snort of a doe he hadn't seen until she bounded away down the hillside, the flash and bounce of white uplifted tails as she pushed her fawn ahead of her.

A few yards from the top, he leaned the shotgun against a pine, careful that it wouldn't slip, and crawled the rest of the way. He felt ludicrous crawling to the top of a ridge, especially dressed in dark clothes and greasepaint, but old habits died hard and he knew he'd feel even weirder if he didn't do it this way.

The slope abruptly crested—higher on his left, descending on his right—like a wave about to break over the valley below, rock outcroppings emerging jagged between intervals of soft mounded soil and grass.

He edged forward on his belly, peering down into the valley. Trees and bushes grew thick along the terraces, which had looked almost bare from down below. The air coming out of the valley was colder and wetter, the noises different. He could see the van in the gloom at the bottom.

He focused the glasses, looking all around the van, trying to count the figures standing in front. Two, for sure; he couldn't quite make them out. The light was going fast. He eased his way back down to the shotgun, his hands suddenly shaking, the shotgun no longer a cumbersome length of metal and plastic, the adrenaline tuning him to its balance and feel.

Something moved on the ridge twenty-five yards below and in front of him, and his eyes widened. He froze, listening to the thump of his heart, the skin at the back of his neck crawling, shotgun still pointed at the ground. He knew no one could see him in the darkness under the trees. Not without night glasses.

His eyes darted, searching for more movement.

It moved again, and he relaxed, laughing silently at himself, as a small herd of mule deer, eight or nine of them, moved silently between rock outcroppings, up over the ridge, and down the side he was on. Gray bodies fine and graceful, their large ears constantly twitching and turning like tiny radar dishes, the fawns unconcerned. He couldn't see any antlers.

He raised the shotgun, sighting on the largest, tracking her as she faded down the slope and across to another line of trees.

He lowered the shotgun. Smiling, he walked to where the deer had come over the ridge, careful to stay below the ridgeline. Relaxed. Glad the deer had frightened him: good to get it out of his system.

Crouching, he quickly ran the few steps up over the ridge and down the other side, scuttling low to the ground, and immediately found what he'd expected to find: a trail leading down. He paused and adjusted the shotgun sling across his left shoulder, adjusting it so he could carry the short, ugly weapon at hip height, barrel horizontal, ready to fire. Old habits. He would walk slowly, as quietly as possible, down the trail, shotgun held at the hip, barrel pointed straight ahead, right hand holding the grip, thumb on the safety, left hand ready to come across and push down on the barrel to control recoil. The trail was much wider than he'd expected, padded with moss at the edges, pine needles and dirt in the center. About two feet across, he reckoned, an elk trail. He'd lucked out; it was probably the only decent trail on that side of the little valley. He knew that, where it crossed the talus slopes, it would be wide, the rocky surface packed tight and level. As he crossed the talus, he'd be a dark blob moving across the lighter background of rocks, but there was nothing he could do about that. He had to be in place before Monster drove the truck into the meadow.

He removed the binoculars from his trousers pocket and carefully scanned the slope and the terraces all the way to the bottom. He could just barely make out the dark symmetry of the van. Nothing seemed to be moving. No voices. Sound would rise. If they were talking, he should be able to hear snatches of conversation, at least. Sometimes it was amazing what you could hear, perched hidden far above a doper's cabin. Especially with a parabolic microphone.

But they hadn't brought the mike—too bulky and awkward.

The air in the canyon was still, not even a night breeze to stir the dampness and humidity. As he passed through thick patches of wet bushes, under and through tight-knit stands of pine and aspen, he could smell the swamp. Dark and cool. Damp like the jungle, where the ground was always damp. Barney's nostrils flared, the thought of the jungle a flash of memory that was an almost physical hurt.

The jungle.

Some people despised it. Some people were driven mad by it. The ground always wet, thick with rotting vegetation and moss. The sun seldom able to reach the ground. Animal life of all sorts, an unimaginable number and variety of birds and snakes and reptiles. Even deer and bear. Tigers.

He smiled to himself as he crunched softly across a rocky slope. Might even be a mountain lion around here, he thought. A perfect place for one.

A mosquito whined past his ear.

Insects. The jungle had thousands of kinds of insects. Weird, fascinating bugs. So many, sometimes it felt as if you were breathing them.

His steps sounded loud and clumsy in the stillness. His boots rasped against pine needles, clinked pieces of shale together as he slowly, gently worked his way down the slope.

In the jungle the noise could be deafening, but you could

still hear human sounds—the clatter of equipment, breathing—as if there were total silence.

He liked the jungle. The colors were beyond imagination, so many different shades of green you couldn't count them all. He remembered sunlight streaming through treetops, casting beams of diffused light, and as he'd walked through the lower plants and bushes, the light beams had blinked and flickered—the jungle seen through an old-time penny arcade video machine. Psychedelic before he even knew what the word meant. The dank musty smell inexplicably clean, each breath cleansing his lungs.

He accidentally scuffed a rock off the edge of the trail. It clattered down the slope and thunked into a tree. His ears strained at the darkness, hearing his heart thump, and he abruptly remembered how the smells and sights and sounds could change, and the jungle, so much alive, could feel and smell and sound like death. A death factory, damp with the vegetable stink of it.

But he'd liked it, felt protected by it. The birds and monkeys and other animals would tell him when the enemy was near. The brush and plants could tell him if someone had passed through the area—how many, which way, how long ago.

He'd felt safe in the jungle, the forest. It was full of life and would protect him if he didn't fight it. It would live forever.

As he neared the base of the hill, just above the meadow, the underbrush and trees became thicker, difficult to move through, thorns and branches catching at his sweat shirt and hat and wool pants. He put the hat in his pocket. His wool pants and the cotton sweat shirt muffled the scrape of branches—branches brushing across denim or nylon made a noise that would lift a deer's head hundreds of yards away. One *whzzzt!* of branch on nylon and they were gone.

The van was an alien symmetry in the darkness fifty yards to the left and below him. He eased his way behind a pine rooted on a rock outcropping at the edge of a rock slide. The slide was about fifteen yards across. Except for the pine trunk, he had an unrestricted field of fire down into the meadow. Dimly, he could make out the lighter mass of the meadow grass funneling into the narrow entrance four hundred yards to his right.

The van rocked, springs squeaking, and he heard muffled voices. The overhead light came on, and he could see one of the men, Lucky or Ears, lean across between the seats and take something out of the glove compartment. The light went off, and for a while, he could hear voices, and then the van was silent again, inert and black against the grass.

Barney lowered himself into a sitting position. He unslung the shotgun and silently tightened the sling, then laid the shotgun across his lap, legs straight out in front of him, and leaned back against a large, square rock. A sudden breeze wafted swamp smell over him.

Monster was right, he thought. This place sucked. From the start of the narrow canyon all the way to the edge of the swamp, it was a perfect place for an ambush. All the dopers had to do was set up on one side of the canyon or meadow and when the truck drove by let them have it—shotguns or pistols or automatic weapons, it wouldn't matter. Slingshots, and they'd have whoever was in the truck. He narrowed his eyes at the van. If anyone got out of it and walked down the meadow or up onto the hillside, that was it. He'd call it off.

It would be tricky getting back up and over the ridge. Son of a bitch. Why hadn't he thought of that? If he called it off and had to outwait whoever came up the hill, Monster would get worried and probably—idiot that he could be—come sneaking over to see what was going on. Then there'd be three or four people running around a hillside already full of deer and snakes and all sorts of little furry critters.

He smiled. Well, maybe he would just shoot whoever came up the hill. That was one solution.

Mosquitoes whined by his ear, fading away, coming back, landing on his nose and cheek, whining off, repulsed by the ointment and the paint.

He chewed on his lower lip. This really was fucking stupid, though. Stupid, like everything they did lately. They'd better get their act together again or one of these fine days they'd end up mosquito bait. He and Monster half-assing their way around like the world gave a shit. Soon as they were done with this they'd get back to why they'd come up here in the first place. Getting set up and just fucking humiliated by a couple of dopers and one crazy female with an M-16. An M-16! A fucking M-16! It boggled the mind. Amateur night at the rest area.

He pulled the hat out of his pocket and slowly, with one hand, put it on. The van was still silent. There was plenty of time. Monster wouldn't be moving for a while yet.

Maybe he should just call it off now. Because here they were again, doing it half-assed. Both he and Monster should have come over the hill. Come over and just hauled those fuckers out of the van, flung them on the ground in front of the headlights, handcuffed them, and driven them right to the Kalispell S.O.

But nooo! They had to play movies again, believing their own propaganda. Wandering around, thinking they were invincible or something, just because they were alive. That was it, wasn't it? Just because they'd survived Vietnam, they thought they were invincible. In 'Nam, they for sure believed it could happen, *knew* it would, and so what, do what you could. But when it didn't, and they were back in the world playing Narcs and Dopers, where nothing was ever like the jungle, they'd gradually assumed that they were invincible.

He slowly reached up and rubbed the side of his nose.

Well, it wasn't just that. As Monster said, it had something to do with the future, with never being able to accept the fact that there might really be a future. Maybe there had already been a future, most of their potential already frittered away, opportunities for a normal life ignored. Because here they were again, still unable to accept it, manufacturing circumstances and conditions that reduced the chances of a future.

Things like this. Not content to just be cops, they had to be narcs. Play James Bond. And then, not content to be just narcs, they had to do things on their own. No backup. Just the two of them playing movies, getting an adrenaline fix. Man, they were fucked up—fucking with themselves, that's what.

And two of those guys down in that van—he looked down at the silent van—weren't into movies. They were for real, and if anything serious happened, it was going to be *deep serious,* and no fucking movies then.

He swallowed, his throat suddenly dry and tight. He felt his hands begin to sweat.

This was it. After this, they were going to get organized, take it serious, he'd make sure of that. Do things right, like his team in Vietnam. Hell, if he and Monster could get their act together, they'd take those dopers out so fast they'd never know what hit them.

He laughed to himself.

That was the problem. You couldn't do that shit here. Because the only way to do it was to plant the fuckers, and that wasn't allowed here. Only bad guys could do that.

Just like Monster said, just like Vietnam: don't go into the DMZ, don't go into Cambodia, don't go into Laos; no fire zones, limited fire zones, free fire zones. What bullshit.

The breeze shifted, swirling around from his right, blowing his scent toward the swamp.

Everybody so worried about rights, nobody had any rights. It was getting to be anarchy, that was all.

Time he and Monster got out, did something else.

But after tonight, and until all this that had been happening lately was over, they were going to play it for real. Like they'd done in Vietnam. He smiled at the dark van. Missions into Cambodia. Nasty little hit-and-runs, and his team fighting the war the way it really was.

A war is a war is a war, Monster would say, but maybe not. Clausewitz, he'd learned in officer's school, said something about war being an extension of politics. But that was only for the politicians. Because war was more than that. Or it became more than that. At least for him it did.

He had enjoyed what he'd done. If you win a battle, an ambush, you win it all. Lose, and you lose it all.

Barney leaned his head back against the rock, watching the van out of the corner of his eye.

At first, and for a long time, he'd felt that he and others like him, dead and alive, were making it possible for the rest of the unknowing country to go about their lives in the freedom Americans take for granted. *Took* for granted. Past tense. Freedom in American was rapidly becoming past tense— becoming freedom for a few; violence, anarchy, fear for the majority. Fear of the air, the food, the blacks, the criminals, the bomb, fear of everyfuckingthing. Useless fear. Fuck that, do what you can, go for it. It.

He smiled crookedly down at the van.

At first it had been idealistic. They taught villagers correct sanitation procedures, how to dig wells, build schools, churches, better houses. They taught economics and agriculture and, of course, defense. They sure did, the Special Forces, they taught all that good shit to help peoples and countries to better themselves.

They did that when the war was young. Then they did a lot of that.

But as the war aged, their idealism was reduced to even simpler terms: teach people to fight and live in freedom—or submit and live under the communist tax collector system. Be free or be enslaved. Fight or die.

He laughed bitterly to himself. Fight *and* die.

When it finally got down to that, all pretenses were put aside and they'd finally got to do what they liked to do. What they had trained best for.

Some of them might have slept through classes on pig farming, but they sure didn't sleep when they were learning all the ways to kill people.

When he'd left, after eighteen months of it, Lang Vei and all, his team had become a machine. A death machine that worked in the death factory—the jungles of Cambodia, North and South Vietnam, Laos. No rules. Except maybe graveyard rules.

He grinned, remembering.

Larsen, a sergeant specially trained in explosives, Sergeant Ennis in weapons. Sergeant Johnson in hand to hand, Corporal Lewis in medicine and first aid, Corporal Werner in communications, and him, the lieutenant, trained in artillery and topography and intelligence. All of them experts by then—not just in their own specialties, but in everyone else's as well. As alike as peas in a pod.

A machine. No rank in the bush. They'd all been in country at least a year, some of them three years. In one year you could do a lot of things. One year was twelve months of fucking with the big It.

Hey, he thought, how would Sarah like to hear this war story?

Ah, Sarah, Sarah, Sarah, that was only one-half of the team. Dear soft and firm and wonderful Sarah, the other half had long been gone. Dead, wounded, missing in the death factory, make a movie of that, someone. Not too entertaining watching a body melt into the vegetable dampness, become food for the living plants and insects, reptiles and whatever else happened along.

But, Sarah, you've got to understand, none of us, the remaining half, feared our own death. Dead is dead. I never really saw myself in that context. What we did fear was to see one another die. We were brothers, you see. Partners. Every death, every mutilating wound, is permanently etched into my memory, Sarah. Every fucking detail, in color, like paging through a tray of slides—click, flash, click, flash. Photos that never fade. Pictures that come complete with sound and smell and everything else.

But—listen to this, Sarah; it'll blow your mind—but they all knew what they were. They all accepted the price tag that went along with it. It.

The thrill of seeing if you could rip off the storekeeper. And if you did, well, nothing else seemed important at the time.

Barney was abruptly completely alert, snatched from his memories, his head smoothly coming forward, eyes searching the dark line of trees and brush just on the other side of the rock slide, slightly below and to his left. Rocks clattered and a branch snapped. The breeze had shifted, once again bringing the stink of the swamp toward him.

It was silent except for the thin rustle of pine needles in the tree above him, the clatter of damp leaves as the breeze ruffled through bushes next to him. Nothing had moved from the van, he was sure of that.

His eyes darted, moving all around the dark patch across the rock slide; his nostrils expanded, sniffing the smells in the breeze. He smelled deer. The unmistakable odor of deer, sharp and rancid like urine.

He relaxed back against the rock, gently wiping his hands on the wool pants.

Chances were the dopers wouldn't try anything, anyway. Probably they were worried about when that redheaded asshole did that fat woman, and wanted to stay out of sight of any gung-ho cop who might remember their description. Anyway, they didn't seem like the type that would try to rip off him and Cookie Monster. Not for that much money.

You could never tell, though.

He could call it off.

Maybe he should. Monster would be starting to move. Well, he'd wait until the last minute. They were in the van, and as long as they stayed in or near the van, it'd be okay.

Monster would be pissed if he called it off. He wanted the redhead as bad as Barney wanted him.

Cookie Monster, Barney thought. Ben. He should have been born back in the Middle Ages, like he'd said. Maybe before then. Back before guns and bombs, when warriors got their hands bloody, face to face. He couldn't have handled the kind of things the team did.

Like the last time the team was in Cambodia, walking down part of the Ho Chi Minh Trail. Listening to the monkeys and birds and bugs buzzing, screeching, chattering. Walking on the edge of the three-foot-wide trail, stepping where the green started, careful to keep out of the dusty tan dirt on the trail itself. Smelling, tasting the air, moving quietly and smoothly so as not to disturb the monkeys and birds. Feeling good, keeping the adrenaline under control.

In midstep, he saw Larsen freeze fifteen yards ahead of him. He completed the step and stopped, listening, watching Larsen. Larsen retraced one step and faded into the jungle on the right side of the trail. Barney quickly took a plastic bag from the pocket of his camouflage fatigues. He removed a folded piece of paper from it and tossed the paper to the other side of the trail. Quickly, silently he moved five steps ahead to a spot where he could ease into the foliage on the same side of the trail as Larsen. Larsen was still ten yards ahead of him, invisible in the jungle. Barney carefully moved five yards into the undergrowth, the ground soft and springy, creepers and flowers, broad-leaf plants of all sorts, and nine yards forward, halting when he found Larsen a yard in front of him, squatting. Right where he was supposed to be. Right where they'd rehearsed.

He squatted next to the sergeant. His face, like Barney's face, was smeared with streaks and blotches of black and green and brown, blending into his fatigues and hands and beret. Even his M-16 was painted the same camouflage colors. Three feet away, and if you didn't know they were there, they were impossible to see.

Larsen put his finger to his ear and then made a motion with his index and middle finger, simulating a person walking. They both looked back toward the trail, barely visible through five yards of jungle. And waited. Calm. Cool. Detached. The taste of adrenaline green as the jungle. Seeing with a clinical clarity the leaves and vines and flowers, the flash suppressor on his M-16.

Almost immediately, he heard them coming. The rustle and slide of clothing. Plodding steps. Breathing. Until he thought they were going to walk right over them.

But he knew they wouldn't because he and Larsen couldn't be seen or heard, and they were downwind and couldn't be smelled. Besides, Americans never went this far into Cambodia. He felt good; it was going to work. He could feel it, glad Larsen had heard them before he'd seen them.

Flashes of uniformed bodies passed small openings in the foliage. A supply train. He could tell by the packs. But he couldn't tell how many there were—how many were NVA regulars.

The lead soldier saw the paper Barney had thrown onto the trail, and stopped. Barney could see him walk to the paper and pick it up. The soldier unfolded it, began to read.

Several other NVA joined him, peering over his shoulder. They began laughing and passing the paper around, the paper affecting them just as Barney and the rest of the team had hoped it would. The beautiful nude Chinese woman, erotic sayings under her photograph, had caused the supply train to come to a stop. The NVA soldiers were thinking that the centerfold must have been dropped by a soldier in another train ahead of them. No American smell on it—no smell of beef or soap or toothpaste—because, along with his other goodies, Barney had put *nuoc-mam*—fermented fish sauce—and tobacco in the bag to erase the American smell. Seven or eight of the soldiers had gathered around the picture, laughing, making lewd remarks. Another soldier—by his manner, an officer—hurried up to them, obviously demanding to know why they'd stopped.

Barney watched the first soldier hand the picture to the officer. And the officer's face—his broad face and narrow, slitted eyes more Mongolian than Vietnamese—creased into a grin. Barney grinned with him. The officer made a remark and the soldiers around him laughed, and then the officer called for a break. An unexpected bonus. Soldiers all along the trail began sitting and lying down, talking, yawning, stretching as they removed packs, unslung AKs.

He and Larsen had been forward scouts for the other four members of the team, scouting for a good ambush spot. As soon as he'd stepped into the jungle he'd signaled the rest of the team—one long press of the talk button on the small portable radio—of the enemy's presence. If it had been a small group, the team would have hidden and let it pass, but Barney felt there were at least thirty soldiers in the group. The small Vietnamese men of the train, most of them weighing no more than 130 pounds, were carrying large, soft packs—brown canvas bags with carrying straps. Each pack, he knew, carried 50 to 70 pounds of supplies and ammunition. All of the soldiers were armed, carrying AK-47s, the officer a pistol only.

There were enough. Even though they hadn't been able to pick the spot, it was good enough. He gave the signal for ambush—three quick presses on the talk button.

He held the radio against his stomach to quiet the sound of the squelch breaks, the volume turned all the way down. The scratch of breaking squelch was inaudible even a few feet away, but even so, to him it sounded like tiny explosions.

He depressed the button again—one long depression that meant he and Larsen would not be able to join the ambush but would cover the rear of the trap. Then he depressed the talk button ten times in a steady rhythm—the number of minutes the rest of the team would have before the Vietnamese entered the ambush zone.

The next code was supposed to indicate the number of men, but he delayed sending, not sure exactly how many there were—around thirty, he guessed, because the officer was a lieutenant and the only officer they'd seen, and because he was ninth in line. But Barney wasn't sure.

One of the small Vietnamese soldiers suddenly rose from the trail and unshouldered his pack. He picked up his rifle and looked straight at Barney and Larsen. Barney felt his palms begin to sweat, his stomach turn hollow. He replaced the radio with a grenade and slowly began twisting the pin from it. The NVA stepped into the jungle and pushed his way straight toward them, stopping no more than eight feet away. Larsen's finger was tight on the trigger of the M-16. When Larsen shot the NVA, Barney would lob the grenade onto the trail and hope it would give them time to get away.

The NVA looked around, his dark, slanted eyes moving over them. He turned his back toward them. Placing his AK against a moss- and vine-covered rock, he undid his pants and squatted, the skin of his buttocks an unnatural color, like old cheese, against the greens around him. The material of his brown uniform was coarse and new.

Barney and Larsen started breathing again, watching the Vietnamese shit a runny brown stream onto the jungle floor; the stench was revolting, worse than just about any other smell in the jungle. The Vietnamese finished, pulled up his trousers, retrieved his AK, and pushed his way back onto the trail. Other soldiers were urinating alongside the trail, but most smoked and talked. The lieutenant gave the order to move out, and grumbling like soldiers anywhere, they shouldered their packs and fell into a column. They started walking. As they passed, Barney counted thirty-six. He depressed the talk button seven long times and one short time—one long for each five NVA, and one short for the number of men less than five.

Barney and Larsen remained motionless. He felt his heartbeat smooth out. They stayed unmoving for one minute, waiting to see if there were any stragglers, or another supply train close behind. Barney grinned at Larsen. The stop, as they'd hoped it would, had bunched the NVA.

They moved to the edge of the trail and started following the thirty-six Vietnamese soldiers, both of them knowing what the rest of the team was doing.

Sergeant Ennis had been in the lead when he heard the four quick squelch breaks on his radio. The squelch breaks shattered the quiet, a thrill knifing up his back to his neck. He turned and motioned to the three men following him. They froze.

Ennis looked around. It was not a good place to set an ambush. There was a straight stretch in the trail approximately one hundred yards to their rear. He pointed back the way they'd come and, making a fist, pumped his hand up and down twice—the signal for double time.

The men turned and quickly slipped back down the trail, their progress not as fast as Ennis would have liked, but still, using the sides of the trail, careful not to break any limbs or plants, they covered the hundred yards with deceptive speed.

As they rounded the last bend, coming into the straight stretch, he heard the code for ambush and then the code telling him they had about ten minutes to set it up. Not very long.

According to their information, the trail they were on joined a larger one heading south about five miles farther on. That was where they'd planned to set the ambush. The lieutenant and Larsen must have run onto a large enough group. They'd have to do it here. Not the best place, but better than most.

They didn't have much time.

The straight stretch was only about ninety yards long—he hoped the group would be small enough to fit into it. If not, Larsen and the lieutenant were in trouble.

The men had stopped at the bend, waiting for him.

"Ambush—ten minutes" was all he said, and the men quickly turned and began to work.

Ennis and Johnson removed one claymore mine from each other's pack and, picking out two trees, one on either side of the trail, strapped the camouflage-painted mines chest high onto the trees, pointed toward the straight stretch. When exploded, the mines would send hundreds of steel balls screaming along the trail, mowing people down like grass being cut for hay. Ennis and Johnson began working their way down the trail, laying wire and det-cord about one yard off the trail, hiding the wire and cord in the thick foliage. The wires ran from the mines; the detonating cord burned so fast it actually exploded.

While Ennis and Johnson laid wire and det-cord, Werner and Lewis quickly moved to a point midway along the stretch. They removed four claymores from each other's packs and attached them to trees at both sides of the trail—two of the claymores facing back toward Johnson and Ennis and the bend, the other two facing in the opposite direction. All of the mines were waist to chest high.

As Werner and Lewis finished attaching the mines, Ennis and Johnson approached, laying the mine wire and det-cord. Werner and Lewis moved quickly to the far end of the straight stretch, farther from the bend. Johnson and Ennis stopped and connected the other four mine wires to the wires they were laying. They continued forward, laying their wires toward Werner and Lewis.

At a point where the trail made a moderate turn to the left, Werner and Lewis removed the last two claymores from their packs and strapped them to a single tree that faced directly down the center of the trail, one chest high, the other waist high. They hooked the wires together, tied a yellow string to them, and moved fifteen feet back down the trail, where Werner removed a leather pouch from Lewis's pack. The pouch was approximately twelve by eight inches and had a flap over the top, tied with a black string. There was a large red star on the pouch.

Werner tied the pouch to a tree beside the trail, waist high and in plain view.

Johnson and Ennis arrived with their wires. "Thirty-six," Ennis said.

Werner and Lewis nodded and moved back to the midway point in the straight stretch. They faded into the jungle, one on either side of the trail, five yards into the jungle, hidden by large tree trunks.

Ennis and Johnson continued to lay their wires to the far turn in the trail. They found the yellow string attached to the wires of the front claymores, and Ennis removed the string and twisted all the claymore wires together, attached them to a small detonating box, and hid himself about three yards into the jungle. Johnson took Ennis's det-cord and twisted the two wires together and dropped the cord across the trail about two yards before the moderate turn. He carefully covered the det-cord with dust and small pieces of foliage. At the side of the trail, he attached two blasting caps to the det-cord—one for backup—and retreated into the jungle to a spot even with Ennis and five yards to Ennis's right. Then he attached the blasting cap wires to a small detonating device.

Sergeant Ennis looked at his watch. Ten minutes had elapsed. He readied his M-16 and the clips of ammunition for it, straightened the pins on several hand grenades. He knew the others were doing the same. He pressed the button on his radio, two long presses, and waited.

The waiting was the worst, Barney knew. While you were

busy setting the ambush, concentrating on wire and mines, careful not to leave any sign, it was okay. You only thought about what you were doing, the activity keeping the adrenaline in check. But waiting, the blood began to pound in your temples, thumping through your body, into your fingertips, and you could taste its green taste, feel the claustrophobia of the jungle as you lay peering through the plants and vines and trees, waiting.

While the other four had been setting the ambush, he and Larsen had been hurrying back along the trail, trying to catch up to the rear of the enemy column. They were not worried about keeping off the trail or leaving any sign.

He could feel they were close.

He heard the two faint squelch breaks on his radio.

Immediately, they both stopped and removed a claymore mine from each other's pack and attached the mines waist high to two trees, one on either side of the trail, facing back the way they'd come. Larsen quickly rigged a trip wire across the trail, made it invisible, and connected it to the claymores. Should there be another troop of soldiers behind them, who could hear the ambush, the soldiers would set off the claymores as they ran down the trail to investigate, alerting the Americans to their presence and, Barney and Larsen hoped, eliminating several of those in the lead and holding up the remainder.

Larsen finished with the trip wire. Barney heard three quick squelch breaks; the ambush was about to begin.

Larsen picked up his M-16, and they started trotting down the trail in the direction of the ambush.

Sergeant Ennis had been worrying. They'd been ready for a minute. The NVA were taking too long. Had they left something on the trail? Were they at this moment being outflanked? He and Johnson could make it out, but the others probably wouldn't. The inside of his mouth tasted sour; his stomach tightened as he lay against the damp jungle floor. He saw the lead soldier step into the stretch. A chill ran up his back to his neck again. He pressed the radio button three quick times.

All right! This was more like it.

GRAVEYARD RULES

The lead soldier walked carelessly, not attentive to his surroundings. If all went well, and it was starting well, the whole column would be in the kill zone when the ambush was sprung. Lucky there weren't more of them.

The lead soldier was walking quickly, the men behind him spaced about three yards apart. They hadn't walked far enough from their last stop to get strung out. They came closer, walking straight at Ennis and Johnson, past Lewis and Werner. Still coming around the far bend, a long line of brown-uniformed soldiers, pith helmets, American helmets, leather boots, canvas boots, no camouflage. Big shapeless packs. AK-47s, all of them it seemed like.

Ennis felt a sudden panic, his mouth as dry as dust on the trail—maybe he'd miscounted the lieutenant's code. Maybe there were forty-six. He could hear the lead soldier's breathing, see his face, the black hair and black eyes, sweat on his forehead. He could smell them, *nuoc-mam* and fish and sweat. His hand tightened on the handle of the detonator. *Look at it. Look at it, you bastard.* He could spit and almost hit him. If they didn't stop, he was going to have to set it off. *Look at it, goddammit.*

The lead soldier's eyes widened as he spotted the pouch, and he stopped. The soldier behind him almost walked into him. The pouch was a common type used by NVA couriers. He walked over to it, his AK still slung, and untied it from the tree. Soldiers clustered behind him, wondering what was happening.

It was working. Ennis smiled crookedly. The whole column was closing up, would soon all be in the kill zone. The front was already very bunched up.

The Vietnamese lieutenant came forward to the lead soldier, asking him what he'd stopped for.

The lead soldier handed him the case, and the lieutenant removed several official-looking papers and maps.

Ennis and Johnson and Werner and Lewis grinned, their eyes dark and brittle-looking. Peas in a pod.

The brown-uniformed soldiers continued to close together.

Ennis could see the soldiers all looking at the Vietnamese lieutenant and the papers. He saw the lieutenant's eyes widen in surprise, his nostrils flare as he read the sentence near the end of the second page: "Fuck you, Charlie!"

Ennis twisted the handle of the detonator, and the whole trail erupted in a blinding flash of flaming powder and screaming steel balls. He heard steel balls ripping the foliage, thunking into trees above his head. At least half the men in the column were killed instantly, like the trees and plants above his head, ripped and torn, riddled with holes. Half of the remaining soldiers were wounded—he could hear moaning and gurgling, screeching, a low keening directly in front of him—writhing in the dust of the trail, bright crimson splashes on the leaves around him; a pith helmet, the liner dark with sweat or blood, rocked in the trail in front of him. Several wounded or slightly wounded men dived off the trail. Five stood unharmed in the middle of the trail, mouths open, slanted eyes wide with shock. It was always amazing how many of the steel balls would be absorbed and stopped by those closest to the mines, their packs and equipment. Amazing how many would still be alive.

Johnson, Lewis, and Werner cut down the five stunned soldiers with short, controlled bursts from the M-16s. The soldiers were abruptly transformed into spastic uniformed puppets, pieces of flesh and skull and equipment flying from them as they were twisted, jerked, and slammed down into the trail and undergrowth. A couple of the NVA off the trail began firing in wild erratic bursts, the sound of their AKs heavier, distinctive against the sound of the M-16s.

Johnson twisted the handle of his detonator. Both sides of the trail flashed and exploded with a roar. Several bodies were thrown out onto the trail, limp before they hit soddenly in the dirt. Two soldiers, unhurt, and one wounded soldier near the end of the column ran back toward the end of the straight stretch and rounded the bend before they could be shot, their running figures indistinct through the smoke that, like a fog, had enveloped the ambush scene. Some of the wounded were trying to fire their weapons or crawl off the trail littered with shapeless brown lumps, legs and arms.

The four Americans carefully aimed their M-16s, squeezing the triggers, as they'd been taught, short bursts, as they'd been taught, that tore a crawling soldier's head apart, that flipped bodies sideways or backwards or forward, the Americans calm and efficient, no two men firing at the same target. A machine. The team.

The shooting lasted only thirty seconds. No one moved. The smell of cordite and blood and torn jungle sifted down around the four Americans.

Barney and Larsen were trotting down the trail when they heard the claymores explode. From the sound—not very loud, muffled by the jungle—they figured the ambush was about eighty yards ahead, and they sprinted another forty yards and then fell to opposite sides of the trail.

They lay there for almost ten seconds, trying to control their breathing, hearts thudding as they watched the trail where it bent and merged into the green.

Three uniform-clad NVA ran out of the green and raced toward them. The soldier in the rear was bent over, clutching his stomach. He carried no rifle. The front two soldiers were ten yards away when Barney and Larsen fired; the six-shot bursts lifted the soldiers and flung them backwards, rifles cartwheeling into the air like clumsily tossed batons. The third soldier stopped. He was slightly bent over, clutching at his stomach, squinting with pain. Barney and Larsen fired at the same time. The bullets tore the soldier's chest open and straightened him—corrected his posture, they'd later joked—slamming him backwards into the dust of the trail, arms splayed.

Barney and Larsen waited for several minutes, but the trail, except for the bodies, remained deserted.

"How's it look?" Barney spoke into his radio.

"Looks good," Ennis replied.

"We're coming up."

Ennis, Johnson, Lewis, and Werner remained motionless until Barney and Larsen came around the bend. And they remained motionless as he and Larsen began checking the bodies, methodically, as they came to them. Twice they discovered a wounded soldier, but both of them were too hurt to talk, and they shot them in the head. As they passed Lewis and Werner, the two men joined them on the trail.

"Gather the packs and put them in the center of the trail," Barney commanded.

The two men began dragging the packs to the midpoint of the trail, not bothering to remove the packs from the bodies. He and Larsen continued toward Ennis and Johnson, carefully prodding and kicking the bodies. They found two more wounded—both of them able to talk and comprehend.

"Put them over there," he said, gesturing with his M-16 to the side of the trail.

After the rest of the bodies had been examined, Johnson and Larsen helped Lewis and Werner pile the packs and bodies in the middle of the trail.

He and Ennis questioned the wounded NVA.

But both of the wounded soldiers—one larger than the other, both of them smaller than the smallest team member; little yellow men, hate in their dark eyes—refused to talk. He stood and looked at them looking up at him and then, picking the larger of the two, fired a burst into his head, three or four; the head burst like an overripe melon.

He turned to the other soldier and began questioning him in Vietnamese. He promised first aid. Promised to leave him for his countrymen to find.

The soldier told Barney what he could, his eyes darting toward the body next to him, trying not to look, Barney knew, but unable to help himself, the words tumbling out like the empty brass that had flipped and tumbled from the M-16.

Ennis wrote it all down, and when the soldier could answer no more questions, Barney shot him, too.

"Sir." Ennis grinned at him. "You really shouldn't lie like that."

Barney had laughed, but now, looking back, he wondered what the laugh had really sounded like. Ah, Sarah. He smiled. Sarah, Sarah. What would you think of that? As the packs and many of the bodies had been gathered, they'd gone through them, looking for information and souvenirs—knives, pistols, canteens, web gear, anything they could carry easily and trade later, NVA money.

Then they'd placed four white phosphorus grenades on the pile, and Ennis rigged a timing device to set them off after they were a safe distance away. They all shouldered their packs and rifles, walked around the moderate turn, and waited a short distance down the trail until they heard the grenades go off, and then they headed back toward Vietnam.

He'd felt good, he remembered. And so had the others. Sometimes they hadn't felt so good, though. Sometimes one of them was killed or wounded. And once, the heavy, shapeless packs had been carried by women. But still, no matter who carried them, the supplies and ammunition were being transported south to kill or hurt Americans and South Vietnamese.

The thirty-six soldiers had been a job well done, but now, sitting in the dark, staring down at the barely visible van, he wondered at the resiliency of their minds then. Feeling good about killing thirty-six men, liking it. A job well done, Sarah. It didn't even have to be the right place and time, it just was. Everyone was, they just didn't know it. Even you, Sarah.

He shifted the barrel of the shotgun across his lap so that it pointed toward the van. Those two down there knew what it was.

When he and Larsen had moved past the three bodies, Larsen had said, "Gawddamn, sir. I think that's the one tried to shit on us."

And he'd smiled, not paying much attention to the body that was only a body, and replied, "Sure smells like it," and they'd laughed and hurried on.

Those two down there had been just like that.

Last chance to call it off; it was time to signal Monster. He eased the radio from its holder and turned it on, holding the speaker against his chest, keeping the volume down. He hesitated.

Fuck it, he thought. This wasn't Cambodia. No matter what they'd been, the dopers wouldn't be into dusting people just to rip them off. They might try to rip him and Cookie Monster off, but that'd be okay; he and Monster could handle that. Maybe they weren't being as efficient as they could be, he and Monster, but this wasn't 'Nam. That kind of paranoia just didn't apply anymore, even though thinking about it made him feel it.

Barney depressed the talk button twice and almost immediately, as he was putting the radio back into its holder, heard the pickup exhaust rumble several times in the narrow defile—Monster revving the engine, letting him know he'd heard.

He heard indistinct voices from the van, heard the side door—the side away from him—slide open, and saw a figure, no more than a dark mass barely seen at the periphery of his vision as he kept his eyes moving, looking all around, but not directly at the van. The figure was at the left rear of the van, silent, those inside silent also.

A mosquito whined past his ear.

His hands began to sweat, the stock slippery in his hand. He quickly wiped his hand on his trousers. Down at the entrance to the valley he could see headlights bouncing through the trees, light striking the cliffs; he could hear the muted rumble as Monster slowly motored toward the meadow.

" . . . time is it?'' Barney heard from the van. The redhead. He couldn't hear the mumbled response from inside, but abruptly the green taste of adrenaline soured his mouth, his stomach felt hollow, his nostrils flared, smelling the jungle smells of the swamp and of the damp hillside. His skin felt oily and tight. There was still only one person outside the van, and that was the redhead. Where were the other two? Inside the van? Maybe one of them had slipped out when he heard the door open and was now hidden somewhere out in the tall grass of the meadow. The truck could drive right by and never see him, even with the headlights on.

The truck cleared the trees and, headlights on dim, trundled into the meadow. Barney knew Monster would hit the brights, the fog lamps, and the landing lights all at once, when he was within about fifty yards of the van, blinding anyone looking directly at the truck. The truck slowed even more, idling forward.

Monster didn't like it either, Barney thought. He could make out the redhead now, standing nonchalantly at the corner of the van, left arm straight out against the metal side, legs crossed. His right arm was in a white sling.

"Here it comes," the redhead said. Barney squinted, trying to see into the tall meadow grass beyond the van as the truck crept closer. The redhead pushed himself away from the van and, legs slightly crouched, held his good hand up to his forehead, shielding his eyes against the glare.

"They're both in it," he said loudly.

Barney smiled, thinking of Suzie Wong. He felt a sudden chill up his back to his neck. The redhead had spoken too loudly. He eased himself up into a low crouch, ass against the rock, ready to pivot in any direction, but keeping his eyes on the meadow, waiting for Monster to hit the lights.

The lights flared on, the landing lights illuminating even

the far end of the valley, the tips of meadow grass silver and sparkling with wet. The truck stopped. Barney could see nothing in the grass. The aspen in the swamp glowed white in the lights, like bones sticking up out of the earth.

The truck inched forward. He could see what looked like another person in the passenger seat. Suzie Wong.

The truck stopped about five yards behind the van; Monster got out as soon as it stopped.

"Hey, Cookie Monster," the redhead said, his voice friendly. "What's happening, man? Turn off some of those lights, will you? They're blinding me."

Barney felt his heart thud; he released the safety, holding the shotgun at his hip, barrel pointed down and to the left, toward the redhead. *How did the redhead know the name Cookie Monster?*

Monster stepped forward almost to the front of the truck, only a foot or two in front of the redhead, but hidden by the brilliant lights. The chrome bumper and rear door handles of the van sparkled and glittered. Barney could see Monster's right hand held against his side, elbow bent, the 9mm pointed directly at the redhead.

"Where's everyone a—" Monster started to say, his words broken by the incredibly loud crack and drumming of a burst of M-16 fire that flashed short red winks of flame from the trees on the other side of the rock slide—where Barney had thought he'd heard a deer—taking out the windshield, hitting the cab, jerking the figure on the passenger side against the passenger door. The first burst was followed immediately by another longer burst, and Barney hardly felt the Benelli kick as he shot from the hip, the five rounds one long continuous roar of noise, long fingers of flame lancing across the rock slide, double-ought and slugs striking all around and into the area the M-16 fire had come from. Five rounds and Barney was moving, running across the rock slide with huge, loping steps, sinking to his ankles in the deep gravel and shale, firing twice more, his face and ears already numb from the stink of cordite, the explosions of shotgun and M-16 rounds. Out of the corner of his eye, he saw the rear doors of the van open, a figure etched by the brilliant lights against the inside of the van, short-barreled rifle or shotgun in the figure's hand belching flame and explosion at Cookie Monster, the redhead sitting down in front of the headlights, and then he was in the trees and bushes, branches and thorns scratching and pulling at his skin and clothing, slapping and digging at his eyes, hearing Monster's 9mm firing, a two-shot burst.

Barney scrabbled up against a small pine, tensed for the flash and drum of the M-16. That many rounds dumped into a small area, so close, he'd hit something, he was sure. Monster's 9mm was still firing, a burst of three rounds. Barney carefully peered into the rocks and bushes around and below him. Nothing moved. He thought he saw the barrel of a M-16, bipod attached, only a few yards below him, silhouetted in the truck lights and, near it, a dark lump, too heavy and soft and smooth to be rock or tree or bush. He fired again—double-ought, by the recoil—and saw the lump flinch with that meaty flinch like bodies on a trail a long time ago.

Monster was screaming incoherent questions at someone.

After Barney left, Monster had dismantled the makeshift shelter, carefully folding and stowing the tarp. He'd stuffed the sleeping bags back into their sacks and straightened up the truck bed, crushing the empty beer cans and throwing them into a corner, surprised to see how many there were. Then he had removed Suzie Wong from the equipment box and placed her on the passenger seat. He laid his bulletproof vest on the driver's seat. The vest would stop most pistol rounds—.44 magnum and double-ought, even—but not a rifle round, not even a .22. Especially not an M-16 round. Nasty things, .223 rounds. They tumbled as soon as they hit something. Get hit in the thigh and the bullet would maybe follow bone and come out somewhere in your gut or back. He put on a dark blue sweat shirt and, reaching behind the seats, pulled out another shotgun, jacked a round into it, and set the safety. Nothing like the solid *cha-chunk* of a shotgun shell being chambered, he thought. Stops people right now; makes them reasonable. He placed the shotgun, barrel pointed toward the passenger-side floor, across the console where he could easily grab it with one hand and fire out the passenger window or pull it out after him if he had to bail out.

Opening the console, he removed the Browning Hi-Power, ejected the magazine, and checked to see that it was full—thirteen rounds of 9mm, hollow-points alternated with solids—replaced the magazine, and pulled back the slide, chambering a round. Leaving the hammer on full cock, he set the safety and placed the automatic on the passenger seat, on top of Suzie Wong, barrel toward the door, next to the portable radio.

Satisfied, he walked to the back of the truck and sat down on the open tailgate, feet dangling, and looked up into the growing darkness toward the ridge Barney was climbing. Funny, he thought, all the years of tramping around the mountains, exploring, hunting, just walking, and it always seemed to be someone like Barney who crept through the woods or jungle or wherever, while he sat and waited on the tailgate of a truck or in the open metal doorway of a helicopter. Hours and hours spent sitting on a piece of metal, watching the sun come up, go down, sweating, being rained on . . . whatever, waiting to fly or drive somewhere for a few brief minutes of adrenaline, into the shit.

He lay back on the metal truck bed, hands clasped behind his head, looking up at the sky, dark blue changing to violet, a few stars already showing. He closed his eyes, wondering how he'd ever come to be lying in the bed of a pickup in Montana, waiting for his partner to get into position so they could play games with some dopers. Once upon a time, when he'd gotten out of the Crotch and started college, the world had looked different. Doing good, too. Playing a little basketball, going to classes, checking the ladies out—pretending it'd never happened, Vietnam. Majoring in engineering. He laughed out loud. That had lasted about four or five quarters of calculus, and fuck that; he knew he'd never be good enough to design anything himself, just little pieces of a bigger something that some genius thought up. Besides, it was boring. He'd changed to history and got heavy into the Vietnam War, read everything, learned everything he could about the Vietnam War, even studied a little Chinese. And he'd come to the conclusion that he didn't know any more than when he'd started. It was Southeast Asia's turn, that's all. No biggie. People killed, got killed, just in general fucked over each other unmercifully. They'd done so since time one, and they sure weren't going to change now. So what? Life. Someday it would be his turn. He'd joined Vietnam Veterans Against the War, not because he gave a shit one way or another—war is just the way things are, that's all—but because he could wear an old fatigue jacket, pin his medals upside down, limp around with a cane—his latest scrape—never actually saying he'd been shot up, but putting that mournful I-been-there-and-it-was-hell look on his face, meeting ladies. Ladies everywhere. That was what he'd really majored in: ladies. The new ladies, into women's rights, protesting the war and Nixon, and, oh, man, practically creaming their jeans watching pissed-off cops throw tear gas and beat people severely about the heads and shoulders. Getting it on in classrooms, in bushes, in the men's room. The'd kept score, he and a few friends. Nothing like a good old campus riot and a beat-up-looking Vietnam veteran to stir the juices. He grinned. Back then, admitting he was a Vietnam veteran was kind of like a queer admitting he was queer. The trick was to convince the ladies, without really saying anything, that he really wasn't responsible for what had happened to him, what he'd done in Vietnam. Appeal to their instincts. Make them think he was just a poor little misguided boy who could be turned around with a little tender loving care and sex. Especially the sex.

He smiled up at the dark pines and sky, but his grin faded as he remembered other women. Asian women. He sat up. Why did he always seem to end up with the same kind of woman? He really liked them. Loved them, but he always ended up fucking it up, no matter how he tried to be.

If not for the country—Montana, his little run-down ranch or farm, or whatever it was—he didn't know what he'd have done. To many ladies. In the end, they always seemed to mess his mind up, they sounded so reasonable. "Life's not like that," he'd say, and they'd say, "Sure it is, give it a chance." And he'd say things like "You only get one chance," and they'd laugh. And of course they were right. In America you could have all kinds of chances. Back in the world. But the world was just a figment of the imagination. Reality, for him, was still lying on the floor of a helicopter.

How do you explain that to a woman and then convince her you aren't just paranoid or manic-depressive or whatever? Impossible. Women wouldn't understand because they didn't have to, most of them.

He peeled off his sweat shirt and hung it over the top of the door as he pulled the door open. Slipping the vest over

175

his head, he pulled the nylon stretch straps tight, fastening the Velcro strips together, careful not to get the vest too tight. The material, little more than a quarter of an inch thick, molded itself to his torso, covering him from collarbone and shoulder to waist. He pulled the sweat shirt back on over the vest and climbed up into the truck.

What he needed was an Asian woman, he thought. A Chinese woman—they understood—but thinking of that always gave him a bad feeling. Made him think of eyes gone faded. He shook his head, as if trying physically to shake the thought away. Maybe it was now looking back on then, but it had seemed to him, even then, that Chinese women understood. He smiled inwardly, perversely thinking of eyes gone faded and flat, letting the zipper come unzipped a little. And, like always, it frightened him. He knew it was a knowledge that he should have looked at long ago, but couldn't ever quite bring himself to. He shook his head again and started the truck, concentrating on the mechanics of driving.

With only the parking lights on, he drove down the road and up onto the road that led into the narrow canyon where the dopers were waiting. He'd drive up the narrow canyon as quietly as possible, with only the park lights, and stop in the trees near the top, where it opened into the meadow, and wait for Barney's signal.

The two squelch breaks made him start, the sound unnaturally loud above the wet noises of the creek and the light rush of wind through the pines. He'd been calm before, not really thinking about it, leaving the decision to Barney, but now he felt a sudden rush that momentarily made him weak; his hands were shaking as he turned the key in the ignition. The truck rumbled to life, the rubber sex doll, Suzie Wong, bobbing and jumping against the seat belt in the passenger seat. He revved the truck loudly, watching her rubber boobs bounce, hoping Barney would hear the sound echo off the rock walls. He turned the headlights on dim. He'd hit all the lights when he got close. Suzie smiled manically at him. In the glow of the dash lights, her plastic eyes were bright and empty, her mouth pouting and smiling and inviting all at once, her arms pinned to her sides by the seat belt. He revved the engine once more. In the dash light, she looked like a corpse under water, the way the current made a corpse bob and sway as if it were alive. He laughed at his imagination, and pointed the truck up the slight incline, toward the meadow.

He felt good now, using the adrenaline constructively, using it to heighten not weaken his senses and muscles. He kissed the air toward Suzie. Barney always put a hat on her head, a shirt or jacket over her shoulders. "Looks more natural," he'd say. "Can't have someone walking by and seeing a naked lady, can we?" But Monster knew the doll bothered Barney. It was just a touch too realistic—realistic in a way that wasn't alive.

Sure was handy, though, when they needed it to look as if there were another person. A joke at first, Suzie had become part of the equipment, part of their act.

He squinted, trying to see ahead of the lights.

Their act.

Not very together lately, that was for sure. His mouth had that familiar sour taste now. This was pure foolishness, now that he thought about it when it was too late, coming into this valley to meet these guys. It'd be okay if the dopers knew they were cops; then they'd assume a backup. The dopers would know they'd have to drive back out of the valley, and only one way out.

Where was that fucking meadow? All he could see was a rutted and still damp track winding through dark, silent pines.

The dopers didn't know they were cops. The redhead just liked to use that word, toad. They thought he and Barney were just a couple of idiots—well, more than that, maybe, after Barney munched the redhead. Likely they'd be wanting to rip them off and then maybe hurt them a little to get even. Maybe hurt them a lot for what they did to the redhead.

He convinced himself that this was the way it was going to go down, working up an anger—motherfuckers think we be two greedy hicks they can lure up here and rip off—using the adrenaline to feed it—we be seeing about that, uh-huh, we be seeing about that—so that when the truck entered the meadow, he was in a rage.

Nevertheless, he stopped the truck just inside the meadow, glared ahead, and opened his door several inches. Barney had taken the bulb out of the overhead light. Monster wedged the 9mm into his belt, the hammer gouging his stomach, and, holding on to the open door, his forearm and elbow along the open windowsill, he drove with his head out the window. Anyone shooting at him would most likely first shoot just over the steering wheel. By then he'd be out and rolling away from the truck.

All around the truck was black, a still, warm, and humid darkness that, if he had not known he was in a small valley, could have stretched forever in any direction. The headlights lit only a small area in front and slightly to the side of the two dark parallel tracks that stretched through the wet, glittering grass. The grass looked silver in the headlights. Next to him, Suzie Wong bobbed and smiled invitingly.

He took his foot off the gas, allowing the truck to idle forward. Chrome glinted at the periphery of the headlights. Suzie nodded. He'd lost his anger; he was calm now, he thought, alert, careful not to try to see too much, just what was.

There were no lights around the van.

He wondered where Barney was.

Someone was standing next to the van. The redhead. Where were the other two?

He hit all the toggle switches at once, and the landing lights blasted on, pinning the redhead in their glare. He couldn't see anyone in the grass, but the grass was too high. He couldn't see anyone except the redhead grinning at him, his arm in a sling.

It stunk.

Motherfuckers.

He gunned the truck forward and, taking his hand off the steering wheel, shifted into neutral, letting the truck roll within ten yards of the van before he trod on the emergency brake. He was out before the truck had completely stopped, not letting the door slam shut as the truck rocked gently several times back and forth. He knew the redhead and anyone opening the back doors or coming out of the van would be blinded by the headlights. He took two quick steps forward, close to the front bumper of the pickup, drawing the 9mm from his belt, holding his elbow firm against his side, muzzle pointed directly at the redhead.

"Hey, Cookie Monster," the redhead said, his voice friendly.

Monster felt the hairs rise on the back of his neck.

"What's happening, man?"

Monster crouched slightly, clicking the safety off, bringing the automatic forward, the click unheard next to the idling engine.

"Turn off some of those lights, will you? They're blinding me."

Cookie Monster!

"Where's everyone a—" Monster started to say, his voice breaking as he heard the snap of bullets close behind him, heard the *sping* and *chunk* of bullets hitting the truck, blowing holes in the windshield, a deafening burst of automatic fire from his left.

He shot the redhead twice, hardly feeling the recoil. One hollow-point and one solid-point hit the redhead, lifting him slightly, as simultaneously another burst of automatic weapons fire slashed and chinked into the cab. The redhead was pushed backwards and down, and the heavy unmistakable roar of the Benelli erupted off to his left, and the back doors of the van were kicked open and he saw a shotgun in the hands of a crouched and squinting figure. The shotgun belched flame. He felt the charge rip past his right shoulder, neck high, and saw clearly that the man was Ears and he was wearing a ridiculous blue Hawaiian shirt and blue jeans, a gold ring gleaming in the white-hot light on the little finger of his left hand. A coil of smoke wisped whitely from the blued barrel of the shotgun. The hand with the ring was wrapped tightly around the rich, polished wood, dragging the action back to chamber another round as Monster fired twice and saw the bullets hit the crouched figure in the chest, ruffling the shirt an inch apart, throwing Ears back inside against the metal wall of the van, shadowing his abruptly widened eyes.

Someone was screaming. Motherfuckers, and so on.

The hand with the gold ring was still in the light, pushing the action forward. The barrel tilted up toward him again. Someone was still screaming. *He* was screaming. He felt a thrill, a sudden sick thrill as the shotgun tilted up toward him, and he shot Ears three more times, as fast as he could pull the trigger—chest, throat, forehead, the final two shots smacking Ears's head back against the metal wall, throwing

179

his arms up away from the shotgun, which clunked onto the floor, then teetered on the edge of the bumper. The body slid soddenly down onto the floor of the van, the head and neck a mass of blood and gore, one slack wrist beating limply against the floor for a moment, like some outrageous queer waving frantically.

"You motherfuckers," Monster screamed. "You assholes. What the fuck do you think you're doing!"

He heard the Benelli fire again, and his finger spasmed reflexively against the trigger of the 9mm; another round smacked into a thigh that was visible just inside the van door. The thigh jumped, like a piece of meat being beaten with the dull edge of a knife; he could see a neat, bloodless hole in the white, almost clinical light of the landing lights.

"Shit," he said, looking surprised down at the Browning.

The redhead was sitting in the grass at the side of the van, his legs spread slightly, sprawled straight out in front of him. His hand and sling clutched at his stomach. His head was tilted back looking up at Monster, mouth working soundlessly, eyes as big and round as buttons in a freckled face.

Monster pivoted and smoothly opened the truck door and switched off all the truck lights, hitting the toggle switches with the barrel of the 9mm. Reaching across with his left hand, he turned the ignition off. Pieces of windshield were all over the dash and seats and floor. The back window was blown completely out. Suzie Wong was a shredded piece of rubber underneath the seat belt. Pieces of granulated glass covered the seat belt and flesh-colored rubber.

He quickly moved to the rear of the truck and crouched next to the wheel. His ears were ringing; the acrid smell of cordite mixed with the thick smell of blood, the fetid smells of the swamp. A mosquito whined past his ear, numb from the explosions. It was totally black, but colored lights winked and pulsed in front of his eyes. He could still see the crouching figure, the black barrel spewing a long tongue of flame and heat at him.

The redhead groaned softly, a small, childish *ooh* sound.

"Barney?" Monster yelled.

"I'm okay," Barney yelled back, his voice startling Monster by its nearness. He'd forgotten the hillside was only thirty or forty yards away.

"I'm okay," he called back. "One dead. One hurt bad." He still couldn't see a thing, just the flame from the shotgun.

"The other one's up here," Barney said. "Turn the lights on and back the truck around so I can see my way off of here."

Monster put the safety on. He climbed into the cab, started the engine, and turned the headlights on. He could see the redhead through the craters and cracks like fine webbing in the windshield. The redhead was still looking up at him, like a little kid just got punched in the stomach, white-faced and still couldn't get his breath enough to cry.

He backed the truck around, switching the landing lights on to illuminate the hillside.

"How's that?" he called, leaning out the window.

"Fine." He saw Barney stand up behind a cluster of rocks and trees at the edge of a rock slide, the light making everything appear two-dimensional. Barney slung what looked like an M-16 across his back. Then he slung the Benelli next to it and, not bending at the waist so that the two rifles wouldn't fall awkwardly forward over his shoulder, bent his knees and picked up two legs, grasping them at the ankles, one on either side of his waist, the soles facing Monster, the body behind Barney, invisible in Barney's shadow, except for the feet and the legs to midthigh. Barney began walking down the rock slide, the limp black-clad body following soddenly behind, arms reaching back, sliding over the rocks. The head moved funny, as if attached by a string only.

Monster watched Barney grunt his way through the grass, pulling the body to behind the van and dumping it in front of the redhead.

"Hi, asshole," Barney said to the redhead.

Monster could see most of one side of the head and neck and shoulder was gone, the chest a gleaming mass of red pulp and wet sweater.

Barney walked over to Monster. Unslinging the rifles, he put them into the pickup bed.

"How you doing?" he asked.

"I'm okay. Ask me in a few minutes."

"Was that you screaming and swearing?"

"Yeah."

"Lost your head, huh?" Barney grinned, but his face was

181

tight and shiny even under the paint, his eye sunken, the grin crooked.

"What . . ." Monster looked from the body to Barney grinning at him. Barney's eyes were brilliant black, like lacquered wood. Monster laughed, a strange, nervous sound he'd never made before.

The redhead groaned.

For a moment, neither of them moved, looking at each other, their expressions unreadable.

They looked at the redhead.

"Here's how it is," Barney said, squatting in front of the redhead. "You talk to us, and we'll get you to a hospital." Monster shut the truck off, but left the headlights on for illumination.

The redhead's slack lips drooled blood down one side of his mouth, down his chin, staining the white cloth of the sling. His eyes glittered feverishly.

"We're cops," Monster explained. He sat cross-legged in the grass next to the redhead, the 9mm held loosely in his lap. There were three mosquitoes on the redhead's forehead and cheek, but he didn't seem to notice.

His eyes swiveled toward Monster. "I know," he said, and tried to laugh, the corners of his mouth curling up and then down as a wave of shock rippled across his face. "Unh," he said, and frowned thoughtfully.

"He called me Cookie Monster," Monster said to Barney.

"That's right, he did."

"How'd you know we were cops?" Barney asked, his voice level.

The redhead stared at a spot between his knees, in front of Barney. "You really fucked up," he said, his voice quiet and matter-of-fact. "Fucked up . . ."

"How'd you know we were cops?" Barney asked again.

"Pigs."

"What?"

The redhead frowned again, his bloody tongue slowly, tentatively passing across his lips. "Pigs," he said quietly. "Pigs."

"He's saying we're pigs, not cops," Monster said.

Barney was silent for a moment, carefully watching the redhead. The three mosquitoes, one after another, their little black bodies swollen with blood, slowly lifted off the red-head's cheek and forehead.

"You're going to die unless we get you to a hospital," Barney said.

The redhead raised his head slightly, eyes glazed with shock, and looked at Barney. "Another pig told us."

"Who?"

The redhead licked his lips again, and slowly shook his head. "Don't know. He talked to the other two." Another mosquito landed at the corner of his bloody mouth. He didn't notice.

"Why?" Barney asked. "Why would another cop burn us?"

The redhead smiled with one side of his mouth. His eyes glittered with shock and hate. "You fucked up," he said in a normal tone of voice. More mosquitoes were clustered around his mouth and throat.

"Tell us why?" Barney said, not hurrying.

"Supposed to hit you . . . Lucky . . . Ears . . . hit you." He frowned, looking thoughtful again.

"Why hit us?" Barney coaxed.

"Don't know. A favor for a friend . . . Some guy . . . big guy . . . lives . . . place called . . . Blackfoot." He suddenly grinned up at Barney, lips thick and red, stretched across bloody gums and teeth. Several of the mosquitoes at the corner of his mouth flew away. "You're dead."

"And you're wasting time," Monster said.

The chalk-white face swiveled toward him, the black button eyes manic, reminding him of Suzie Wong's. "Dead."

Monster felt a chill down his spine.

Barney gently lifted one of the redhead's legs six inches off the ground. He dropped the leg. The heel of the redhead's shoe thudded into the soft dirt.

"Nuahhh!" The redhead's face went even whiter, lips stretched tauntly across clenched teeth. Globules of yellow sweat broke out on his forehead. Only a few of the mosquitoes were disturbed.

"*You're* dead, unless you get to a hospital," Barney said. "Why'd you wait to try it here?"

Monster thought the redhead was going to pass out. Barney picked the leg up again.

"Didn't know for sure," the redhead said, looking anxiously at his leg, as if it was his leg that was hurt. "Then . . . rip off buy money. Ohh, it . . . hurt bad."

"If you knew we were cops, you must've figured we'd have backup?"

"Knew you wouldn't." His eyes winded. "Ahh," he said.

Barney watched the mosquitoes for a moment. "He's not going to make it," he said to Monster.

Monster nodded.

" . . . backup, we'd've known."

"How?" Monster asked.

"The pig . . . unhh." They could see sweat begin to trickle down his face, onto his nose, into the rivulet of blood and mosquitoes.

"What cop?" Barney asked.

"Don't—"

"Tell us!" Barney said, raising the leg higher.

"A captain . . . Don't know . . . Fuck, it hurts. Ohh, help me, someone. Help me!"

"A captain. You mean a lieutenant?"

"Yeah. That's it . . . whatever." The redhead lifted his head, his eyes clear and free of pain for a moment. "Fuck you, pig-fucker," he said. "You fucked up now. You're both dead."

Barney dropped the leg, and the redhead's mouth dropped open, screaming soundlessly, lips flaccid, drooling blood. His eyes glazed. They could see that he knew if he screamed or cried or did anything, it would hurt more. Mosquitoes lifted off from his face and neck, replaced by others equally hungry.

Barney and Monster looked at each other for a moment. Barney nodded to the 9mm in Monster's hand.

"You ever kill a cop, like you said?" Barney asked. "Or anybody else, for that matter?" He stood and took several steps back. Monster raised the 9mm, the barrel pointed slightly up, just behind the redhead's ear.

The redhead grinned his terrible chalk-faced, bloody-mouthed grin. "What . . . you think . . . pig!" he spat.

"Shoot him," Barney said, and Monster did, the muzzle blast lifting the redhead off the ground, limp before his body settled back onto the grass. He toppled backwards, legs splayed apart, bandaged arm across his chest, the other arm out away from his body, the back half of his skull gone, exploded, the spray just missing the still seated Monster, some of it striking the van behind him.

He stood up, easing the hammer down with his left hand.

A mosquito whined past his ear. He swatted at it, terrified suddenly of the image of a mosquito mixing the redhead's blood with his own.

Pieces of skull, the underside pink, were scattered into the grass like broken pieces of clay pottery. There was a large clot of dark substance gathered around the top of the head, but from their angle the redhead looked intact, eyes staring up at the night sky, hair matted into the tiny pool beneath his head. Monster could see a large clump of brains a foot or so from the shattered head. For a moment, there were no mosquitoes on the redhead's face.

"How you doing?" Barney asked, carefully watching Monster.

Monster shook his head. He turned and walked back to the pickup. He felt weak and sick, unable to walk the few steps. His hand was shaking almost uncontrollably as he put the 9mm on the driver's seat, and sat on the metal running board, elbows on knees, hands holding his head as he looked down between his feet at the shadowed grass bent and trampled by the truck and van. A part of him recognized that old, familiar emotion of long ago—part sickness, part disgust, part horror, part hurt, and feeling all of that, not because he'd killed someone, but because all those parts made up an understanding. A felt knowledge of how little separated him from what the bodies had become, how little separated anyone from them. But in his case, even less. Wu Chi had said the field of battle is a land of standing corpses. Well, he had survived, and he was sitting, but it was the same.

"Let's get the bodies into the van," Barney said quietly.

Thirty minutes later, they sat in the truck. They'd loaded the bodies into the van, clouds of mosquitoes rising off the bodies as they heaved them through the side door. Then they'd gone back to the truck and with their hands swept the glass off the seats. Barney had thrown the shredded remnants of Suzie Wong into the back.

He cleared his throat. "We'd better have our shit together from here on out, if we're going to make it through this."

Monster grunted.

"Ever since up the Blackfoot," Barney went on, "when those assholes left us handcuffed and sitting in the dust, we've been out of step with the whole thing—a step behind."

Monster looked over at him.

"But we lucked out, and now we're a step ahead. We've got the initiative; we've just got to figure out how to use it."

"I feel bad, Barn. Real bad."

"Well, hang in there, you'll feel better."

"I never did that before."

Barney shook his head. "He never would have made it. Besides, it's not so different."

"Maybe for you, but I never done anything . . . felt like this before."

"Well, hey, what the fuck is this? You need a war or something to make it okay? For your information, this was a war—a little war between us and them. It just took you by surprise, that's all. Me, too. But if we'd had a choice, if we had known who they were and what they were really up to, we would've done the same thing—just a little more efficiently and less dangerous for us, is all."

Monster was silent.

"Look. We decided days ago—probably when we were handcuffed and lying in the dirt—we weren't going to do this legally. Remember that?"

"Graveyard rules," Monster said.

"That's right. Graveyard rules. The only rules these people know."

"Well, we can't be blowing away the whole fucking world!"

"*These* assholes"—Barney gestured toward the van and the bodies—"were going to blow *us* away. We lucked out. They could've done it. Except they got lazy and greedy."

"They just underestimated us," Monster said. "That's all."

"They—" Barney stopped. "That's true. I wasn't thinking that way, but that's right, they underestimated us. Maybe they knew we were cops, but somebody forgot to fill them in on the particulars. Somebody forgot to tell them that working narcs means you're on your own, anyway. And that gets to be a habit like anything else.''

"It doesn't matter.'' Monster sighed. He could smell the reek of cordite and blood. "If we'd done it right, this wouldn't have happened.''

"Wrong! You heard what he said: they were going to hit us. They had a contract on us. Man, he even said they would have known if we'd asked for backup. And if we had, they wouldn't have showed. They would have hit us some other time, some other place, where we would have had a whole lot less of a chance than we did.''

Monster stared out the side window up at the stars. The valley was a dark pit. A fitting place for what had happened, he thought.

"Still,'' he said, seeing the flame erupt from the black barrel, feeling the heat and energy of the shot so close. So close . . .

"We're done screwing around,'' Barney said. "These motherfuckers want to play games, we'll play games. And we'll play them by their rules—even if some of them are probably too ignorant to realize what the rules are.'' He looked at Monster. "What do you say?''

Monster rubbed the side of his face; his cheek felt hot and oily to the touch. He sighed and shrugged. "I guess we don't have much choice.'' He looked at the dark bulk of the van through the cracked windshield. "We didn't exactly follow procedure. And we've sort of tampered with the evidence, and all that.'' He looked at Barney. "What the hell? What have we got to lose?''

Barney laughed. "Only what we've always had to lose.''

Nothing.

CHAPTER 18

Body Bags

The van drove well, but it was noisy, the sound of the big radial tries reverberating between the metal walls, reminding him of helicopters—flying medevac, the thin magnesium-alloy walls of the UH-34 a lot like the thin metal walls of the van. Even the bodies jiggling under the canvas tarp were almost the same. He and Barney had thrown the bodies in through the side door, both of them wearing rubber kitchen gloves. He used the gloves to clean out deer and elk—more grip when you pulled on the esophagus, and a lot cleaner; warmer, too, in the cold weather when the hot, steaming blood froze and crusted on your hands.

He made the right turn that would take him and the van and the bodies around the northern end of the lake to the highway that turned and went up the Swan River Valley to Clearwater Junction and then down the Blackfoot to the dopers' ranch.

"You drive the van and the bodies down the Swan to the dopers' ranch," Barney had said. "I'll take the truck back to town, pick up your beater, and meet you up that old logging road we went up that time we climbed the hill above their ranch."

"Okay."

"I'll have to drive pretty slow because of the windshield, so take your time."

Then they'd searched the van and found nearly six hundred rounds of .223 loaded into thirty-round magazines; a CAR-16—a shortened version of the M-16—with a government-issue silencer in a custom-made case; fifty rounds of shotgun ammunition; three boxes of .357 ammunition, including one box of Teflon-coated bullets—Teflon bullets penetrate any bulletproof vest; they penetrate even an engine block; several Colt revolvers; three Walther PPK 9mm semiautomatic pistols; and a large red metal toolbox, the pull-out shelves neatly stocked with hand tools—wrenches, pliers, screwdrivers, multimeter—and a variety of wire splices, tape, and terminals. The PPKs were new, in boxes. They hadn't found any 9mm ammunition to go with them.

"A regular arsenal," Barney said. "Boys had a serious case of paranoia."

"Or a good business. I wonder where they got the CAR-sixteen and silencer."

"Vietnam, maybe."

"I don't think so. The silencer looks new."

They'd also found several pounds of what looked to be high-grade sinsemilla—the large plastic bags loosely filled with buds only; a small vial of cocaine—maybe five grams, Monster estimated; and about two hundred small white pills with crosses on top—pharmaceutical-quality speed.

"Good thing there's not more," Barney said. "I don't know what we're going to do with this."

"Toss it in the swamp."

"Good idea."

"Or make the lieutenant eat it all at once."

Barney laughed. "I'll throw it into the swamp."

"What are we going to do about him?"

"Let's not worry about it now. Let's just take one thing at a time. First, we got to get rid of these bodies and the van, and do something with the truck before daylight. Then, when they're all running around screaming and shouting, wondering what happened, we'll worry about the lieutenant."

They'd also found $3,541.32 on the bodies, most of it on the redhead. Barney had placed the money in a small green backpack along with the magazines of .223 and had put the pack plus the weapons and toolbox into the bed of the pickup.

The rest of the stuff, the clothes and toilet articles and miscellaneous equipment—things like fishing poles and sunglasses and groceries—they'd left in the van. Using the stock of Ears's shotgun, Monster had helped Barney break the rest of the windshield out of the truck.

"You got another barrel for your nine-millimeter, don't you?" Barney asked, looking through the open windshield at him.

"In my jacket pocket." He patted his windbreaker. "I'll stop somewhere and change barrels. Throw it into the woods or something."

"It's a used barrel, isn't it?"

"Of course."

And then Monster had gotten in the van and slowly driven out of the meadow, through the narrow defile, and onto the highway that ran next to the lake—I drive Highway 93, pray for me. It wasn't more than a mile as the crow flies from where he was now to where he'd killed the two men, and he knew that no matter how long he lived, each time he drove by the turnoff to that canyon he'd smell the swamp, feel the damp air and mosquitoes, smell the stink of fear and death, and his world would twist a little, the bright Technicolor of lake and sky and mountains would become muted. He'd feel whatever it was—the residue of that night. Ghosts, and he'd drive slower, not faster, for a few miles. Maybe even take the highway on the other side of the lake. No. He wouldn't do that. He'd feel gray driving by that canyon, but he'd do it. He glanced behind at the lumped canvas. Fuck them, they deserved to die if anyone did. He'd do it again. And he'd always feel that way, so fuck them.

He made the turn onto the Swan River Highway. Traffic was sparse; not more than twenty cars so far. Be lucky if he met more than two or three more, this time of night. He held the van at forty-five to give Barney time. Barney would have to throw the dope in the swamp, drive back to Missoula without a windshield—nearly a hundred miles—unload the truck, and get it back to their snitch and sometime dope dealer and truck dealer, who would raise hell. Barney would probably get nasty with him and everything would be cool. The snitch would take Barney home. Barney would get Monster's International out of the garage and drive up the Blackfoot to meet him.

The van was smooth, but the metal sides vibrated, reminding him of helicopters and medevacs, and, thinking about helicopters and medevacs, he was reminded there'd been a worse time in his life. But that didn't help.

He wondered what Evy was doing right then, and felt his face turn hot, tight, his skin greasy as it had been that day a long time ago.

She was probably thinking it had been only a one-night stand. Just him counting coup. Maybe it'd turn out that way. Probably it would. For sure, it'd be a while before he and Barney would be in a position to be chasing women. Who knew what would happen next? Holy shit. Montana, not 'Nam. But three bodies jiggling around back there like this was a medevac helicopter or something.

Inexplicably, his eyes misted, the highway ahead suddenly seen through a warp of tears, a memory of himself sitting in a worn metal doorway, the helicopter vibrating two thousand feet above paddies that looked like silver windowpanes.

He shook his head, blinking his eyes. Oh, think of something else, he thought. Anything. Think of Evy, her long, smooth legs drawn up against her breasts as he pressed his weight down onto her, into her.

No. Don't think of that, either. That'd make you crazy, too.

Don't think of anything. Just drive. Watch out for deer. Remember the first time you drove this highway. It was summer, the sky filled with fluffy white clouds, the pines and thick underbrush brilliant greens, the highway white and clean as the six of them, in an old 1957 Pontiac, hollered and whooped and drank cheap beer out of quart bottles one year before he joined the Marine Corps. Before two of them joined—the other now burned out on drugs and memories. "Woman! Get back in the wagon!" he'd yelled at every woman they'd seen, regardless of age or looks. And the six of them had thought that was hilarious, and driving down that highway they'd taken to yelling it at everything—bridges, trees, deer.

"Woman. Get back in the wagon," he murmured, but the

words spoken out loud frightened him, his voice a stranger's voice.

He turned the radio on, but it was just a jumble of noise, a few bits of rock and roll and talk stations that faded and whirred back into static. He shut the radio off.

Music. He needed music.

He turned the overhead light on. The radio had a tape deck built into it. Tapes were littered across the dash. The Doors, the Stones, Simon and Garfunkel. Simon and Garfunkel! Jesus. Punk rock and heavy metal groups—probably the redhead's.

He inserted the Doors tape into the radio and heard, low and soft . . . *become a funeral pyre. Come on, baby, light my*—he pushed the eject button, but too late to stop emotions rekindled. Vietnam, Vietnam, Vietnam, go a-way! his mind screamed at the highway.

He reached up to turn the overhead light back off and, knowing better but doing it anyway, glanced back. The canvas had worked partway down one of the bodies. An empty skull gaped up at him: an oval darkness the size of a post hole. The redhead.

He switched the light off and turned forward again, looking at highway lit by headlights. But that was worse because he started imagining the van was driving into that hole, the headlights looking ahead into the darkness. Here it comes, he giggled to himself. The Magical Mystery Tour.

Cursing, he pulled the van off the highway onto a graveled shoulder bordered by tall pines.

He shut off the lights and engine and climbed out. Had to get rid of the barrel anyway. And walked around the back of the van, pulled the Browning from his belt, and dismantled it by touch, putting the magazine and parts in his jacket pocket.

He reared back and threw the barrel high into the air, arching it over the first row of pines, into the trees and bushes beyond.

He waited, but all he heard was the popping of the exhaust pipes as they cooled. He took the other barrel from his windbreaker pocket and reassembled the Browning, smacked the magazine in and, not bothering to chamber a round, placed the gun back at his waist just behind his right hip, only the grip and hammer above his belt. Gravel crunched as he walked back toward the van.

He paused for a moment at the side door. Might as well sit and relax for a while, he thought, and twisted the handle and slid the door open. The door rumbled on the rollers. Barney would probably be several hours behind him, anyway.

He sat down in the worn metal doorway. And the doorway, the feel of the metal, the smell inside—oil and exhaust mixed with the smell of stale clothes and blood and death—reminded him again of a day worse than this one could ever be. One of those memories, he thought, that he remembered but not quite remembered. One of those locked-away, zipped-into-bags memories.

Head tilted back, he stared past the pines, into the stars that seemed so close he could fall into the spaces between them. "Hey!" he yelled up at the stars. "Why me? Why's it have to be me?"

His voice sounded puny, absorbed by the pines and the interior of the van.

He let his head fall forward, thinking. Thinking what?

He was thinking of— His mind was abruptly filled with a soft, pale expansion that seemed to stretch his eyes apart.

He blinked. And blinked again, trying to make the pines and the mountains, the stars and the van seem real. He reached back behind him and felt a leg, and the touch, instead of centering him in the present, blasted a piece of memory into his consciousness.

A memory sharp and clear, the understanding of it organic but as hard for him to accept as the cold, limitless spaces between the stars. And he realized in that instant that he'd been dreaming about it for years and not knowing it. Memory seen through warp of heat or blur of tears, he didn't know, and he shuddered, frightened, knowing he was going to sit there and remember it all, unable to stop it, afraid he'd find out he wasn't what he thought he was. Knowing already, as he remembered sitting in the doorway so much like the doorway of the van, that he wasn't.

Sitting in the doorway of the helicopter, eating a can of C rations—cold beans and meatballs—watching the sun come up.

Other helicopters were scattered about the landscape, one

193

to each desiccated rice paddy, security against nightly rocket attacks. The air was free of dust, almost cool. Pilots and crews, dressed in green or tan flight suits, carrying M-60 machine guns, cans of ammunition, flight helmets, spare parts, field packs, straggled out to the helicopters.

Morning heat roused the smells: hydraulic fluid, oil, human fertilizer still embedded in the dusty rice paddies, partially filled sawed-off fifty-five-gallon barrels set underneath the outhouses. And himself: greasy, his clothes torn and rotten with sweat, dust, oil.

Flies flew from shitter to mess tent to rice paddy to people to his can of beans and meatballs, laying their eggs.

But the flies didn't matter because he'd stopped eating and was thinking about Mei-Li and Taipei.

Taipei, he thought with wonder, looking up at the dark row of pines as if the pines should know too, *he remembered Taipei.*

The damp, cool, air-conditioned bar was a jolt that made him forget the honking taxis and platoons of motorcycles charging up and down congested streets, the crowds of Chinese laughing, shouting, bartering, staring. His body yielded to the sudden relief, and, eyes adapting to the gloom, he noticed a fat, middle-aged Chinese woman eating peanuts at the far end of a polished wood bar. She was the only person in the bar.

"Hello there," he said.

"Have seat." The fat woman climbed off the stool and walked behind the bar, her image reflected in the long mirror hanging behind the clutter of bottles. "Need beer, have. Need hard stuff, have, too. Girls come soon back."

He walked to the center of the bar and sat down on a vinyl-covered stool. "Beer," he said, feeling off-balance in the empty room.

"American, Chinese, both have."

"Uh . . . Chinese," he said, and immediately wondered if he'd made a mistake.

The woman smiled, a silver tooth glinting like fresh shrapnel, and placed a tall brown bottle, already beginning to sweat, in front of him.

"Thank you," he said, and placed a wad of money on the

bar. He took a long drink, shivering with pleasure, the beer bouncing and foaming in the bottom of the bottle. He belched softly, and smiled, embarrassed. "Excuse me."

Warmth bled through the opaque eyes, and the wrinkled face smiled. "You wait. Have special girl for you. Speak good English."

"Where are they?" he asked, but he didn't care, content to hold the wet bottle in both hands, slide it in circles and watch smears of water follow it along the rich wood.

"Go see doctor. Get check. Very clean girls. Students. You wait, okay?"

"Okay." He took another drink. The cold beer numbed his thoughts.

Three beers later, he stood in front of the juke box, the bar empty and silent but for the hum of the air conditioner and the occasional quiet crunch of peanuts. Neatly ranked tables and chairs sat rigid in the gloom behind the jukebox. He imagined them filled with the men who had been in his boot camp platoon. More than sixty percent of the platoon already dead. He pushed buttons at random, and a crowd of young, well-dressed Chinese girls burst through the door, chattering and laughing, two American men, one a black, caught in their midst, the black slim and gangly, the other man tall and broad-shouldered, hair close-cropped. The mass of girls, jabbering in Chinese and English, escorted the two men to a table.

Grunts on R and R, Ben thought, but he was watching long black hair, and long nylon-encased legs, sleek muscles flexing as the women crowded about the two men. Almond eyes.

The girls left the two men and gathered in front of the bar, laughing and talking all at once to the old woman. One, tall and graceful, hair to her waist, was the center of attention. The old woman demanded silence and talked to the girl for a moment, and the girl took a seat behind the cash register. Flunked her checkup, I'll bet, he thought.

The other girls dispersed, several to sit with the two men, the remainder to sit at tables in the rear. None of them had noticed him.

"Hey!" a voice boomed. "In front of the jukebox. Come over and have a beer!"

Ben's head jerked toward the two Americans, a startled

195

chorus of "ai yah's," from the girls, greeting his movement, and he felt himself blush. Women stared and murmured. The black grinned at him.

And later there was a fresh beer in front of him, and he was seated at the table with the two grunts. The big man a recon sergeant, loud and aggressive, a lifer, bovine in his competence, the black a PFC who looked seventeen. The black's eyes reminded Ben of a deer he'd wounded, its large brown eyes soft, liquid, not knowing the nature of the wound that steamed in cold mountain air. He'd shot it again, through one eye, and stood watching until the wounds no longer steamed and the other eye turned almost gray. His first kill.

"Jeezus H. Christ, Sam. Can't you fuckin' hold still for even a minute?" the recon sergeant said. "You fidgetin' son of a bitch."

"Can't help it." Sam grinned at his girl. "Just nervous, I guess."

"Fuckin' boot camp is what you are."

"Ain't no boot camp! I been in 'Nam six months, and wounded once."

The big sergeant laughed. "Look at this silly shit," he said to Ben. "Six months in 'Nam, and he's ready to pee his pants because he's about to get a little ass from a zipper-head."

And from behind him Mei-Li had said hello in her soft, husky voice, and her hand had lightly caressed the back of his neck. "I am Mei-Li." And he felt the press of her warm hip against his cheek. Tall and slender Mei-Li, silky hair soft and long to her breasts. He could still smell her, still feel the panties under the thin fabric of her slacks.

"Mama-san say you number one."

Ben felt a breeze cool his face. His whole body felt hot, the same kind of hot he'd felt that night with Evy. Last night? He could smell the interior of the van, oil and metal and bodies, and he was once again sitting in the worn metal doorway of a helicopter. It seemed as if he'd spent most of his life in that worn metal doorway, the helicopter thrashing and vibrating its way above rivers and paddies and villages, his feet dangling out into the sky, shoulder slumped against the well-used barrel of a M-60 machine gun swiveled inside the doorway, cartridge belt meandering from the M-60, across the folded flak vest lying on the empty seat, and into the almost full ammo can. Conversation squealed and crackled and hissed in the headset of his flight helmet.

"Here we go," announced the pilot, and the rhythm of the rotor blades changed, the floor tilted, and they began the long spiral descent toward the jungle. He grabbed the gun mount and pulled himself up into the seat and put the flak vest on. The helicopter was headed for a clearing, the only break discernible in the pastel green jungle.

At five hundred feet he spotted them: four rectangular gray-green bags, each approximately the size of a man, side by side in the clearing, punctuated by one smaller square gray-green bag. From five hundred feet they were an alien symmetry in the confusion of jungle, but as the helicopter settled to the earth, their flat planes became bulges and folds, and only their color separated them from the jungle.

A squad of marines stood next to the bags, wind from the helicopter rotors rippling their fatigues, pressing the material against their bodies. One man at the foot, one at the head, they bent and picked up the bags, the bags limp, centers sagging, and dragged them along the ground and heaved them onto the helicopter's floor.

A single man easily picked up the fifth bag, folded into a square, but pieces of body inside bulged and distorted the gray-green covering and made it difficult for him to keep a solid grip on the bag. When he threw it onto the other bags, the contents continued for a moment to move and slide, as if some small animal were zipped inside, struggling to find a way out.

"Okay," Ben said into the microphone, and the helicopter lifted, engine bellowing as it fought for altitude.

He stared at the bags crowded into the narrow cabin, the nearest almost touching his leg. Don't look like they've got boots on, he thought, watching the bags jiggle loosely together on the vibrating floor. The zipper on the nearest began to work open. The helicopter banked and the zipper opened nearly a foot. A thatch of dirty brown hair quivered up through the opening. Underneath the hair the remains of a face emerged, eye sockets and ears squirming with colonies of gray-white maggots. The head appeared to rise out of the slit in the body bag. Fetal.

Ben vomited—no warning gag, just a solid spew of partially digested meatballs and beans—before he registered the smell. Burned, putrefied flesh and hair. He reached down to zip the bag, pulling the bag up by the zipper seam, but the zipper stuck, caught in the hair. And he vomited again, spraying the bags and floor. He forced the zipper shut, shearing off shards of brittle hair.

The pilots had grounded the helicopter. "Bag failure," they'd written in the log book, and left it to him to tell the maintenance sergeant what they'd meant by that.

"First day back from Mei-Li," he explained to the pines. He could hear them swaying in the darkness, see them tilt and lean across the stars. Mei-Li.

Sitting waist deep in the hot, steaming pool, trying to teach him a little Chinese, her figure almost obscured by rising wisps of steam. The steam-fog creating the impression that the room had no boundaries; it felt as if he were suspended in a void.

"Wo ai ni," Mei-Li said. "I love you. But Chinese never say that. Only Americans." Sweat mingled with pool water made her flat stomach sleek, oiled her body. Her nipples were erect despite the heat.

"Foreigners come rarely here," she said. "It is for Chinese and their guests. But when foreigners do, they always are fat and old, with bellies like bean curd."

He pulled her up against his chest and crotch. "Ai, yah," she breathed.

The pines moved against the stars, sighing.

Later that same day the pilot was grim: "Khe Sahn," he said.

Khe Sahn. The name Khe Sahn seemed to reverberate from inside the van out across the paddies, and he remembered Mei-Li, her head thrown back, dark hair trailing in the water, her little cry echoing through the fog as he watched her eyes change.

* * *

He'd been shot down at Khe Sanh once already, blood from the copilot spattering down onto his helmet as the helicopter autorotated crazily, the metal matting rushing up at them.

But this time they slipped in unharmed, taking only a few rounds in the tail section. Through the dust and debris thrown up by the rotor blades he could see a hazy row of body bags lying alongside the metal matting. Artillery and mortar rounds struck 150 meters to the right. Three marines ran through the dust and turbulence, carrying a dark bundle between them, helmets knocking together, legs tripping, stepping on one another. They threw the bundle into the helicopter. It landed sodden and fresh on the metal floor, blood pooling.

"You fuckers, where's the fucking body bag!" he yelled at the pines.

But they were gone, sprinting for a bunker, mortar rounds hitting the matting, charcoal-brown puffs walking toward the helicopter.

"Go! Go!" he screamed into the mike.

And later, slumped in his seat, clear of Khe Sanh. Oh, fuck, oh, dear. He'd looked down at the corpse shivering loosely on the vibrating floor, fatigues reduced to a uniform brown, right leg gone, torn off at the knee, shredded edge of bloody material flapping wetly in the wind blowing through the open doorway. Sometimes the wind blowing through the open doorway and under the edge of his flight helmet just behind the ear made him remember old songs like "Black Is Black." Raw meat on a butcher's block—just like the Beatles' album cover. Bone-white and obscene. Its mouth open in a shout, as it had been when Ben had watched him dancing in the bar in Taipei—Tai*bei*, Mei-Li had said. Tai*bei*—a bar girl gamely trying to learn a new dance step from him. He dipped, shook, pivoted, graceful and relaxed, at one with the pulsating music, shirt whipping, head thrown back, neck muscles rigid, the vein prominent. Mouth open, shouting to the music, he looked up at Ben. Looked at everything, looked at nothing. A black with eyes that had been soft and liquid. No boot camp, wounded once already, and now his leg was gone, Khe Sanh, and Mei-Li's eyes stared at him, soft and dark and forever as the corpse continued to shout, quivering with the floor. Ben bowed his head into crossed arms on top of his knees.

The corpse stared; he could feel it.

He jerked upright and looked around the cabin for something to cover it with, and stood and took his flak vest off and laid it over the corpse's head so that it covered the eyes.

But the chest gaped raw and dirty, and the pantleg continued to flap, and the raw meat winked at him. Mei-Li had winked at him.

He unbuckled his gun belt; the .38 fell on the floor as he tossed the belt toward the open radio compartment in the tail section. He unzipped the flight suit, forgetting the leg zips, and fought it over his boots, barely aware of the open doorway inches away. He laid the flight suit over the chest and leg of the corpse. And then sat back in his seat, clad only in jungle boots and green skivvy shorts and flight helmet. *Black is black, I want my baby back.*

"Everyone say they come back," Mei-Li had said at the airport, and smiled at him, but her eyes didn't really see him.

"Wo ai ni," he whispered, and the flak vest shifted with the plane's vibration, and one eye, now almost gray—*gray is gray, since you been away*—stared up at him through the arm hole. He stared back, for a long time, it seemed like, and then picked up the .38 and shot the eye, the shot a small pop over the engine, wind, and radio noise. The eye blinked out. In its place the flak vest's armhole stared—a small oval darkness the size of a post hole. Mei-Li's eyes had been soft and liquid until he'd whispered *"Wo ai ni,"* and then they'd turned dull, and he remembered that his first kill had been a doe and when he'd first shot her, she'd cried—a thin, wavering cry eerily human.

Monster sat in the doorway of the helicopter, watching the pines shift against the stars. Sweat ran down his face. His first day back from Mei-Li, and he was once again in the doorway of the helicopter, eating C rations out of a can—pears this time—watching the sun go down, a huge ocher ball suspended on the horizon. *Maybe I will go back,* he'd thought, still thought. *Maybe.*

He extended his arm straight out toward the pines and slowly tipped the can of pears, watching the syrup and slippery clots leak out, red and viscous in the dying sunlight. When the can was empty, he rotated the open end toward himself and stared into it for a moment, an oval darkness, like the top of the redhead's skull, and threw it out into the dried-up rice paddy, toward the pines, where it rattled and tinked and came to rest among the other empty cans.

CHAPTER **19**

Woody Woodpecker

There weren't any beer cans in the van, Monster thought.
Just the dope and a few empty plastic orange juice containers.
He was seated in the pine needles at the base of a large ponderosa, his back resting against coarse ridged bark, watching
the old logging road, barely seen winding down through the
pines. Lucky and Ears hadn't drunk much, and he didn't
think they'd done much dope, either, because they'd both been
in good shape. Selling dope and killing people for a living—
for a way of life.

He glanced over at the dark square bulk of the van parked
among the trees off to his left, and shivered: how you could
get. He found it hard to be angry at the two men. The redhead—no problem there. Garbage. Just garbage was all the
redhead had ever been. He could understand the other two:
given the right circumstances, it could just as well have been
him doing that kind of shit.

The old logging road, the trees and bushes and the open
grass-covered slope across the road were starting to assume
their shapes as the sky lightened in the east.

Could have been him! What was he talking about? He'd
just blown two people away, and no matter how Barney looked
at it, he'd had a choice. A whole range of choices.

But so what? Did it make him bad? The only people who'd

been hurt were two professional killers and one piece of garbage. He'd done the world a favor.

So kiss my ass, world. Maybe he was bad, evil, because no matter who or how many Lucky and Ears had killed, maybe those people deserved it more than Lucky and Ears had. Hell, if you wanted to do the world a favor you'd round up a bunch of people like Lucky and Ears and plant the people who really deserved it: the people who since Time One had fucked over God and Creation unmercifully, the few who forced a life-style right down everyone else's throat, a life-style that included large doses of war and pollution and, in general, a fucked existence for almost everyone on the face of the earth. And for what? So the really bent few could chase after power. Power, power, power, that's where it was at, where it always had been. Men over men, men over women, women over men, women over women. All of them bent and becoming more bent. He and Barney had become bent a long time ago.

Like the elk: men had driven the elk into the mountains. For the elk it was either hide or be killed. And in just a few generations the elk had changed, become bigger, stronger, smarter, hiding in thick brush and timber. One-thousand-pound bulls would lie still until a hunter had passed and then silently stand and melt into forest so thick a man could barely squirm through. Once he'd seen a bull with a harem of five cows grazing on an open slope, the cows spread out in a circle around the bull, one cow at the top of the ridge, one fifty yards below the bull, one thirty yards in front, one thirty yards behind, and one next to him. Elk had learned all that in just a few generations, some of them sneakier and more clever each year.

And if elk had learned that in a hundred years, imagine what people had learned after countless generations of fighting and killing and generally fucking over each other unmercifully.

He smiled at himself, at his persistent naiveté. Nothing would happen. You'd just replace one set of assholes with another. Power, that was all. Down on the bottom, where people like him and Barney were up to their necks in shit and blood and brains, things would always be the same.

He heard the grumble of his old beat-up International coming, and the dark, awkward shape of the truck emerged down-slope from behind a stand of trees. Like some massive nearsighted bear, it lumbered toward him, puffs of gray dust rising around the wheels.

A morning breeze whispered down the hill, eddying around the big ponderosa, ruffling his hair. He shivered; the air was coldest just before dawn.

He stood and walked to the middle of the road so Barney could see him. The truck grumbled up to him and turned off into the trees on the opposite side of the road from the van, the wooden rack on the back jumping and rattling as the truck crawled up the rocky shoulder and into the forest. Barney killed the engine and climbed out, slamming the door shut.

"Hi, there," he said.

"What's that you've got?"

"Doughnuts." He rattled a white paper bag in his other hand. "And coffee." He handed Monster a silver Thermos.

"All right!" Monster said, abruptly incredibly hungry and thirsty.

Barney followed him over to the big ponderosa, and they sat down, Barney lying back into the pine needles. He stretched. "Man, that truck of yours feels like someone forgot to put shocks on it."

Monster poured steaming coffee into the Thermos cup, the smell somehow always perfect in the morning among the pines. Memories of hunting trips: a last cup before setting out, climbing, sneaking into position before first light.

"How'd it go?" he asked.

"Not bad. There was an old pair of ski goggles in the box, so I made pretty good time." Barney waved the cup away. "No, thanks, I've had about a gallon already."

"Any trouble with Frederick?"

Barney laughed. "Old Fred? He took one look at me, at the dried blood on my shirt and pants, and must've said, 'Don't worry. I'll take care of it. Don't worry,' about ninety times. I gave him the three thousand to pay for the damages."

Monster smiled and bit into a maple bar.

"How about you? I see you got here in one piece, anyway."

Monster sipped loudly at the coffee, chewed the maple bar. He shook his head. "I stopped for about an hour somewhere up the Swan. Changed the barrel. Sat there for a while." He sipped the coffee.

"How long you been here, then?"

Monster shrugged and reached into the sack for another doughnut. "Not too long." He took a huge bite of doughnut. "This sure hits the spot," he mumbled. He raised the cup at Barney. "Appreciate it."

Barney struggled to his feet. "Well, you're back to normal," he said, hands on hips, stretching his back.

Monster finished the coffee and doughnut and twisted the cup back onto the Thermos. He stood and took the last doughnut from the paper sack and crumpled the sack with one hand. "Better go do it," he said. "Getting light."

Forty-five minutes later, they were lying behind a jumbled mass of blow-down—five trees, one on top of the other, like huge pickup sticks thrown down, bark long ago peeled off, branches reduced to bleached bone-size bits strewn over pine needle–covered dirt and rocks. They were on the edge of the treeline, about eighty yards uphill, next to a meadow that ran from the top of the ridge far above them, down across the valley, and up into the treeline about three-quarters of a mile away. In the center of the valley, a large house constructed of square logs sat half completed, barbed-wire fence, whole sections of five or six posts rotted and fallen to the ground along one side; a large wooden barn and several outbuildings, obviously the remnants of an earlier working ranch, were scattered weatherworn on the other side of the road from the house. The house was two stories, wood shingles and big windows. Through the binoculars, Barney could see the porch was made of weathered and curled pieces of plywood tacked on to two-by-tens. Steps only, about four feet high, with no handrail. A fancy Dodge PowerWagon was parked a few feet from the steps. A cat wandered about in front of the barn.

The dirt road ran from the house east about three hundred yards to a large metal gate directly below them. From where they sat, the gate was only about fifty yards as the crow flies, but over a hundred yards if they ran down the hill and through the gulley lined with bushes that lay between the hillside and the gate. The van was parked twenty yards inside the gate, off the side of the road, facing directly toward the house. One end of the gate was twisted and smashed down into the middle of the road.

The gate had been padlocked with a large hardened steel lock connecting the ends of a thick chain looped through the gate and around a railroad tie set on end into the ground. Monster had simply driven the van up to the gate and railroad tie and pushed the bumper against the tie and gate until he'd uprooted the tie. Then he'd driven over one end of the metal gate, the metal crumpling and bending as the heavy van drove over it, and over the corrugated iron cattle guard.

"Knock, knock," he'd said. "Guess who's here?"

The bodies were already becoming stiff with rigor mortis, and it had been difficult to set the redhead up in the driver's seat and make him stare straight ahead toward the house, his fingers bent around the steering wheel, seat belt cinched tight, holding him in place. He looked like a wax dummy, dull, flat eyes seeming to follow Monster and Barney no matter what angle they were away from him. The blood and brain matter had dried, leaving his hair tufted up behind his head, like the topknot on a woodpecker.

"Fuck you, Woody," Monster had said, and slammed the door, laughing like Woody Woodpecker. "Ha. Ha-ha-ha. Ha-ha-ha-ha-ha-ha."

The other two they'd hung by the knees over the top of barbed wire, each straddling a fence post, one knee on either side of the wooden post, head down toward the ground. They'd tied the legs around the posts and top strand of wire, and tied hands to belts to keep them off the ground. Barney had cut the sweater off Lucky and the ridiculous Hawaiian shirt off Ears, so that the wounds could clearly be seen. It was like meat hung in a butcher's shop, Ears's throat furrowed open by the 9mm, two neat little holes in his chest and another neat little hole just above his right eyebrow, a piece of skull the size of a baseball blown out of the back of his head, his eyes rolled back, only the white showing, thick, gelatinous mass of blood and brain clotting the hole at the back of his head; most of Lucky's upper arm and shoulder and neck gone, bone splinters showing; one shotgun round— one solid ounce of lead—had opened up his stomach and pulverized his backbone at the small of his back. The stench was overpowering, torn guts leaking. One side of Lucky's chin was mostly gone, teeth and gum showing.

"Not so fucking lucky now, are you?" Barney had asked the corpse staring upside down at his shins. He threw an unzipped sleeping bag over it. "What a mess."

Monster threw another sleeping bag over Ears. "Maybe we should take his ears," he said. "Might come in handy later."

Barney handed Monster the knife. "Go ahead."

"You do it."

"It was your idea."

Then they'd carefully folded the canvas tarp and walked back across the cattle guard and up the hill, Barney carrying the small green pack and the M-16, Monster the canvas tarp.

When Monster had run the van over the gate, there'd been just enough light to see the barbed-wire strands, but now, as they sat silent behind the blow-down, watching the house for movement, the first rays of sunlight began to hit into the trees and meadow at the upper end of the valley, the colors all crisp greens and pale yellows. It was going to be one of those great summer days, Monster thought. Not a cloud in the sky. A morning like summer mornings when, as a boy, he'd wake up to the smell of fresh dew on grass, meadowlarks singing in the field just outside his window. He'd climb slowly out of bed, grinning just to feel himself grin, throw on an old pair of cutoffs, and go out and sit on the front steps in the sunshine, warm and chill at the same time. He'd close his eyes and, turning his face directly into the early morning sun, he'd feel his dog's chin across his bare leg, and he'd reach down and scratch him behind the ear, feeling how warm the fur on his dog's head and neck was, warmed by the sun as he had waited for Ben to come out and pet him and enjoy the morning, glad to be alive.

The van was silent, cold in the shadow of the hill. The two sleeping bags hung from the fence, like huge green cocoons.

Barney raised the binoculars. The valley, lit by the early morning sun, was beautiful and fresh, except the house. The sunlight only accented its tar paper and insulation, cement foundation stark gray and out of place between the logs and the packed, weed-infested earth. A litter of kittens played on the flimsy-looking steps.

The sun warmed the left side of Monster's face, reminding

him again how he'd felt as a kid, living only for the moment of sunshine. Empty now, he thought. All of us, our juices poured out, sucked out, spooned out.

He closed his eyes and tilted his face toward the morning sun.

Barney leaned forward. There was movement behind one of the windows. The sun's reflection had turned the windows into big silver mirrors, and he couldn't see who or how many.

"I'll tell you what," Monster said. "I can think of a whole lot of people I'd rather've dumped." He sat up and squinted toward the house. "But blowing that fucking redhead away just can't be bad."

Barney put the binoculars down. "It's not a case of good or bad. You'll just get yourself crazy if you let yourself get tangled up in that kind of Catholic bullshit again."

"Well, what is it, then? I'm having a little trouble with the 'I like it' part."

Barney smiled thinly and picked up the binoculars again. "You were born this way, that's all." A woman, barefoot, dressed in a faded calico bathrobe, opened the door and put a pan of something on the steps.

"Yeah," Monster said sarcastically. "That's convenient for me. What about you?"

"Your girlfriend just came out and fed the cats."

Monster looked over the log. "Did she notice the van?"

"I don't think so. Here, you watch for a while." Barney handed him the binoculars. He rubbed his eyes. "Whew. This is getting to be a long day."

Monster raised the glasses. "Why don't you put in for overtime?"

Barney smiled. "That's a good idea. I can see it now: the lieutenant picks up the time sheets and sees ten hours' overtime for dusting his good buddies and hanging them up to dry on a barbed-wire fence."

"Sure hope they don't call the cops."

"Who cares? We wiped the van clean and we'll burn our clothes and the tarp. In fact, if it comes to that, we might even get to be the investigating officers."

"Somebody is standing behind one of the windows. Not sure, but I think whoever it is, is using binoculars."

"Get down. They might look up here."

Monster lay back, resting his back against a broken branch partially covered with pine needles. He looked at the cloudless summer sky. "I don't think we have to worry about it," he said. "That big bastard is smarter than that."

"Where's the pack?"

"Right next to you, on the other side of that log you've got the M-sixteen against."

Barney pulled the small green pack onto his side of the fallen tree. He rummaged around inside, pulling out a small white box that looked like a small cake box. Then he pulled out a slingshot and handful of rubber bands.

"Find some rocks," he said. "We'll wrap the M-eighties to them."

Monster brushed through the pine needles and broken branches, looking for likely-size rocks to attach to each of the powerful firecrackers—squat yellow cylinders about the size of the first two joints of an index finger, each the equivalent of an eighth of a stick of dynamite. He stretched a rubber band around a small rock and one of the M-80s. "Wait until these start going off." He grinned.

"He sees it," Barney said. The slingshot and ten M-80s were arrayed neatly on the log in front of them.

"Who is it?"

"It's that scumbag Harold. And he's wearing my good luck hat."

"Let me see."

Barney handed him the binoculars.

Monster propped his elbows on the log and adjusted the glasses. Harold was standing on the steps to the house, squinting toward the van, shading his eyes with his hand. He was wearing old, patched Levi's. Barney's faded camouflage hat sat on the back of his long, greasy-looking hair. He was barefoot. Curly black hair grew thick on his muscular chest and arms. Monster snickered.

"What you laughing at?"

"I'll bet he sleeps with it on. All that greasy hair."

Barney picked up the M-16, hit the beavertail with his thumb, and the bolt chunked forward, chambering a round. He checked the safety. "Well, we'll see how happy he is with my hat in a few minutes."

"He just went back in. The big one just came out. The girl's behind him. He's got a pair of binoculars, looking at the van."

"The sun's in his eyes; I'll bet he can't see much even with the glasses."

"Boy," Monster said. "You got to give Debbie credit. She ain't half bad looking." The girl was wearing tight cutoffs and a skimpy string top that barely covered her breasts. Her long brown hair gleamed in the sunlight. "Ab-so-lute-ly perfect tits."

"You ought to know. Let me see."

"Fuck you."

"I want to look at him, not the girl."

"Sure you do." Monster smiled and handed him the binoculars. "Sure beats that camouflage jumpsuit all to hell."

Barney adjusted the glasses. "Ah, hmmm. Maybe you're not so stupid after all. It never occurred to me that underneath all that hippie junk she wears—"

"Takes a connoisseur."

Barney laughed. "You got the con part right." The big man was standing one step down from the girl, but he was still nearly a head taller. His bald freckled head gleamed in the sunlight. "She sure makes that big bastard look ugly, doesn't she?" The big man's walrus mustache moved up and down on either side of the binoculars as he talked to the girl. He was wearing jeans and a gray sweat shirt. Both of them had on purple jogging shoes. "A real sweetie. Maybe you could go jogging with them."

Monster reached around behind Barney and picked up the M-16.

Barney glanced over at him. "Now, don't be shooting anyone."

"Heaven forbid."

"Here they come. All three of them." Barney hunkered farther down, resting the binoculars on top of the log.

Monster craned his neck and head upward, looking over the log, like a ground squirrel coming up out of his hole.

"Get your head down."

"What for? They can't see us. They're looking at the van and the sleeping bags." He giggled.

"I don't see any guns," Barney said.

"Of course not. They know the van."

Barney chuckled. "I'll bet they think their friends were too polite to drive the van in in the middle of the night and wake them up."

"I hope so."

"Although I can't imagine anyone expecting politeness from the redhead."

"He's going to be even ruder this time."

"They're stopping."

Monster sat up and peered anxiously over the log. The three figures had halted in the middle of the dirt road. "The gate?" he said. "We should've closed it again."

"They'll just think they were drunk or stoned," Barney said.

"Maybe. But Ears and Lucky didn't drink much. There weren't any beer cans in the back of the van, or roaches in the ashtray."

"Well, it's too late now. We couldn't have bent it back anyway. Hey, that big one looks pissed off about it."

"Which way is the wind blowing?"

"Isn't any."

The slope they were sitting on was gradually warming, flies and bees buzzing in and out of the logs. A string of ants had suddenly appeared, moving across one of the lower logs. A horsefly as big as a bee floated down the hill toward the green cocoons.

"They're moving again," Barney said. "Get ready." He put the binoculars down and picked up the wrist rocket, put his hand and forearm through the metal brace, and gripping the slingshot firmly, inserted one of the M-80s banded to a rock into the leather pocket.

"Lob the first couple as high as you can," Monster said, "then a couple lower down, so they all get there one after another. Like a mortar."

Barney nodded.

Below them on the road, the three figures—the big man followed by Debbie and short, muscular Harold—approached the van. They stopped, and the big man called something. He walked to the van and peered into the front window.

Monster and Barney both grinned.

The big man stepped around to the driver's side and opened

the door. He reached in, touched the redhead, and recoiled, slamming the door shut.

"Guess who's coming to dinner?" Monster said. "Ha-ha-ha. Ha-ha-ha-ha-ha."

The big man walked around to the rear of the van, stopping momentarily to stare at the crumpled and uprooted gate.

"All kinds of surprises," Monster said. "My goodness."

The big man pulled open the rear doors, and the other two slowly walked forward to the driver's side of the van, the girl first.

"She's going to faint," Barney said, and she slumped back, knees buckling. Her hand gripped the door handle. The door swung open, twisting her around as she let go and sank onto the dirt road, one leg folded underneath her. Her head nodded forward, like a student falling asleep in class.

"I'll bet that's the first dead body she's ever seen," Monster said.

"The other one better not lose my hat."

Harold squatted behind the girl and, putting his hands and arms through her armpits, hoisted her to her feet. Unsteadily, she walked several steps away from the van, back into the middle of the road. Harold looked inside and turned and vomited into the grass at the side of the road.

"You wanted to play games, you silly shits," Barney said. "Here it is."

The big man closed the back doors and walked back toward Harold. They could see only his head moving along the far side of the van. He pushed Harold, wiping at his mouth with his forearm, back toward the girl. Harold stumbled and almost fell, righted himself. The girl was crying. They could see her breasts moving under the string bra, but at that moment her sexuality was grotesque, almost embarrassing.

"Show's not over yet, folks," Monster said. "Don't leave now."

The big man, hands on hips, considered the sleepings bags. Slowly, deliberately, he walked over to the nearest and lifted the green Gortex material. From where they sat, Ears looked like a kid playing on the parallel bars in the schoolyard, hanging upside down to impress his girlfriend. But even from there, they could see the body was not right. All the internal muscles had softened, allowing the innards to slide down into the chest cavity, making the chest appear unnaturally large, the waist too small. The big man took a step back and looked away, across the meadow toward the opposite side of the valley.

"Trick or treat, fucker," Monster said.

Barney laughed. But it was the same laugh he'd laughed on a trail a long time ago.

The big man stepped up to the other sleeping bag and ripped the bag off the corpse, and immediately stepped back and away, averting his face. They could see the dark entrails at the corpse's waist, hanging down toward the head.

"Looks a little pale there, all of a sudden," Barney said.

"Smells great, I'll bet," Monster replied. "Something to work up your appetite on a nice sunny day like this."

The big man must have said something when he stepped away, because the other two looked toward him. Harold screamed and the girl tried to, her eyes bulging, mouth opening and closing, hyperventilating.

Monster knelt forward, aiming the M-16 carefully, holding the plastic rest firmly against the log. "Now?"

"Now," Barney said, and with his thumb, Monster snapped the selector to full auto and began firing six- and seven-round bursts, the brass flicking and winking in the sunlight across the logs in front of Barney, the rounds raising puffs of dust ten yards down the road from the girl, snapping five yards above the head of the big man, smashing into the dirt and grass of the meadow between the big man and the other two. Thirty rounds, the smell of cordite heavy in the air as the noise of the last burst rolled across the valley.

The girl was screaming now, her arms rigid, out away from her body. The big man ran to the van and hid behind it. Harold dived to the ground, heedless of his bare chest, and pressed Barney's hat down on the back of his head. The girl screamed and screamed.

Monster quickly laid the M-16 against the log and pulled a Bic lighter from his windbreaker pocket.

Barney had the wrist rocket pulled back, pointed at a sixty-degree angle up toward the sky, the surgical tubing pulled back to the max, the M-80 just behind his ear.

Monster flicked the lighter, holding the flame to the fuse.

The fuse sparked. Barney let go and the M-80 whizzed high up into the deep azure of the sky.

Almost in one motion, Monster handed Barney another M-80, and Barney drew it back as Monster lit it, and Barney released it. Four M-80s in the air before the first one exploded, a large bang, louder than most hunting rifles. *Bang! Bang! Bang!* Two of the explosions were airbursts, showering bits of rock on the road and on the girl. The other two hit and exploded in the meadow.

"See if you can hit the van," Monster said. "Get him out from behind it."

"Fire in the hole," Barney said, and the M-80 arched out and down, bouncing off the grill, exploding in the dirt. The girl just stood and screamed, holding her hands over her ears, breasts pushed out between her elbows.

"Nothing like a little trauma," Monster said. "Try again."

"Fire in the hole," Barney repeated, and the M-80 arched out and down, exploding with a sharp *blaang* against the metal roof. It made him think of sitting on top of that bunker, watching the NVA rocket the shit out of the ships on the river. The fat, muddy river.

"Nice shot."

"Thank you."

The big man abruptly ran out from behind the van. He yelled at Harold and grabbed the girl by the wrist, tearing her hand away from her ear, and pulled her after him as he ran toward the house. Harold looked up and then jumped to his feet, sprinting after the other two.

"Quick," Barney said, and they began lobbing the remaining five M-80s after the running figures. The girl tripped and fell, and the big man left her behind. Harold ran past her, holding on to Barney's hat. She scrambled up and, limping, followed them, the M-80s exploding harmlessly thirty yards behind.

Monster and Barney sat for a moment, watching the fleeing figures, the woman limping frantically behind the other two.

Monster stood, slinging the M-16 over his shoulder. He picked up the folded canvas tarp.

Barney picked up the green pack and put the white box of M-80s and the wrist rocket back into it. He zipped the pack shut.

They stood for a moment, looking down at the brown custom van and the crumpled gate. Looking at the bodies hanging upside down from the wire, and Monster felt a familiar ache that, for a moment, faded the bright, clear sunshine, made everything pastel.

Wordlessly, they filed into the trees and headed for the truck.

Driving past the LaFray Creek Rest Area, they were still silent, each lost in his own thoughts.

"What do you want to do now?" Monster asked, as they pulled off the Interstate and headed into the city. He felt a deep tiredness, wishing none of it had ever happened—Vietnam, the dead men on the fence, none of it. Wanting it to just go away and leave him alone, let him be the way he was when he was a kid sitting in the morning sunshine.

"Drop me off at my place and go home and get some sleep," Barney said. "Home is the last place they'll expect us to be. Give them time to figure it out. A day or so. Then we'll just wait and watch."

"What if they report it?"

"They won't. But I'll call John; he'll let us know if anything weird happens."

"If anything weird happens," Monster repeated. He laughed tiredly.

When he let Barney out, Barney said, "Get some sleep. Feed your cat. Don't forget to burn your clothes and the tarp."

Monster nodded. "Later," he said.

"Later," Barney replied.

CHAPTER 20

Kids

Quarter to two in the afternoon, and Monster was aimlessly driving his battered truck around the city. After he'd dropped Barney off, he'd driven home, showered, and collapsed face down on the mattress, unmindful even of Fu Manchu kneading the skin between his shoulderblades. He hadn't slept long—six hours, maybe—but it had been an exhausted sleep, and he'd awakened slowly, feeling bruised from the inside out, skin tight and dry, smells still in his nostrils. He'd dreamed of a bloody corpse lying on a helicopter floor—not the black, but a buddy he'd gone through survival school with, who kept sitting up like a grotesque jack-in-the-box and winking, sitting up and winking, sitting up and winking. He'd staggered stiffly to the shower again, shaved in the hot, steaming stall. Made a breakfast of scrambled eggs and elk steak, and shared it with the cat. Fu in a chair at the table across from him, eating raw elk off a plate. Just like a people. Then he'd burned the clothes and tarp, running shoes, and rubber gloves, surprised at the amount of dried blood spattered on his shoes and pants, the sleeves of the windbreaker.

He turned the truck onto a street that led into the Rattlesnake Valley.

The buddy in his dream he hadn't seen since they were at survival school. They'd lived off rattlesnakes. Killed them with rocks. Gutted and peeled the flaccid bodies with a pocket knife. They weren't supposed to have the pocket knife. Slivers of raw rattlesnake. Not bad, especially when you were as hungry as they'd been. Hot. Dirty. Tired. Sitting in the dust. Laughing until tears made muddy rivulets through the grime on their cheeks. Throwing a fat five-and-a-half-foot headless rattlesnake at each other, blood spattering all over their faces and dusty fatigues.

He smiled at the memory.

Survival school had been just before Vietnam. They'd been proud and arrogant, like the elk.

He drove farther up into the Rattlesnake, looking at all the new, expensive, energy-efficient houses erected on slopes formerly occupied by elk. Houses for the most part owned by affluent migrants from the big cities. Each winter the pollution from wood burning got worse and worse, and when people were asked to cut back, use alternate sources of heat, it was the poorer people, the people who could least afford to, who complied most readily. The wealthy ignored air alerts, smug in the knowledge that winds would nearly every night blow out of the Rattlesnake, flush the smog down into the larger valley, dump it on the riffraff.

He laughed to himself.

People were just fucking hopeless. If they were rich and they'd do shit like that, imagine what they would be capable of if times got really rough. The richer, the better educated, the more they were capable of whatever rationalization it took.

Hell, world. Vietnam was nothing.

He drove back out of the Rattlesnake, but turned onto the Interstate before he reached the city.

Maybe they'd done enough already, he and Barney. Who really cared if the lieutenant was on the take? Who cared if the lieutenant had been at least partly responsible for almost getting them killed? Who cared about anything?

He laughed out loud at his silliness, his ability to feel sorry for himself. As if the world gave a shit. Fuck, oh, dear. Who cared that he'd blown the redhead into pieces of pink pottery?

A few minutes later he turned off the Interstate onto Highway 93, barely aware of what he was doing, no longer really thinking or noticing, just letting the battered pickup rattle and bounce down the highway, through a small town, off onto a gravel road, rocks pinging against the underside and fenders, off the gravel onto a rutted and potholed dirt road, third from the highway, no mailbox—"Call before you come," she'd said, her voice thick with sleep—and saw ahead the road curve between deep green alfalfa fields into cottonwoods and elms clustered around an old white farmhouse, and beyond the trees, to a red barn and sheds with sagging roofs.

The truck rumbled to a stop next to a low wire and wood fence surrounding the house. The lawn was mowed and trimmed, fence painted. In front of the truck, a flock of chickens pecked at the driveway; a tabby cat in their midst was looking at him. The cat turned and strolled through the chickens, headed toward the alfalfa field.

Wonder if anyone is home, he thought, and a huge collie ran around the corner of the house, ears alert, tail in the air, pushed through the gate, and trotted around the front of the truck. It looked up at him, head cocked to the side.

"Hi, there."

The collie cocked its head farther.

"Kiss my ass."

The collie barked and wagged its tail.

Ben laughed and opened the door and climbed out. The collie sniffed at his boots and pants, rubbed and shoved against him.

"Hell of a watchdog you are." He reached down and scratched the collie's back. He heard the screen door slap shut, footsteps on the cement walkway.

"Can I help you?" Evy asked.

He straightened and turned toward her. She was wearing faded blue jeans, gray sweat shirt, running shoes, torn and paint-splotched. Her hair was tied behind her head, emphasizing her cheekbones, the Indian in her.

"Ben! What are you doing here?"

He shrugged, grinning uncontrollably. "Just wandering around." The collie shoved its cold nose against his hand. "Thought I'd drop in and say hello."

"Mac! Come here."

"He's okay." But the dog trotted over to her, wagging its tail. It barked.

"Shush! Sit down."

"Nice-looking dog," he said. "Looks like Lassie—I guess

everybody probably says that . . ." Had he really talked and laughed and made love to her? Only a few days ago. His smile faded. It seemed like miles.

"I didn't expect to see you," she said.

"Just driving around, thought I'd drop in, is all." She didn't have any makeup on, and the old clothes made her look sort of rangy, and she had a few miles on her, he could see that, but he could also see she'd always be a handsome woman, the whites of her eyes so healthy they had a bluish tinge to them, Indian eyes, dark irises; the tiny wrinkles at the corners would be crow's-feet someday.

"Go play," she said to the dog, and pointed toward the barn. "Go on. Go play."

The dog turned and ambled, head down, over to a tree and lay down heavily. It sighed and put its head on its paws and stared at them.

"A real character," Ben said. He could smell horses and cattle, the fields.

"Oh, don't get him wrong. He just thinks you're all right is all." She frowned. "You look tired."

"It's been sort of tough going the last few days." He looked over at the dog.

"Anything I'd want to know about?"

He shook his head. "Nothing you'd want to know about."

"More war stories?"

"More war stories." He laughed, but it was an awkward sound.

"Then I won't ask."

He nodded, and they were both silent.

She folded her arms across her chest. "So to what do I owe the honor of this visit?"

He grinned at her. "Just driving around."

"Look, Ben . . ." She considered him for a moment. "The other night was a combination of a lot of things, and not something I'm in the habit of doing, especially with someone I've just met. I'm divorced, got a little boy to raise, this farm—such as it is—and a part-time job three days a week, and to tell you the truth, even though I enjoyed the other night, I've had my fill of men who insist on their freedom and independence except when they want to come by and lay their problems on my doorstep . . . or their head on my breast.''

He stared blankly at her for a moment. What was she talking about? Freedom? He looked down at the dust of the driveway. His freedom had been shared with a buddy and a rattlesnake, with eyes that looked at everything, looked at nothing, with bodies stretched in an inseparable jumble of pieces from the belly of a helicopter to upside down on a fence in Montana. So many they didn't seem real.

He smiled at her. ''I didn't come here to lay my troubles on you or to jump into your bed. I don't know why I came here; I just sort of found myself here.''

''Something bad happened, didn't it?''

''Something bad is always happening.'' But it wasn't that. It was a question of which life he wanted to live: the dark side, sour-sweet moments of adrenaline, or that other side, the more painful side.

''Think I'll ever get over it?'' he asked.

She considered him for a moment. ''Maybe. Some men do, I suppose. Although I've never met one.'' She paused. ''But to most men the question doesn't seem to be whether or not you'll get over it—whatever *it* is—but what you've done for yourself, what you've accomplished.''

He looked at the dog and patted his leg. The collie got up and trotted over to him.

''Not a hell of a lot,'' he said. He scratched inside its ear. The dog made groaning sounds, pressed its head harder against his hand. ''But I've come this far; I'll see it through.''

''And after you see it through, what are you going to do then? What's it going to get you?''

''Hell,'' he said, surprised she didn't know. ''I'm going to get exactly what everyone else gets.''

Thirty minutes later, rattling back toward the highway, he passed a serious-looking little boy walking along the gravel road, jeans, red T-shirt, and small blue day pack. The boy had Evy's cheekbones and coloring, already lanky.

''I'm sorry I can't invite you in,'' she'd said, after they'd strolled around the barn and sheds—''My father left me this, not my ex''—and looked at her horses, a brown mare with palomino foal; her ''herd'' of cattle, three fat and healthy-looking black Angus that wanted to chase the collie; her herd of chickens, a name for each one; and her duck, a handsome mallard she called Clark Duck. "But I can't invite you in until Jason meets you." She'd smiled, obviously thinking of her son. "He's impossible most of the time, but it's his house, too. Maybe I'll introduce you someday," and he knew, looking at her eyes, that even saying that wasn't easy for her.

He slammed the brakes on, skidding the truck to a stop, ground the gearshift into reverse, and backed up to the boy.

"Hi, there."

The boy watched him warily.

"Nice day, huh?"

The boy nodded.

"Too nice to be in school, I'll bet."

The boy nodded.

"You ought to be fishing or riding horses or something."

The boy smiled. His smile was exactly like hers.

Monster put the truck in gear. "So go fishing, Jason," he said, not aware of the sudden harshness in his voice or of the tears in his eyes.

"Tell that mother of yours I said to let you enjoy it while you can."

The boy frowned, and Monster drove off, watching in the side mirror the tiny figure with the day pack standing in the dust, staring puzzled after the dented old truck. A kid filled with dusty road and sunshine and thoughts of fishing and horses. Monster was only dimly aware of the tears running down his cheeks.

Kids, he thought. That's all I'd need.

Monster knocked on Barney's screen door, banging the aluminum door against the frame. The house was dark and silent.

"Barn. It's me," he shouted. "Open up."

He felt the vibration of footsteps inside.

"It's me," he said to the door.

Barney opened the door. It was dark behind him, but Monster could see Barney was dressed only in jeans; his arm hung straight down, a revolver in his hand, barrel pointed toward the floor.

"What's wrong?" Barney said.

Monster laughed. "Well . . . things being as boring as they've been . . ."

"C'mon in." Barney walked back into the dark house.

He switched a lamp on and put the revolver, a four-inch Smith and Wesson .357, down next to the lamp. "Why aren't you home sleeping?"

Monster walked over to a reclining chair and sat down, sinking into the imitation leather.

Barney shook his head and went into the kitchen.

"Want a Pepsi?" he called.

"Okay."

He walked back into the living room. "Here," he said. "To the Pepsi generation." He sat down in one of the beige overstuffed chairs.

"What happened to all your plants? Looks kind of bare in here without them."

"I guess the ex-old lady came and got them while we were gone."

"I thought she was getting the house and everything. Why bother to take the plants?"

Barney shrugged. "Who knows what women'll do?"

"I thought I'd crap out on your couch," Monster said.

"Help yourself. As long as you're here, though, we might as well figure out what we're going to do next."

"We could go capture the lieutenant."

Barney looked up at the ceiling. "Might be a little soon for that."

"You figure Bruce's involved?"

"Nah. Not smart enough. I figure Lucky and Ears couldn't figure out who we were because we'd cleaned up our act, so the lieutenant sent Bruce up there to find us." He took a drink of Pepsi. "Bruce probably called the lieutenant and told him he'd found us, and then the lieutenant called Lucky and Ears and told them."

Monster put the can of Pepsi down next to the chair; the light reflected off its red, white, and blue surface. "So what do you want to do?"

Barney patted his bare stomach. "I think I'm losing weight," he said. "I couldn't even wear these old pants a few weeks ago."

Monster smiled. Barney *was* losing weight. Trimming up. No fucking wonder.

"We ought to talk to Debbie and Harold before we talk to the lieutenant," Barney said. "Those two idiots are going to rabbit. And since neither of them has a car, as far as I know, they'll have to take a bus or an airplane."

"Or hitchhike."

"They've got too much money to do that. And they'll be afraid it might be us picking them up."

Monster rubbed the side of his face. "Means surveillance," he said.

Barney stood and picked up Monster's empty can. "You looked tired," he said. "Why don't you catch a little shuteye? I'll get dressed and drive out east of town and wait for them to come in."

"You sure?" Monster adjusted the chair to recline and folded his hands over his chest and closed his eyes. "I can ride along. Catch some z's in the truck."

"No, that's okay. This way we'll have two vehicles. Just don't leave until I call."

A few minutes later Barney walked back into the living room. Monster was already snoring, mouth open, head tilted back against the head rest.

Barney silently opened the door, careful not to let the screen door bang shut. He looked back through the window at Monster sleeping, and kicked the screen door hard with the side of his foot, making a loud crash that brought Monster up out of the chair.

Barney laughed. "Turn the light out," he shouted, and turned and walked down the steps.

CHAPTER 21

I'd Rather It Was You

Meet me at the print shop next to the bus station," Barney said.

"Okay." Monster hung up the phone, rubbed the side of his face, and stretched. He pulled open the drapes and looked up at the wedge of blue above the roof of the house next door. He grimaced. Another perfect day.

The bus station was amazingly inconspicuous: a covered passageway between buildings, wide enough to accommodate two buses side by side. Buses entered through a parking lot behind the buildings and exited onto the street in front. There was a print shop on one side of the passageway, a repair shop on the other side. The actual station—two cramped and grimy rooms that opened onto the passageway—was in the rear behind the print shop. Sometimes Monster would drive past and see people standing in front of the print shop, small groups of blacks and Chicanos—Job Corps people—and tired-looking men in out-of-fashion slacks and sport coats, women in rumpled dresses and lank hair, and he'd wonder why all the strange people were standing around the middle of the block.

The block was deserted now, no one on the sidewalk except him. Mountains were framed by the bank buildings on either side of the street a block away—Hellgate Canyon, where the

Indians used to ambush one another. Heat reflected off buildings and cars.

Sometime between his childhood and when he'd returned from Asia, the city had become ugly, grimy, and polluted just like the really big cities—no wonder the people getting off the buses looked confused. They thought they'd be in Big Sky country—mountains and lakes, cowboys and Indians—but it looked like downtown anywhere. Less than fifty thousand people in the city, but you'd swear—if you didn't look at the mountains—that it was a little bit of L.A., pollution, traffic problems, and all.

Barney came out of the print shop, putting his sunglasses on. He was dressed in jeans and tennis shoes, a green T-shirt hanging loose over his belt.

"Nice day, y'all," Monster said.

"Think so, huh?"

"Yup."

"Well, I'm glad it has your approval."

"Your gun is showing." Monster nodded at Barney's T-shirt.

Barney shrugged. "He drove the van in. It's parked out back in the parking lot."

"Farm out. Who's he?"

"Harold."

"Ah, ha! Is he still wearing your hat?"

Barney smiled. "Even he's not *that* dumb."

Monster looked into the shaded passageway. The passageway smelled of diesel and tired bodies.

"C'mon," Barney said, "y'all," and turned and led the way into the passageway. "He won't even recognize us."

The waiting room was lined with black-cushioned chrome chairs that looked like rejects from a doctor's office. The walls were painted institutional light green, black and white linoleum squares on the floor, Coke machine and coin lockers along the wall.

"Excuse me, sir," Barney said politely.

Harold looked up from a battered magazine. He was dressed in jeans and hiking boots and brown T-shirt. Matted black hair on his muscular arms accentuated the darkness of his tan. A dirty blue canvas bag with carrying strap lay on the floor between his feet.

"You probably don't remember us," Barney said, as if he

225

was apologizing for something. "I'm Barney and this here's my partner, Ben, and we're narcs"—Harold's eyes widened—"and . . . uh, well, if y'all do anything unreasonable . . ." Harold's face paled, panic beginning to leak into his eyes. Monster grinned hugely down at him. Barney frowned thoughtfully. "Well, what I mean to say is . . . if you even breathe too hard, we are going to *shoot you right in the fucking head!*"

Harold looked wildly around. They were the only people in the waiting room; the ticket agent was out of sight in the storage room.

Barney pulled the four-inch .357 from the pancake holster underneath his T-shirt and pointed it between Harold's eyes.

Harold stopped breathing. "Ah . . . ah . . ." he said.

Barney cocked the hammer back, the click abnormally loud in the empty room. Monster could see white all the way around Harold's pupils.

"I'm going to count to three and pull the trigger," Barney said, his voice again calm and reasonable.

Harold's mouth opened and closed silently.

"One." He pushed the barrel up against Harold's forehead; Harold's eyes crossed watching it, his face shiny beneath the fluorescent lights.

"Two."

"Going to be messy," Monster warned.

"Don't . . ." Harold said, a tiny sound they could barely hear.

"Three," Barney said, and pushed the barrel harder against Harold's forehead. "Say, good-bye, scumbag." He pulled the trigger. The clunk of hammer on empty chamber reverberated through the small, grimy room.

Harold squeaked.

Barney laughed and replaced the revolver in the holster underneath his shirt.

Harold collapsed back into the chair, sweat running down his forehead and cheeks into his tangled beard.

"Isn't it just amazing?" Barney said, shaking his head. "Just amazing how fast the human body sweats. I swear, twenty seconds, and look at this."

Harold raised a hand to the little round indentation on his forehead. He looked from one man to the other.

"Well, don't just sit there, say something," Barney said.

"I—"

"That's enough," Barney interrupted. "Let's go."

The brown and gold van was parked in a far corner of the lot. Monster opened the rear doors, swinging them wide. The carpet had been ripped out, the interior cleaned and scrubbed, obviously hosed out; a few wet spots were still visible between some of the metal side supports and the floor. He turned toward Harold. "Have a seat," he said, patting the edge of the floor above the bumper, the exact spot where Ears's shotgun had fallen. He saw the black, ugly barrel, the streak of flame ripping past.

Harold glanced nervously from side to side. A few people walked to and from cars in the parking lot. He licked his lips, and they saw his leg tense.

Monster grabbed the front of Harold's T-shirt. "Are you going to try to rabbit on us, you fuck?" He pushed him away. "Go ahead." He pushed him again, and Harold stumbled. "Run." Monster shoved him again. "Come on, scumbag. Run."

Harold crouched, the skin across his cheekbones tight and shiny, eyes stark against black, greasy hair and tangled beard. He held his hands up and out from his body in an obviously practiced martial arts stance. "Leave me alone," he whined. "I didn't do anything. It wasn't my idea."

"What is *this?*" Monster said in amazement. He looked back at Barney. "Can you believe this guy?"

Barney laughed. "Harold, come over here and sit down. You look silly."

Monster jumped at Harold. "Booga-booga."

Harold flinched and jumped sideways.

"Look, Harold," Monster said reasonably, as if about to do Harold a favor. He winked at Barney. "I see somebody cleaned up this van—maybe it was you. Was it you, Harold?"

Harold looked at him; he looked ready to cry. He nodded.

Monster lifted his polo shirt so Harold could see the butt of the 9mm above his belt. "Well, Harold, you scumbag, we don't know no ka-ra-te or kung fu, but we know something better."

Barney rolled his eyes upward.

"Gun-doh, Harold, gun-doh. And you probably noticed we're pretty good at it." He paused. "You did notice, didn't you, Harold? All that blood and guts and stuff."

"What do you guys *want?* Why are you doing this? What do you want from *me?*"

Monster looked up, as if seriously considering Harold's questions, gazing past the top of the van and the buildings across the street, at the wooded mountains a few miles away etched against the blue sky.

"You guys are *animals!*" Harold's voice quivered with emotion—with that special emotion they'd been hearing since Vietnam—the emotion of someone trying to understand *how they got that way.*

Monster dropped his gaze to Harold.

"Tell us about it, Harold," he said, his voice flat and emotionless.

Harold's eyes twitched back and forth, looking between the two men. He swallowed and licked his lips. "About what?"

Barney folded his arms across his chest.

Monster could feel the afternoon sun hot on his back, smell the asphalt parking lot. Here and there, people walked across the lot, threading their way among parked cars, getting in and out of cars. Three kids in jeans and cutoffs, no shirts. Two women in sandals and shorts and sunglasses, their legs white and flabby, little rolls at the backs of their thighs. A middle-aged balding man in a rumpled suit, sweat stains under his arms.

"I don't know anything," Harold whined. "He didn't tell me anything." He ran a hand through his greasy hair and looked down at the pavement, shaking his head.

Barney glanced at Monster.

"What did you do with the bodies?" Monster asked.

"He made me—"

"Who made you?"

"Martin . . . the big guy. You know." He looked from one to the other, his eyes pleading.

"Made you do what?"

"Made me take the backhoe—"

"What backhoe?"

"He's—Martin's got an old backhoe he keeps in the barn."

"And?"

Harold looked down, shivering despite the hot, bright sunlight. "He made me dig a hole with it . . . out in the field behind the house, way up against the trees. He made me help him throw the bodies in. . . . Oh, God. Why did you guys do that? I've never seen—"

"How'd you know it was us?" Barney asked.

Harold's eyes were red and pathetic. "Martin said it was you. He said he put a contract out on you with those three guys."

"How'd he know them?" Monster asked.

"I don't know." Harold looked at Barney. "I didn't mean anything. He made me come along that night." He looked toward the bus station. "I just want to get out of here—"

"How'd you know we were narcs?" Monster asked.

"Somebody told Martin a long time ago, way before we saw you up by Kalispell—"

"Who?"

Harold swallowed; they could see his Adam's apple move just below his beard. "I don't know. Honest to God, I don't. Somebody in the sheriff's department, but I just heard Martin talking on the phone to him once."

Monster looked questioningly at Barney.

Harold's eyes darted back and forth. "That's the truth. I know it's important to you. That's the truth."

"Why'd he put the contract out?" Monster asked.

"I don't know. He didn't say." He brightened. "But I know a big shipment is coming in any day. Maybe it—"

"Shipment of what?"

"Cocaine, I guess. We—he only deals coke."

"When?"

Harold looked down and shook his head.

"You don't fucking know very much, do you?" Monster snarled.

Harold's head jerked up.

"On a fence just like those other two." Barney smiled. "Martin can put you in that hole you dug, alongside the other three. How's that sound?"

Harold stared at him, his mouth open.

Two buses turned into the far end of the parking lot, big, ungainly blue and white and gray buses, their windows reflecting sunlight. They waddled through the lot, roaring in low gear, the diesel smell nauseating, and into the passageway, one behind the other. "How'd Martin know Lucky and Ears and the redhead?" Monster asked.

"He—he met them in Seattle. They weren't supposed to do it."

"Do what?" They could hear the sudden commotion of people inside the passageway, metal cargo doors opening, people talking. The buses idled, tendrils of diesel fumes gathering at the end of the passageway.

Harold looked toward the bus station. "That's my bus."

"Do what? What weren't they supposed to do?"

"They aren't—weren't supposed to take contracts on their own."

"What the hell do you mean by that?"

"They worked for somebody; they weren't supposed to do private business."

Barney and Monster looked at each other.

"That's all I know. Honest to God!"

"Shit," Monster said, and turned and walked a few steps away. "I just fucking knew it."

Barney turned to Harold. "Who's the cop?"

Harold shook his head. "I don't know. I really don't know—"

"I don't know. I don't know," Barney mimicked.

"I don't know! I swear to God I don't know! You've got to believe me!"

"We don't *got* to do anything."

"Does Debbie know?" Monster asked.

"I don't know!" He paused. "Yeah. Maybe! I think so. He talks to her a lot." His eyes were watery. "I don't know them very well. I just met them a few months ago when—"

"What's she going to do?"

"She's leaving. She was screaming and crying half the night. . . . He gave her some Valium or something. They had a big fight this morning, and he said he'd drive her to the airport today."

"When? What time?"

"Six . . . or three, I'm not sure. He made me drive the van in. He told me to leave it here."

Monster looked at Barney.

"Where's my hat?" Barney asked.

Harold winced. "In my bag," he said in a low voice.

"Where are you going? Which way? East or west?"

"Seattle. I'm going to Seattle."

"You buy your ticket yet?"

"No, I was—"

"Where's your money? I'll buy it for you."

"In my bag. I—"

"Back in a minute," Barney said to Monster.

Harold watched him walk away. "What's he going to do?"

Monster stared at Harold. Fucking hair monster, he thought. Educated. Probably from a family with money. A fucking spineless ex-hippie flower child, peace and love, and now just doing whatever it took—small-time dealing, ripping off the people he used to profess peace and love with, ripping them off for a few bucks, cheating them on o.z.'s of pot, hundred lots of speed, whatever. A used-car dealer of the counterculture, that's all he was now. Playing games.

"Harold," he said, "believe me, I'd rather it was you in that hole. So just fucking shut up until Barney gets back." He looked up at the mountains, longed to be up on top of one of the ridges, shirt off, feeling the hot sun and breeze, smelling pine and grass. Maybe seeing a bear, like he'd seen once, beating feet across a clearing at the top of a ridge along the edge of an old clear-cut. A big blond bear, healthy and happy, running along for no reason at all, straight at him standing motionless in the trees. When he'd cocked the .357, the bear had stopped abruptly, comically, back legs skidding through the front feet, sniffing the air, trying with nearsighted eyes to see him, smell him. Wondering at the alien sound, the tiny click as the hammer came back.

"Fuck you," said Monster. "Just fuck you."

Barney laughed, as they stood in front of the print shop, watching the bus pull out.

"What're you laughing at?"

"He thinks he's going to Seattle."

"So?"

"So we put him on the bus to Chicago."

They watched the bus cross the intersection and pass between the two bank buildings, headed east through Hellgate Canyon.

"We ought to get an Oscar for that performance," Barney said. "Isn't it amazing the shit you can get by with?"

"Yeah. Amazing. But I don't know how much we're getting by with."

Barney smiled. "If we could only get rid of all the other assholes around here that easily."

"There wouldn't be anyone left," Monster replied. "Not even us."

CHAPTER 22

A Little Present for You

Well, at least you got your hat back."

"It'll never be the same."

Monster smiled and glanced out the window of the patrol car. You can say that again, he thought. He held the steering wheel loosely with one hand. The air conditioner was on maximum, muting the crackle and garble of the radio. Outside, under a deep blue sky, fields of grain and straw and stubble stretched in a patchwork of gold toward the blue mountains. Commercial industries—construction and trucking companies and smaller, related industries—encroached on the fields.

He felt uncomfortable in the uniform: brown shirt, gray pants, and ridiculous clip-on tie, heavy leather belt equipped with handcuff case, nightstick holder, belt keepers, ammo pouches, holster. Both of them carried .357 magnums— Barney the Smith and Wesson, Monster a Colt Python.

"Been a long time since we were on patrol, hasn't it?" Monster said. "I sort of miss it. Working patrol is kind of like this car: black and white. Not like working narcs."

Barney stared out the window.

"What are you thinking about?"

Barney turned toward him, adjusting the aviator sunglasses

on the bridge of his nose. "I hope he was wrong about those guys working for somebody."

"Yeah, I hear that." Monster turned the air conditioner down. "But I had a feeling about that."

Up ahead they could see the control tower, the hangars and rows of commuter aircraft; the main building was new, made of brick and glass and shingle. It looked from a distance like a gigantic drive-up hamburger stand. A pickup was pulling out of the airport access road onto the two-lane highway.

"Is that who I think it is?" Barney asked.

"Sure looks like it."

The pickup approached, a fancy Dodge PowerWagon, Martin's bulk behind the steering wheel.

"Sure enough." Monster grinned.

The two vehicles met and passed each other, Martin obviously not paying much attention to them—just two deputies in a black-and-white, sunglasses and uniforms—the pickup's exhaust a quick rumble as they passed, reminding Monster of sitting in the dust and gravel of the LaFray Creek Rest Area, listening to that same rumble fade down the river.

"Want to pull him over?"

"No. I don't think so. He didn't recognize us. Probably just dropped her off."

Monster was silent.

"He won't scare easily," Barney said.

Monster glanced over at him. "We could always shoot him, too," he said sarcastically. He signaled for the turn.

Barney smiled. "I wouldn't mind," he said. "But we don't have to. When you're in the middle like he is, you really don't have much say about what happens; you just have to go with it."

"I guess we can just park anywhere," Monster said as they cruised into the airport, past the departure and arrival building. He parked the patrol car in the shade of the building, next to a sign that said No Parking Any Time. Tow Away Zone.

"I sure feel conspicuous in this uniform," he said.

They climbed out of the vehicle, automatically locking and slamming the doors shut. Inside, the radio crackled. With both hands, Monster hitched up his belt and holster and joined

Barney on the sidewalk. It was hot, but the heat was dry and comfortable, the sky a perfect blue above the control tower.

"I'm glad I'm quitting," Monster said as they walked toward the doorway. "I sure see how this could get to be a habit. How it could be abused."

"Could be abused!"

The electric doors opened. Inside, the ceilings were high, the counters dwarfed by the space from floor to ceiling. The floor was tile; the ceiling wood planks. Chairs, orange and plastic, were arrayed in small groups, like platoons on line. There was a lot of space, but most of it was unused—expanses of tile under a wood ceiling almost three stories high.

They stood for a moment just inside the door, putting sunglasses into shirt pockets.

"I always feel disoriented when I first come in here," Barney said, looking up at the ceiling. "The ceiling looks like a boat dock or something. Makes me feel upside down."

Clusters of people—ranchers in boots and hats and Levi's slacks, salesmen in summer suits, fun hogs with backpacks, dressed in shorts and hiking boots and T-shirts—stood at the counters, baggage to one side. People waiting for incoming passengers wandered up and down the long expanse of tile or sat, scattered, in the plastic chairs.

"She's down at the other end," Monster said. "Looking at photos on the wall. Sundress and sandals."

"I see her." They walked toward her, conscious of the attention their uniforms attracted, always attracted. Until you got used to it, Monster thought, the attention felt weird, a composite of hostility and interest and fear. The uniforms and guns were supposed to intimidate, but it felt uncomfortable to intimidate people without meaning to. Some cops got off on it. For some, it was the only reason they were cops. Sometimes, though, the intimidation helped.

"Let me do the talking," he said.

"Be my guest."

She was dressed in a thin cotton sundress, black and white stripes with red flowers, medium-heeled sandals, nylons. Long brown hair healthy and clean. Tanned back toward them. She was looking at pictures of houses and ranches for sale.

GRAVEYARD RULES

Barney halted a yard behind Monster, to one side, so she'd see him also when she turned around.

"Hello, Debbie," Monster said softly, gently running a fingernail down her exposed backbone.

She sucked in a breath, her shoulders rising with the intake of air, and whirled around, large brown eyes wide and frightened, and then confused by the uniform and the lack of hair and beard.

"Your favorite 'chauvinist fuckers.' " He smiled. "Remember?"

She was wearing makeup, lipstick and eye shadow. She was even wearing a bra. Just goes to show you, he thought. He had a vague memory of lips warm and soft, and of lying on the ground just inside the trees fifty yards or so behind the bar where Barney and he had first met them. Then she'd been wearing khaki pants, boots, and sweater. No bra.

"You're looking very middle-class today," he said.

"You!" she said, her voice filled with loathing. She glanced past his shoulder at Barney. "Both of you." The loathing had turned to fear.

"Ma'am." Barney nodded to her.

"We just saw you standing here," Monster said, one part of his mind thinking, I don't want to do this. "And I said to Barney, maybe she needs a ride somewhere. I mean, what are friends for, anyway?"

He could see she was having trouble accepting who they were, the two clean and well-groomed sheriff's deputies at odds with her image of a frayed and weird and half-hippie, half-biker Cookie Monster. He watched her pupils shrink to dots.

"What . . ." She cleared her throat. "What do you want?" There was a tremor in her voice.

Fucking cunt, he thought. Playing urban guerrilla with an M-16. Fun and games until—Surprise! Bullets actually kill people. Running back to Mommy and Daddy, probably. A new story to tell at parties: the world is a real jungle; I know, I've been there. Well, not this time, bitch. This time you won't even want to *think* about the story, let alone tell it to a bunch of jerk-offs making absurd conversation.

236

She crossed her arms across her breasts, hands clasping her shoulders, and her body seemed to shrink. A little girl. A pretty girl, another brown-eyed doe, trapped by his eyes and smile.

"What are you going to do to me?" she said, tears gathering in the corners of her eyes.

"Think about that van," Monster said softly. "Think about what was in it." His smile was cruel. "Think about what was on the fence." His eyes glittered.

Her mouth quivered.

"Think about you fucking around with that M-sixteen," he said, allowing his voice to rise a little.

Her face abruptly turned ugly—a little girl about to cry, a rictus of creased skin pulling away from gums and teeth, squinting eyes.

Barney quickly stepped up next to her and, grasping her elbow, pivoted her toward the real-estate pictures so that anyone walking past would not be able to see how upset she was. "Now, don't get upset, ma'am. We just want to talk to you."

"About what?" she cried, her shoulders shaking. "Haven't you done enough to me already?"

Barney's eyes narrowed, and he flushed slightly, the skin tightening at his temples. He bent his head closer to hers. "Look, bitch," he said, his voice low and intense, "don't start any of your poor-little-girl bullshit with us or we're going to throw the cuffs on you and drag you bodily out to the patrol car." His hand tightened on her elbow, fingers digging into her skin. "Do you understand?"

Her eyes were wide, mouth slack and slightly open. Tears ran down her cheeks.

Monster frowned.

Barney let go of her arm. "You will answer our questions," he instructed, giving equal emphasis to each word. "You will not bullshit us. If you do we will know it and then we will take you somewhere and do bad things to you until you tell us what we want to know. *Do you understand?*"

She looked at him.

"Do you understand?"

She swallowed and nodded, her eyes never leaving his.

237

"Good. Now follow this officer over to that corner over there, where we can talk undisturbed."

The three of them sat in the corner, the two officers clean-cut, athletic-looking—the way cops should look—the girl pretty, obviously the girlfriend of one of them, distraught at having to leave. The two officers smiled at people wandering by. They avoided prolonged eye contact.

Behind them, outside the narrow windows, small planes took off and landed, the buzz of engines and propellers barely heard. The room was filled with summer light.

"How'd you like those bodies?" Monster said conversationally, not liking himself much for asking. "Pretty neat stuff, huh?"

She shuddered, staring down at her hands folded in her lap. "Please," she said in a small voice. "Please don't talk about it."

Monster reached over and patted her hands. "Not to worry," he said. "Not to worry. Tell us about the lieutenant."

She was silent for a moment. "He's always trying to make me," she said.

Barney laughed. "That's our lieutenant, all right."

Her gaze ran across his face—a little girl trying to understand something. She looked down at her hands again.

"C'mon," he prompted. "You know what we want."

Voice distracted, she answered, "Martin pays him for information."

"For what?"

"For selling dope. What else?"

"Why'd they put the hit on us?"

"That was Martin." She stared at the brick wall behind him. "I don't know why. He just came home one night—the night after . . . after we did that to you up the Blackfoot—and said he'd called some friends. He said he put a contract out on you."

"Why?"

She shook her head, looked back at her hands. "I don't know. He has another partner somewhere. Maybe he had something to do with it. He was worried about you guys finding out about the deal they've got going."

"Who was worried? Martin?"

"No. His partner."

"The lieutenant?"

"No. No. Someone else. I don't know who."

"What deal?" Monster asked.

"I don't know exactly," she said. "But they put up everything they've got—about three hundred thousand dollars."

"Where'd they make a connection for that much coke?"

"Martin knows some people in Seattle or Vancouver, or somewhere."

Monster and Barney were silent for a moment.

"I just want to go home now," she said tonelessly.

Barney and Monster stood, adjusted their gun belts.

She looked up. "What are you going to do now?"

"We're going to give you a little present, something to remember us by," Barney said. "And then you're going to get on the plane and never come back."

Monster pulled open the flap on his handcuff case. He pulled out a small package wrapped in wrinkled brown paper.

"Here you go," he said, handing it to her. "A going-away present. Don't open it until you get on the plane."

She nodded, frowning up at him, and he almost took the package—the ears—back.

"Okay," she said.

"Let's go," Barney said, and they turned and walked away, leaving her sitting there, a pretty girl in a sundress and sandals, summer light gleaming off her long hair—a pretty girl thinking of bodies hanging from a barbed-wire fence.

"Fuck," Monster said. "That really made me feel rotten. Shit."

"You probably did her a favor. Besides, we don't want her blabbing as soon as she gets out of here."

In the patrol car, Monster removed the small Norelco mini-recorder from his shirt pocket and put it on the seat between them.

"What d'you think?" he said.

"About the partner bit? Too much money, wouldn't you say?"

"Well, that, and Lucky and Ears worked for somebody who might not be too happy with us."

Barney shrugged. "You know what they say: sometimes you eat the bear; sometimes—"

"I know," Monster said, and started the car. "Boy, do I know. But how long before we meet the bear, do you suppose?"

CHAPTER 23

The Bear

Late afternoon, and Barney and Monster sat shirtless in lawn chairs out behind Monster's house shooting with the M-16 Barney had taken from the dead Lucky at beer cans tied with pieces of clothesline cord onto the branches of a big cottonwood. The cottonwood was at the edge of a rocky creek bed that ran along the edge of the back lawn, only a few inches of water trickling among the rocks. The creek curved out of a thickly wooded crease in the pine-covered mountain a few hundred yards behind the cottonwood, through a broken-down and decayed pole fence, into Monster's crude trout pond, out of the pond, across the back of the yard, around the side of the house, under the cattle guard, and down the valley, running parallel to the dirt road. In the spring most of the backyard between the house and the cottonwood was under water; the high, earthen, grass-covered sides of the trout pond well above the high-water mark.

The cans hung motionless in the hot, still air, reminding Barney of pictures he'd seen of partisans hanged by the Nazis in World War II.

He slouched in the chair, holding the M-16 by the pistol grip and thirty-round magazine, cheek halfway down the plastic stock. It was difficult to aim, with his eye that far from

241

the sights. The M-16 fired, the flash-suppressor kicking upward.

"You're never going to hit anything like that." Monster was eating potato chips from a bowl; cans of Pepsi and the green pack containing magazines of ammunition lay on the ground between the chairs. Fu sat in the grass at the other side of his chair, staring inscrutably up at the bowls of chips.

Barney flicked the selector to safe. "Want to bet?"

"Sure."

"Okay. Watch this." He pushed the selector over to auto.

"Hey, don't do that! We'll have to tie the cans up again."

Barney pushed the selector to safe, leaned over, and placed the rifle in the grass next to his chair.

Monster handed Fu a potato chip. The cat instantly snatched the two-inch chip out of his hand, and ran across to the shade of the house, running tail down, as if he had a rodent rather than a potato chip in his mouth.

"Fu the hunter," Monster said.

Catching movement out of the corner of his eye, he turned to look down the dirt road, squinting against the sun. "Somebody's coming." A small white dot, dust billowing behind in sooty contrails, was coming toward them, the vehicle and the dust cloud an intrusion in the green expanse of hay and alfalfa on the other side of Monster's road, the dust cloud stark against the dark blue of the mountains on the other side of the valley.

"Looks like it," Barney said.

They both stood and watched as the vehicle continued past the turnoff that led to the nearest neighbor's.

Fu slowly walked to the corner of the house and looked at the approaching vehicle; his tail twitched.

The vehicle, a white Chevy Citation, clean and new, slowed as it neared the end of the road. The road ended across the cattle guard in Monster's front yard.

"Rent-a-car," Barney said. "Only one person in it. A man." He cradled the M-16 in his arms.

Fu lay down, only his ears and top of his head showing above the grass.

The vehicle turned into the yard, rattled across the cattle guard, and pulled in next to the old International, parking on their side of the pickup.

"You recognize him?" Monster asked.

"Nope." Barney allowed the M-16 to drop barrel down, holding it by the pistol grip and front rest.

Monster heard the snick-snick of the selector going to auto.

A man stepped out of the white Citation: late fifties, early sixties, bald on top, hair close-cut around the ears, face tanned and wrinkled and creased into a smile. Despite the age and creases, he looked fit and healthy, a slight paunch showing above the belt. His gray slacks were twenty years out of style. Brown polished shoes. Black tie unknotted, the ends hanging loose. Sleeves neatly rolled to mid-forearm. A suggestion of old-fashioned tank-top underwear through the white shirt.

About Barney's size, but with the hands and forearms of someone who'd worked hard most of his life, on a farm, maybe.

"Oh-oh," Monster said.

The man put his hands in his pockets. His eyes were like black buttons in his weathered face. "Hello, fellas. How you doing?" He smiled, and Barney pointed the M-16 at his chest.

"Just fine," Monster replied. "How you doing?"

"Just fine." He smiled and walked toward them. "Just fine. Had a nice flight." He halted five yards away, ignoring the M-16 pointed at his chest.

Fu sauntered across the sunburned lawn toward them.

"What can we do for you?" Barney asked.

The almost black eyes regarded Barney. Wrinkles above and at the sides made them reptilian, unblinking in the harsh sunlight. "You must be Barney."

Fu rubbed himself against the old man's leg, purring loudly.

The old man's eyes rotated toward Monster. "Nice cat you got here, Ben," he said, smiling again. He bent down and scratched the base of Fu's tail. "How you doing, Fu Manchu?"

Fu arched and pressed against his leg.

The man straightened and, still ignoring the M-16, looked around at the run-down house and property. "Reminds me of where I grew up," he said.

"And where might that be?" Barney asked.

The smile faded, and the eyes for a moment contemplated Barney. "You want to watch where you point that made-by-Mattel Star Wars Special."

Barney stared at the old man.

The old man chuckled. "I'm not armed." His eyes were brittle.

"What's that got to do with it?" Barney asked.

The old man smiled again. "Everything."

Monster sighed.

Barney glanced over at him.

Monster shrugged. "You can always shoot him later."

Humor bled into the old man's eyes. "You're too smart for that," he said.

Monster laughed. "You have certainly got to be shitting. We're dumber than a box of rocks. You ought to know that. We'd shoot you in a second."

"You're not so dumb that you don't know you're dead men if you do."

"Right," Monster said sarcastically. "Right."

"It occurred to us that we might already be dead," Barney said.

"That contract was a mistake."

"It sure was. But so far not for us."

Monster gestured toward the aluminum lawn chairs. "Might as well sit," he said. "So far the bullshit is only ankle deep."

The old man smiled.

"How 'bout a beer?" Monster said.

"A soda would be nice," the old man replied. "If you've got one."

"Pepsi?"

"That'd be fine."

"You two remind me a lot of the kids I had in my platoon," the old man said. He smiled. "In the Battle of the Bulge—that was in World War Two," he added.

The three of them sat in the shade of the old house. Monster on the worn wooden steps, Barney in a lawn chair to his left, the old man in a lawn chair between them. Fu Manchu lay on the old man's lap, kneading his leg. Barney had the M-16 crossways on top of the aluminum chair arms, pointed toward the old man. It was hot and still; shadows were beginning to lengthen.

The old man scratched Fu's belly and took a drink of Pepsi.

"Not many people can get near him," Monster said.

The old man smiled. "Animals and kids I get along with just fine." He took another drink. "The problems I had with some of them," he said. "It was cold, and some of them would zip their sleeping bags up, no matter what I said or did. Smart kids, too, good fighters, but some of them just didn't give a damn anymore. Done too much, seen too much, I guess. Everyone has a point when they just don't give a damn anymore." He smiled and scratched Fu. "I felt that way once myself, so I know how you feel."

Monster and Barney were silent.

The old man smiled. "So you think me and, uh, my associates want you dead?" He paused, eyeing first one, then the other. "As I said, that contract was a mistake. . . ." Fu looked up at him. "Otherwise, I wouldn't be here; someone else would."

Barney and Monster remained silent.

"What looks like happened is you two got too close to a drug deal and someone made a bad decision." He smiled. "And they employed some of my people to implement that decision."

Fu relaxed back on his leg.

"But my people, you need to understand, are *not* available for such things. Repeat: *not*. The two men you killed were not even available for work in the United States. They were acting, from what I understand, out of boredom." He smiled. "They work primarily in Asia, and things being the way they are these days, they hadn't been used for some time."

He stroked Fu's back, looking with his brittle, hooded eyes from Monster to Barney. "They were good men, you see, but they didn't give much of a damn anymore."

Barney and Monster watched him.

"So you've got nothing to worry about from me on that account."

"There were three men," Monster said.

Fu raised his head, ears alert, tail twitching on the old man's lap. He abruptly stood and jumped down off the old man's leg and walked up the step and lay down next to Monster. He stared balefully at the old man.

"So there were. So there were," the old man said. "The third was my nephew." Barney's hand closed around the pistol grip on the M-16. "The other two were supposed to be keeping him out of trouble."

Barney glanced at Monster. Monster opened his mouth to say something, but thought better of it. "We did the world a favor," Monster finally said, then raised his voice. *"I did the world a favor."*

The old man arched his eyebrows.

"And *I* told him to," Barney said, keeping the rifle pointed at the old man. "And maybe we ought to do the world another favor."

The old man chuckled and shook his head. "You two," he said. "You remind me of myself when I was younger."

"Never like you," Monster said.

The old man's smile faded. *"Just like me,"* he said. "I was young and stupid like you once. I fought for my country. And I'll bet I believed in my war a damn sight more than you believed in yours." He smiled. "You're thinking Mafia or Colombians, because drugs are involved. And you're thinking that maybe you can put up enough of a fight so that whoever it is will simply write off his losses and forget about you. More-trouble-than-you're-worth kind of thing."

"You got it," Monster said.

The old man chuckled, a friendly, grandfatherly chuckle. "The people I represent are most certainly not Mafia. You've been around enough to know that everything is connected—government, business, legal and illegal crime, whatever. That's why my bosses employ people like Ears and Lucky: so they don't have to worry about the Mafia or the Colombians or anyone else." His smiled. "The people I work for would never just write you off as not worth the trouble; they don't do business that way."

He smiled again, and Monster abruptly realized that the reason he smiled so much was because he thought it masked his eyes: the old man's smile was a nervous tic, a mannerism, nothing more.

"Connections," Barney said sarcastically. "Fuck your connections."

The old man gazed thoughtfully at him for a moment. "I find your ideals more than a little hypocritical," he said. "If I'd found you before all this happened and offered you a job doing what Lucky and Ears were doing, and at the salary they were getting. And"—he held up his hand, stilling Monster's reply—"if I'd told you that anyone you killed would, *by your standards,* warrant killing . . ."

He looked from one to the other, his hooded eyes unblinking.

Monster looked past him at the blue mountains across the valley.

"You sound like you're getting ready to offer us a job," Monster said.

The old man laughed. "When that fellow—what's his name? The big one giving you such a bad time of it . . . Mark?"

"Martin," Monster said.

"When Martin told me what had happened and what you two had done . . . well, I reckon I knew right then all I needed to know about you."

"Fuck you," Barney said.

"What about your nephew?" Monster asked.

The old man shrugged, the corners of his mouth turning down in disgust. "I could have killed him myself." He looked at them and didn't smile. "Nevertheless, family is family."

"But . . ." The old man smiled, the skin at the corners of his eyes wrinkling with humor. He looked up at the mountain behind the cottonwood. The top of the mountain was bathed in rosy golden light. "I can handle his old man, who is himself probably very happy to be rid of him. His other kids are nothing like that little redheaded bastard."

Monster and Barney glanced at each other.

"What do you want, then?" Monster asked. "You didn't come all this way to drink Pepsi and play with my cat."

The old man sighed. "This was something Lucky and Ears were involved in on their own—boredom, as I said." He smiled. He looked at Monster, and for an instant Monster was reminded of an old Chinese lady eating peanuts in a bar in Taipei, her eyes like chips of mica.

The old man stood and stretched. "These old bones ain't what they used to be," he said, looking around. "But the trip was worth it; this sure does remind me of the old homestead." He put his hands in his pockets. "What they say they care about, the people I work for," he said, "is legalizing gambling in this state. That's the bottom line. And even though they are *not* the Mafia, if all this shit gets into the public eye, the public will *assume* that the Mafia is involved.'' He looked thoughtfully at the cottonwood and the cans dangling from its branches. ''It would be a real mess. Especially in the press.'' He looked toward them. ''And if that happens, my young friends, you will be out of luck, no matter how much I like you.'' He smiled and looked down at his shirt, and absently pulled a small white box from the pocket.

He looked at it for a moment—a small white box, the kind suitable for a piece of jewelry, one of those little boxes containing a necklace or ring lying in cotton or on top of blue felt cardboard—and opened it and pulled out a small .25 caliber five-shot automatic. He let the box fall to the ground and pointed the automatic at Barney's head. He smiled. ''Don't be stupid, Ben,'' he said to Monster, his voice clear and unhurried. He walked two steps closer to Barney. ''Now,'' he said to Barney, ''put your right hand under the butt of that Mattel toy and tip it over onto the ground. Slowly, slowly.''

Barney tipped the M-16 onto the ground.

The old man walked over to the chair, automatic pointed at Barney's head, and with one foot dragged the rifle closer. He squatted slowly and with his left hand reached out and picked up the M-16. He flicked the selector to semi and backed up several yards, pointing it at a spot somewhere between Monster, seated tensed, ready to spring, and Barney, equally tense in the lawn chair.

He put the .25 auto in his pocket and, grasping the M-16 with both hands, flicked the selector to auto. He placed the butt firmly against the right side of his crotch, one hand on top of the front rest, pushing down on the barrel, and pivoted forty-five degrees and fired. One long burst that hit most of the cans suspended by cords from the cottonwood, brass flipping up and out, into the dried-up grass. Several cans fell to the ground; the others bounced and swayed in the rose-tinted light.

The silence was deafening, the smell of cordite thick in the air.

Fu streaked around the corner of the house.

The old man laughed and hefted the empty rifle in his hands, looking down at it. ''I just love these little toys,'' he said, and with a quick motion he jammed the rifle barrel into the ground. "You can have a lot of fun with them."

Monster and Barney stared at him, the skin of their faces tight.

The old man grinned, embarrassed—a friendly-looking little wrinkled and tanned old man, tough from years on the farm. "I guess the old fart's still got some life in him, after all.

"Now, here's what I'd like you to do," he said. He raised one finger. "Number one, get rid of this Martin fellow—he's bad for business . . . and he whines." He raised another finger. "Fix it so your lieutenant comes out looking good." He paused, thinking about it. "Just make him look good." He held up another finger. "And three, stop being such a pain in the ass."

"And what do we get out of all this?" Monster asked.

The old man smiled. "You get to stay alive."

"Gee, thanks."

The old man raised one eyebrow. "Well, yes," he said. "I understand all that, but I'm not concerned with your personal problems. Just put a lid on this business, and I'll be satisfied, and then you can get back to whatever."

He looked from one man to the other. "I realize some of this will probably come out somehow, in some way or another. You just make sure that way is not detrimental to the people I work for."

He smiled, nodded. "Good," he said, and turned and walked back to the car. He opened the door, waved once, and climbed in—a friendly old man, looking as if he'd just gotten a little lost and had stopped for directions.

They watched the white rent-a-car pull out of the yard and head back down the road, raising a cloud of dust, a gray pall suspended against the dark blue mountains and green fields.

The air was cooling already. A mosquito whined past Monster's ear. He swatted at it, catching and squashing it in his hand.

"What do you think?" he asked.

Barney was silent for a while. "I believe him," he said. He looked at Monster. "But he wasn't much help."

"He knows we might blow it."

"He never even mentioned the lieutenant, or that partner of Martin's that Debbie told us about."

"Well, it's not the old man, that's for sure."

"Maybe he doesn't know."

They both thought about the chances of that.

"He never did say he was offering us a job," Monster said.

"When hell freezes over," Barney replied.

They smiled at each other.

"Well, let's go get something to eat," Monster said. "Let's go talk to the lieutenant."

CHAPTER 24

Sudden Escalations

Monster walked into the narc room from the men's room, wiping his still damp hands on his jeans and on the front of his gray sweat shirt. Barney was just hanging the phone up.

The narc room always seemed a different place at night; fluorescent lighting lent the clutter of gray desks and the litter of papers and files and typewriters a stark and washed-out appearance. The scuffed tile floor and the dusty assortment of drug paraphernalia and marijuana plants made the room grimy.

"He says he'll be right down," Barney said.

"What'd you tell him?"

"I told him we were going to make a bust, and if he wanted to get in on it, he'd better get his ass down here."

"Won't he be suspicious? He must know something about what we've been up to."

Barney leaned back in the chair, hands clasped behind his head. "He probably does. But he doesn't know we know what *he's* been up to. I told him we just got a hot tip from an informant that something was going down here in town. He'll think it's something new that just came up. At worst, he'll just be curious to see if we say anything about what happened."

251

Monster frowned, pacing between the desks, picking up things—papers, staplers—putting them down.

"If he calls the desk," Barney said, "they'll tell him we're here, and that'll make him feel secure, just like we figured. And, anyway, maybe Martin hasn't gotten around to telling him what happened."

"Did he sound surprised to hear from you?"

Barney thought for a moment. "No. Now that you mention it, he didn't. Just his usual asshole self."

"Well, maybe he doesn't know, then."

Barney smiled. "If he doesn't, he will soon enough."

"Someone's coming." Barney leaned forward in the chair, drawing the Magnum from the holster on his belt, holding it pointed down at the floor, out of sight under the desktop.

Footsteps echoed off the tile floor in the hallway.

Monster took a position behind the wall leading to the conference room, out of sight of anyone coming through the door, arms folded loosely across his chest. It was amazing how calm he felt, he thought. He could feel the Browning underneath his sweat shirt, the barrel pressed into his hip as he leaned against the wall.

The lieutenant walked into the narc room. "This better be good," he said. He was dressed in baggy cotton pants and T-shirt and tan jacket with padded shoulders. His hair was tousled, as if he'd been called in out of bed. They'd once seen him tousle it as he got out of his car and headed for the wire gate at the back entrance to the sheriff's office.

"Well," he demanded, "what is it? Who's the informant? How much dope are we talking about?"

Barney smiled. As if he would tell the phony son of a bitch who *any* informant was.

"Evening, Lieutenant," Monster said, stepping out from behind the wall. "What's happening?" He walked around a desk, toward the lieutenant. Relaxed, smiling. He stopped three or four feet from the lieutenant, not too close. "We met a good-looking girl who said she knew you," he said. "She said you really know how to put the moves on."

The lieutenant frowned, confused by Monster's sudden appearance, his friendliness.

Monster grinned, knowing the lieutenant misunderstood the

grin. It felt like prickles of electricity in his fingertips. Scurvy son of a bitch, he thought, letting a little of it leak into his consciousness.

The lieutenant smirked. "Where—" he began, and Monster hit him in the stomach, hard, pivoting into it, feeling his fist sink inches into the relaxed flesh, grazing the belt buckle. The lieutenant folded together instantly, like a piece of elastic suddenly let go, crashing into a metal filing cabinet just inside the door. "Unh," he gagged, hands clasping his stomach.

Monster grabbed him by his tousled hair and half dragged, half threw him across the desk Barney had been sitting behind.

Paper and files, a stapler, fluttered and skittered off the desk onto the floor.

The lieutenant looked like a fish out of water, mouth working for air, eyes filling with tears. "Unhh. Unhh," he said, as Monster jerked his arms behind his back and handcuffed him.

He pulled the lieutenant off the desk, one hand in the lieutenant's hair, pulling his head back, the other hand pulling back on the chain that joined the cuffs together. He guided the lieutenant around the desk. The lieutenant made weird, quick little grunting sounds, tears trickling down his cheeks. Monster threw him into the chair Barney had pulled out for him.

The chair careened backwards on its rollers, smashing against the radiator, the lieutenant's head snapping back and then forward as he bent at the waist, hands cuffed behind his back. "Unh. Unh. Unh," he said.

Monster stepped forward, feeling *good*, not like the way he'd felt with Harold and Debbie, ready to work out on the lieutenant, smash his pinched and squinting face, break his legs, any fucking thing.

"Not now," Barney said quietly, and grasped Monster's upper arm. "Not now."

"Hunhh," the lieutenant said. "Hunhh."

Monster looked at Barney, not really seeing him, into it, his neck and shoulders and arms swollen with the rush of energy, the release of pent-up rage.

"Not here," Barney said.

Monster jerked his arm away from Barney's grasp and turned and walked out of sight into the conference room.

"Ohhh," the lieutenant said. "Ohhh."

Barney heard a crash from the conference room—a chair thrown against the wall. Another crash. He sat down on the edge of the desk, waiting.

Monster came back out of the conference room, walked purposefully toward the lieutenant. The lieutenant looked up toward him, eyes squinted in pain.

Monster roughly frisked him. He tossed the lieutenant's .38, and a .25 automatic he found in a leg holster, onto the desktop. He stepped back, his jaw muscles jumping, and leaned against the wall and radiator.

"Wh-why'd . . . you . . . do that?" the lieutenant asked.

Monster and Barney didn't say anything. The lieutenant's eyes were watery, his face white. The fluorescent lights made his skin look like the skin on a corpse.

"What . . . are you doing?" He managed to look bewildered.

Barney whistled tunelessly, rocking his foot back and forth at the edge of the desk. How many had he met just like the lieutenant in Vietnam, and since? he asked himself. Corrupt, cunning men not brave enough to really do it right—doing for a few dollars what others with courage were doing for a lot of dollars. Not that the others were any better—they were all assholes—but at least they had courage.

The lieutenant sat back, taking a deep breath. He looked from Barney to Monster, back to Barney. They could see the fear and evasion in his eyes.

"You'd better—" he began, but halted, flinching when Monster straightened away from the wall.

Monster leaned back against the wall.

Wordlessly, Barney pulled out the mini-recorder and switched it on. Immediately they heard Debbie's distracted voice saying, "Martin pays him for information," and Barney's voice asking, "For what?"

"For selling dope," she replied. "What else?"

Barney shut the tape recorder off. "Recognize that voice?" he asked. He'd seen the recognition in the lieutenant's eyes.

The lieutenant frowned and they knew he was going to deny it, but before he could, Monster stepped forward and with the toe of his boot kicked the lieutenant just below the kneecap, hard, but not hard enough to disable him, then went back to the wall.

"Don't . . . Oww!"

"Do you recognize that voice?" Barney asked again.

The lieutenant opened his mouth to speak. Monster straightened away from the wall. The lieutenant's mouth closed.

He looked from Monster to Barney. He looked back at Monster.

Monster's eyes glittered.

The lieutenant licked his lips nervously. He looked down. He looked back up at Monster.

"Well?" Barney said.

The lieutenant nodded.

Barney looked expressionlessly at Monster. "I guess we'll go for a ride, then," he said.

"What do you mean?" the lieutenant asked, knowing what he meant. "What do you mean, go for a ride? What are you doing? You can't just—"

"We'll give you a choice," Barney interrupted. "You can come with us and answer our questions, or you can stay here, back in the slammer with all those wonderful people who'd just love to get their hands on you." He paused. "What'll it be?"

"I don't know what you're talking about."

Barney looked at Monster. "Call the county attorney and the sheriff. Tell them we just arrested the lieutenant."

"Okay," the lieutenant said. "Okay. Okay."

Barney smiled.

"What are you going to do—" the lieutenant began, but Monster grasped him by the arm and jerked him to his feet. He pushed the lieutenant, limping, to the door and out into the hallway toward the elevator.

"Where are we going?" the lieutenant asked, the panic and fear in his voice as ugly and grimy as the narc room they'd just left.

Barney turned out the lights behind them. "You'll see," he said.

* * *

GRAVEYARD RULES

A chill breeze ruffled their hair. Tall pines swayed and creaked in the darkness. They could hear the rush and swirl, the slap of water against rocks, the chuckle of tiny waves against the rocky shore. The air smelled of water and grass and pine, and of the lieutenant's fear.

The lieutenant was kneeling at the edge of the shore, in the grass, head bowed, hands still cuffed behind him. Barney stood to one side, a dark, almost invisible presence, Monster to the other, his gray sweat shirt a ghostly blur. Above the pines, the dark bulk of the mountains pressed in against the narrow valley, the ridge a fine black delineation against the star field.

The lieutenant was hyperventilating; they could hear him. Neither of them had spoken to him during the ride up the Blackfoot. They'd taken an unmarked sheriff's car and driven out of the city and up the Blackfoot to the spot where they'd stopped on their way to the LaFray Creek Rest Area. The same spot Barney used to like to drive to on quiet nights when he was on patrol, a spot where, listening to the waters of the Blackfoot, he could think.

"Tell us again why you tried to have us killed," Barney said.

"I told you I don't know what you're talking about!" the lieutenant screamed, his voice inconsequential and puny, lost in the sounds of the river. "I don't know what you're talking about!"

"Debbie says you're partners with Martin selling dope."

The lieutenant's breathing was ragged and fast.

"Well?" Barney prompted.

"I wouldn't do that," the lieutenant said. "Not sell dope. You know I wouldn't do that."

Monster laughed, a harsh sound in the darkness. "Let's just shoot him and get it over with."

"If not dope, then what?" Barney said.

"You'll never prove it in court."

Monster leaned down next to the lieutenant's ear and said, "Look, you fucking idiot, we don't give a shit about court. If you don't start telling us what we want to know, we are going to hold *court* right here! And in about two weeks some fisherman is going to find your body downstream, floating among the rocks and weeds."

256

The lieutenant sank back on his heels. "Just information," he said. "That's all. I swear to God that's all! Where the narc team is, who's working on what, that's all. That's all! I swear, I don't—"

"That's all!" Monster interrupted. "Fuck, oh, dear."

"You knew about them jumping us up here," Barney said. "You knew about it before it happened."

The lieutenant was silent, a dark form between them, breathing raggedly.

"Nice night," Barney said conversationally. "Enjoy it, Lieutenant," he snarled.

"I didn't," he moaned, rocking back and forth. "I didn't."

"But you've been selling dope, haven't you?" Barney asked.

The lieutenant groaned.

Monster looked down at the dark kneeling form. Back in the narc room, he had wanted to kill the lieutenant with his bare hands. Beat him to death. But out here among the pines and mountains, breathing the clean air, feeling the breeze against his face, in his hair, listening to the river, he couldn't muster that anger. Didn't give a damn, he thought. Too gray and sick with the killing and bodies. Terrorizing people out of some righteous anger. Kill the lieutenant. Kill Martin. Kill them all, and it wouldn't make a shit. It was more than just a few people; it was the whole fucking world.

He looked up at the ridgeline. In Vietnam it had been the same way. In the beginning it had just been soldiers fighting soldiers, and that was okay. Despite the death, the bodies, and the wounded, it had been what he'd figured it was supposed to be. But suddenly they were blowing apart hooches with M-79 grenade launchers, just to see them blow apart, and firing tracers that ignited buildings and sometimes people, just to see things burn.

He looked down at the lieutenant. And here they were again. And sure it was partly by their own choice and inclination, idealistically or otherwise, but mostly it was because some low-rent asshole was fucking with their lives, other people's lives. Here they were again, back where things always seemed warped, sudden escalations out of the acceptable into the horrible.

He squinted at the dark form. But once you were in it,

you had to see it through, no matter how crazy it got. Unless you really didn't give a damn. Otherwise, it would eat all of you, not just a part of you.

He motioned Barney back, the gray of his sweat shirt–clad arm phosphorescent in the dark. He drew the Browning and, holding it a few inches from the lieutenant's face, cocked it and then slowly withdrew it out of the lieutenant's range of vision.

"Answer the question—you been selling dope?"

"Ye—" the lieutenant began, and Monster fired the 9mm, flame lancing out of the darkness behind the lieutenant's head, toward the river, the explosion quickly lost in the wind and river and trees. The lieutenant fell over on his side.

"Jesus!" Barney said. "Jesus!" He peered down at the dark form huddled on the rocks. "You crazy— Did you actually shoot him?"

"No. But if we're lucky, he had a heart attack or something."

Barney bent down, feeling for the carotid artery. He laughed and pulled on the padded jacket. "Get up, you stupid shit; you're not shot. Jesus!" He hauled the lieutenant back up to his knees.

"Next time," Monster said. "Next time, Lieutenant," and as he said it, he remembered that was what the big man had said to him.

"Have you been selling dope?" Barney asked again, loudly this time, because he knew the lieutenant's ears were numb from the explosion.

"Yes," the lieutenant said, his voice dazed.

"It's not the dope; it's the people who sell it," Monster said to Barney. "Remember when I told you that?"

Barney was silent, considering the lieutenant. Damn, he'd sure thought Monster had blown him away. And if he had . . . well, so what? They ought to do him right now. They would just have to take whatever that old man wanted to dish out. Got to go sometime. He and Monster'd sure as hell take a few of them out first.

Well, that was bullshit: movies always getting in the way. They'd never know what hit them. He mentally shrugged. But not a bad way to go: if the old man wanted to take them out, it'd be over in a hurry.

"Why'd you try to have us killed?" he asked.

"I didn't," the lieutenant said. "I didn't. Martin and the others were just supposed to scare you, warn you off. I told him it wouldn't work. I told him how crazy you guys are."

"Well, somebody put the contract out, because sure as shit they tried to kill us."

"It wasn't me. I wouldn't put another cop in any real danger. You know that."

"The fuck you wouldn't!" Monster said. "You're just too low-rent to do it right."

Barney tugged on the sleeve of Monster's sweat shirt, pulled him toward the car.

"Something wrong here," Barney said in a low voice. "He's in shock. Did you smell him? He pissed his pants."

Monster shrugged. "Who wouldn't?"

"That's not what I mean: he really doesn't know anything about the hit."

Monster was silent.

"What do you think?" Barney asked.

"Shit, I don't know. You're right, though. Anyway, we can't dump him. Remember what that old fart told us?"

"Yeah. But I'm not sure I give a damn."

"Let's talk to him some more," Monster said.

The lieutenant was sitting, feet sprawled out in front of him on the rocks.

"Why'd you try to scare us off?" Monster asked.

The lieutenant looked up, his face a pale oval in the darkness. "Martin was convinced you guys were getting too close to this deal, even though I told him you weren't working on it at all."

"What deal?"

"The thing tomorrow."

"Don't start fucking around again. Tell us."

"Early tomorrow—this morning—a plane is flying in with three hundred thousand dollars' worth of cocaine."

"Where?"

"That old strip—farther on up here, past Potomac."

"What time?"

"Daybreak."

Monster looked up at the stars. No mosquitoes, he thought. Water's probably too fast here. The lieutenant hunched forward, relieving the strain on his lower back, his hands cuffed behind him.

"Did Martin tell you about the three guys we killed?" Monster asked.

The lieutenant's head jerked up. "No." His voice rose, strained. "I told you I don't know." His head slumped forward, and his voice trailed off. "I don't know. . . ."

For a moment, Barney and Monster looked down at the dark form in front of them.

"Did you send Bruce up to Kalispell to check on us?" Barney asked.

"Why would I do that?" the lieutenant mumbled.

CHAPTER 25

Breakfast

Monster felt his teeth begin to chatter; he willed his muscles to relax. It didn't do any good. It was just plain cold lying on the ground, and there was nothing he could do about it. He could see dew heavy on the blades of grass directly in front of him, and on the leaves of the bushes around him; he could feel it on his head and sweat shirt. Beads of moisture glistened dully like oil on the barrel and receiver of the shotgun. In the distance, about a hundred and fifty yards away, an old unpainted barn began to take shape in the gray early morning light. An orange wind sock at the peak of the barn, above the hayloft door, rotated in the chill morning breeze. The barn was at the end of a mowed grass runway.

They'd loaded the lieutenant into the unmarked car and driven into the city, to Barney's house, where they'd picked up the shotgun, the CAR-16, ammunition, binoculars, and then driven back up the Blackfoot, past Potomac, to the old landing strip, stopping only to pick up candy bars and orange juice at the Circle K. They'd left the lieutenant about half a mile back, handcuffed to the steering wheel of the car. The car was hidden in the bushes off a little-used logging road.

Barney was ten yards to Monster's right, sitting under a tiny stand of young fir fronted by a screen of low bushes, watching the old barn through the binoculars.

Monster shivered. Fuck, it was cold.

He rolled over onto his back, looking up at the gray morning sky, waiting to hear the distant drone of an airplane or the grumble of a vehicle driving out to the barn.

The air smelled of fall, the heavy dew almost a frost. Time to go hunting pretty soon, he thought. Up early before light, candy bars and orange juice, a bag of granola, knife, a last cup of coffee. Sneaking through the woods.

That was the best part, sneaking up on deer and elk.

Sometimes, though, elk and deer were just as stupid as people; sometimes they would stand right out in the open like cows and let you shoot them.

He reached in his pocket and pulled out a Snickers candy bar. "Hey. You. Sergeant Rock," he stage-whispered to Barney. "Want half a candy bar?"

Barney frowned through the branches of a fir at him. "Shhh!" he said.

"What for?" Monster said loudly. "Ain't nobody around but us chickens. Us wet, armed-to-the-teeth, ready for World War Three chickens."

Barney scooted over to him, holding the CAR-16 up out of the wet grass. "You crazy fuck," he said in a low voice. "You know how voices carry in the early morning. Somebody could be in that barn."

Monster tore the wrapper off the candy bar, wadded it up, and put it in his pants pocket, which was bulging with shotgun shells. He offered half to Barney. "Shee-it," he said, as Barney accepted the candy. "We've been her for an hour and a half; busted our ass in the dark to get here, and nothing has moved. Maybe the lieutenant wasn't so truthful, after all."

Barney munched thoughtfully on the candy bar. "They're coming," he said. "Too much is on the line."

"We've been wrong before." Monster chewed vigorously, tasting the caramel and peanuts and chocolate. One of life's major pleasures, he thought. Junk food in the great outdoors.

"That's right. We've been wrong before. So let's just keep quiet a little longer and see what happens." He turned to look toward the runway and barn. The sky was lightening, colors beginning to intrude upon the grays, the barn now a dark brown, the leaves and grass wet, pastel greens, the runway a pale tan of mowed grass.

"One time in 'Nam, up by the DMZ, we were clearing some NVA bunkers—" An image of the bunkers flashed through Barney's mind: holes dug into the red and yellow clay, covered with layers of logs and more clay, the brown-uniformed NVA wide-eyed with surprise before they died.

"Hadn't lost a man. Hadn't taken even a single wounded. And I was walking around the corner of this bunker, just checking things out. Being a little careless, holding my sixteen with one hand." He held the CAR-16 up by the pistol grip, showing Monster how he'd held the M-16. "And there's this fucking NVA standing there with his AK pointed right at my chest. Man, I knew I was dead. I *saw* his finger pull the trigger." He glanced toward Monster. "I brought my sixteen up—just a reflex, I guess. Figured what the hell, maybe get at least one into him before he took me out." He smiled. "Three or four out of that AK and I would have been breakfast for the jungle."

"What happened?"

"I greased the fucker. Put about half a clip into his chest."

"Why didn't he shoot you?"

"When we checked his weapon, we found out he'd had a misfire. The primer was dented and everything, but it hadn't gone off."

"No shit?"

Barney nodded. "It still makes me itch all over thinking about it. No way you can ever figure something like that."

"Okay," Monster said. "I get your point."

"Thanks for the candy bar," Barney said. He scooted sideways back into the stand of fir.

Monster sighed and rolled over onto his stomach. Barney was right, he thought. No time to get lazy and impatient just because he didn't believe it was going to happen. The important thing to remember was that it *could* happen. The lieutenant might be telling the truth, but that didn't mean the lieutenant knew what the truth really was.

He rubbed the side of his face, feeling the stubble. I'm tired, he thought. It's getting harder and harder to give a damn.

In the distance, he heard the drone of a light aircraft, and his senses and reflexes were abruptly alert. He crawled, cradling the shotgun, underneath the bushes.

The barn was silent; the Dodge was nowhere in sight.

"Do you see it?" he said.

"It's coming from the west. He'll probably make a pass from west to east and then land out of the east just as the sun is breaking over the ridge."

The first rays were just beginning to slant across the ridge down into the valley. Droplets of moisture glittered on grass and leaves.

They squinted toward the sunrise, careful not to raise their faces toward the sky; faces, they knew, reflected light, pale ovals easily seen from overhead.

The plane flew low, passed directly above them, the roar of its engine increasing, diminishing as it flew into the sunrise, a single-engine Cessna, white and gold, sunlight reflecting off its flight surface. It climbed, banking to the north over the blue mountains, and curved around to the east, coming back at them straight out of the sun.

No sign of the PowerWagon.

The plane dropped suddenly, as if on an invisible elevator, gliding, its engine shut down to an idle, coming in quiet, wing tips wagging slightly just before the pilot settled it onto the mowed strip. The propeller wound down, spinning loosely, as the white and gold aircraft taxied toward the barn.

Barney propped himself up on his elbows and raised the binoculars. "Nice plane," he said. "Looks like a four-seater. Two people in it that I can see."

The plane made a short half-circle through the mowed grass, its wings dipping and bouncing, and stopped about thirty yards from the barn, facing back the way it had landed.

It sat there for a few minutes, obviously waiting for someone to meet it.

A door opened on the side facing them and a man jumped down, a stubby rifle in his hands.

"Looks like an H and K, folding stick. Looks like he's done this before."

"I wonder why that old man just didn't stop it before it got here."

"Maybe he did." Barney stared intently through the glasses. "Maybe these dudes are going to take out whoever meets the plane."

The man ran over to the corner of the barn and peered

through a crack in the boards. The pilot climbed out the same side, a small briefcase in one hand, rifle in the other. He ran over to the barn and set the briefcase down, leaning it against the wall.

The first man pushed open the half of the barn door that swung away from him, and the second man ran inside, crouched, the butt of the rifle held steadily against his side, one hand on top of the barrel, as he ran through the door to the other side, disappearing into the shadows. Almost simultaneously, the first man ducked around his side of the doorway and slipped inside the barn.

"Too bad there's not a cow or something in there," Monster said.

"This is weird," Barney said.

"I hear that! What do you think is in that case?"

"Dope, probably. Shit, I don't know."

"It must be full of dope," Monster said. "Otherwise, why bother with it? And if it is, that means the old man and his people really are not involved."

"This is getting out of hand again," Barney said. "I can feel it."

The two figures emerged from the barn, rifles held loosely. They walked out into the field, looking around. One of them, the first one out, slung his rifle over his shoulder and, cupping his hands, lit a cigarette. The other man began walking back toward the briefcase, and his arms flew out from his sides as he was lifted backwards off his feet, throwing the rifle yards away, body slammed down into the golden stubble of the field as they heard the heavy crack of a large-caliber rifle.

"Shit!" Monster grabbed the Benelli. "Where'd that come from?"

The other man spun toward the barn, unslinging his rifle as he began running toward the side of the barn.

"Hayloft!" Barney said.

The door to the hayloft had swung open. The running man raised the H and K toward it and was jerked sideways off his feet, slammed head down into the stubble as they heard the heavy crack again, his arms and legs asprawl, the submachine gun next to him.

Through the binoculars Barney saw the first body, about one hundred fifty yards away, flinch suddenly as the rifle cracked again. And even without the glasses Monster saw the head of the second body rebound off the ground as the rifle cracked yet again.

"Damn," Barney said. "Damn."

A camouflage-clad figure—tiger stripes, they both noticed—ran out of the barn toward the aircraft.

"Bruce!" Barney said, looking up from the glasses. "It's that fucking Bruce!"

Monster squinted toward the figure. "Let me see."

Barney handed him the glasses.

Monster focused on the plane. The running figure had disappeared inside it. His head reappeared as he looked down at the ground around the plane, then glanced toward the barn. "It *is* Bruce."

Bruce, his face shiny with sweat, jumped out of the plane and ran to the briefcase propped against the barn. He scooped it up and ran inside the barn.

"Shoot that son of a bitch," Monster said, ejecting the first round from the shotgun, chambering the second, a slug.

"No!" Barney said, grabbing his arm. "Not now. Let him go for now. You're too far away, anyway."

Monster looked at him as if Barney were crazy. "What!" he said. "That son—"

"Not now," Barney said, his fingers digging into Monster's arm. "Not now."

Bruce ran out of the barn, wearing tan coveralls and gloves, and went to the nearest body, grabbed it by the armpits, lifted it—they could see a large stain at the chest—and dragged it to the airplane. He picked the body up under the shoulders and knees and threw it into the aircraft. He ran to the other body and did the same thing, the misshapen head dangling to the side. He stripped off the coveralls and gloves and threw them in on top of the bodies. They could see a large pistol in a shoulder holster that stretched from his armpit almost to his waist.

Monster's knuckles were white around the stock of the shotgun.

"I didn't think he was that strong," Barney said.

Bruce ran back inside the barn, and a few seconds later they heard a motorcycle rev inside the barn, a ring-ringing sound. A yellow dirt bike skidded out of the barn, Bruce crouched over the handlebars, a long-barreled, scooped hunting rifle slung across his back, the briefcase fastened with elastic straps to the rear fender, and darted out to the aircraft.

"He sure likes cannons," Barney said. "Look at that pistol."

Bruce threw something into the aircraft, then revved the bike, skidded around in a tight half-circle, and accelerated past the barn and down the tire tracks worn into the grass that led away from the landing strip.

The aircraft exploded, and exploded again, a ball of rolling flame as the fuel cells went up, pieces of airplane flying into clear blue sky, the heat of the shock wave buffeting Barney and Monster as, instinctively, they pressed face down into the grass and dirt.

Barney jumped to his feet. The area for yards around the plane was scorched, small grass fires burning, orange flame licking out of the stubble. He slung the binoculars around his neck and tucked them inside his black windbreaker. "Let's get out of here." Smoldering chunks of metal were all that was left of the plane. The small grass fires were already beginning to die out in the dew-wet stubble.

He turned and began running though the wood, along the hillside, the CAR-16 slung over his shoulder.

Monster checked the safety on the shotgun, and picked up the ejected round and put it into his pocket, and quickly turned and followed Barney.

Barney halted about a hundred yards from the car. Panting, he walked over to the dirt embankment and sat down.

Monster wiped sweat from his forehead and temples with his fingertips and gently placed the shotgun against the embankment. He squatted down on the road.

"It's been Bruce all the time," Barney panted. "He's been Martin's partner all along. Using the lieutenant through Martin." He wiped the sweat from his forehead with his forearm. He spit into the grass at the edge of the road.

Monster grunted. He picked up a pebble and flipped it across the road into the trees and bushes on the other side.

"You know what he's doing, don't you?" Barney said.

"Yeah. He's getting rid of everybody. He figures we know about the connection between Martin and the lieutenant."

Barney nodded and wiped his forehead again. "He wants all the blame on the lieutenant."

Monster stood and stretched. "The ranch?"

Barney nodded. "Whether or not he's already killed Martin, that's where he's got to be headed. He wouldn't dare go very far on that bike, dressed and armed the way he is."

"He'll probably want the lieutenant to go out to the ranch," Monster said. "He'll dump the lieutenant and make it look like Martin did it. That way he won't have to worry about the lieutenant on a polygraph, screaming his innocence, talking about another partner." He smiled without humor. "He doesn't know about the old man."

Barney was silent, his breathing back to normal.

He looked at Monster.

Monster cleared his throat, not willing to meet Barney's gaze. "I know what you're thinking."

"Well, it gives him a chance, at least—which is all he deserves. It was his choice to play with the bear. Nobody twisted his arm."

Monster shook his head. "The bear, he be getting awful fat."

Barney nodded. "That's a fact."

Monster walked over and picked up the shotgun. "Well, let's go do it," he said. "We've come this far."

"What happened?" the lieutenant asked, as Monster unlocked the handcuffs. "I heard shots, an explosion."

"We haven't got much time," Barney answered. He handed the lieutenant his .38. The lieutenant looked at him, surprised. "I'm going to tell you what happened, what's been going on, and what you have to do," Barney said. "So just shut up and listen until I'm done."

CHAPTER 26

A Nice Group

The bike's there," Monster said. Barney and the lieutenant were sitting in the unmarked sheriff's car, parked out of sight just down the road from the crumpled gate. "I couldn't see any movement."

Barney climbed out of the passenger side. He had shed the nylon windbreaker and was wearing a green O.D. T-shirt. He handed Monster the shotgun and slung the CAR-16 over his shoulder.

He bent down and looked in at the lieutenant. "Give us fifteen minutes," he said. "And remember what I said: if we don't get you, that old guy will. This is your only chance to come out of it whole."

The lieutenant swallowed and nodded.

"Okay." Barney straightened and winked at Monster. "Let's boogie," he said, and they began jogging down the road, turning off into the treeline just before they reached the gate.

They hurried through the trees, over falldown, and down into the thickly wooded gulley that bisected the fields, out of sight of the log house, fighting their way through the brush and thorny bushes. It was hot already, flies and bees buzzing around them as they sweated down the gulley toward a spot downhill from and behind the old barn and outbuildings across the road from the log house.

They ran up the open slope behind the barn and outbuildings, both of them remembering the heavy crack of the hunting rifle.

And panted, out of breath, up behind the barn. Sweat stained their shirts at chest and back, ran down their faces, dripped off their chins. Monster propped the shotgun against the weathered boards of the barn. They could smell horse manure and hay, old musty smells.

Barney wiped his forehead with his arm. "We should be able to stay behind the barn and sheds until we get to that old chicken coop. Get across the openings as fast as you can. We'll wait behind the chicken coop until asshole goes in. Then we'll run across the road to the PowerWagon and front-end loader parked in front of the house."

A few minute later, they waited crouched behind the chicken coop, Barney at one end watching the house, Monster at the other end watching the road for the lieutenant.

"What if he doesn't show?" Monster said.

"He'll be here."

Monster felt the sun against his face, smelled the barn smells, the old wood of the chicken coop. He looked down the valley at the pine-covered hills and, in the distance, the dark blue ridges of the higher mountains. Vietnam was like this, he thought. A beautiful country. "Here he comes," he said, as the rust-colored Chevy Nova slowly drove around a curve, headed up the road toward the house.

The Nova pulled into the driveway and parked behind the PowerWagon.

The lieutenant climbed out of the Chevy and walked across the dirt yard toward the flimsy-looking steps.

Monster scuttled over behind Barney at the other end of the chicken coop. He checked the safety on the shotgun.

"Anybody comes out besides the lieutenant," Barney said.

"Roger dodger."

The lieutenant disappeared into the house, the .38 held out in front of him. "Martin?" they heard him call, and Barney sprinted for the Dodge, Monster passing him on the right, darting across to the front-end loader, shotgun pointed toward the open doorway.

"Martin?" they heard the lieutenant call again, fainter this time, and then the blast of a large-caliber handgun firing magnum loads, blending with the smaller whack of the .38. The magnum fired again.

Barney rose up over the hood of the PowerWagon and, resting his hand on the hot metal, flicked the selector to auto, aiming toward the open doorway.

Monster moved to the front of the tractor and, using one of the thick rubber tires for a rest, pushed the safety off and watched the windows. Come on, you bastard, he thought. Come out and see what a nice day it is.

A shadowy figure appeared just inside the doorway, moving uncertainly.

"He's hit," Monster said.

Bruce appeared in the doorway, a large revolver in his hand, clutched to his belly. He had changed his camouflage fatigues for jeans and a blue tank top. He leaned against the doorjamb, squinting into the bright sunlight. There was a fist-size stain above and to the right of his big, silver belt buckle. He was dragging a large white and yellow gym bag.

Monster and Barney both aimed at the buckle. Bruce stepped out into the sunlight, the muscles of his arms and shoulders like cables under the pale, sweaty skin. He looked directly at Barney.

"Bruce!" Monster shouted.

Bruce struggled to point the revolver.

"Fuck you, Bruce!" And he and Barney fired at the same time, Monster feeling the heavy, vicious kick of the shotgun against his shoulder and cheekbone, Barney the light recoil of the submachine gun.

"Nice group," Barney said.

CHAPTER 27

Skins

Some time later—they weren't sure just when, but a few weeks after the team of investigators from another county had concluded the official investigation and the public furor had died down and they'd quit the sheriff's department, at that time of the year when the sky is supposed to be a perfect Technicolor blue, when pale yellow larch needles sift to the ground and bull elk, so much the color of the larch needles, lift their head to the gray dawn and half scream, half whistle their challenge to the mountains—some time later, almost to winter, they received a telegram.

"Any time you need a job, let me know," it said, and it was from Hong Kong.

"Hong Kong," Ben said. *"Hong Kong!* What the hell?"

After they'd shot Bruce, they'd retrieved the yellow and white nylon clothing bag, ignoring the body crumpled into an awkward pile on the ground to the side of the steps, a large pool of blood and other things soaking into the dirt. Monster had been careful not to look at the eyes, concentrating on the contents of the bag—yellowish cocaine wrapped in plastic, taped with freezer tape, and covered with $300,000 in assorted bills, nothing smaller than a twenty. The bundles of money were wrapped with rubber bands; it was amazing how bulky $300,000 could be.

Barney had gone inside and found the briefcase the dope had originally come in. He'd also found the lieutenant lying at the base of the steps, made out of sections of log, that led to a loft above the large living room. The lieutenant had been shot in the leg and in the chest; his eyes stared out the sliding glass doors across from the steps.

The big man, Martin, had been upstairs in a queen-size bed, propped up against the heavy oak headboard, covers to his waist, a surprised expression on his big freckled face, two large holes in his torso, one in the middle of his chest, the other where the heart should have been. Hell of a way to wake up, Barney had thought.

They'd put the dope back into the briefcase and thrown it so it fell open, face down next to Bruce, the cocaine spilled out, as if Bruce had fallen off the steps with the briefcase clutched in his hand.

Then Monster had stowed the yellow and white bag of money in the trunk of the rust-colored Nova the lieutenant had driven, and called Dispatch on the radio, requesting assistance, one officer KIA, two bad guys KIA, and a mysterious explosion and fire to the east, but not to hurry because it was all over, and the fire was just a grass fire that had probably already burned itself out, and so on, location, times, and all that, and then they'd sat on the hood of the Nova, shirts off, soaking up a few rays while they waited, drinking a couple of Coors beers Barney had found in the refrigerator, ignoring the flies around the body. Sitting there had reminded Monster of sitting in the belly of a helicopter parked in a paddy somewhere, the sun bright and hot, his flight suit peeled to the waist, sweat trickling down his chest and stomach, puddling around his belly button. What would it feel like to take a round of double-ought and four or five rounds of .223 in the stomach and chest? he thought. All at once. A serious case of indigestion, at least. Fuck, oh, dear. More bodies. Why did colors always seem so washed out?

"I love this country," he said.

Barney took a drink of beer.

"I mean the country country," Monster said. "The mountains and rivers . . . you know."

Barney had nodded, and they'd sat there, silent, until in the distance they heard the sirens and watched the four or five vehicles, black-and-whites and unmarked cars, wail and whoop-whoop-whoop up the road, skidding around the corner, sliding into the drive, across the dirt lawn, dust billowing everywhere.

"You must've turned the radio off," Barney said. He drained his beer and threw the can end over end through the dust, out into the yard, sunlight glinting as it tunked into the parched earth.

Monster smiled at the commotion. "Must have."

Their story was that the lieutenant hadn't waited for them to get into position, but had gone in by himself and wounded the bad guy—they had known beforehand that Bruce was the bad guy because the lieutenant had told them so, don't ask us how he knew, it's not ours to reason why—before Bruce had put two rounds of .44 magnum into the lieutenant, just goes to show you, .38 rounds aren't worth a shit. They'd arrived just in time to shoot Bruce as he was trying to shoot Barney.

Subsequent investigation indicated Bruce had killed the two men in the aircraft—there was plenty of physical evidence to support this theory, bullets and rifle, fingerprints, and all that—and, some time well before meeting the plane, had killed the big guy in the bed, a known drug dealer, anyway, too fucking bad.

A renegade cop, the newspapers called Bruce, much to the chagrin of local law enforcement—the only one, however, the papers implied, much to the delight of the sheriff.

They'd laughed, he and Barney, at the stories. Real John Wayne stuff that, of course, since it was John Wayne stuff, everyone believed, the investigators included. No one even questioned how Barney had acquired the CAR-16, not to mention where. And the sheriff was smart enough not to make them take a polygraph test, which was standard procedure.

They'd stashed the money out at Monster's place. No one had even much wondered about the money, either, assuming, if they thought of it at all, that it had accidentally gone up with the aircraft.

No one really cared.

They had a good story.

The newspapers and TV loved it.

The sheriff loved it. Even though it had all happened because of a bad cop, it still showed how dangerous the job was, and therefore it gave the sheriff an excuse to ask for more money for more men to be better equipped and trained.

For more power.

Just like 'Nam.

The lieutenant was a hero, albeit a dead, stupid hero, and was buried with full honors, cops from everywhere, it seemed, at the funeral. His widow didn't seem all that broken up, nor, Ben noticed, did the secretary.

And much to everyone's relief, Barney and Cookie Monster quit the department, collected their sick and retirement pay in a lump sum, and declared they were going into the outfitting business, becoming professional hunters, as it were.

Everyone understood that; it must have been hell.

But Barney and Cookie Monster couldn't seem to get organized. They kept wandering into and out of town, up into the hills. Going fishing. Barney looking for women. Drinking too much again.

Barney had flown back to Virginia for a visit, returning a week later.

"Hey," Ben had said, "when you first came out here, you came out for the country, didn't you? Then you took the cop job. Well, now you got the time and money to get into the country, so do it, instead of just dragging around."

"Speak for yourself, asshole."

They couldn't think of anything to spend the money on. All their plans were for the future, and, well, the future always ends the same. So no rush.

And now, sitting in Monster's battered pickup, listening to a new tape deck that he'd bought with his retirement money, they read the telegram and looked out at the day that was supposed to be a perfect autumn day, Technicolor blue sky and all, but was instead cold and muddy, rain mixed with sleet falling from low, slate-gray clouds onto sodden piles of maple leaves that lay under trees and in storm drains.

"Hong Kong," Ben said again. "How'd you like to go to Hong Kong again?"

Barney snorted. "Not hardly likely."

"Well, the thought of playing baby-sitter in the woods to a bunch of fat businessmen from Minneapolis or someplace ain't exactly turning me on, either."

"I've gotten a few calls and a couple of letters about cop jobs in other places around the state."

"Yeah. Me, too. Letters," Monster said.

"You get one from Frank, the sheriff we worked with up north?"

"Uh-huh."

"He's a good man."

Ben looked across at Barney. "I've had it with that kind of work, Barn. I hate to say so. But I just can't do it anymore. It's not a case of burnout; I'm afraid I'm going to turn into something like the old guy who wrote this telegram."

Barney smiled. "If you don't want to baby-sit hunters and you don't want to be a cop, what else you going to do? What else *can* you do? Hell, you won't ever be like that old guy." He shook his head. "Impossible."

Ben looked across the valley toward the mountains hidden by low, sullen clouds. Impossible, he thought, and abruptly, for no reason, except that it had gone on long enough, he laughed, and it felt as if he were shedding skins, the depression and ugly somehow wicked away by the weather that reminded him of monsoons a long time ago.

"I don't care," he said. "I'll find something else. The money don't matter. If you need my share to do something, you're welcome to it."

"It's in your blood," Barney said. "What else you going to do to make life interesting?"

"It might be in my blood—it's in everyone's blood—but there's other things in my blood, too." He grinned. "I know what you're thinking: give him a few months."

Barney shook his head. "Some assholes got blown away. So what? We did the world a favor."

"For sure." Ben nodded. "But there's no end to the assholes." His grin faded. "And you handle that a lot better than I do. You look at killing people as if it's a science or something—they need it, let's go do it, kind of thing." He raised his hand to halt Barney's reply. "I know you feel it. You feel the loss of friends and all that, but the rest are just meat to you." He shrugged. "I just can't make my mind work that way, Barn, no matter how much it might be doing the world a favor.

"World don't give a shit, Barney; it just don't give a shit. Otherwise, things wouldn't be the way they are."

"I give a shit," Barney said. "Fuck the world."

"Don't get me wrong. All I'm trying to say is, you can do what has to be done without it eating at you." He shook his head. "I can't. It really gets to me, makes me crazy in the wrong ways. If I keep doing this kind of shit, I really am going to turn into a monster. Hell, maybe I already have."

They were silent for a while.

"I think I'll take Sheriff Frank up on that job," Barney said. "Nice country, good department."

"Sheriff Barney, one of these days."

"Fuck you. I just want to ride around in a marked car, in a black-and-white, where things are black and white, get a little adrenaline now and then. Do what I'm good at. Handle it."

"Nah. You got ambition, I can see it. That's why you was a lieutenant in the SF and why you was a sergeant on the department." He laughed. "You goin' to be a sheriff, all right." He laughed. "Crazy fucker."

Barney grinned. "I'll bet I see you in a few months—gun and badge in hand."

"Not this time. Not anymore. You're the leader. Not me. And I don't want to be."

Barney looked narrowly at him. "What are you going to do, then?"

"Oh, I'll think of something."

"Yeah. And I know what it is." He shook his head. "You'll be sorry."

"You're back," she said, her eyes as wary as her son's had been. She'd been working out in the pasture, and her boots were crusted with mud and manure. A few strands of black hair straggled out from underneath her worn and stained cowboy hat. "What are you up to now?"

He grinned. "I'm retired, at the moment." Her skin was tanned and healthy with the outdoors. She smelled of horses.

"Yeah. I read about it. Seemed like there might be a bit more to it, though."

He shrugged. "No matter. I'm retired permanently from that sort of thing."

Anger flashed in her eyes. "Sure," she said. "And I'm a virgin, too."

"Well, hey—" he began, but then he saw her eyes, and he looked down at his hands, not knowing what to do or how to say it.

She pushed her hat back and regarded him for a long moment, her eyes clear and brown and not especially friendly.

"There's something my father used to say to a friend of his he was in World War Two with, who'd come over to our house all the time, drunk and crying about the war. My father would always say, 'Look, George, if you don't want to be there anymore, then just don't be there anymore.' " She paused. "All I got to say to you, Ben, is if you don't want to be there anymore then *just don't fucking be there anymore!*" She blushed. "That's all I've got to say about that," she mumbled.

Ben looked up, surprised at the anger and frustration in her voice, but even more surprised by what she'd said. He grinned.

"What're you grinning at? It's not supposed to be funny."

"I'm grinning because it feels good to grin."

She put her hands in her back pockets, looked down at the ground, scuffed her boot back and forth.

She looked up at him. "So you're back," she said. "Why?"

"Well." He smiled. "I thought maybe you'd introduce me to your son."

"He's not here right now."

"That's okay; I'll wait."

"That was you who told him to tell me to let him go fishing, wasn't it?"

He didn't answer, waited.

"This ain't a damn movie," she said, angry again. "Isn't that what one of you said? This isn't a movie."

"No, I guess it isn't," he said, and thought, It never is.

She stared at him for a moment.

"Are you serious?" she finally asked. *"Really* serious?" a tinge of hope, like the last colors of a sunset, in her voice.

He smiled, "About what? Going fishing?"

"Meeting my son, you know what."

Her eyes, like so many other eyes, searched his, and he had to look away. Behind her, through the almost bare trees, he could see slate-gray clouds obscuring all but the base of the mountains.

"Oh, yes," he said, and smiled crookedly, focusing his eyes on hers. "I'm just about as serious as you can get."

SUSPENSE, INTRIGUE & INTERNATIONAL DANGER

These novels of espionage and excitement-filled tension will guarantee you the best in high-voltage reading pleasure.

____**FLIGHT OF THE INTRUDER** by Stephen Coonts 64012/$4.95

____**THE LANDING** by Haynes Johnson & Howard Simons 63037/$4.50

____**DEEP SIX** by Clive Cussler 64804/$4.95

____**ICEBERG** by Clive Cussler 67041/$4.95

____**MEDITERRANEAN CAPER** by Clive Cussler 67042/$4.95

____**THE PLUTONIUM CONSPIRACY** By Jeffrey Robinson 64252/$3.95

____**DIRECTIVE SIXTEEN** by Charles Robertson 61153/$4.50

____**THE ZURICH NUMBERS** by Bill Granger 55399/$3.95

____**CARNIVAL OF SPIES** by Robert Moss 62372/$4.95

____**NIGHT OF THE FOX** by Jack Higgins 64012/$4.95

____**THE HUMAN FACTOR** by Graham Greene 64850/$4.50

____**WARLORD!** by Janet Morris 61923/$3.95

POCKET
B O O K S